The English Department's Whores

The English Department's Whores

A novel about education

Douglas Maddon

Writers Club Press
San Jose New York Lincoln Shanghai

The English Department's Whores
A novel about education

Writers Club Press
an imprint of iUniverse, Inc.

For information address:
iUniverse, Inc.
5220 S. 16th St., Suite 200
Lincoln, NE 68512
www.iuniverse.com

This is a work of fiction

ISBN: 0-595-20594-1

Printed in the United States of America

For Rosamund Edwards, whose fault this book is, with love and thanks.

ACKNOWLEDGEMENTS

I should like to thank everyone who helped with this book, but particularly Sheri Dawson, Julie Dodd, Martin Nichols and John Attridge. The inspiration of several generations of students from the county of West Sussex was also invaluable, as was the hospitality of the Bedford Arms and its clientele.

My thanks must finally go to successive Secretaries of State for Education, who, for the last four decades, have worked tirelessly to make England's state school system the flower of Western civilisation.

INTRODUCTION

Extracts from the *Handbook for Staff*, Sir Fulke Mercier's College (formerly Mercier's Grammar School for Boys), Hengistley, Sussex, September 1998 edition

Staff Roll

Senior Management Group
The Role of the Senior Management Group is to formulate strategic policy for the College and to ensure its financial well-being. Each member of the SMG is responsible for a defined area and reports to the Principal .

Principal : Dr B Godley, MA (Oxon) DPhil (Kentucky Bible College)
Vice-Principal (Finance & Premises) : Dr V Walpurgess PhD
Deputy Vice-Principal (Curriculum) : Mr J Speer BA
Under-Vice Principal (Planning) : Mr J Bleach BSc
Assistant Vice-Principal (Quality Control) : Mrs S Lewerthwaite BEd

The Faculties are responsible for the delivery of the curriculum and report to the SMG

Faculty of Humanities
Acting Head of Faculty : Mr M Alcock MA (Cantab)

Humanities (A) English & associated subjects
Head of the English Department : Mr M Alcock, MA (Cantab)
Head of the Drama Department : Miss S Halsbury BA (new appointment)
Head of the Media Studies Department : Mr J Monks MA

Humanities (B) History & associated subjects
Head of the History Department : Mrs J Miller MPhil
Head of the Law Department : Mr A MacDonald MPhil
Head of the Politics Department : Mr W Fenneck MA (Oxon)

Social Science Faculty

Personal & Social Awareness Programme
Co-Ordinator : Mr B Worthington MSSc

PROLOGUE

The abolition of its popular hanging fairs had been the ruin of Hengistley. Once the region's entertainment centre, whose market-days had resounded to the happy cries of stallholders, farmers and capital punishment enthusiasts, it had become the most tedious town in Sussex, a title for which there was some competition. Nights in the little town were even more still and hushed than the excruciatingly placid days; people who dropped pins were rumoured to receive stern letters from the council. The war had given the silence a national sanction. As the blackout settled onto the town like a fat man engulfing a small chair, Hengistley could enjoy the conceit that it wasn't quiet because it was dull, but because Britain's very survival depended on it. This made life both better and worse for the two men who were standing in the grounds of the old grammar-school. They were quite well shielded from view by the high fence which ran around its perimeter, and there was no-one to see them, but the comprehensive nature of the darkness and the silence made whatever noise and light they created seem a million times more significant than in fact it was. Unloading a heavy, coffin-sized wooden box from the back of an old shooting-brake was never going to be a quiet job, but it seemed like a whole dockside of tuba-wielding elephants at work to Kevin McCabe.

1

"Will you not make so much bloody noise?" he hissed, irritably.

"There's no need for swearing," his new comrade, Evans, sniffed rather pathetically. McCabe did not think much of Evans, who was the kind of person that was called a big Jennie-Anne back in Belfast.

Evans was trying to lift the box off the floor of the car so that it did not make the agonisingly loud scraping noise which they feared would attract attention. Despite his powerful commitment to revolutionary Welsh nationalism, he had never really outgrown the strict Methodism of his youth, and found the coarseness of his Irish companion somewhat distressing. However, as Professor Griffiths had explained, the IRA's objectives were the same as their own. The liberation of historically oppressed Celtic peoples from the slavery of London could not be achieved by one nation alone, but by all of them acting in concert. A helpful Germany was aiding the cause with sporadic drops of arms, some of which the IRA had generously offered to share with their Welsh comrades. This particular batch was to be stashed prior to its allocation to a variety of fifth columnists deployed throughout the oppressor's home territory. Had the IRA leadership enquired any more deeply into their allies' order of battle, they would have discovered that these units largely consisted of rather odd Welsh students, scattered around the big towns of England. Most of these young men were friendless and, frankly, bored. Professor Griffiths had been partly driven by the desire to prevent them from masturbating themselves to death by giving them something more positive to do with their time. Dai Evans had never even held a gun before, and had no idea at all how a grenade worked. He imagined that he would pick it up as he went along. But he did not really like the beastly things. Especially not since he had got a splinter from the crate. It hurt, and he harboured a secret desire to go back to Llandudno to be with his mam.

For McCabe, however, the crate was a selection box of the most erotically charged objects he had ever seen. A Christian Brothers' education had, in his case, actually worked, and he did his best to keep his mind pure and free from thoughts of girls and their sinful ways. Unfortunately, the Brothers had not thought to mention that firearms, too, might lead to activities of which the Good Lord could reasonably be assumed to disapprove. Indeed, they had contributed to Kevin McCabe's present frame of mind. Brother Innocent's history lessons were a particular favourite for the young McCabe, and he had eagerly drunk from the fount of romanticised descriptions of armed struggle against the Saxon oppressor like an alcoholic with an account at the Crown. The descriptions of Padraig Pearse's heroic, doomed uprising of 1916, when the Mausers were broken out to proclaim Ireland's freedom by force of arms, had enchanted him. So much so that he absently passed on to his neighbour, without so much as a glance, the porno-graphic postcards which Francis Sullivan's cousin had brought back from a business trip to Egypt. After the lesson, Francis Sullivan com-mented that, "Paddy Pearse sounds like a right tosser to me," and Kevin did not respond that this was a bit rich coming from a dealer in stroke materials, but flung himself in an unco-ordinated frenzy of patriotic fervour at the defamer of the hero. The subsequent beating he received merely confirmed in his adolescent mind the need to stay true to the struggle. Francis Sullivan was, after all, the scion of a family whose head worked for the Civil Service at Stormont, and was thus an agent of the continued British oppression of Ireland. His death at the hands of the Luftwaffe whilst piloting a Hurricane in the Battle of France had caused Kevin some guilty satisfaction.

He was particularly pleased that inside the box were several Mausers, one of which had been adapted for sniping. This, to Kevin, was a reminder of the old days; again, Britain's enemy Germany had con-tributed to the struggle at home. It would be like 1916 and the Tan War all over again, rising up with their forefathers' weapons, supplied by their forefathers' allies, against their forefathers' foes. The fact that Kevin's own forefathers had sat out these momentous occasions run-ning a fairly profitable bakery in Belfast was neither here nor there. The

Germans had also kindly supplied a number of sub-machine guns and a box of grenades, and he had taken delivery of it all in his capacity as Officer Commanding in the Brighton Area. This had been a source of immense joy to him, and then, almost immediately, of guilt at his pride in handling the equipment of death, so he had surreptitiously crept off to confess. The priest, who had been a padre to the Irish Division at the Battle of the Somme and had thus acquired a vision of 1916 somewhat different from that of the excited boy on the other side of the grille, was so tormented at his new knowledge that he went to the nearest bar and drank himself into oblivion. Lurching back to the Presbytery, he failed to notice an oncoming lorry in the blackout and was run over.

"Don't talk to me like that, you wee bollocks," McCabe snarled to the Welsh boy, "Take the other end of the damn thing and we'll carry it down to the cellar door."

Puffing audibly, they lurched from the car and went to a small door at the base of the building, well away from its imposing main entrance. It was unlocked and they staggered inside.

"This is the basement of the school," he explained, "we used to come here for cups of tea when I was the caretaker's assistant last summer. On the left is the boiler-room, on the right is the caretaker's office and workshop. We go straight ahead."

Straining at the weight of the box, they advanced up the gloomy, dusty corridor to a small store-room.

"It's not used much, as you can see," Kevin said, "There's all sorts of crap here. Old books, boxes of nails, you name it. This box should fit exactly under that table at the back. We cover it with other bits of shite and leave it. No-one seems to come in here. It'll be pretty safe."

"And then what?" Dai panted, relieved that soon he would be free from this horrible, heavy thing. His back was killing him and he still wanted his mam.

"Put it down. Here, you gobshite, not there. Feck almighty, are all Welsh people as bloody stupid as you?"

Dai glared at Kevin through the murk, then sneezed.

"Stop making that fecking noise," Kevin snapped.

"I can't help it," Dai whined, miserably, "It's the dust. It does all sorts of mischief with my sinuses. And please don't swear like that."

"Jesus, Mary, Joseph and the wee donkey," Kevin snorted in disgust, "What the Army Council was thinking of when it teamed us up with you useless Taffy bastards I'll never know. And if the Germans discover what you're like they'll probably team up with the bloody English."

"Why do you have to be so horrible?" Dai whimpered.

"I'm a gunman, you fool," Kevin barked, "What did you expect me to be like, Florence sodding Nightingale? Anyway, when the Germans come, we break out these weapons, and rise up alongside them. Alternatively, if they don't come, we divide up the guns between our respective troops, and use them for guerrilla activities, like Tom Barry. Got it?"

Dai nodded damply. Kevin looked at him with contempt. Then a thought struck him.

"How many troops do you actually have?"

The little Welshman thought for a moment.

"Well, there's Ivor in London, and there's Thomas in Reading, and Blodwen in London too."

"Three people? Bloody hell. And what sort of a name is Blodwen? I bet he got the ride taken out of him at school."

"Blodwen is a girl," said Dai, with dignity, "And a very beautiful one."

"Bloody hell," Kevin said, again.

They were driving back to Brighton in the shooting-brake when the lone Heinkel came ambling out of the darkness, very low. Its crew had not done very well in their attempts to find the designated target, and had lost the rest of the bomber stream.

"I bet the others are home now," the ventral gunner complained.

"We're going to get tons of abuse from the CO when we get back," the bomb-aimer added.

"Hell, yeah," the gunner said, "Remember what he did to Dieter Hoffmann's crew? Those poor sods were doing press-ups outside the mess for a week. Proper little Hitler, he is."

There was a discreet cough from the bomb-aimer. The bomb-aimer was a Party member and allowed no-one to forget it.

"Stop gossiping like a pack of old women," the pilot yelled, "We're still over England. Keep your eyes peeled. There could be a dozen night fighters out there and we wouldn't know they were there until they'd turned us into a flying colander because my halfwit crew were too busy whingeing."

"It wouldn't be a flying colander, though, would it?" the radio operator interrupted, "Because if they'd filled us with that many holes, we'd crash, wouldn't we?"

"Yes, and it is precisely that eventuality which I want to avoid," said the pilot in exasperation.

"Can't we go any faster?" the ventral gunner asked.

"We could get rid of the bombs. That would increase our speed quite a bit," the radio operator suggested.

"Good thinking," the pilot said, "Open the bomb doors."

"Look!" the bomb-aimer shouted, almost giving his crew-mates heart-attacks, "There's a car driving along that road. I bet you a round in the mess I can hit it."

"Oh, all right then," the pilot said, "Have a go and see if you can hit the damn thing."

He steadied the aeroplane and the bomb-aimer started counting down for release.

"Is there any need for you to drive quite so fast?" Dai asked, querulously.

"Strangely, yes," Kevin retorted, "The sooner we're back in Brighton and seen there by people, the more we have by way of alibi. We can say that we were there all night."

"What's that noise?" Dai would, had he been a dog, have pricked up his ears.

There was a kind of throbbing sound which was becoming steadily louder and more insistent. Dai put his head out of the window. Above and behind them was a large cigar with enormous bat-like wings.

"It's an aeroplane," he informed Kevin.

"Really?" asked Kevin, with weary lack of interest. Like most people, he would have liked to have chosen some clever or inspiring last words, but he had to make do with "Bollocks" because at this point the Heinkel's load of Five-hundred kilogramme bombs thumped down onto the Sussex countryside around the car. The night was briefly lit up by a series of bright flashes and the silence chewed apart by a succession of thuds. Kevin's car, on fire from the first bomb, was flung sideways into a field by the second as if picked up and hurled there by a spiteful toddler of unnatural strength. It bounced twice, rolled onto its back and exploded.

"Beautifully done," said the ventral gunner appreciatively, as the Heinkel picked up speed and droned away, "That English bastard's going nowhere in a hurry, I can tell you."

CHAPTER ONE

HENGISTLEY, FEBRUARY 1998

The beer badger, the beer badger. Portia Bates woke up with the distinct feeling that she had just gone five rounds with the furry little sod. It was one of the multifarious beasts of Sussex mythology about which she had been warned by grinning locals when she had moved there. Unlike the dragon of St. Swithin's forest, which Portia's rational, scientific mind discounted as a particularly large and unruly horse, the beer badger was very real. Every Friday night it took all her money, hit her over the head and left its fur on the roof of her mouth. Ha ha. Attributing the self-inflicted wounds of alcohol abuse to a non-existent animal was all very well, but some motor system in her head told her to move and get on with her life. She shook her head muzzily, trying to get some feeling back into it, then whimpered in self-pity as her brain lurched towards the front of her skull with a resounding crash. Moaning softly and wincing at the brutal assault of the electric light on her delicate vision, she padded into the bathroom to look for aspirins. As she did so, she absent-mindedly switched on the little transistor radio which was strategically positioned in the hallway so as to be audible, provided no-one spoke or moved, in every part of the flat. Her cat looked at her with a languidly inquiring gaze as she pulled the entire contents of the medicine cabinet into the sink. Portia swore.

The cat continued to stare with unblinking self-possession, full of the smugness of its kind. An enormous and robust coal-black tom, it was unfazed by strong language. It was notorious in the area for the ripeness of its own vocabulary when defending Portia's flat against intruders or simply putting itself about. The radio squawked unkindly into a jingle and the cat moved into the kitchen, as far as it could get from the noise.

"Well, I hope you're having a great morning out there in the North Sussex and Surrey Downs area," the disc jockey burbled, "Because we sure are here at Radio Therapy, the hottest sound across the A23-A24 corridor."

"Uuurgh," said Portia, who didn't do early-morning conversation. Scrabbling in the basin, she found an old packet of painkillers.

"Yes," the disc jockey continued, "Make the most of it. It's a lovely morning but we're gonna have a pretty miserable afternoon. Heavy rain is forecast for the region, I'm afraid. Oh, well, it's not as if it's going to ruin a perfectly good Saturday, is it?"

Portia thought about this for a moment as she stared at the bathroom mirror. Her reflection looked back at her with unconcealed disgust. The green eyes, which had been known to enchant young men, had acquired a repulsively bloodshot hue, and the bloom of her normally healthy apple-red cheeks had gone to the colour of processed peas. The capacity of alcohol to make people sexually irresistible was clearly rather short-lived. Portia was twenty-eight but could add ten years to her appearance with the judicious application of lager and Scotch. But why wouldn't the weather ruin her Saturday? The song on the radio—a saccharine paean to lost love by an angel-faced young man who was adored by teenage girls but rumoured amongst teenage boys to be a confirmed homosexual with a rubber fetish—came to a close, and the disc jockey resumed his inane ramblings.

"Let's face it, who cares what sort of weather it is on a Monday? We're all at work anyway, so it might as well be pouring."

Portia lurched to attention like a guardsman and turned to the little radio.

"What do you mean, Monday, you little creep? It can't be Monday," she screamed, wincing as her throat constricted around the last words, squeezing them out as a desperate croak. How much had she smoked last night? Was there a karaoke? Oh, hell, hell, hell.

"And now it's time for the news here on Radio Therapy, the sound of today for Gatwick Airport and its associated trading estates," the man on the radio announced, with callous indifference.

"Pooh and perturbation," Portia said, colourfully.

"Good morning. This is the independent radio news at eight a.m. for Monday, the twenty-first of February, nineteen-ninety eight," a different voice said.

"You're joking," Portia begged.

The announcer went on to describe in pithy generalities a mammoth government bill to restructure the welfare state, and to paint in vivid colours every detail of a party hosted the previous evening by a topless model who was fornicating with an actor in a soap opera. If he was joking, he was in no hurry to let the audience in on it.

Portia rasped a succession of thoroughly unpleasant words. But she was a practical young woman at heart, and went to hurriedly to wash and dress. If she put her skates on, she might just get to work in time for the official Monday morning staff briefing. There would be no time for breakfast but she didn't really feel like one after the eight pints of Guinness she had a horrible suspicion she had consumed the previous night. She could worry about what had happened to the weekend as she drove into town.

"Look after the house for me, Behemoth," she called to the cat, who yawned with amiable indifference in reply. Portia slammed the door as she left the flat, stuffing her blouse frantically into her patterned dark green skirt as she moved. She found that the scholar gypsy look not only disarmed people but was easy to put on in a hurry. Or take off, if you got the opportunity. Not that she did. Wrenching open the door of her rusty Fiat, she clambered in and turned her key in the ignition. After a few sickly splutters and wheezes, the old car's engine came grudgingly to life and Portia gunned it out of the peripheral estate she lived in and towards the centre of Hengistley.

As she drove, the sharp air blasting though the open window started to unblock the pores of memory and a picture began to emerge of the weekend. She had spent Saturday with Kieran Holby. That was it. She remembered now. He was one of her old students. Two years ago, he'd left College. He had made a bit of a hash of his A levels but had got it into his head that he might still be able to find a university course that would keep him occupied for three years. Portia had doubted it, but Kieran was an agreeable enough lad with a degree of roguish charm, so she had unlocked her office in the College and gone through a variety of options with him. Eventually, after many hours' hunting, they had found an aeronautical engineering course at a university in Wales which suited the boy down to the ground. He had been overjoyed and insisted on treating her to Sunday lunch at his parents' pub, an oak-beamed four-ale bar in a village five miles from Hengistley. One thing had led to another and Portia had ended up spending the day there, her stay prolonged by the discovery by the pub's quiz team that she was a teacher. This resulted in her recruitment for their joust against rivals from Surrey, and a victory celebrated in the rural style with life-threatening quantities of beer, and Portia had somehow been loaded into a taxi and sent home without remembering a thing about it.

She pulled up at the College with a minute to spare, and dashed from the car park through the quadrangle to the staffroom, high in the old building where the Principal would be about to hold court.

*   *   *

Sir Fulke Mercier's College, through which Portia was running, was a considerably older institution than its late Victorian main building and rather seventies status as a Further Education College might have implied. It had once been Hengistley's grammar school, and countless middle-aged and elderly men in the northern parts of Sussex owed it a great deal. For four and a half centuries, the school's policy of robust bullying and violent sports had trained village lads and small-town boys how to handle themselves in the big bad world.

It had been founded for precisely this purpose by Fulke Mercier, a local thruster made good, in 1502. Old Fulke had accumulated considerable wealth in the course of a long and thoroughly wicked life as a merchant in London. Seized by religious fervour as the grave approached, he had founded the school as an act of penitence in the hope that the Almighty would overlook the string of frauds and petty dishonesties which had marked his career. He had originally intended to leave his cash to his sons, but every last one of the little swine had inconsiderately died in a cholera epidemic which Fulke had prudently avoided by sailing to Antwerp. This had added to his feelings of guilt and heightened his sense of urgency in endowing charitable works.

The school was to be free for any boy who might reasonably be expected to benefit from studying there, and the masters, a collection of semi-civilised fourth raters from the backstreets of Oxford, had been enjoined to batter literacy and numeracy into their charges with a minimum of pity or restraint. Life, in Fulke's experience, was cruel, hard and competitive, and a boy at his school would learn that very quickly indeed. In return for the investment made in the salaries of the teachers and the education of the boys, Fulke's immortal soul was to be prayed for each day in services conducted by the school body.

Mercier's had prospered along with the town, surviving such minor hiccups as the discovery that Simeon Brocklebank, Headmaster in 1609, was a practising occultist who regularly tried to summon up the powers of darkness to deal with unruly pupils. Indeed, his burning on the town common only served to prove the old adage that there is no such thing as bad publicity, for his wily deputy had distributed flyers amongst the gathered spectators and gained another fifteen pupils. A Victorian refit and the acquisition of bourgeois respectability helped buy in a few teachers who could actually count and spell, and the school began setting exams for the first time in 1891. The injection of money provided by the 1944 Act meant that Mercier's offered such a good education, at least in comparison with the local secondary moderns, that the eccentricities of a few of the teachers, such as the notorious "Dirty Bertie" of the Mathematics Department, was overlooked by parents whose sole concern was their offsprings' examination results.

The school, like most of its kind, had become a sound and worthy institution, good at what it did and playing an important role in the life of the town. Needless to say, it was just at the point that Mercier's and its fellow grammar schools felt that they were doing best that the government ungratefully decided to close them down. The edicts of Shirley Williams had filled the town with horror, but the quick-witted headmaster acted swiftly to prevent the school's traditions of excellence through robustness from being subsumed in a tide of progressive conformity. Elbowing the headmistress of the local girls' grammar school out of the way, he had announced that Mercier's was henceforth to be a further education college, offering bespoke qualifications to such young folk of the town as were aged sixteen and above and could meet the entry requirements. A very few older staff had grumbled at the abolition of uniforms and the arrival of girls, fearing the collapse of civilisation and mourning the loss of their freedom to wage unrestricted physical warfare on their charges. Most, however, were delighted to be spared the trauma of comprehensivisation, and overjoyed not to have to teach spotty thirteen-year-olds, wrestling with the spiteful anaconda of puberty, any longer. Some younger staff had been particularly pleased to see female students arrive, and a number of affairs bloomed in the stock-cupboards and departmental offices.

Mercier's sailed on, ruthlessly crushing any local institution which dared to compete against it in the provision of education to the young adults of the town. An attempt by the short-lived Liberal Democrat regime at the district council to open a less elitist College, offering courses in hairdressing and beauty treatments, was stopped in its tracks by acts of arson and a whispering campaign about the sexual proclivities of its principal. Mercier's portrayed itself simultaneously as an historic and prestigious qualification emporium and as a go-getting university substitute where teenagers might find themselves. The questionable accuracy of both of these claims was known only to the staff, who did their best to ensure that debate and understanding of educational issues in the town was kept to a minimum. Publicity for the College was handled by a shadowy clique of male teachers who were so spectacularly amoral that it was noted in the staffroom that they would have made ideal collaborators in the event of the Nazi conquest of England. Carefully edited exam results and tales of happy trips abroad filled the pages of the town newspaper, with grumblings suppressed by means of a closed relationship with the editor. An old Mercionian himself, he had convinced himself that the beatings and rote learning of his youth had made him the man he was today. He never printed a letter complaining about his alma mater and never changed a word of its official press releases, even if these were manifestly untrue, as had been the case with the report of how an upper sixth boy had saved a child from drowning in the local park. The boy had actually knocked the infant into the water by accident, whilst staggering drunkenly back from a liquid lunch, but had been forced to go to the rescue when the indignant mother accosted him. He had then squelched miserably into the college, where his teacher, recognising a useful photo-opportunity, dragged him back to the park and offered the mother twenty pounds to recreate the scene for the camera.

Mercier's was an academically efficient and pleasantly appointed institution. Its middle-class students were willing to learn, for the most part, and the staff were paid just enough to afford the little town's expensive prices. Teachers were free from the National Curriculum and were allowed considerable latitude in the delivery of their personal subject-related hobby-horses. The relative ease of their lives was kept secret from other schools and, apart from self-congratulatory puffing in the press about exam results, from the world at large. It was a happy land indeed for any teacher lucky enough to get a post there. Such, at least, was how things appeared to Portia, as she wheezed into the staffroom and flopped down in an armchair next to one of the English teachers, and waited for the Principal to make his announcements.

*   *   *

By ten o'clock, Portia was keeping her richly-deserved hangover at bay by oscillating between cups of bad coffee and glasses of gin and orange juice. She had hurriedly made photocopies of various pictures before the lesson and had given them to the students, who were discussing them in groups. Portia wandered amongst them, nudging the wayward back onto the subject in hand and encouraging the rest. A collection of distinctly unacademic girls from the mixed comprehensive were poring over a copy of an oil-painting of a muscle-bound athlete wielding a javelin. Portia inclined her head—she was keeping her hands firmly in her pockets in case they shook—at the picture.

"So what's that, then?" she asked

"It's a naked man, miss," offered one of the girls, whose name was Amazon ("After the ship, miss. My dad served on it. Then he was on *Antelope* in the Falklands, so that's my brother's middle name. Poor little sod.").

"Don't you know *anything*?" her friend asked.

"Indeed," Portia said, "Youthful and inexperienced though I am, I have seen one before."

The girls tittered. They lounged in their seats, simultaneously displaying, and declaring their indifference to, their chests, and darted occasional glances at the boys to see if they were looking. The boys had a football magazine, and weren't.

"But is there anything distinctive about him?" continued Portia.

"I can't speak for you, miss," the girl said, "But I sure as hell don't know any blokes like that. He's far too fit. It's not very realistic."

Another girl took time out from a piece of chewing gum to demur.

"Yes, he is. He looks like a Chippendale. I saw them at the leisure centre."

Portia had too and prayed that the girl hadn't noticed her in the crowd.

"Or that bloke in the footer team, the one who got his kit off for rag week."

"Bet he's hung like a baby's arm."

"You can't see though, can you, miss? Because of the way he's standing."

"He's got a great bum, though."

The girls cackled.

"Why would they show this sort of thing?" Portia asked, through gritted teeth. She was beginning to wish she'd given the girls a picture of a building instead.

"Because people want to see it. It's like page three."

"It was painted before the War. They didn't have page three then."

"Really? What was in the papers?"

The question was asked in genuine innocence. Portia shuddered.

"News, possibly," she snarled, "Though I'm just hazarding a guess there. Look. Think politically. You don't, as you've said yourselves, see blokes like that every day. So why make—as these people did—loads of posters and paintings and sculptures of this sort of figure?"

"It's romanticised," contributed a shy girl, who tended to sit at the back and say little, "It's a kind of ideal bloke. Do they want all blokes to look like that?"

"I can think of worse things for blokes to look like," Amazon sniggered, and leaned back in her chair to wave the picture at a boy on the other side of the room.

"Oi, Rob! How come you don't look like this, then?" she shouted.

"'Cause I haven't any incentive," Rob said, "If there was some half decent totty round here, I'd think about it. No point building up muscles just to impress an old bag like you, is there?"

"Bastard," Amazon replied, affectionately.

"Christ," Portia said, "What's the significance of this thing *politically*?"

"He looks pretty macho. Do they want people to be sort of fit and healthy and tough?"

"Well done," Portia said, "They certainly do. What can a load of fit, healthy tough blokes get up to?"

There was more tittering.

"I can think of a thing or two," said an earthy girl whose father was a prominent local Methodist clergyman.

"Fighting?" the shy girl volunteered again.

"Quite right. So which twentieth century leader would be likely to encourage this sort of art, then? Mahatma Gandhi? Nelson Mandela? John Major?"

"Hitler, Miss," said several of the students simultaneously, naming the only twentieth-century leader they could actually remember.

"Good show," Portia said, "Well done. Excellent."

She felt a welling up, like an over-shaken tin of lemonade, of that feeling of achievement which all teachers get when, by dint of bullying, cajolery or bribery, they manage to get the right answer out of children without actually telling them beforehand. Portia was widely considered to be good with students, and enjoyed this gratifying sensation regularly. She genuinely liked teaching, which had the capacity to lift her up when she was down, especially when concepts of potentially night-marish difficulty penetrated the students' minds without the use of agricultural machinery. Having satisfied herself that they had got the basic idea, she went on to elaborate for the whole class the significance of art in National Socialist Germany. Time began to fly by and she began to enjoy herself. With a minute to go before their break, the students were sufficiently interested and engaged not to commence their habitual shuffling and rattling of pencil-cases. Portia roared into a grand summary of her topic.

"So, when you go into the exam and you get asked about culture in Nazi Germany," she declaimed, her voice rising to a crescendo, "Think of this," (she waved a picture of a buxom nude) "as vulgarity, this," (a chocolate-box picture of peasants in the fields) "as sentimentality, this" (the naked man) "as brutality and the whole damn lot as unoriginal, boring and opposed to individualism of any kind."

The class cheered. Breathless and exhilarated, Portia bowed and blushed. As the students filed out to go to their next class, Portia called the normally quiet girl, who had joined in the discussion with an unusual degree of enthusiasm, over to her desk.

"That was a good point you made about the paintings in Russia being the same as the ones in Germany, Susanna," she said.

The girl looked at her feet.

"Thank you," she said, hesitantly.

"Have you been reading about the topic?"

"No," Susanna said, "It's my grandfather. He's Ukranian, you see. He ran away from the Red Army, and worked for the Germans in the war, and then the Americans. He said it was pretty much the same with the Communists and the Nazis. The same style of propaganda pictures, I mean, and getting bossed about all the time. And always eating cabbage soup."

"Gosh," Portia was impressed, "Well, you must ask him all about it."

"I do, miss," said Susanna, suddenly animated, "It's awfully interesting. I didn't before I came here. Ask him, I mean. But it's interesting, isn't it? History was a bit boring at St. Eva's, but it's, erm…better here."

She smiled. Portia blushed for a second time.

"You're kind," she said. On the foundations of such little words of comfort, together with the ego-massaging knowledge that she could lift even the most feeble students to a slightly higher level of mediocrity, was the happiness of her life constructed. Portia understood the one great truth of teaching; it was a process in which individuals who wanted to be liked came together in a room and rewarded one another. Not all of her colleagues believed in this, and others simply had not grasped it at all. Portia's success lay in the affection she had for her students. Mercier's had been her first teaching post, and she had amply rewarded the Principal's faith in her by boosting both her department's results and its standing in the College. She was universally beloved and seen as the heart and soul of the Humanities Faculty, and had, through the years, built up a retinue of deeply loyal former students, known to envious colleagues as the Family, who kept in touch with her years after they had left Hengistley.

"A shining example of professional brilliance," the Principal had said, as he introduced her to the Governors on Prize-Giving Day. Mercier's was her life.

Portia walked into the Humanities office feeling a hundred times better than she had three hours previously, and lit a cigarette. She found Mike Alcock, who taught English and Drama, looking at a computer terminal, presumably searching for mentions of his name on internet reviews of independent theatre productions on the south coast. As Portia came in, he ran his fingers through thick blond hair which was—to what she knew was his secret delight—still there, whereas that of the glamorous Head of Law was said to be thinning. His hands were thrust into the pockets of his rather fashionable waistcoat, where they rested against a stomach considerably firmer than that of the Head of Politics, whose vast expanse of beer gut was a College landmark. Portia did not think Mike an unduly vain man—in fact, he had a fairly low opinion of himself—but she was well aware that the knowledge that he was less repulsive than some of his colleagues helped him to sleep at night.

"Hello, gorgeous," he said.

"All right, big boy?" responded Portia, who found that flirting with Mike worked better than slapping him about, "How are things?"

"Bloody hopeless with this thing," Mike said, "But not as scary as what's in the staffroom."

"What's in the staffroom?" Portia asked.

"All of us have had photocopies of the relevant situations vacant pages of the *Times Educational Supplement* crammed into our pigeon-holes."

"What?" Portia snorted smoke incredulously from her nose, a dismissive dragon.

"There's also an enormous poster which says "Voluntary Redundancy—opening a new door to the future". It urges us to submit suggestions to the Principal about what we'd like to see in our personal references, were prospective employers to ask him for such things."

"What on earth for? We've got loads of money. They've just started to rebuild the Clutterbuck Hall and last year they stuck up an enormous gym with a fitness suite. The Vice-Principal, whatshisname, Walpurgess. He was wittering on at staff meetings last month about how Mercier's will look thoroughly beautiful after he's finished spending thousands of pounds on his refurbishment programme."

"It's not as simple as that, apparently," Mike said, "I've seen some of the paperwork, though I can't say I understand it. That was a separate budget. The budget which pays for the staff is different, and it doesn't cover enough for all of us."

"But if they get rid of people, won't the class sizes go up?"

"Presumably. But that's an efficiency gain. Weren't you listening in the staff meeting last week?"

"I was doing my marking. Everyone does in staff meetings."

"We're a business, Portia. Not a real one, of course, but we're meant to behave like one. Be efficient and slimmed down and virile and that. A tiger in the educational jungle."

"Oh, well," Portia said, "It can't affect us, can it? Humanities has great results. We work much harder here than anyone else. It would do them good to get rid of some of the dead wood."

*   *   *

"'Mercier's College, Greene Road, Hengistley, etcetera, 20th May 1998. Dear Portia, I am writing on behalf of the governing body to inform you that I am giving you three months notice from 31st May 1998 that your post will be made redundant with effect from 1st September 1998. Your final day of employment with the college will be on 31st August 1998.' Then it goes on to talk about redundancy payments and how they're worked out," Portia's voice tailed off into a whisper as she sank into the overstuffed armchair in the Humanities office.

"No 'sorry to lose you' or anything like that?" Mike asked.

"Not a sausage," Portia said.

"So that's it, then."

"Mmm," said Portia, and helped herself to a glass of whisky from the filing-cabinet. She stared around the room where she had spent her breaktimes, given revision tutorials, and cuddled weeping students whose lives had been temporarily wrecked by boyfriends, girlfriends or her colleagues.

The axe had not differentiated between the successful and the unsuccessful, the diligent and the indifferent. The last few months had been
horrible, as rumour and counter-rumour circulated as to who was to be
culled. Then, towards the end of the Spring Term, the word flew around
the College that the Principal was issuing preliminary black spots in
person. As lunchtime approached, she had felt giddy with relief. He had
not come for her. Five minutes before the end of her lesson, there had
been a knock on the door. The Principal came in and smiled amiably at
her. Portia had carried on teaching, with the Principal occasionally
offering the benefit of his knowledge, much to the confusion of the students, until the end. After the students had gone, he broke the news. He
was polite and genial, but the fact remained that difficult economic
times required sacrifices to the gods of the account ledger headings, and
she might well be among the victims.

Portia was furious. It was not merely that she knew perfectly well
that a number of other staff—who, for instance, had worse attendance
records than truanting teenagers or couldn't actually spell—were
regarded by colleagues and students alike as useless whilst she was
universally worshipped. It was not even that the government's pious
homilies on schooling were being flouted in an institution over which
the Department for Education (now there was a misnomer; if ever
ministers had run a system so as to be against education, it was in
England) exercised such rigid control. What really irritated Portia was
the fact that, as she trudged miserably from office to classroom, she
could see all around her the building projects, largely cosmetic, into
which the Vice Principal was channelling so much money. Having discovered the joys of corporate rebranding, he had redecorated the
entire College in blue, its official colour, down to shiny notices in the
toilets suggesting that problems be reported to the maintenance staff.
It was after seeing these that Portia had had a series of nightmares in
which the senior staff played a prominent part. In one of them, the
Principal and Dr Walpurgess had dragged her from her classroom and

stuffed her into a van along with the other people who were being made redundant. They were driven through the night to an unknown destination. Eventually, they were pulled from the van and bundled into cells in a grim, barrack-like building in what looked like Eastern Europe, or perhaps Liverpool. Walpurgess, dressed in a black shirt, had summoned a drably uniformed guard.

"Watch her," he said, "She's trouble."

"You bastard," she shouted, "You're only management because you can't teach to save your life."

Walpurgess leered sadistically at her, and took the guard's rifle.

"Any last requests?" he asked.

"My job back, you overpaid scum," Portia had bawled.

"You can't have it," Walpurgess sneered, "Under the directives of the Strategic Plan's Accommodation Programme, your classroom is to be demolished and turned into a car park for government inspectors. There will be pretty flower beds all around it, and a rather attractive water sculpture. Now that your department's been slimmed down and made more efficient, they'll appreciate the view."

Then he walked over and shot her. Portia had woken up in a cold sweat of terror and anguish.

And now she arose from her armchair, the coup de grace still in her hand.

"I'm going to the pub," she said, and walked with dignity up to the Hertford Arms, where she drank fifteen large gins.

"Stop here," she slurred to the taxi driver as he drove her home later. He pulled the car up to the kerb by the College. Portia lurched out and staggered into the senior staff car park. She stared up at the old building, which loomed above her in the darkness. At one time she had found its bulk vaguely comforting. Portia would work late into the night on projects for her students or reports for her masters, hammering away on computers or reviewing the latest tapes of crudely sensationalised programmes from the History Channel for use in lessons. Even alone, the darkened corridors held no fears for her. She knew by instinct how to move about the building, welcomed the strange gurgling sounds that the Victorian piping made in the twilight hours, knew the cycle of the boiler in the staffroom coffee machine off by heart. The unevenly fitted paving slabs by the sports hall made a funny plonking sound if you rode your bicycle over them, as she did when she came in at weekends and was feeling healthy. The English corridor had little red emergency lights that winked at you in the darkness if you went downstairs to borrow fags from Mike's desk. The big windows of the Politics room gave a fine view over the town park which she would not see again. All gone. It had been her home, where she felt as safe and secure as a child in the womb, and now she was to be expelled from it.

The Principal had gone, but the Vice-Principal, whose profligacy on the issue of blue paint Portia had come to identify with her redundancy, was working late, and his BMW was still there. She stared at it for a moment, aimed carefully, and hurled the bottle of lager she had taken for the road through its windscreen. It made a satisfyingly large hole, but no alarm went off.

"Cheapskate," muttered Portia, vaguely.

She dropped to her knees on the grass, and wept.

"Cheapskates," she sobbed, "Cheapskate bastards."

Portia would recall, when it was all over, that it was at this point, as the despair and misery flowed out of her, that the iron had entered her soul.

CHAPTER TWO

HENGISTLEY, SEPTEMBER 1998

The red wallpaper of the Conference Room was looking particularly brazen as Jonathan Bleach, the Under-Vice-Principal, walked in to join his colleagues on the Management Group. The winter term had just begun and the senior staff always held a grand summit meeting on the day the students arrived back. As he entered, some young teachers in the staffroom next door took the opportunity to peer in, and sniggered into their tepid coffee. Not for the first time, Bleach found himself wishing that all College decisions should be put through a screening process to test whether or not cheap jokes could be made about them. In the case of the Conference Room, which had once, like most of the other administrative areas, been used for lessons, a highly expensive refit had left the place with red wallpaper, brass fittings and the nickname of "The Brothel". An object of derision for all the staff, who would take guests there and gleefully point out the room's assorted vulgarities, the Brothel's bizarre appearance was partly due to the success of a plausible former student, who claimed to be an interior designer, in persuading Dr Walpurgess that this style was the very latest thing in the more go-ahead institutions of London. Walpurgess was also impressed by the lad's announcement that, as a good Old Mercionian, he would happily do the job for half the going rate. The fact that the ex-student had been taught by Portia Bates, who had just received her redundancy notice and was discreetly encouraging her loyal acolytes to make life unpleasant for the Mercier's management, was not realised until the finished job was unveiled to the rapturous disapproval of all concerned.

Bleach sat down on one of the expensive chairs which were ranged around an incongruously Scandinavian-looking table, checking first to see that it had not been sabotaged in any way. Portia's students had been known to go around putting everything from chewing gum to small fireworks on the chairs of the senior staff. The Principal's secretary had almost lost a hand opening a parcel which turned out to contain a Catherine Wheel intended for her master. The seat seemed safe; a small mercy, given what Bleach suspected was to come. He waited for the rest of the management to arrive and sipped listlessly at his coffee.

Mercier's, in the view of the more radical staff, was a dictatorship, governed through the conspiracy of a power crazed group of individuals in their own interests or in those of the wider bourgeoisie of which they were a part. Such people pined for a Rousseauesque State of Nature in which the staff would be free citizens who gathered together to discuss, on an equal basis, the way forward for the next year. The General Will of the people, not an oligarchy, would make decisions. The Principal and his myrmidons did their best to prevent such a picture from becoming reality through refusing point blank to allow voting of any kind to take place amongst the staff.

"That way, chaos lies," intoned the old man, much to the annoyance of the radicals. After leaving the Army he had enjoyed a career at Oxford, which, if not glittering, had at least been impressively shiny. There he had been transfixed by Karl Popper's *The Open Society and its Enemies,* his somewhat idiosyncratic reading of which was to inform his management style for the next four decades. A careful analysis of Popper's work led the Principal to conclude that the open society of the title was, in fact, himself and, to a lesser extent, the College. Its enemies were those who, with their obsession with voting and free discussion, merely undermined the open society, in ways too irritating to mention, so he found it best to keep such things to a minimum.

In his mind, Mercier's was a living, breathing, organic entity, every part of which was constantly evolving, with a function which might vary through time, just as a leaf was required at one point to photosynthesise and at another might find a new role as mulch. The image preferred by the Principal was that of the garden, with himself as the gardener, forever weeding, pruning and laying out the saplings. Cynics amongst the staff, having noticed a great enthusiasm for particular forms of fertiliser in the speeches of the management, agreed entirely. Others preferred the image of the Animal Pack, with the Principal as Alpha Male, ruthlessly destroying enemies and discarding the weak in a constant struggle for survival. The Principal himself was not wholly averse to this vision. He had once watched a television programme about huskies in Canada, in which the man in charge of the sledge gave food directly to the alpha male of his pack, and to no other animal. The most important husky then gave out the resources to the other dogs as it saw fit, just as the primary hunting wolf did. Given that the Principal had to abase himself before the Further Education Funding Council up in London in order to get hold of the funds which kept the college alive, he felt that it was only right and proper for him to dominate the beasts of his pack. Politically lazy members of staff colluded in this vision, preferring to spend their spare time honing their ability to slaughter moose or developing the resources of their clans. They disliked the idea of ploughing through the minutiae of management issues which made a meeting of a Bulgarian Cement Collective sound like a night out with Elvis. Radicals seethed in impotent fury and bewailed their misfortunes.

The Principal entered and beamed around the room as he took up his position at the end of the table. At these meetings of the dozen or so people who made up the Management Group, he liked to station himself here, like a Victorian paterfamilias. In staff meetings, he preferred to sit in the middle of his managerial colleagues, gazing down upon the assembled teachers in the manner of Christ at the last supper. With the students, he stood alone, like Moses giving the Commandments to the Children of Israel. This was partly because of the psychological advantages which the old man felt it gave him, based on the ideas he had read about in an American corporate management handbook suggested to him by another College head at a conference. A result of this widely noted habit, however, was that many members of the Mercier's community, as he grandly called it, thought that he was mad.

"I'm sure you all know the new financial arrangements," he said, cheerfully, "The government cutting our funding and so on. We have come up with a new solution to this, which, in my view, will radically reform the way we do things and take us into the twenty-first century as a dynamic, enterprising institution."

Bleach held the old man's gaze. How annoying it was, he thought, that the Boss could still have a twinkle in his eye at his age, and especially given what he was about to announce.

"Yes, I know I shall have retired," he nodded at Bleach, "But whoever leads you into the next century—nay, millennium!—will, I am confident, see this idea as the best way forward."

"Well said, Principal," said Sally Lewerthwaite, the Assistant Vice Principal and token woman, obligingly. The others looked at her with contempt. Jim Speer, the Deputy Vice Principal, stared at a hairline crack in the cocaine-white ceiling and recalled a hymn from his childhood containing the line "The cry goes up 'How long?'" Jonathan Bleach doodled a large hatchet on his notepad. The College management, and indeed its core values, were almost entirely male. There had been a female Registrar and a female Bursar once upon a time, but they had gone. Their departure had led to Sally's promotion from the post of part-time Needlework Adviser in order to preserve the fiction of equal opportunities. She was a portly, blousy woman who had the faintest hint of vulnerability, and no-one really disliked her as such, but she did have a rather tragic, not to say embarrassing, tendency to cling to the

Principal's side. This was partly because her job was a rather bogus one, having been invented solely to keep her occupied whilst simultaneously denying her access to anything difficult or important. Sally's life revolved around printing off more or less meaningless questionnaires about quality assurance and sending them to teachers, who were meant to tick boxes indicating how happy or otherwise they were. At regular intervals, Sally would collate these and use a computer to analyse the number of ticks to see how the College was performing in its role of nurturing the professional wellbeing of its employees. To Sally's surprise, this irritated the staff and led them to make her life unpleasant. Initially, this took the form of withholding the sheets of paper, whereupon she complained to the Principal that the staff were picking on her, thus earning the childish nickname of Sally the Snitch. She had reinforced her reputation in this field by raising Cain when she discovered that the staff who had been made redundant were using the College photocopiers, which she saw as the chariots of her own career advancement, to print invitations to what they disloyally called their P45 party. Since then, the cruelties had been refined. A popular way of spending free periods was to ask her to explain what the statistics meant and refusing to understand. The Head of Law had once spent three hours with her, painfully getting her to go through the minutiae of quality assurance, and when, in the end, she had collapsed in tears, had put his arm around her and said soothingly, "There, there, Sally. If it's all too much, we'll understand if you want to resign. Of course it gets too much sometimes. Maybe becoming AVP was just a bit too much of a step, eh? Perhaps it would be best just to go back to teaching the remedials and forget this silly management nonsense."

"Our idea," the Principal continued, "Is based on the Financial Management Initiative in the Civil Service in 1982, and the Ibbs Report into the same organisation in 1988. These reforms revolutionised the culture of the Civil Service and made it into the efficient and dynamic operation it is today."

This is it, Bleach thought; he's gone off the rails now.

"I have written a poem which, I think, sums it up rather well. Dr Walpurgess will now read it out."

The Vice-Principal's cheeks turned to the kind of red normally associated with a damaging fire at a distant paint factory on a summer evening.

"I do feel, Principal," he said, with an almost despairing tone in his voice, "That you would do it so much better than me. After all, you're the one with the classically trained mind, and it is, of course, your poem. I'd get the cadences and the rhythms and the, ah, pentameters and so forth all wrong."

"Nonsense, nonsense," the Principal replied, jovially, "Give it a stab. If you don't do it very well, then perhaps Jim Speer could read it out at the General Staff Meeting."

An explosive "Shit!" hissed from the other end of the table, as the Deputy Vice Principal spat out the chewed biro which was his substitute for a cigarette at meetings.

"Sorry, Jim?" the Principal asked, innocently.

"Just realised, Principal," Speer smiled glassily, "I've got to be at that seminar on Managing the Millennium on Monday. In Worthing. I shan't be back until, oh, six at the earliest. Sorry—I'll have to miss the staff meeting."

"Well, never mind," the Principal said, "I'm sure Jonathan can do it instead."

Bleach shot his colleague a look of concentrated malice. Speer stuck his tongue out.

"Anyway, without further ado, the Vice-Principal and the poem."

Walpurgess looked desperately around the room, as if pleading with his colleagues for forbearance. It was the last time for a week that he would be able to look any of them in the eye. He was an economic man, who saw the College as a machine, where one bit definitely went *there* and did *this* and cost *x*. He could not abide the intrusion of emotion, territorialism or tradition into the equations which governed his picture of the life of the College. Walpurgess had also had to take the brunt of the students' hatred over the redundancies of their favourite staff. Unlike most other teachers, he lacked a fan base of loyal students who would listen to his side of the argument, and the previous few years had been a nightmare for him. His wife had still not really recovered from the horror of going down for breakfast to discover their hallway overrun by rats which had been fed in through the letterbox in the middle of the night. He had not disliked teaching, but had been glad enough to replace the unpredictability of the classroom with the logical and comprehensible world of administration. The downside of this was that the students did not know who he was, and, at Mike Alcock's suggestion, regularly called the police to report a pervert prowling round the buildings. At least in his office, all was order and reason. The Vice-Principal passed happy hours there, exploring the computer-generated model of the perfect College which his assistants had created for him. Unfortunately, irrationalities had begun to creep in even at the level of the management, as the Principal became more determinedly eccentric with every passing day. He was becoming worse than the bloody kids, and was smiling at him now, like some sort of all-powerful Cheshire Cat. Walpurgess swallowed uncomfortably and looked down at the poem.

"Ahem," he began. The Principal smiled at him encouragingly.

"Ahem," he said again.

"Our College funding's rather like
A little flopsy bunny,
Except instead of lettuces
It needs a lot of money.
Now in the past we used to get
Our money out of tax
But that's been cut, and so we must
Face up to horrid facts."

He swallowed. A clammy silence had descended upon the room. The Principal was still smiling broadly. Everyone else was staring at the grain of the wooden table.

"Like little bunnies in the wild
All lonely in the snow
We must get cash from someplace
But where, we do not know.
And so, our teachers shall arise
And look for things to eat
Or, to put things another way,
Make subjects make ends meet."

Walpurgess breathed a sigh of relief. He mopped his brow and looked furtively around.

"That's it."

Tonight he would not tell his wife about this, but she would notice a slight change in his behaviour, such as telling the cat to go out and rip the throat out of that bloody flopsy bunny rabbit that kept coming into the garden.

"That was, er, very interesting, Principal," Bleach said, daringly using the strongest word of condemnation allowed by College etiquette. The fact that interesting was a term of abuse spoke volumes for the attitude to education which the senior staff had developed, and went a long way towards explaining why many of them had not been seen in classrooms for years.

"Yes, I thought you'd say that," replied the old man, whose long years of experience as a schoolmaster had given him a skin so thick that armour-piercing bullets would have been needed to assassinate him, "Essentially, the idea is that we set the Departments free to manage their own budgets and indeed to raise their own funds. Like little businesses, if you will. It will create a much more dynamic ethos, better to serve the client base. What they did in the Civil Service, you see, was to split up the big, unwieldy monolith into lots of little agencies with specialised functions. It made it ever so efficient, you know. Huge savings. I was watching a programme about dinosaurs last night which reminded me of it. A pack of little Velociraptors knocked the living daylights out of a big Brontosaurus, even though it was many times their size, and why? Because they were small and nimble and specialised. That's what I've got in mind for the departments, if you follow me."

"Do you think the teachers will run with it, though?" Speer asked, "Now, we know what that lot are like when it comes to change, and this idea—I'm not criticising it myself, you understand—well, it raises all sorts of practical and ethical questions."

"Oh, there will be doubters," the Principal waved his hand in an airy gesture, "There always are. I remember when I first started here, trying to get them all to wear jackets and ties. That was hard enough. But look at us now. Best dressed staff in Sussex."

"This is, ah, arguably of course, a bit different," Bleach said, "You're effectively asking them to be businessmen, with all that that entails, as well as their teaching responsibilities. They'll go bananas. And with a new Principal due to arrive in less than a year, we just can't afford that."

"We'll see," the Principal responded opaquely. Gathering his notes, he ambled from the room and went down to his office, where he switched on his computer, put a Gilbert and Sullivan compact disc into it, and settled down for the afternoon.

The Senior Management stared at one another in horror.

"He's gone stark staring mad," Speer said.

"It was a nice poem, though, wasn't it?" Sally piped up, brightly.

Dr Walpurgess stared at her wildly.

"Leave it," Speer warned, "She's not worth it. Smacking her would feel good for about two seconds, but then you'd have an industrial tribunal to face."

"Who's talking about smacking her? I'm going to strangle the dozy bint," Walpurgess snarled.

"There's got to be a subtext here," mused Bleach, whose memories of O level English had not entirely left him, "It's not just about efficiency gains or capital acquisition, is it?"

"Probably not," Walpurgess said, "If you think about it, we've made several staff redundant and put a lot of others onto part-time contracts, but we're still losing money hand over fist. If—or perhaps I should say when—the whole shooting match rolls over and plays dead, there will be a hunt for scapegoats."

"And that's us," Speer said, "Unless…"

"Unless we have a system whereby the teaching staff are seen to be responsible for the College finances," Walpurgess filled in, "They can take the blame when the solids hit the fan."

"It's brilliant," Sally breathed, "I wish I could think up great things like that."

"Don't even try," Speer muttered, "You'll only hurt yourself. Sort out your shoelaces first."

"Yes," Bleach said, "But isn't it potentially dangerous? I mean, first of all we have to persuade a load of teachers, most of whom work in the public service because they're too crap with money to do anything else, to become captains of industry. How the hell are we going to manage that? And what if some bright spark decides to just take all his department's dosh and do a flit to Tierra del Fuego?"

"I don't think they will," Jim Speer was sitting back in his chair, his hands folded behind his head, in the manner of a primitive sun-worshipper. "They're professionals. Most of them will try to make the system work. What we need to do is to make it sound like fun to them. Encourage them to see the possibilities. And also imply that we aren't comfortable with it. That ought to help—to them, it proves that something's good."

"Well, I have to say that I'm not remotely happy with it," Bleach said, "It's morally questionable in the extreme."

"That's a bit rich coming from a man who used to be the Casanova of Continuing Education," Speer snapped, "You've become remarkably responsible in your old age."

"I resent that," Bleach tried to look dignified, "Er…"

Jonathan Bleach had once been an imaginative young teacher of Biology whose fertility had not been confined to ideas about the dissection of larvae. He had had the pick of the Upper Sixth girls until the introduction of the Environmental Science syllabus. This had required the appointment of someone to teach those parts of the peculiar new subject which he did not understand, and the Principal had thoughtfully left the final say in the choice of candidates to Bleach, with the comment that if it was up to him he'd go for the one he fancied. Bleach had done just that and within a few months he had set up home with his attractive new colleague. Domestic responsibility had heightened his ambition and he had worked his way onto the management, partly because no-one else wanted to do the jobs he now did. He had found an aptitude for the jargon of administration and could baffle a staff meeting for hours on end with talk of optimum operating densities and transforming the culture of learning.

The downside of this was that his interest in the student body, or at any rate the bodies of specific individual students, had had to be curtailed. His old laddishness had been replaced by a level of political correctness which made Andrea Dworkin look like a character in a Harold Robbins novel. The Head of English had yet to forgive him for an incident in the summer term, when they had appointed a new Drama teacher to replace one of several staff who had sucumbed to nervous breakdowns, alcoholism or Myalgic Encephlomyelitis in the general atmosphere of paranoia which had suffused the college. The candidates had been a chubby and rather camp man in his fifties and a bubbly redheaded young woman who was looking for her first appointment. Mike's innocent "yes" to a student's inquiry as to whether he had appointed "the pretty one" had led to a lengthy lecture from the Under-Vice-Principal on the use of unprofessional and sexist language. Many people felt Bleach that had become a bit weird since stepping onto the straight and narrow path to power.

"I think that one of us ought to bounce it off one or two of them," Walpurgess said, "I reckon that Jonathan's acting skills ought to come in handy here. I think you'll be surprised at how well it's received, you know."

*   *   *

In the English Department, Mike Alcock was fighting a losing battle with his students' inability to understand the text before them. They seemed to have spent their long summer break letting their brains lie fallow as part of a European-funded set-aside scheme.

"You really are Thatcher's children, aren't you?" he snorted in despair, "Your horizons are limited by the desire for instant gratification and the profit motive. Just because you don't understand something immediately, you reject it. *Engage* with the *facking* text, for God's sake."

Two dozen seventeen-year old eyes stared blankly back at him, as he thought, not for the first time, that he was too good for these little sods.

Why should I give a monkey's that they're all thinking I'm a sad old bastard? he thought. What does some teenage slapper whose sole interest is what Bazza said to Shazza about Razza last night know about me? I *do* things outside this dump. I have a life. I live in Brighton, for one thing, not in a suburban shanty-town that makes Stepford look like 1920s Berlin. This place is so tedious that train-spotting's regarded as a dangerous sport.

"Is it about sex, sir?" asked a blonde girl.

"In what sense?" the lecturer's head snapped upwards as he hoped against hope that some intelligent observation was about to be made.

He had terrible trouble with the female students. It wasn't his fault. One mixed comprehensive apart, Hengistley District Council maintained that it was best for the sexes not to meet until the age of sixteen, when they would go to College at a suitably mature stage in their development and meet the life partners of their dreams. The staff at Woodlands, the local boys' school, were, accordingly, the unhappy organisers of what amounted to a containment pen for untamed adolescent beasts, whose end of term parties were the occasion for a rash of sick leave throughout the Sussex Constabulary. Oddly, however, their products were less of a problem than those of St. Eva's, the girls' school, whose teachers saw their role as the efficient drilling of examination success into their charges. The typical St. Eva's girl was neat, diligent, and polite, but her critical imagination had been suppressed like an illegal newspaper in a Stalinist dictatorship. This was not a problem for more old-fashioned departments such as Mathematics, which provided her with a series of conundrums to be solved by the power of reason, or Politics, which held up a succession of theoretical hoops through which she could be trained to jump. It was English at which the St.Eva's girl bridled. Attempts to grapple with distasteful underlying causes or difficult subtexts represented an unpleasant intrusion into the ordered, happy world which her teachers had assured her represented the sum total of human experience. Mike had a particular difficulty with the girls' absolute refusal to countenance the possibility that literature was anything other than it said it was. A poem about a flower was a poem about a flower, not a repressed scream of Freudian panic or a subtle political metaphor. Why could the teachers not just give them a nice set of notes explaining how beautiful the poem was? The St. Eva's girls would look after them carefully, in elaborately-constructed files with pictures of Disney characters on the covers.

"I'm not sure," the girl said, "It's just that it's usually about sex."

"Ah," sighed the Head of Humanities, his hopes of insight dashed like an egg on a cricket bat. Looking on the bright side, at least there was one former St. Eva's girl who didn't regard the invasion of that sort of thing into literature as a form of harrassment.

"I'm sorry," he said, "But Marvell's *Horatian Ode on Cromwel's Return from Ireland* is not, strictly speaking, about sex."

He was just about to explain that it was an heroic treatment of genocidal oppression when the rattle of pencil-cases and snapping of ring-binders signalled that the students, who were clock-watchers of a type made famous by television satires of trades unionism in the seventies, were due to have their lunch. Mike sighed again.

"Think about what this means for tomorrow," he yelled above the tintinabullation, "Why not ask your History teachers what Cromwell did in Ireland?"

He was on his way to the canteen when he realised that the only member of the History staff who specialised in the seventeenth century taught the period with a robustly British nationalist approach which the St. Eva's girls and Woodlands boys absorbed with uncritical loyalty. Mike swore. His words were, fortunately, lost in the canteen, a maelstrom of noise and confusion at the best of times and particularly so on a wet day such as this. The students had, as was their wont, transformed it from its early-morning tidiness into a morass of torn-up paper plates, crisp packets and drinks tins. House music thudded from speakers mounted high on the walls. Shrieks of girlish laughter came from the centre of the room as female students pretended to be less intelligent than they actually were in order to appeal to their thuggish male counterparts. Neanderthalic grunts of concentration were audible from boys clustered around the pool tables in the corner. Mike collected a plate of roast pork from a woman in a tabard which had been colour-co-ordinated with the College theme and sat down at the empty staff table. He had just polished off his lunch and was ruminating on the possible views on Oliver Cromwell which the girls might regurgitate the next day when Jonathan Bleach came in and sat down next to him, looking upset.

"I'll get straight to the point," Bleach said, "Rumour has it that you keep a stash of alcohol somewhere in your office. Is that true?"

"Absolutely not," Mike said, "It's a disgraceful lie. Just because a man has a few pints here and there doesn't make him some sort of old soak. I appreciate that my impression of Bob Dylan on top of a table at Portia's P45 party may have struck some narrow minds as the act of someone who'd had a few too many, but I can assure you that it was merely the ebullience natural to an artistic persona such as my own."

"Oh," Bleach mumbled, "I really wanted a large Scotch. And I'd pay ten quid for a half bottle of vodka."

"Ah, now that's different," Mike beamed, ingratiatingly, "I've got some of that. I confiscated it from one of the kids."

"Really?" asked Bleach. Normally a composed, not to say suave figure, it now appeared that he was shaking like a leaf and staring wildly at some point in the middle distance. Mike knew enough of the byzantine College decision-making process to know that this weakness had to be exploited ruthlessly, and information or concessions extracted.

"Yeah, come down to the Politics office. That's where I put it," Mike grinned.

They shambled down to the Politics office, where Mike triumphantly hauled a bottle of expensive Swedish lemon-flavoured vodka from a small fridge.

"Now, tell me all about it," said Mike, comfortingly.

Bleach looked up, fear of Mike's almost certain anger—the Head of English was known to have at least some radical tendencies—when he told him what was going to happen, wrestling with his desire for a confessional experience. His need to pour out the truth, or as much of it as his colleagues felt would be good for the foot soldiers to know, won. Plied with vodka and cigarettes, encouraged by Mike's non-committal grunts and vague smiles, he told him that he and his colleagues were going to have to become businessmen, and fund their own activities.

And when he had finished, all Mike said was, "Mmm. Lots to think about there, eh?"

Jonathan Bleach left Mike Alcock deep in thought. He felt better in himself but did not understand why he hadn't been lynched. He was conscious of a new development over which he had no control, but, unlike the Principal's idea, no-one was telling him what it was.

CHAPTER THREE

Susan Halsbury strode into the College with the confidence she felt was expected of a Drama teacher. The students in the quad made way for her with a politeness to which she was unused as she made for the English Department, where she was to meet her new boss. The students were eerily nice here, rather different from the yobs in the dump where she had done her teaching practice, who conducted their affairs in an Brummie whine punctuated with aggressive swearing. Susan had also been rather disconcerted by her first trip around the College campus. In addition to its impressive redbrick old building, it had sunlit flowerbeds around two quadrangles, composed of buildings gradually erected through the course of the century. Its enormous library featured a plaque commemorating the Men Of Mercier's Who Gave Their All For Our Freedom and a huge framed portrait of the founder, a sinister-looking, stoat-like man in a ruff and a fur coat. This was not the image of education she saw on the television, nor indeed the one she experienced in school. It wasn't exactly how she imagined a college, either. Where were the tower blocks and pre-stressed concrete?

"Council won't allow it," Dr Walpurgess had said, "But we do have plans for such times as when they do. Great big tower, six storeys, German architect. Award winning, innovative. Dominate the skyline for miles. Have to put lights on top to stop aeroplanes bouncing off it, you know. Ah, but I can dream. I'll show you the blueprints if you like."

Entering the old grammar school building, she walked along a corridor decorated with the produce of the Art Department and found room 14. A plastic notice on the door informed her that this was the English Office, Head of Department Mr Michael Alcock, MA (Cantab). She knocked briskly.

A muffled voice from the interior said something indistinct. Susan knocked again. There was a sound of argument between male and female voices. Susan caught the phrase, "You damn well open it," and suddenly the door was wrenched open and a tweedy young man appeared. He was short, rotund, and irritable.

"Yes?" he said, neither charm nor interest colouring his voice. Susan was assaulted by the stench of whisky and tobacco.

"I've come to see Mike," she said.

"Mr Alcock to you, young lady," the man snapped, in the reedily formal tones of Edinburgh, "He's not in."

"Erm, yes, sorry," Susan said, "He said I should wait here for him."

"Oh," the young man opened the door more widely, looking distinctly ungracious, "I suppose you'd best come in, then. Sit down and for goodness' sake don't touch anything."

Susan came into the office and looked around her. It was an untidy room, with bookcases on virtually every inch of wall space, stretching to the high ceiling and crammed with tatty volumes on virtually every non-scientific subject on the curriculum. A ladder was propped up against a set of shelves opposite the door; the young man climbed up it and stared at a row of Shakespeare plays, occasionally picking one out and peering intently at it. Beside the grubby window stood a desk, on top of which a young woman of about twenty was sitting, clutching a sheaf of paper. She was tall, slim and dark, and she looked at Susan with interest.

"Found *Coriolanus*," said the man on the ladder, dropping a battered paperback to the floor, "What's next?"

The young woman picked it up and added it to an enormous pile of books on her desk. She stared at him.

"I can't *believe* you," she shouted.

"What?" the man looked at her in confusion and some irritation.

"You are so *rude*."

"What have I done *now*?"

The girl stood up on the desk and looked at him, gesturing downwards towards Susan with her papers.

"Someone comes in and you just completely ignore her. I don't know how you can do that. I really am embarrassed to be seen with you sometimes."

"There are a thousand students in this College. I teach one hundred and twelve of them, and I'm damned if I'm going to be nice to any more of them than that. This (he flung an indifferent hand in Susan's direction) is not my student. Not my responsibility," the fat man snarled.

"Open your eyes, you idiot. She's not a student, she's too old," the girl snorted. She turned to Susan and smiled apologetically.

"Not *old*, old. Just older than a student."

"Oh, really?" William peered at Susan, "I suppose she is. I didn't look too closely."

Alice climbed off the table and extended a hand to Susan. The two appraised one another. The girl had an educated accent which tended, perhaps understandably, towards shrewishness when she addressed William, and clear brown eyes.

"I'm sorry about him," she said, "Are you Susan, the new Drama teacher? Mike said you were starting today. I'm Alice Jameson."

"Susan Halsbury," Susan shook the girl's hand.

"He's William Fenneck," Alice continued, "When he's not being horrible, he teaches History and Politics."

"I am the *Head* of Politics," William corrected.

"Only because the last one had a nervous breakdown," Alice cackled, "Largely as a result of having to work with you."

"You can't prove that," William shouted, his face purple. Alice had clearly touched on a sore spot. "I gave that bloody woman my full support. It was the Quality Audit that did for her."

Alice smiled triumphantly.

"Ha!" she cried, "Yes, because she lost her marbles trying to work out polite ways of expressing how useless you were."

"What the hell do you know, anyway? You're only an undergraduate. Shut up and don't speak until you've learned enough to have something worthwhile to say."

Alice ignored him and asked Susan if she wanted a drink.

"Don't give her any of my Swedish vodka," William barked from his ladder, "Some thieving gypsy bastard hoofed loads of it out of the office yesterday. If I find out who it was I'll have his knees on a plate."

"I'm not giving out any vodka. It's ten o'clock in the morning," Alice said.

So what, Susan thought.

"Erm," she said, "Coffee would be lovely. What do you do here?"

"Officially, nothing. I used to go here, you see, and I'm still at university. But I want to be a teacher and sometimes this lot let me have work experience. And sometimes, like today, William lets me borrow books for my course. Other times I help with admin and so on."

Susan looked at the enormous pile of texts which tottered precariously on a table.

"You're borrowing all those?" she asked, incredulously, "Don't the students here need them?"

"Well, yes," William said, "But we aren't allowed to issue them. As of last year, College policy has been that students must buy their own textbooks. We have an arrangement with the town bookshop; they have an outlet next to the canteen where the kiddiwinks can buy books at inflated prices. We get a bit of a rakeoff. Good, eh?"

"Seems a bit dodgy to me," Susan said.

"It's an absolute disgrace," Alice agreed, "But it does mean I get access to this great big stock of books that no-one's using."

Susan looked at the pile of books again.

"These are Eng Lit texts," she observed.

"Yes, you wouldn't catch me doing mouldy old History or pompous rubbish like Politics," the girl said, "I'm going to teach English."

"Only because no educational institution offers qualifications in shopping," rasped William.

There was a knock at the door and another young man came in. Unlike William, he had eschewed the traditional uniform of academia for a collarless shirt with Indian patterning on it and a rather fashionable sequinned waistcoat. He had also grown a beard and a pony-tail.

"I've brought next week's Personal and Social Awareness materials," he announced, carefully placing a bundle of photocopies on one of the few clear areas of desk space. William and Alice ignored him, so he looked at Susan.

"Hi," he said, enthusiastically, "You must be Susan, the drama person, yah? I saw the announcement on the boss's noticeboard. Great to have you on board here in the madhouse."

He chortled.

"Thank you," said Susan, "And you're, er…?"

"Barnaby, call me Barnaby, everyone does," he said, ignoring William's comment that the boys in the rugby team had a quite different name for him, "I'm from the Social Science Faculty, yah? We teach stuff like Sociology and, like, Economics and that, and we also run the Personal and Social Awareness course which all the students take, right?"

"I see," Susan said.

"It's really great," continued Barnaby, who was still enthusiastic despite the fact that William and Alice were ostentatiously looking at the materials he had brought with visible distaste, "There are scheduled lessons, whole-College lectures and, like, workshops. All the staff contribute whatever they can from their subject backgrounds, interests or personal experiences, right? And, hey, as a female member of staff I think you'd have a lot of ideas to offer. Women are very much in a minority here, and the patriarchal power structures are skewed against them, what with it being a very bourgeois, traditionalist environment, you know?"

"Women aren't in a minority here," William said, vaguely, as if to himself, "There are fifty-six women and forty-eight men."

"Maybe so, William," Barnaby said, seriously, "But they're treated as a minority. Men have all the important posts."

"Like yours, for instance," Alice commented, idly contemplating her fingernails, "I must say that when I went here I really appreciated being taught about toxic shock syndrome by blokes who think periods are something to do with geology."

"Do you *have* to talk about that sort of thing in mixed company?" William asked, with palpable revulsion, "You really disgust me sometimes."

"There's nothing disgusting about natural human activity," Barnaby said.

"I'll remember that," William said, "When next I have to go to the toilet in the Social Science Block. Your office is handier than trekking down to the gents."

Susan wished Mike would hurry up. He had explained to her on a previous visit that there was a degree of inter-subject rivalry in the College. This was partly due to the climate of fear engendered by the redundancy programme but had also been inadvertently encouraged by the Principal, who was not averse to making jocularly disparaging remarks about the less traditional subjects. The enthusiasm of the Sociologists in particular for radical causes had led to their being regarded by some other teachers as a political correctness thought police. This was not wholly fair, since when they were on their own the Sociologists were perfectly capable of discussing football and pornography with an enthusiasm which would have impressed even the crassest members of the football team. William Fenneck and other right-wing members of staff did not see this; they only saw the white poppies at Remembrance Day and bizarre essays which referred to the National Health Service as a capitalist plot. William had interpreted the old man's remarks about Social Sciences as carte blanche to indulge his natural proclivities towards conflict. From his rooms in the old grammar school, known to the cognoscenti as the Wolfschanze, he waged an ideological war against the Marxist anti-Christ. Disingenuously offering to arrange a joint educational tour with the Social Science Faculty, the Historians had taken the students to Eastern Europe, where they were shown round labour camps, lectured by former dissidents and driven through bleak housing developments. Faced with what they were told were irrefutable physical proof of the realities of Marxism, the students subsequently refused point-blank to believe anything they were told in Sociology classes.

Inter-subject co-operation had broken down and been replaced with open hostility, which the students clearly enjoyed and indeed stirred up, gleefully running to William with claims that they were being denied freedom of speech in Sociology lessons whilst reporting William's blatant political incorrectness back to Barnaby. Mike had warned Susan not to get sucked into their cold war, as the teachers had developed a tendency to dump their worst students in one another's subjects. William took particular pleasure in suggesting to the least civilised thugs from the first fifteen that Sociology would be just the thing for their cvs, and Barnaby retaliated by flooding the History and Politics classes with long-haired boys who pursued a distinctly laid-back agenda. This struggle was rendered one-sided by William's cheerful use of tactics of bullying, hatred and contempt to force students he disliked out of his classes. Barnaby clung desperately to the belief that the most dim-witted student could be lifted to a more constructive level of awareness through kindness and understanding, and was driven to despair by the refusal of William's rugby players to spout anything other than a crude social Darwinism in lessons.

These setbacks apart, however, the Social Sciences Faculty was undergoing a renaissance. Whilst the Principal was known to disapprove of them, their subjects were popular with students who took them largely on the grounds that they were different from what they had done at school and not especially difficult. They could also claim a high degree of social relevance, which impressed ambitious local parents anxious to be thought up-to-date. Their control of the Personal and Social Awareness course enabled them to extend their agenda throughout the college, as did the Equal Opportunities Committee, which monitored the numbers of female and ethnic minority students taking each subject and sent piously-worded letters to those department heads who presided over noticeable imbalances. Secure in their fastness in a smart modern block, strategically overlooking both the car park and the lower quad, they were happy in their work. Susan had been advised to be nice to them.

"This pile of stuff," William said, "It's incomplete."

"What do you mean?" Barnaby asked.

"Well, it's about the arms trade, but you only give one point of view."

"You can't mean that we should include the viewpoint of the weapons manufacturers? You must be joking. The whole thing's morally indefensible."

"Nonsense," William said, "We could use a topic like this to instil a bit of civic pride amongst the students. Did you know that, as a nation, our arms exports rose by a good five per cent last year?"

"That's not quite the point of view I think we want to encourage. These materials concentrate on the damage, waste and cruelty of the arms trade."

"Ah," William said, triumphantly, "I think you'll be pleasantly surprised by some of the new thinking in the defence industry. I've got some brochures from British Aerospace for a new aeroplane. It's got the kind of economical, multi-mission adaptability that small developing nations have been crying out for. And you can target some of our latest munitions onto the actual CND badge in the back window of an individual Citroen 2CV. A whole Gay Pride march can be taken out with minimum collateral damage."

"You," Barnaby said, "Are a sick man."

"I thought we were teaching them that there are two sides to every argument," William said, "You were quick enough off the mark to do that when I introduced the lower sixth to *the Bell Curve*."

"That was different," Barnaby snapped, "And if you don't know why you ought to be sacked."

"If anyone ought to be sacked it's you," William retorted, "These documents are littered with exclamation marks. That means you've either got the literary skills of a six-year-old or, since only pooves use exclamation marks, you're insidiously promoting homosexuality in contravention of Section Twenty-eight of the Local Government Act. Either way you're out on your ear when I grass you up to the *Daily Mail*."

He smiled with all the affectionate warmth of a guard at the Lubianka.

Barnaby looked disgusted. He turned from William, who had found a bottle of correction fluid and had begun carefully to erase all the exclamation marks, and addressed Susan.

"William, as you can see, is our resident National Socialist," he breezed.

William muttered that he wasn't any sort of bloody socialist. Barnaby paid no attention and continued to breeze.

"Susan, hey, great to meet you. I have to go and deliver more of these things to departments which appreciate the work we put into this programme. See you down at the canteen sometime, or perhaps you'd like to join the Equal Opportunities Committee."

He left, ignoring the raspberry which William blew at his retreating back.

"He's going to have to work on those chat-up lines," Alice observed.

"Who was he chatting up?" William was bewildered.

"You," Alice said, then snorted as the little man looked even more puzzled, "Susan, you idiot. Wasn't it obvious?"

"Was he chatting her up?" William asked.

"William, you dozy sod, some men do chat up women. They're actually interested in them."

"Oh," William said, "Why?"

"Because we're great. Hadn't you noticed?"

Alice tossed her dark hair theatrically. Susan smiled. William didn't.

"The only female I know is you," he said, "So no, not really."

"Twat. What did you think he was doing, anyway?"

"Being patronising. You know what his sort are like. Skirt, ethnics, bum-bandits, cripples—they always want to co-opt them for some damn-fool ideas. Ever since the native English working class were shown up for the bone idle, racialist, scrounging bastards that they are, your commie type has been on the lookout for a substitute proletariat. Hence totty, sausage-jockeys, our chums from exotic climes et cetera are constantly being harrassed by bearded mummy's boys to join their polytariat. I read about it in the *Spectator*."

William returned to the shelving. He stared at another book and dropped it onto the floor.

"For goodness' sake, William," Alice hissed, "You mustn't talk like that. I've told you before. You'll get into serious trouble some day. Some of those words you use are probably illegal. Anyway, I have to go. I've got to dish out pharmaceuticals to the sickly folk of Hengistley. Nice meeting you, Susan. I'm sure I'll see you about. I work in Boots in the holidays if you want a discount on life's little essentials."

Susan smiled and watched the girl leave.

"She's nice," she said.

"No she isn't," William said, shortly, "She's a bossy old trout."

He picked up a copy of the *Daily Telegraph* with a prominent "Not to be removed from the Library" sticker on the cover, and lay down on the floor with it. From a pocket in his tweed waistcoat he produced a metal cigarette lighter.

"Do you have any cigarettes?" he asked.

"No," said Susan, "Sorry."

"Ah, dear," said William, sadly, "I suppose I'll have to smoke one of my own."

He fumbled in the pockets of his jacket and found a tattered packet of tobacco. He rolled a cigarette and lit it with a sharp clacking sound. Sprawled on the floor with his green and brown clothes, he resembled a smouldering pile of compost. He pored over an article in the *Telegraph* linking juvenile crime to hamburgers and television and made contented little puffing noises.

"Oh," said Susan, and, as it seemed to be what William wanted, sat quietly reading a book. She wished Mike would hurry up.

Mike was on his way, positively alight with joy. He had, in fact, been quivering with excitement since his encounter with Jonathan Bleach the previous day. After their conversation, he had collared William in the office and explained the new system to him in raptures of excitement. William had not seen him like this before. Teachers at Mercier's were not encouraged to go into raptures.

"This is it! My big break!"

"It just sounds like more work to me."

"Oh, the narrow ideas of lesser men. Don't you see the possibilities? This is your chance to make your mark."

"I've already made my mark."

"Yes, and an unhealthy, yellowing sort of mark it was too. No, we want another kind of mark. We could divert the money somehow and use it for our own projects."

"Like what? I don't have any projects." "Not since that nice brunette who taught Russian left, anyway. But *I* have projects. I have vision. Great vision."

"Doesn't sound like it to me. I'd see an optician if I were you."

William fiddled with the workings of a retractable ball-point pen. Propelled by the spring, its ink cartridge shot across the room and landed in a waste-paper basket. William smiled with the innocent joy of a four-year-old who has discovered a new trick. He trotted over to the waste-paper basket, collected the cartridge, and reloaded his pen. Mick groaned in exasperation.

"Christ, you Scotch berk. That's the most interesting thing you've ever done, isn't it? Little things for little fucking minds."

William looked hurt, like a four-year-old child who has just discovered that his new trick has not met with parental approval. Mike ignored him.

"By diverting funds from this thing, I can finance the biggest dramatic extravaganza ever to grace the boards of the Progressive Horizons Theatre, Brighton."

"I dare say," William was sulky, "What did you have in mind?"

"Picture the scene," Mike was acutely conscious that, in dealing with a person with no imagination, this might be difficult, but, as Sir James Goldsmith had once said, it was worth the fight, "The Millenium production. The audio-visual spectacular of *Our Mutual Friend*."

"Not *Our Mutual Friend* by Dickens?"

"No, *Our Mutual Friend* by Tina fucking Turner. Of course the one by bloody Dickens."

"But it's about a billion pages long. There's drowning and stuff in it. How the hell are you going to get that on stage?"

"That's where the money from the College comes in," Mike looked out of the window with a visionary stare. He saw one of his students smoking a joint in the shrubbery, realised that reporting the fact would involve filling in a detailed form, and looked back at William. William looked dubious, but then he usually did.

"But how will you divert the cash? There's bound to be some sort of monitoring built in."

Mike paced into the centre of the room and stopped being visionary. He adopted a more encouraging tone.

"But, but, but; for pity's sake, man, you sound like a moped. Would Britain have built the Empire for which you retain a very suspicious level of affection if everyone had gone around saying 'but'?"

"It would be pretty difficult to build anything if one just said 'but', or indeed any other word, all the time. I'm just saying that you'll need to generate cash from the lump sum they give you, then divert the profits, and feed the money back somehow. How are you actually going to make money?" William squirted some hot water into a paper cup with instant coffee granules, then carefully poured the resulting grimy fluid into his favourite mug, which bore an image of several Moomins at play. Even the way he did this seemed to indicate a Calvinistic pedantry. Mike tutted.

"I haven't thought about that yet. That's the problem about being a teacher, I suppose. No instinct for the profit motive. It's why the internal market in hospitals didn't work. I don't imagine doctors were very good at money-making schemes either."

"Well, quite," William had gathered his papers together and stuffed them into an old brown leather briefcase. He lit another cigarette and peered out of the window at the fine drizzle which was descending on the town and pulled a battered tweed trilby from the pocket of a shabby overcoat that hung from a hook on the back of the door. He drained his coffee and grimaced.

"How beastly the non-alcoholic drink is. I'm off. Coming for a snifter?"

"Can't. Want to look around cyberspace for entrepreneurial visions."

"You'll go blind."

William had struggled into the overcoat, jammed the trilby on his head and ambled off. A few minutes later, through the open window of the staffroom, Mike could hear the rhythmic squeaking of the Head of Politics' ancient bicycle, overlaid with a thoroughly unpleasant wheezing sound, as his colleague pedalled off for the customary pints which would form his pre-supper aperitif or, if it was raining, supper itself. Then Mike had worked long into the night.

Eventually, he had gone home, his head in a whirl of ideas, and his mind was no less excited now as he made his way to the English office to meet his new colleague. Pulling a packet of Silk Cut from his pigeonhole, Mike walked to the staffroom drinks machine, took a cup of tea from it, and drank it and smoked, nervously, excitedly, as he moved. There were possibilities here. There was a chance to make *OMF*, as he already referred in his head to the stage version of his favourite novel, into a dramatic production of such power that it would radicalise, or at least mildly divert, all who came to see it. Already, in his mind's eye, Mike had conjured up sets and themes, selected actors from amongst Brighton's thespian community for various roles, and weaved progressive themes into the story. A bold and innovative exploration of class, selfishness, prejudice and duty—*Jerusalem* come alive on stage—no more tedious minimalism for him and his troupe. Mike was fed up with productions done in the round so as to save on backdrops and settings, with Samuel *fucking* Beckett. The theatre was the part of Mike's life which liberated him and was like a big placard above his head; *I am not just a teacher—I do other things—I don't have to do this.* This was his chance to make more of it. It wasn't even intrinsically dishonest; the College would get its money back eventually. He exhaled a thin jet of smoke as he entered his office.

"Susan, Susan," he carolled, "Great to see you. Has William been looking after you? No, I don't suppose he has. No matter, no matter. Have you ever thought about dramatising *Our Mutual Friend*?"

"Leave the wretched woman be," William snorted from behind the newspaper.

"Actually, William," Mike said, "I've got a bone to pick with you. Did you tell Annelise Featherstone that Cromwell's activities in Ireland were the moral equivalent of the United Nations today?"

"No," William was indignant, "You know perfectly well I disapprove of the United Nations. She must have put that spin on it herself. Now Cromwell, on the other hand, was a great—"

"Shut up," Mike said, impatiently, "Let's go and have lunch in the pub. I've got a great idea to put to you."

CHAPTER FOUR

"Three pints of four star, John, a slimline tonic for the charming person on my right, and whatever for your good self," Michael Alcock boomed across the bar of the Hertford Arms. William, who lived in Hengistley and often drank in the Hertford, was exchanging pleasantries with some seedy-looking young men who were playing pool and swearing a lot. Susan tried to ignore the fact that these people were staring at her with frank interest. She was not merely being mentally undressed but subjected to a medical inspection.

"Sorry," William called over to her, "Young women don't often come in at this time of the day. They don't mean any harm. Most of them used to be our students, you know." This did not inspire Susan's confidence.

"Thanks now," the barman said to Mike, "I'll have a half with ye. That'll be eight pounds and fifty pence."

"Faaack," the Head of English gyrated slightly, "I'm not sure I have enough. Susan, could you sub me a tenner for the weekend? I'll pay you back on Monday."

His eyes opened wide and he gave a winning smile of inspiring openness.

William Fenneck ambled over. Susan had last seen him leaning over a brightly-lit gaming machine, into which he had been cramming coins, murmuring, "Come on, now, my precious, daddy needs a win, do it for daddy, hey?"

"I say, Susan," he murmured, running his fingers nervously through his hair, then entwining them amongst one another in an almost spastic gesture of awkwardness, "Could you possibly lend me a bluey? I'm on a winning streak on the quiz machine, and I'm convinced I can make it a brownie. We could split the profits."

"No, William," Mike said, "You never win, you know it. Remember that time in the pub in Brighton? Twelve pounds you put into that thing. And what did you get back? Sweet Fanny Adams. Your glory days on the quiz machine are over, don't you understand? They were back in 1995. Those days are gone. And Susan's going to lend *me* some money anyway."

"That was different. It was a Brighton quiz machine. Questions about new age music and vegetarianism and such. This is a Hengistley quiz machine. I can do those. Anyway, my glory days need not end. I see myself enjoying a comeback, like Elvis at Vegas in the seventies."

Susan had a mental picture of William in a rhinestone catsuit. A wave of nausea passed through her.

"Come, let us sit," Mike announced, and settled the group around a high table. Perched on tall chairs, they leaned inwards awkwardly.

"These are really awful tables," Mike said, "Where the hell did they come from?"

"It was the refit," said William, who loved the Hertford more than anything else in the world and could not bear to hear criticism of it, "It's supposed to combine the best of an American sports bar with a traditional English look. And if you drop your drink, it's got longer to travel before it hits the ground, so you might, conceivably, catch it."

"Which means that we are stuck four foot off the ground around a very high, very wonky table, which, for the sake of looking olde worlde, weighs two tons because it's made of solid bleeding oak? Nice one. What if it tips over, eh? We'd be crushed like ants."

He swigged heartily from his pint of lager.

"I think it looks rather good," Susan offered, "It reminds me of a place in Southport I used to drink in."

She was immediately conscious of having committed a faux pas through the expression of unteacherly opinions.

"But with the greatest possible respect, Susan," Mike said, "We are in Hengistley, a town known for its ancient alehouses and its traditional drinking environment. This lot looks a bit out of place here, don't you think?"

"It has to be said that most of the alehouses in Hengistley aren't especially traditional," William commented, morosely, "The majority are just beer machines for teenage proles."

A familiar figure in most of the pubs of the town, William knew what he was talking about. Virtually all of the central bars were populated entirely by sub-Essex wide boys who had left school at sixteen and were doing awright, as they put it, in local trades. They were homogenous, boisterous and intolerant, with a high opinion of their own virility and honour which led to violent altercations at closing time. They were suspicious of people like William, who at twenty-eight they considered too old to be in pubs and whose refusal to wear anything other than tweeds they regarded as a sure sign of incipient homosexuality, an interesting irony given his belief that society's toleration of sodomy was a step on the road to national collapse. The Mercier's students had their own favourite pubs, which changed from year to year as the local licensed victuallers went through annual purges of under-age drinkers. The Hertford was, despite its unusual high tables, virtually the only pub in town which served a cross-section of Hengistley society. Its owners, an intelligent and hard-working Scottish family, had cleared out the nastier regulars when they took over, and established it as a community pub in which no one clique was permitted to dominate. They had also refurbished the main bar, creating a bright and airy space where previously there had been twilight gloom in the middle of the day, and installed a television facing the bar in order to watch Rangers-Celtic matches and check on their shares via Ceefax. The Hertford was one of the few pubs where most of the clientele on a Friday night was over the age of twenty-five and there were no confrontations between adolescent gangs. It was the official watering-hole of the Mercier's staff.

"Of course, it could be argued that in the late twentieth century, we are inventing our own traditions," Mike contributed, "The pictures and artefacts on the walls representing a post-modern statement about where we are currently going."

"Well, we aren't currently going to the point, and I rather wish we could," said Susan, who had been told that you had to be firm with the other English teachers, "I mean, we aren't here just because you want to show me your favourite bar, are we? And we're supposed to be going to that play later on."

"No, indeed," Mike said, "To business, to business. Now, you may have seen Jonathan Bleach, our esteemed Under-Vice-Principal, weaving an unsteady path home last night. This is because of an excellent piece of detective work carried out by myself with the aid of some vodka I found lying about."

"So that's where it went," William growled, "Thieving scumbag."

"Well, look on the bright side," said Mike, "That's a bottle of vodka that didn't go down your throat. Think of the benefits to your health. Anyway, getting on, we stand on the edge of a brave new era at Mercier's."

"Which will involve what, exactly?" asked Susan.

"Well, apparently, in order to save money, they're going to abolish the position of Bursar, and turn the departments into mini-businesses. The heads of the departments will have a budget from which they will set their own pay and work out what they're going to spend on books and so on for the kids. They'll have to make up any shortfalls themselves."

"But that's appalling," Susan cried, "You can't treat education like a business. It's totally immoral. Whatever happened to the idea that teachers were driven by love for their subjects and enthusiasm for learning?"

There was a momentary pause whilst the others tried to think of sarcastic remarks about this, and failed. Mike broke the silence with characteristic breezy enthusiasm.

"Well, putting aside the moral issue—not that I want to, you understand, but just for a moment—let's look at the structure of it. All the subjects will carry on being grouped into big super-departments, the faculties. This is where the financial planning would be done. We in English are grouped together, along with History, in the Humanities Faculty. The Head of this Faculty, a position which will be up for review before the new machinery comes in, would take responsibility for the budget, being, in effect, a kind of chief executive or government minister. He or she would then allocate funds to each subject area. So, just like, say, the Minister of Defence, the Head of Humanities would give a budget to his Army," Mike indicated himself, "his Navy," he pointed at Susan, then jerked his thumb at William, "and his Home Guard. They could pool their resources or spend or invest them individually. It's supposed to encourage creative financial responsibility."

"The potential for corruption here," Susan said, "Is immense."

"Yes," Mike said suavely, "It is, isn't it?"

Six hours later, Susan was in the foyer of the local theatre buying tickets whilst Mike charged about trying to count a milling crowd of students. Her first task as Head of Drama had been to organise a visit to the theatre with which to start the term, and she had been delighted when Andrew MacDonald, the Head of Law, had agreed to come along and help. She was perfectly well aware that he was freeloading at her department's expense and that he probably wouldn't have been interested in helping had she been other than young, slim and red-headed, but she didn't care. She had never done this before and needed all the moral support she could get. It had also been useful to tell someone about the plots that Mike Alcock was hatching.

"This production of *the Tempest*," Andrew mused, "It's pretty avant-garde, isn't it?"

"Yes, so I hear," Susan answered, "I do hope the kids like it. It's the first trip I've organised. It's really good of you to come and help."

"Not at all," Andrew said, smoothly, "Always glad to help out. And don't worry about Mike's scheming. He can't do anything with that money unless he's Head of Faculty, in the full financial sense. Strong chance that Jane Miller, the Head of History, could get that, rather than him. And she's as honest as…as me."

Susan was still concerned. The Head of English seemed to feel that the new budgets represented a giant slush fund into which he and his immediate friends could dip in order to gratify their desires. Susan did not want to think about what these desires were. He claimed he wanted to put on a play, but how was she to know that this was true? Mike's ideas, she felt, were singularly inappropriate for someone who was supposed to be a card-carrying member of the Labour Party.

"And who's that girl, Alice, who hangs about in the English office?"

"Oh, A Town Like, we call her. One of our old students. William's Official Friend. Only girl in his social circle which is otherwise entirely composed of soaks from the Hertford and the Conservative Club. Only person younger than him allowed to use his Christian name. Only person he knows who, despite being close to him, still wants to be a teacher. I think that's why she hangs around with him. She's also pally with Portia Bates, who was made redundant last year. Some people say Alice knows more about Mercier's than a lot of teachers."

"Are she and William, er..?"

"Hell, no, and don't ask either of them that or they'll bite your head off. Understandable in Alice's case. He treats her like an annoying little sister and she treats him like a fat oaf who wouldn't know reality if it kicked him in the arse. He once said that he hangs around with her because she appreciates the concept of an ever-expanding body of knowledge. He should know all about ever-expanding bodies, given the amount he drinks. Funny pair."

Mike came up to them looking dishevelled.

"If this play is shit," he said, "I must make it clear that I shall regard it as my absolute duty to put on a better one with the aid of cash borrowed from the College."

Susan went into the auditorium with a sense of foreboding.

The interval saw the theatre bar throb with students, all intent on squeezing as many pints as possible into twenty minutes. They would pay for this in the second act, as their bladders screamed angrily for relief and they were trapped in the middle of the auditorium. Susan was sipping glumly at a small lager shandy.

"It's awful," she wailed, "I've never seen such a dreadful production of any play, ever. Whatever drugs they were on when they thought up those costumes are clearly a major threat to British culture. And they can't even act. The kids must hate me."

"Nonsense," Mike said, comfortingly, "Look at them. Happy as Larry. They like to see bad productions because it gives them something to talk about. No-one remembers that fantastic performance of *An Inspector Calls* which I took them to see because it was good. After they'd enthused a bit, it evaporated from their minds. This, on the other hand, they will remember for years to come."

Mike considered the learning process to be at least partly experiential and wholly good. Whilst he had a sceptical attitude to human nature, he believed that a better society could be created if everyone pulled together in the right way. The fact that this had yet to happen occasionally depressed him, but he was just as often buoyed up by some happy event such as a student's discovery of a new author or the defeat of right-wing candidates in local elections. Of such things would the new collectivist millenium be made.

Susan did not know this, but, had she done, it would have raised awkward questions in her mind about Mike's willingness to manipulate the College funds in some as yet unspecified way. Mike would not have been fazed by such questions. He had no intention of stealing from the place, merely using the money to generate more so that he could mount a production of startling brilliance with his amateur theatre group in Brighton, with which he worked in order to sustain a viable existence away from the cultural desert of Hengistley. He was being a tiny bit dishonest in order to bring a greater truth to bear on the world via the great play which he was going to unleash. This was, he felt sure, a deeply moral act. It was just more fun to make it look a bit shady. Mike had not been a keen, if unsuccessful, student of female psychology for nothing. He was perfectly well aware that all the most interesting girls liked a rogue, and girls of any sort liked something to complain about. It was excellent training for married life. Similarly, students were wary of teachers who were always right. They liked a streak of humanity, apart, obviously, from the St. Eva's girls. Susan would gain a safe place in their affections after tonight's debacle.

"And they won't hate you anyway," Andrew pointed out, "Because they think Mike booked it. I heard them talking about vandalising his car."

"But I don't have one," Mike said, puzzled, "I was banned after that, ah, incident."

"Oh, yeah, so you were," Andrew remembered, "I wonder whose car that is that they've written all over, then?"

"No matter," Mike said, "Let's all look on the funny side, shall we? It's so dreadful it's amusing. What more could you ask for?"

The play was indeed a bizarre spectacle. Banal in the extreme until Scene II, the only people enjoying it were a group of twelve year olds from the local boarding school. Suddenly, Ariel had arrived. The airy spirit was a ten foot high black tepee on legs, whose goat-like papier-mâché head bobbed about as he weaved about the stage in peculiar dances, waving enormous, spindly hands at the end of broom-handles.

"Hell's bells!" Mike yelled, beer having dulled his sense of propriety, "Look at that!"

If the person inside Ariel's costume heard this, he or she gave no indication. It was not immediately possible to ascertain to which of the sexes this person belonged, so muffled was the speech which emerged from the depths of the pirouetting wigwam. The fact that the cast was made up of three actresses and one actor added to the difficulty. Caliban, who appeared on the stage looking like a giant turtle, was played by a woman, giving his passion for Miranda a rather confusing edge. Andrew, who lived in Brighton and had, accordingly, a higher level of pretension tolerance than the students, was initially prepared to accept that there might be some rationale behind it all. When Miranda was transformed into a goddess, and donned a fifteen foot high silver marquee and a headpiece that resembled a shaving-brush to symbolise the event, even he gave up, and joined the students in helpless sniggering.

"For a play with touchingly romantic overtones," he remarked to Mike, "This production has the dispiriting effect of putting one off relations with the opposite sex for life. If that bloody bacofoil junkheap was supposed to represent the summit of all human desire, then I'm opting out of the whole babes thing."

"Speaking of human desire," Mike said, "Or the lack thereof, I wonder what saucy doings our esteemed colleague is up to with A Town Like back at his bachelor love grotto?"

"Oh, is William cooking for Alice again? I'm not entirely sure that I want to think about that," Andrew giggled, "But then, I've always been squeamish."

"In that case, I regret to have to tell you that Act Two is upon us. Do you want to take an Alka Seltzer before we go in?"

William was, in fact, experimenting with a small saucepan of gravy in the uncharacteristically tidy little kitchen of his flat. Alice rested her willowy frame in the doorway and crunched at raw vegetables as she watched him play with various ingredients.

"Do you like it any more peppery than that?" he asked, "It's just that I don't want to drown out the taste of the quail. A delicate meat, you see."

"After what you've drunk and smoked over the past ten years, I'm surprised you can taste anything," said Alice, sipping from the proffered spoon, "But it's fine like that."

"I wasn't thinking of me, I was thinking of you," he replied, vaguely.

"There's a first," she remarked.

"It'll be a last, too, if you don't desist with the smartarse comments," said William, putting his hand into the oven to see if it was hot.

"What are you doing now, you old fool?" asked the girl.

"I am not old," he barked, testily, "I'm twenty-eight."

"You neither look nor act it," said Alice with asperity, "You dress like the last war hadn't happened, your views on life are out of the dark ages and your physical condition is that of a man twice your age."

"You'll never find out about my physical condition," responded William, "I'm saving this carcase for someone a hell of a lot sexier that you."

"What, like Calpurnia Woodard, you mean?" Alice sneered, naming another former student with whom William had had a brief relationship some years previously, and for whom she had developed an intemperate degree of loathing, "She's welcome to find out about your bloody physical condition, but I'm in no hurry. I'd sooner go to bed with a farmyard animal."

"As indeed you have," William snapped, poisonously, "Naming no names."

"You bastard," Alice yelled, "That was uncalled for."

"So was your remark about Calpurnia," muttered William, who was stubbornly loyal to his ex-girlfriend, even though, all things considered, it had been a little unfair of her to abandon him in favour of a member of the Crowborough Grease Warriors motorcycle gang. William saw himself as a worthless and iniquitous sinner, so, in his peculiar value system, Calpurnia had demonstrated a degree of intelligence by getting rid of him. This had confirmed both what passed for his esteem for her and his overall misogyny. "At least she's got a plural number of brain cells."

"Honestly! You're like a six year old child."

"Make your bloody mind up about my age, would you? While you're doing so, and I imagine it'll take you a while, given that you'll have to find a mind first, take these plates into the dining room. I'm about to dish up."

Conversations such as this brought Alice and William very real happiness and maintained a useful barrier to the development of an inconvenient romantic relationship. The mutual disgust that each felt for the other's former partners ensured that they could never bear the thought of being added to a list containing people they so disliked. In any case, Alice had a boyfriend at university, whilst William was unable to contemplate the difficulties which acquiring another girl-friend would entail.

Brought up, following the death of his parents, by an uncle who was a clergyman in a remote part of Scotland, his reading matter as a child had consisted entirely of books written before the sexual revolution, the end of the British Empire and the introduction of decimal currency. His first visit to the shops on his own had bewildered him, whilst the girl behind the counter of the village tobacconist had been equally confused to find the minister's nephew demanding sixpennyworth of brandy balls and half a crown in cinnamon lozenges. His view of women had been romantic to a degree which even the readers of Barbara Cartland would have found naïve. His rank idiocy had lost him a girlfriend at university, whilst a relationship with a colleague which might have made him more socially acceptable had been wrecked by her discovery that he kept a shrine to Queen Victoria in his bathroom. His disastrous relationship with Calpurnia had turned him into such a thoroughgoing sexist that it was widely believed at the College that when Alice had introduced him to her mother, it had doubled the number of women whom he actually liked. His discovery that the entire world which he imagined lived beyond the bounds of his childhood village and isolated boarding-school no longer existed had made him bitterly cynical about virtually everything. If Mike's world was like a James Stewart film, and Barnaby Worthington's a production by Eisenstein, William looked out onto the Hobbesian state of nature featured in the works of Clint Eastwood. In that amoral, cruel landscape, life was a desolate struggle for survival in which happiness could only ever be a transitory illusion, for sin and wickedness would always intrude. This did not depress William; on the contrary, he felt a gloomy Eeyorean smugness about it.

Alice, for her part, found that spending time with William was a more restful experience than the frantic and energetic life she pursued at university, and it flattered her to know that she was believed by many of his friends to be a good influence on him. An essentially good-natured girl, she liked the idea—which some of William's friends, who were eager to see him married off and saw Alice as useful practice, assiduously cultivated—that she brought out what passed for the nicer side of his character. Her ambition to become a teacher helped in her dealings with him. She was fascinated by staffroom gossip, whilst his apparent enjoyment of her enthusiastic chatter about her favourite literature confirmed her belief that she could definitely pursue this career. Being waited on and cooked for not only gave her the cosseting she did not always receive from boys her own age, but satisfied her that he was eating as well. Alice was well aware that William was sufficiently absent-minded to forget about feeding himself, so by having dinner with him she could make sure that he had proper meals every so often.

It was obvious to her that the meal was merely a device to accompany heavy drinking on his part, and that he preferred having dinner with girls because he believed they should not be allowed into pubs, but Alice didn't mind.

No-one, especially not Alice and William, was really sure how or why they had become friends. They just had.

"What was Mike Alcock looking so excited about yesterday?" she asked as she poured gravy over the small birds which sat brownly in the middle of her plate, "He looked like a puppy in a tripe pit."

"I can't remember," William said, sadly, for he couldn't, and hated his poor memory, "After you with the vegetables."

He thought for a moment.

"It might be this new funding thing. Jonathan Bleach told him about it. Essentially, as I understand it, and I can't swear that I do, we'd be given much more responsibility for the cash our departments spend. Like a business, you see. This would mean that we could get up to all sorts of fiddles. Great fun. Alcock reckons we could make a fortune. He wants to spend it on a big play, I think."

Alice's bright, warm brown eyes met his tired, cold grey eyes across the table. The candles lent extra light to her gaze as she fixed him with a stare which reminded him, for a poignant second, of the way Calpurnia had looked at him when he had absent-mindedly used her perfume to clean a model aeroplane paintbrush.

"Now you listen to me, you stupid bastard. You are not going to try to fiddle anything. You can't teach. You can't womanise. You can't tidy your own flat. What the hell makes you think that you are remotely capable of defrauding scheming bastards like Walpurgess and Bleach, eh? You're too bloody incompetent, and you'd get caught. And you know why? Because I'd tell on you. So forget it, and forget it now. Or there'll be trouble."

A candle guttered as a gust of wind hit the window. To William, it seemed as if the flame had been bent by the strength of Alice's gaze and the vehemence of what she had said. He swallowed a mushroom the wrong way and choked unattractively. Meeting her gaze with a degree of reluctance, he looked at her defensively.

"It's only an idea," he murmured, "I'm sure we shan't go ahead with anything."

Alice's look softened slightly.

"Make sure you don't," she said, "For goodness' sake, if they can sack Portia Bates, the most popular teacher in the College, so as to save a few quid, getting rid of a dozy sod like you for corruption will be child's play. You just don't think, do you?"

"No, I don't suppose I do," William sighed, and returned to his food.

The play had ended, to the undisguised relief of all in the theatre. The natural reserve of the Sussex audience prevented the curtain call from degenerating into a welter of flying fruit. Mike and Andrew bolted across the road into the nearest pub. Susan followed them slowly, trying to pick up on the vibrations from the students. Her colleagues had been right; they were in hysterics at how amusingly bad the performance had been. She found Mike and Andrew in a corner with a fashionably-dressed man in his late thirties.

"Ah, Susan, my sweet, come join us," carolled Mike, whose alcohol tolerance, Susan realised, was as limited as his moral tolerance was vast, "Do you know Jonathan Bleach, our Under Vice Principal? He drinks here when his wife lets him out of the house because this is where the Czech au pair girls hang out."

Bleach gave a sickly smile.

"Don't mind Mike," he said, "It's actually the closest pub to my house."

"No it isn't," Mike shouted, "The Station Hotel is. But it's full of lorry drivers and what used to be called commercial travellers. Fuck knows what they're called now."

Bleach looked irritated.

"Look, do you want to find out about this big meeting or not?" he asked.

"Yes, yes, Jonathan," Andrew said, reassuringly, "Ignore Mike, he's pissed."

"So I see," said Bleach, doing his best to preserve an image of bonhomie, "Well, the Boss has got it into his head that we should loosen up a bit. He's becoming conscious that staff meetings are a bit stiff and formal. So he wants to take us all out, at College expense, to have the next meeting in a restaurant."

"But what about the cutbacks?" Andrew asked, incredulously, "We were making people redundant last term. Going out to a restaurant strikes me as pure madness. If someone like Portia Bates finds out she'll go to the *County Advertiser* for sure. One of her old students is a journalist there. The one who exposed that District Councillor who took a bung in return for knocking down the primary school to extend the golf course. We'll be made to look like fat cats or something."

"Andrew, not with the wildest and most elastic stretchings of the most flexible imagination could someone with your impeccable socialist credentials be made to look like a fat cat," Mike purred, "Not to mention those snake-like hips."

Andrew shrugged self-deprecatingly to Susan.

"Well, we shall see on Monday. That's when the solids hit the fan in no uncertain terms. I'm worried about the danger of a rash of M.E.," Bleach sighed, "We could all be at risk."

"For fuck's sake, that's a bloody middle class myth," yelled Mike, who insisted that because his grandfather had been a Welsh miner, he was therefore a working man and the salt of the earth.

"So's New fucking Labour," Bleach retorted, "But we still let you believe in that."

"Only women can get M.E.," Mike's political correctness had been known to evaporate under the assaults of extra strong lager, "And you're not one of them. Actually, I don't know. You've become a right bloody old woman in the past few months."

"Do you think you gents could quieten down please, and cut out the swearing?" the barman intervened.

"Or what?" Mike said, belligerently.

Andrew slumped beside Bleach on the wooden bench, put his head in his hands, and thought about Cameron Diaz. He found it helped at moments like this. Susan slipped out a back door and was just getting into her car when she heard the sound of breaking glass. She decided to see Alice at the earliest opportunity.

CHAPTER FIVE

Boots was, fortunately, fairly empty as Susan picked the cheapest brand of Aspirins she could find and made her way to the till where Alice was stationed. It would have been excruciatingly awkward to have had to try to develop social contact with the girl whilst an impatient queue of personal hygiene products purchasers built up.

"Oh, hello," she said brightly, as if in sudden recognition.

"Hello," Alice replied, which was not, in conversational terms, a wholly unreasonable contribution, "Did you enjoy *the Tempest*? Fenneck said that's what you were off to see the other night."

"Er," Susan said.

"One of those, eh?" the younger woman laughed, "Michael Alcock used to take us to see some absolute crap when I was there. Often produced by himself. Was this one of his as well? Forcing eighty-odd students to attend a performance was his way of making sure that his productions made some sort of profit. So Fenneck says, anyway. Though you can't always be sure with what he says. His memory's rubbish. Some of it's the booze, but I think he had a brain like a sieve in the first place. And working in Mercier's just makes him worse."

"Absolutely," Susan smiled, not wanting to go into who had booked the theatre tickets purely on the strength of a very promising, but highly misleading, flyer, "Look, what time do you finish? Could I take you for coffee later? I'd like to have a discreet chat about something."

A flash of momentary doubt hurtled through Alice's mind, but was quickly gone. Whilst some institutions would appoint a predatory lesbian for the sake of political correctness, Alice realised that Mercier's was not one of them. Its male-dominated hierarchy was robustly heterosexual and saw the slightest expression of feminist thinking as a threat not merely to itself but to civilisation as a whole. Lesbianism would terrify these people, for all their laddish jokes about it. In fact, everything terrified these people. The Principal was afraid of the government, the management were afraid of the Principal, and, thanks to the policies pursued by the management, the teachers lived in a permanent state of paranoia and dread. In one of his more morbid lessons whilst she had been his student, William had taught her class a Slavic proverb; "What is large and black and scary and knocking at the door? The future." He had then paused, coughed vigorously and horribly, and added, "That, or big Mohammed, the Moroccan drug dealer from Brighton Road." That William had never been sacked for this kind of thing was a source of constant amazement to Alice.

"Four," she said, "The same as the College. Do you want to come down here and meet me? There's a place at the back of the shopping centre which we could go to."

"Great," Susan replied, relieved that it had been so easy, "I'll see you then."

The Humanities office at Mercier's was a sprawling oaf of a room, reflecting the kind of people who represented the bulk of the faculty staff. Overflowing bookcases dripped paper onto faded carpet, and tottering silent babels of notes, registers, videotapes and texts rose from the scuffed wooden tables which dotted the room. In a dusty corner, a small, dank fridge abounded with more cultural life than the entire North West of England. A scrawled note in Andrew MacDonald's handwriting, pinned to the door along with a playground duty rota from 1975 and a washed-out photography of the English department party in 1989, declared "Arbeit Macht Frei." It was the intellectual answer to the shop notice "You don't have to be mad to work here, but it helps."

Susan joined Prudence and Jane, the other women in the faculty in a huddle in the corner of the room. Prudence, the only female English teacher in a Department largely composed of hard-faced men who had done well out of their Waugh, was reclining gracefully on two old chairs which had been artfully covered with an even older curtain to resemble a chaise longue. She arose languidly, a long menthol cigarette in a black holder describing plumed arcs in the air as she invited Susan to sit with her.

"Susan, dearest, have a chair, do," she trilled, and Susan found herself being reminded, as she so often was when she met women who taught English, of the character Ermyntrude in the popular 1970s television series *The Magic Roundabout*, "We girls must stick together against this great wall of testosterone."

"Yes, indeed," Jane Miller, the Head of History, chimed in, "Left to their own devices, this lot would just talk about football all day."

"That's a disgraceful slur," Andrew said, "Which relies on the perpetuation of cheap sexist clichés. We'd do no such thing. Chiefly because none of this lot know the first thing about football. I have to go and talk to Hannah in Business Studies to get a decent chat about footer."

"But also because we are here to discuss tonight's parents' evening," interjected Mike, whose black eye, tousled hair and torn shirt would have given him a faintly Bohemian air had Susan not been aware that he had acquired this picturesque wear and tear by rolling drunkenly off a table in the Drama Studio, where he had spent the night after being unable to cadge a lift to Brighton, "And I propose we make a start. Now, are we following the usual drill? Parents come up to classrooms, where we are concentrated in groups of half a dozen for protection, see us for seven and a half minutes, then go away?"

"I do wish we could cut it to five minutes," Prudence said, "Some of them can be so difficult to talk to. Especially the ones who were scared of teachers when they were little, and are still intimidated by us. They sit there, like little mice, frightened in case you're going to hit them or something."

"I like that kind," Mike protested, "They're no trouble at all. You could tell them the moon was made of green cheese and that cutting their kids' heads off was part of the syllabus, and they'd go along with it. But they're a dying breed, unfortunately."

"This raises an interesting issue," Jane said, "Susan's about to have her first parents' evening. What would you have liked to have known before your first go at one of these horrible experiences?"

"Well, they aren't really horrible experiences," Andrew pointed out, "Given that we never see the parents of the absolute hellhounds. Most of the parents we see are the decent, supportive kind, who have normal kids who aren't any problem. At worst, it's a pleasant little social ritual in which each side pays lip service to caring about what the other has to say. At best, it's the formation of partnerships with people who see us as their allies in the successful rearing and training of the students, and want to be useful."

"Good, middle-class stuff," Mike sighed, "They just want us to perpetuate the kind of values that they have."

"What exactly is wrong with that?" barked William, who normally said little in meetings because he had a limited understanding of what was going on, and was devoid of interest in anything educational.

"Surely our job is to challenge entrenched prejudice and get them to think for themselves?" Prudence asked. William looked as if she had proposed teaching them about group sex with animals. He put down his copy of *Greenmantle* and made a crochety snorting noise.

"No, it's not. It's to get the brutes through their exams and imbue them with the kind of ideas that they need to succeed in that Darwinian hell-hole which passes for a society out there," he said, crossly, "These parents worked damned hard to be able to live in an over-priced tip like this and it's our duty to make sure that their kids don't become long-haired drop-outs who'll be a disappointment to them."

"Not that it matters either way for William," said Andrew to Susan, "Given that, after two years with him, most students can neither think for themselves nor have any exam results."

"Just because you teach an easy subject," William snarled defensively, "All the buggers have to do is learn a load of court cases off by heart and Bob's their uncle." He lit a cigarette and curled up into his armchair, puffing away like an angry laboratory beagle, "Carlill versus Carbolic Smoke Ball Company. What a load of bollocks."

"Ah, there's another piece of useful advice, actually, admittedly disguised amidst William's customary wreath of thistles," Mike said, "All subjects are easy, except yours. So, if a kid's doing well, make the parents feel good. If he or she isn't, explain that the subject's really difficult and he or she needs to pull the old socks up. Never fails. Absolves you of any responsibility."

He poured a cup of coffee from a frighteningly dirty cafetiere, slopping some over the table, and looked pleased with himself.

"And they *always* need to read more," Prudence said, "Parents often ask for advice on what they can do to help, and, unless there's something specific, like little Billy should stop fiddling with his parts in lessons, this is the thing. The child has not been born who wouldn't benefit from reading another book. Talk about how it develops literary skills as well as imparting information. The interesting thing is that most of the money around here is new, and whilst the parents have the cash, they spend it on consumer durables rather than intellectual self-improvement. This passes on rather unfortunate values to the kiddies. The parents will often say that the child doesn't like reading, and this is super, because then you can put the blame for this on television and primary schools or whatever, and shrug your shoulders, and...oh, it's great. You now have the reason why the brute fails exams, if he does. Immediate arse-covering. Even better if they feel guilty themselves, as they damn well should in my opinion. You can play on it. Though it does get a bit embarrassing if they then decide to blame one another for the swine's illiteracy. 'If you hadn't given in and let him have that computer game…I said buy him the *Encyclopaedia Britannica,* but no, you said let the lad have his fun, he's only seven, give him a Ford Capri'…"

Susan felt slightly better about the whole procedure.

"But what if a parent turns nasty with you?" she asked, meaning with herself.

"That's relatively rare," Mike said, "But we do have this small third category of pains in the arse. There are different types. There's the bastard who despises teachers because they're poncey middle-class intellectuals who don't know what real graft is and are social failures because they haven't made any money. Then there's the pushy parent who thinks little Johnny is God's gift and hates you because you bring it home to them that he isn't."

"Do excuse my colleague's ungrammatical, if politically correct and non-gender-specific, use of the word 'them' to describe this sort of parent," William interrupted, "He should say 'she' because it is invariably a mother doting over her son. Women are blind like this. The fathers are much more realistic. They see a long-haired workshy pain in the arse, much as we do. One chap even said I could feel free to hit his son. Bloody marvellous. Mothers still see the little cherub they dandled on their knees as an infant. You can get a lot of sadistic pleasure from puncturing their balloons, I can tell you."

He smiled in fond reminiscence as Prudence stoked up her fires of righteous indignation and prepared to fall upon him in feminist wrath.

Susan was thinking about this when she met up with Alice outside Boots that afternoon. Alice sensed a degree of distraction and asked if she was all right.

"Sometimes I wonder," she said slowly, "No, actually, every day since I went into teaching I've wondered about some of the people I work with. Why do they do the jobs they're doing? They don't seem to like other human beings very much." She pondered William's remark that a boy from Mike's form ought to be drowned in a bucket.

"Oh, they do really," Alice said, "It's just a game they play. They want to look all tough and macho because you're new. They are awfully caring when they want to be, though Fenneck in particular will never use the word to describe himself because he thinks it's girly. And because he isn't, come to think of it. But they all want to be liked. That's their guilty secret."

She shrugged.

"It's mine, too, I suppose, if I'm being honest. Deep down, I love the idea of lots of kids thinking I'm brilliant and believing my every word about literature. But the thing about the teachers at Mercier's is that they can't show it. It would reveal too much of themselves, make them look weak. So they talk tough. But they're pussycats, every last one of them. In different ways, of course."

The shopping centre, like all of its kind, was bright and antiseptic, with the plastic shopfronts of every British high street conveniently stashed under one roof along with a token reminder of the local past, in this case a rather hideous statue of the Saxon warrior Hengist, for whom the town was named, standing in a fountain. One of the students had added a packet of soap flakes to this attraction and the centre of the arcade was a frothing mass of suds. Children romped in it as if it was winter snow, occasionally running in tears to their mothers as the true nature of the substance made itself manifest on contact with their eyes.

The coffee shop was an undistinguished but clean establishment, tucked away in a corner of the building. Susan ordered two coffees and slices of chocolate cake. Alice clearly did not feel any need to make the obligatory noises of horror, and she attacked the dark slab with gusto. Susan suspected that this was why William ate with her; she could not imagine him having any patience with a woman who daintily picked at food and whimpered about her figure. Then she realised that Alice was one of those women who could get away with eating things like this and not get fat. Repressing a desire to hate the girl, Susan looked around her.

"Is there any chance one of the others could see us here?" she asked.

"None," Alice said, firmly, "Of the teachers you'll know, only William Fenneck lives in Hengistley. And he would never come here."

"How do you know?"

"Look at the menu. It's a coffee shop. No beer. What this place has for sale is of no interest to him. And he used to come here with some bitch he was going out with a couple of years back. He won't set foot in it now. He's funny about things like that. He's an idiot sometimes," Alice snorted and then smiled, "Most of the time, in fact."

"Are they all like that?" Susan asked.

"No," said Alice, hooking a tendril of dark hair behind her left ear with a pre-Raphaelite finger, "They're all different sorts of idiots. It's like a gang of little boys. They're very clever in their own ways and they love the things they teach, but I wouldn't say they're very grown up."

Susan pondered the nature of a world in which a girl just out of her teens could comment with what she suspected was some accuracy on the mentalities of educated men, the youngest of whom was eight years her senior. Women needed this edge, she thought.

"Michael Alcock is like the tortured adolescent," continued Alice, who was actually making things up as she went along, embellishing the impressions she had formed as a student with the slivers of gossip she had picked up since. The most important thing she had learned from William was to make use at all times and in all places of the Divine gift of authoritative bullshit. "All sex and tension and rebellion and that. He's the only one who makes any attempt to understand what it's like to be young. Most teachers just assume you're being a typical idiot teenager if you have any problems. It's such a pity he doesn't have a girlfriend. We used to ask him about his unending attempts to pull during lessons."

Susan looked puzzled.

"I mean, during lessons, we'd ask him about his attempts to pull," Alice said, helpfully, "Though of course none of them would be averse to pulling students, which they've all done, by the way, though I'm not sure that William's activities count as pulling as normal people use the term. 'Disasters' is a better word. Anyway, as I imagine you've guessed, Mr MacDonald is the most fancied. He's the most grown up of that crowd, and clever in every sense, not just academic. He's like the oldest boy in the group, who's learned to drive and stuff. He knows about music and football, and goes clubbing. Cool bastard, and knows it, despite being old. I get the impression that he has real relationships, not sad affairs. All the girls go for his arse. Well worth a look."

"I'm in a long-term relationship," Susan said, responsibly. She sipped her coffee and cast another anxious glance around the coffee shop.

"And?" Alice responded pertly, wondering if Susan had had to say that line a lot, with the male staff at Mercier's romping around her, panting and leering, like a load of randy elephant seals, "Anyway, then there's William Fenneck. The useless one. Fat, short, wheezy boy who's shit at sport."

"What about Barnaby Worthington?"

"I don't really know him. The Sociology people think they're too cool for Hengistley. They probably are, but either way I don't see them about much. William tries to bully them. He calls them the Gibeonites, the hewers of wood and drawers of water. Do you know what that means? I don't."

She was interrupted by a short, bosomy young woman who appeared at her shoulder.

"Darling," she carolled, "How are you?"

She kissed Alice with genuine warmth and flopped down beside her, lighting a long cigarette with a plastic lighter and blowing a column of smoke skywards.

"This is Portia Bates," Alice explained, "She taught History at the College until the bastards made her redundant."

"But now I've got a miles better job at the local comp.," Portia extended a hand, "I do careers advice and stuff like that. It's great. I'm earning loads more than those arseheads at Mercier's, too. Oh, Alice, poppet, I've got that sports car I told you about. The throbbing bright yellow trouser arouser of a boy magnet with leather seats and built in machine guns for blowing away the Principal of Mercier's and that turd Walpurgess should the twats cross my path. It's a good job I'm a person of deeply held humanitarian convictions, because in the wrong hands this baby could destroy Europe. I'll give you a ride in it sometime, if you like."

She had lively green eyes behind which a keen intelligence and a capacity for mischief made themselves obvious to Susan.

"Susan Halsbury," she said, "I'm the new drama teacher."

"And you've met Alice already," Portia beamed, "You *are* doing well. A divine creature, is Alice."

Alice preened. She and Portia had a high degree of mutual admiration and affection. Portia, with her energy, popularity and passion for her work, represented the kind of teacher the girl wanted to become. Everyone liked her. Alice, Portia felt for her part, was the only positive element in her old friend William's life. She was a real person, not an intellectual construct attached to a very different reality in the way that William's girlfriends tended to be.

"Why the discreet tete-a-tete?" Portia asked.

"I had wanted to ask," Susan said, "About some of the teachers at Mercier's. Their capacity for corruption."

"Oh, the departmental finance initiative?" Alice said.

"William told you?" Susan was faintly surprised.

"He tells me more or less everything which he can remember or understand, which isn't, to be honest, a vast amount," Alice said, "And he talked about this thing last night. I suspect they're capable of the idea but they aren't up to the reality. As with so much else in life."

"What is this, exactly?" Portia asked.

"There's a rumour that the Principal is going to downgrade the position of Bursar and let the departments run their own financial affairs, like businesses. Mike seems to think this is an opportunity to make a few quid on the side," Susan explained, "Is he really likely to try something? And, I suppose, most importantly, would I get into trouble for it?"

"Well done," Portia said, "You've established the first rule of Mercier's. If someone's involved in something dodgy, don't get involved in it yourself, or at least make sure there isn't any evidence if you do. I have to say though, that the thought of the boys ripping off the College gives me a lot of sadistic satisfaction."

Alice's right eyebrow arched like a tiny black mamba ready to strike.

"Do you really think they'd be able to get away with it, though?" she asked, "You forget that they aren't as smart as you. They're men, for one thing. Complete knowledge of all the songs of Bob Dylan and their relevance for contemporary English literature and pulling, or being able to describe in suspiciously enthusiastic detail the inner workings of the Black Shirts, is of no use whatsoever if you're trying to be a criminal."

"Have you said this to William?" Portia asked.

"Yes, though obviously I didn't use so many big words. If he knows what's good for him, he'll steer well clear," Alice said, firmly.

"You could argue that someone who smokes thirty cigarettes a day and spends every lunchtime in a public house has absolutely no idea what's good for him," Susan suggested.

"Well, I don't think they'll do it. William says Michael Alcock wants the money for some sort of play, but he's unlikely to risk anything criminal," Alice opined, "A mixture of cowardice and incompetence is enough to hold any of that lot back."

Susan felt reassured, though why she should feel like this on the basis of the word of a university student whose chief source of information was a confused and morally questionable soak was unclear.

"Pity," Portia said, "Because it would be good to see the College take a financial beating. Serve them right."

She developed these thoughts as she drove home. Revenge had been a major theme in her dreams, even after she had got her marvellous new job, but she hadn't been able to get her teeth into anything. The bottle through Walpugess' windscreen had given a moment's release, and she had enjoyed both the stories of her students' antics and the ritual of expressing surprise about them to the Principal. She had also spoken very solemnly to her form in morning briefing.

"Someone," she said, "Is putting around the rumour that the Principal and Dr Walpurgess were seen in Brighton at the weekend, wearing dresses and asking to be addressed as Marilyn and Judy. I need hardly tell you that this rumour is almost certainly untrue, and even if it is true, to spread it in a malicious and homophobic way is a terrible thing to do. I'd like you to ask around and find out who is saying this, and report back to me."

This had given her some satisfaction, but, again, it had been rather limited. Portia, for the first time in her life, wanted to cause pain, and thought that now she had found her weapon.

Portia was not the only person who was trying to think of a way to exploit the potential goldmine of the Departmental Finance Initiative.

"We need to find a way to borrow the money, invest it, make a return and then fund my brilliant new play. You must have some ideas," Mike said.

"I don't, really," William said.

"But you're virtually amoral. You're bound to have had some thoughts about what to do to get at the bloody money," Mike was becoming exasperated.

William blinked at him, surprised.

"Well, no. I've got everything I could possibly want. I've never thought about making money."

"You don't have a car. And what about impressing the totty? Alice would be into your trousers like a shot if you had a flash motor."

"If that cow comes anywhere near my trousers I'll give her a jolly good slap. I can't drive, anyway."

"You could learn."

"Don't want to. I have a bicycle. Anyway, it was your idea to rip off the system. You think up the brilliant plan. I'm not sure I want to. This is wrong. It's corrupt. We kicked out the last government precisely because of the sort of nonsense. Alice says…"

Mike put his foot down. He leaned over the smaller man in what he hoped was an intimidating way.

"Who gives a toss what Alice says? She's twenty and by your own admission a cow. Think for yourself."

William moved out of Mike's shadow without haste, and unwrapped a Kit Kat.

"No, I mean, I know she's female, and young, and these two things generally combine to make someone automatically wrong. But she might be right about this. What would happen if we got caught? Doesn't that worry you?"

"We can't actually *get* caught," Mike took a piece of William's chocolate as a tax on his uselessness, "The system's flexible enough. We aren't talking about stealing, anyway, just borrowing."

"We can't get caught because we don't have any ideas for what to do."

"If there's one thing worse than being a criminal," Mike sighed, "It's being a criminal without a crime."

CHAPTER SIX

"Don't book anything for next Monday evening," the Vice Principal announced to the staff at morning briefing, "We're all going out to dinner."

"Why?" one of the Maths teachers asked.

Walpurgess looked perplexed. It was bad enough having to relay strange news from the Principal without having to explain it as well.

"We just are," he said, eventually.

"That's not a proper answer," the Maths teacher said, "We don't say that sort of thing to the kids."

"I do," William said.

"*Normal* people don't," the Maths teacher told him, firmly. The Mathematics Department was always right.

"This is an announcement from the Principal," Walpurgess said, "If you're saying he's not normal, that's up to you. But I'm just saying that we're all having dinner together at a restaurant next week."

"Which one?" the Head of Information Technology asked, "I only ask because curry plays merry hell with my insides."

"Yes, it does, doesn't it?" her deputy said, "I remember that awful night when we had the Christmas Dinner at the Rajah of Baluchistan. Chained to the porcelain for hours, you were."

"Bagsy Chinese," Mike called, "I like that stuff."

"Yes, but after three pints you start doing racist impressions and causing a fuss," Andrew said, "We can't go back to that place in Hove after you called the waiter Chairman Mao and accused him of serving stray cats. I've never been so humiliated. I mean to say. 'Flied lice' just isn't funny."

"Mere juvenile high spirits," Mike mumbled.

"You're forty-one," Andrew said, simply and cruelly. Mike winced.

"There's a very good pub on Albion Way which does a lovely venison casserole. I had it for lunch on Sunday," William offered, "It was awfully nice."

"That might be good," Walpurgess said, "Could it take all of us?"

"No," William said.

"Why did you tell us about it, then?" the Vice Principal snapped.

"Because I liked it. I had a lovely time. I thought you'd be happy for me," William curled up in a little ball and looked as if he was going to cry.

"I am, William," Prudence soothed.

"You aren't William," William said, "I'm William. You're Prudence."

"Jesus wept," Jim Speer muttered.

"That's lovely, that is," Mike said, "Blaspheming members of the Senior Management Team. Having just given my life to Jesus, I find that bloody offensive."

"Don't be sanctimonious, Michael," Prudence said, "Remember that we have people here of all faiths and none."

"I knew a former nun once," Jane contributed, "Used to do aromatherapy in Bognor."

"Stop it!" Walpurgess screamed, "Stop using these blasted non-sequiturs, you surreal bastards. You're just trying to annoy me, I know you are. It's not my fault I have to read these things out."

"But of course," Andrew said, "You were forced at gunpoint to take a job paying ludicrous amounts of money."

"They're not ludicrous enough to justify what I have to take from you lot," Walpurgess muttered, "You're worse than the bloody kids."

"Can I tell you about Jesus?" Mike asked.

*   *   *

One of the joys of Portia's new job was that she got to liaise with local businesses in order to find work placements for her pupils. In addition to the deluge of free corporate gifts which splashed across her desk, this provided her with a wide range of contacts which might prove useful should the comprehensive go the same way as Mercier's and make her redundant. On the downside, there were some local employers who had a rather more intimate understanding of the word contact than she was prepared to regard as within her job description.

"I'm sure I don't know what you mean," she said distractedly to the chief engineering officer at the local airport. They were driving around the tarmac in a special lorry designed to pull aeroplanes. The aura of testosterone was almost as pungent as the more traditional stench of Avgas as the forty-seven-year-old engineer offered her the benefits of his experience with bodywork and thrust.

"Oh, don't be coy," he grinned, wolfishly, "You're a mature woman. I'm sure you've got what it takes."

"I know you're sure," muttered Portia, who had already noticed the way he liked to cram her into the smallest lifts and insisted on giving her a helping hand to get into aeroplanes.

"There's nothing like it, you know. All that stuff about the mile high club is bollocks. You don't have to be airborne, unless you can get that baby in an inverted loop, which isn't a good idea in a 747. No, so long as those big turbofans are running, you've got all you need."

"Really?" asked Portia, who might have been fascinated had the chief engineering officer not had a disturbing resemblance to Lenin, whose embalmed corpse she had once seen on a school trip to Moscow.

"Too right. The whole structure of the aircraft is throbbing and screaming—just like us, if you play your cards right, honey."

"You're very kind."

"Once you get those engines turned on, and ourselves, it's very special."

"I don't doubt it," Portia said, wriggling away from the engineer's oil-covered hand as she tried to position herself closer to the emergency alarm. He lunged at her and she pressed the button, which turned out to be the fire extinguisher. There was a loud hiss and foam engulfed the lorry's cab.

"Hell's bells," the engineer yelled, "I can't see."

The lorry swerved violently into the path of the 14:30 Estonian Airways flight to Tallinn. The pilot dragged the Boeing out of its way just in time to avoid having the wheels of his aeroplane ripped off.

"There's a complete arse playing dodgems on the apron," he bawled to ground control.

"So I see," ground control said, with the unflappability the pilot had previously admired about the English.

"Well, do something, damn it," barked the pilot, who had flown Sukhois against the Afghans in the days of the USSR and had his own ideas about how to deal with people who got up to this sort of jiggery-pokery.

"Oh, it'll sort itself out," ground control said, "You Russians are always so excitable."

"I'm not a bloody Russian," the pilot shouted, "I wouldn't be a Russian if you paid me."

"Keep your eyes on the runway," the stewardess screamed, as the big aeroplane drifted towards the 14:20 Aeroflot flight to Moscow.

"Get out of my way, you Baltic twat," its pilot yelled.

"Sod off," the crew of the 14:30 shouted.

"Where's that pratt in the lorry gone?" the stewardess asked.

"The only pratt I can see is making crap attempts to steer a Boeing with Estonian Airways written on it," the pilot of the Aeroflot plane said, "Have you been drinking?"

"No," replied the Estonian pilot, "I'm not the President of Russia."

"At least everybody knows who our President is."

"They know what he is, as well."

"And they know where our country is, too."

"With a smell like that, it's hard to miss."

The two big aircraft were weaving erratically and almost bumping off one another. Amongst the passengers, panic was beginning to look like a reasonable option.

"Do you want to sort this out on the tarmac, you cheeky little sod?" the Russian pilot shouted.

"What the hell are you idiots doing?" the pilot of the 14:40 Lufthansa Airbus to Dresden bawled. His grandfather had been held as a prisoner by the Russians and forced to work as a slave until 1950, and certain of the old man's attitudes had been passed on through the family. The Lufthansa pilot wished he was in a Messerschmitt.

"You can piss right off," snapped the Russian captain, whose grandfather had, in 1943, been shot as a partisan by the SS for the treasonous crime of stealing a loaf of bread, "You're not running the Reich now."

"Give it time, fat boy," the German yelled, "I've got to fly eastbound and I'd appreciate it if you'd get the hell out of my way."

"You lot didn't have any problems finding your way east in 1941," the Estonian said, unhelpfully.

As a major diplomatic incident fermented on the taxiway, the lorry weaved erratically away towards the maintenance area and bounced gently into a hangar. Portia and the chief engineering officer staggered out, covered in foam. They stared at one another like snowmen on the apron.

"Sorry about that," Portia said.

"No, it's my fault," the engineer sighed, "It's just that you're such a damned attractive woman."

He shook himself like a damp dog, scattering foam all around.

"You're very kind," said Portia, "But I think your wife, who's on the Board of Governors of my school, might have something to say."

"Honestly. Bloody women and their feminist solidarity. She doesn't understand me, you know."

"How very foolish of her," Portia commented, "I've got some sex education materials you can borrow if you like."

"Got to get my thrills from somewhere, I suppose," the engineer said, glumly, "There's just so little to do around here that's fun."

Portia commiserated, thinking as she did so that there were possibilities here which might be exploited.

*   *   *

On Monday afternoon, the staff gathered round the Principal's noticeboard. In his distinctive flourishing script, he had written a note.

"To all staff.

Tonight's General Staff Meeting will be held in El Ranchero's Tex-Mex Diner and Bar-B-Q Grill, North Road. This is the closest restaurant to the College. Our meals there will be paid for from the Principal's Special Fund.

The Topic for the Meeting will be the new Departmental Finance Initiative.

Attendance is mandatory."

"What's that place like?" Susan asked.

"Doesn't the name tell you all you need to know?" Mike said, gloomily, "It's bound to be some sort of American-style hell-hole. Why couldn't we have gone down to Brighton?"

"Because the College is in Hengistley?" Susan suggested, brightly.

"But Hengistley is a cultural vacuum," Mike sniffed.

"Oh, I don't know," Susan said, "The parents weren't bad."

Susan's experience of Parents' Evening had been entirely positive, partly because, as a Drama teacher, she tended to work with the off-spring of progressive families who were delighted to discover that she was a friendly young woman, and had given her an easy time.

Positioned between Andrew and William, she had learned a great deal about different strategies for coping with potentially awkward parents. Andrew had piled packets of Lemsip, aspirin and other pharmaceuticals on his desk in order to make the parents feel guilty about taking up his time, and then bombarded them with a bewildering barrage of technical, theoretical and occasionally fictitious educational terms before ending with the remark that the student really needed, above all else, to do a bit more reading. William had cravenly but successfully gained the loyalty of the parents he met by agreeing vehemently with whatever prejudices they displayed. In the course of half an hour, Susan heard him affirming that, whilst he wasn't allowed to say so under the College regulations, these people were exactly right that the collapse of educational standards was due to the Conservatives, to Labour, to the Europeans, the ethnic minorities and the ingrained racialism of primary school teachers, and that children needed to read more.

Mike snorted.

"Look out of that window, and what do you see?"

Susan peered out.

"A road. Mike, they have those in Brighton too, you know. It doesn't necessarily make Hengistley a bad place."

"No, no, in the distance."

"A big chimney. That's Thruttock's brewery, isn't it?"

Susan had heard that the brewery was a source of pride for half of the population of Hengisltley. The remainder were less fond of an institution which was instrumental in their menfolk's arrival at the hearth at four o'clock in the morning. Susan had also heard that the Mercier's staff were instrumental in keeping the place in profit.

"Yes, but I meant in the near distance, and to the sides."

"Semi-detached houses, and a big modern block over there."

"Right. Right! You see, this is the heartland of Home Counties bourgeois stuffiness. Semi-detached microwaveable ready portions of life, all nicely blended in our factory to serve the interests of that thing over there, and that, my esteemed and gorgeous colleague, is the headquarters of Imperial Union insurance. That glittering edifice is a temple to our need to appease the Gods of financial misfortune, and it dominates the town. Everything that happens here is something to do with those bastards. This town is not real. It's shrink-wrapped suburbia for the millenium. It exists in a cultural vacuum where the only values are economic."

"Bloody hell," Susan said, impressed despite herself, as Mike panted with exhaustion.

"And because we are in this cultural wasteland, we have to face a hideous restaurant which probably has a menu composed entirely of carcinogens and e-numbers," Mike continued. He was in his stride now.

"I'm sure it'll be possible to get a salad or something," Susan said.

"Nonsense," Mike said, "It'll be buckets of fat or nothing."

Like most young, unmarried staff, Mike preferred the seedy Bohemianism of the South Coast to what was seen as the stodgy respectability of Hengistley. The little town was the epitome of classless wealth; no traditional feudal structures remained against which to rail, and anyone with cash to spare could fit in nicely. There was no university to inject a fluid and lively element into the population, and the absence of manufacturing industry meant that there was no working class to speak of. As the years wore on, the town grew increasingly to resemble an American suburb. The younger staff at the College saw the effect of this on their pupils and were aghast. Neither as raffishly cosmopolitan as privately-educated students, nor as streetwise and sorted as most other state school alumni, they were amiable, homogenous and hard-working. Barnaby and the other radical teachers fretted at the lack of adolescent rebellion amongst teenagers who preferred to spend their weekends manning tills at the supermarket to protesting against things. They desperately tried to needle the students into some sort of activism, and despaired when they were politely ignored in favour of excited discussions about the merits of various second-hand cars. Brighton was,

therefore, a refuge in which staff could pursue their interests in alternative theatre, environmentalism or socialism, none of which was
regarded as acceptable in Hengistley. The young and dynamic lived on
the coast, and only the older, married teachers lived in the town. The
exceptions to this rule were William and, when she had worked at
Mercier's, Portia. She liked to be on hand to help her students and was
immensely sociable, with no interest in the fashionable bars near
Brighton beach in which her colleagues liked to pose as non-teachers.
William was unable to drive and could not bear the thought of travel-
ling into work every morning with sociology lecturers. Hengistley, in
any case, gave them almost all they could have asked for. It had a supermarket, a theatre, churches and pubs, and its people were agreeable and
diligent. Portia and William did not ask for much in life. They were
both regarded as profoundly odd, though admittedly no-one was very
sorry about not having to chauffeur William up and down the A23
every day.

Susan's first impression of El Ranchero's was that it looked like a fun
kind of place. However, as she had learned to her cost, Brighton Man
had a rather different definition of both fun and place to the rest of
humanity. El Ranchero's, whose main elements had clearly been built as
a low-slung modernist pub in the 1970s, was fooling no-one with the
strips of log which had been nailed to its frontage, or the rickety
wooden veranda which protruded from the entrance like a lame child's
calliper. A miniature covered wagon stood forlornly in the scabbed garden by the side of the restaurant, and the entrance to the car park had
been decorated to resemble the OK Corral. Not that anyone was driving. It was obvious that this establishment had been selected largely, if
not entirely, for its closeness to the College. No other reason could have
stood up to the argument that this was probably the least suitable venue
in the south of England, apart, perhaps, from one of the gay nightclubs
in Brighton, in which to hold a meeting of schoolteachers. That said,

even had it been further away, there were plenty of staff whose intention was to exploit the situation to the full by drinking themselves into a coma at someone else's expense.

A crush formed as fifty thirsty teachers crowded round the narrow bar, which was decorated with authentic Americana such as number-plates stolen by the proprietor whilst drunkenly staggering through a suburb of Delware in 1992. Unused to the crush, the large wooden barrels which served as pretentious and highly impractical bar tables overturned and rolled into the restaurant, knocking over a teenage waitress who was carrying a tray of glasses. A ragged cheer went up as the girl was sent to the floor and her cargo spattered dangerously around the room.

"That'll teach the little minx to bunk off my lessons to work in pubs," one of the Physics teachers chortled, with what Susan would one day come to see as an admirable sense of detachment from his students' personal problems.

Susan became conscious, in her position in the middle of the queue for the bar, of a little presence at her elbow. It was Mike, holding his cigarette up like an Olympic torch as he slithered through the mass of bodies.

"Can you let me through, please?" he asked, plaintively, "I need to speak to that woman at the bar. It's a bit urgent. Sorry."

Susan let him through, as did the teacher in front of her.

"Thanks ever so," Mike said, "It is very important."

He clung to the bar and spoke directly to a blonde woman of about thirty.

"Large jug of beer, please, to my table," he said, politely but loudly, holding a twenty pound note before the woman's eyes.

"And what table would that be, sir?" she asked, putting down the glasses into which she was going to pour other people's drinks and pick-ing up a glass pitcher. Mike looked confused, or rather more confused than normal.

"The one I'm sitting at, obviously," he said, and sidled out again. Susan found him later, sitting proudly in front of his large jug of beer, but without a glass.

"Even geniuses can't think of everything," he said, furtively stealing a tumbler from the Head of German. Susan wandered off to sit beside Andrew, who looked as if he was going to stay sober, and William, who had more faults than a tectonic plate but could be relied upon not to chat her up, partly because he couldn't actually focus on her and still didn't really know who she was.

Mike commandeered a table in a dark corner of the restaurant where he could hold court with some easily-led members of the Media Studies Department, and had covered it with glasses of beer. Propped up before him was a copy of the menu, which was one of those giant laminated affairs which resemble blades from ceiling fans.

"Well, comrades, since we must eat this pseudo-American nonsense, let us order," he cried, radiating good nature and high spirits like an atomic device, "Miss Waitress! Can you come over here, please, and hear our demands?"

The waitress approached and looked at him suspiciously. Like most waitresses in Hengistley, she was a student at Mercier's. Unlike most students who were waitresses, she was dressed in a cowboy hat, a gingham shirt and a pair of cut-off shorts, which put the Head of Media Studies in mind of a bit part actress in an early episode of *The Dukes of Hazzard*. She felt faintly ridiculous, and knew that she looked that way, because Andrew was her form tutor and he had helpfully drawn her attention to the matter by summoning her over and saying, "You look, if I may say so, my dear, thoroughly stupid." Sometimes it wasn't advantageous to have a tutor who was so unutterably honest.

"I'd like a gullet-bustin' rack o'ribs surprise, please," Mike announced, "And for starters I think I'll have a Mount St.Helen's of corn chips covered in cheese melt. Oh, and more beer, please."

"Of course, Mr Alcock," the girl replied.

Mike noticed something on the menu.

"Hey, what's this?" he asked, pointing at a highlighted item in the dessert section.

"That's our Big Fat Birthday Boy Boomer," she said, "It's basically an enormous chocolate sundae with a firework in it. All the staff come out and give a sort of speech to whoever's birthday it is, and give them that."

"It's Mr Bleach's birthday, isn't it, lads?" Mike said, "I think we should have one of those for him. It'll be a lovely surprise."

Meanwhile, the Principal had decided that he would announce his plans to the staff between the starter and the main course.

"Do you think that's a good idea, Principal?" Walpurgess asked, "If they don't like the news, they'll have access to bigger and heavier pieces of food with which to express their displeasure. Why not between the main course and pudding?"

"Well done," the Principal said, "That's the sort of forward-looking thinking I like to see in the senior staff. Of course, the downside is that they will all be drunk. But then, I suppose their aim won't be as good. So they'll hit you instead of me. That is a good thing, I think."

"Of course, Principal," Walpurgess said. He cursed inwardly.

Mike Alcock's table stumbled from course to course in a singularly unattractive way. Initially, it featured a Mount St.Helen's of corn chips. What appeared to be a stack of thin pieces of tree bark crouched on a huge plate, drenched in a glutinous mass of melted cheese. Mike and his friends were relatively quiet as they ploughed through the culinary insurance risk. The only noise was the occasional yelp as someone found a chilli pepper which had been concealed beneath the lava.

The main course, before which William had recoiled in Calvinist horror, was an enormous slab of meat, which sat smugly beneath its coating of suspiciously bright chemical sauce, daring the customer to touch it with his puny cutlery. Mike's gang had fallen upon this with vigour, alcohol numbing their objections to its cultural reference points.

Suddenly, the Principal stood up. He produced a cowboy revolver normally kept behind the bar and fired a blank round into the air. There were screams and shouts of "Christ, he's actually flipped," and "Missed me, you bastard."

"Dear friends," he announced, having gained everyone's attention, "You may be wondering what the Departmental Finance Initiative is. Well, I'll tell you. From the beginning of next term, those of you with executive subject responsibility will each be given a sum of money. From that you will pay your own salary and those of any junior members of staff in your subjects. You will buy the books your students need and anything else that occurs to you. If you run out of money, you will have to get it from somewhere. I suggest the students. Jonathan Bleach will now explain the rest."

The Principal sat down to stunned silence, and sucked through a straw the large purple cocktail with an umbrella on top which he was rather enjoying.

"Fundamentally, the ethos which is driving this reform is one of efficiency, excellence and enterprise," Bleach announced, smoothly, "And the core rationale is the better delivery of an educational product to the client base."

He got no further. From the kitchen emerged a troupe of restaurant staff, clad in wild west outfits and hammering on frying pans with metal spoons. They gathered around the Senior Management Group's table. The Principal blinked in mild surprise and returned to his cocktail. A spotty teenager was energetically battering away just behind Jim Speer's ear. Recognising the boy as a particularly half-witted Business Studies student, Speer politely suggested that if he didn't stop that nonsense right now he would have his fucking arm broken.

"Now hear this," the blonde woman from the bar bawled, in a Texan accent which sounded, in places, like the illegitimate offspring of an act of congress between an Irish brogue and a Dorset burr, "Today is the birthday of Big Chief Birthday Boy hisself, Jo-nay-than Bleach, and we here in the posse are gonna honour him in the time hallowed way, y'all understand?"

A small girl in a chef's uniform produced an enormous Red Indian head-dress and placed it on Bleach's head. He smiled glassily and looked profoundly afraid.

"And because it's his birthday," the blonde woman continued ("It's not, you know," Bleach whispered, desperately), "He's gotta eat a Big Boy Birthday Boomer aaaall by his self while you all claps an' hollers."

From the kitchen, to the sound of a cavalry bugle, came a fat boy carrying what appeared to be a vase full of chocolate ice-cream, the top of which was emitting a shower of sparks. This was set down in front of Bleach, who was, by now, sweating profusely and panicking.

"Bloody hell," he whimpered, "That thing'll turn my arteries into concrete. I can't eat that. I'm on a diet plan out of *Men's Health*."

"Now you all are going to cheer Big Chief Birthday Boy on while he eats this mother aaaawll up, yeah?" screeched the blonde woman, for whom Bleach had developed a profound, and quite justified, dislike. The kitchen staff stood around whilst the Mercier's staff, their inhibitions ripped into shreds by unaccustomed alcohol consumption and the profound moral confusion of being told that they were to become business managers, cheered deleriously and hammered their cutlery on the tables. This had the partly merciful effect of hastening the onset of the vomiting attack which would, for Jonathan Bleach, for ever afterwards pop into his head whenever he heard an American accent.

At Mike's table, the beer had taken its most deadly effect. Robust and manly comparisons were being made between different female students. This was a rather sad feature of college life and one which would have been stamped out if anyone had genuinely believed that it was serious. A swaying socio-economic development adviser, best known for his ferocious interpretations of Marxist Feminism as the only coherent idea for the new century, had just explained his theory that one of Mike's favourite upper sixth girls resembled a pit bull terrier licking piss off a nettle, and Mike was getting ready to launch into a vivid description of her merits, when the waitress reappeared.

"Would you like your coffee now, sir?" she hissed.

"Yes, indeed, comely wench," Mike bawled, "Bring it hither. I'm just away to the little boys' room."

The waitress reflected that this was not a wholly inappropriate term. She watched Mike weave unsteadily to the toilets and suddenly shoot sideways into an alcove. This didn't happen in Pizza Express.

Mike had been rather surprised when an invisible hand had reached out and grabbed him. As a member of the Labour Party, he felt that this concept had been somewhat discredited by modern economics. This particular hand belonged to Portia, who had underestimated both her own strength and Mike's vertical instability.

"Get off me, you bastard," she growled, as he sprawled on top of her.

"Well, make your mind up," he said, "You haul me in here for what a casual observer would have to assume was a torrid sexual liaison and then go all coy. Don't fight it, Portia. You know that I can be your Mister Lover Man."

Portia's eyes rolled like lottery balls.

"Listen, you arsehole. I know why you're here."

"Look, I know you may have overheard some of our conversation, but I can promise you, I'm not going for a Jodrell Bank. I just want a piss."

"No, you tosser," she barked, "The Departmental Finance Initiative."

"Fucking hell," Mike said, "I knew you wanted to keep in touch with events at Mercier's, but that's amazing. This lot only just found out about it."

"Alice told me," Portia explained.

"Alice? Oh, A Town Like. How the hell does she know about it? She's twenty, for the love of sweet buggery arse, and spends half her life nightclubbing in Leicester. Since when did she become the all-knowing fount of truth?"

"She works very hard at university, which is more than you ever did. And if she's only twenty, she's still twice your mental age," Portia said, "Anyway, I can see big possibilities in this for us. Big big ones. Ask yourself—do I want lots of money?"

"I don't have to," Mike said, "The answer, as always, is yes, provided I don't have to do any work."

"Well, this is your big chance to fulfil that surprisingly popular career goal. Ask yourself another question. What's the big problem that stops clever folk like you and I from setting up successful businesses?"

"Rank incompetence."

"Sorry, I meant clever folk like just me, then."

"Oh," Mike thought for a moment, "Lack of capital?"

"Good boy. Have a chocolate drop," Portia patted his thigh, and recoiled as Mike leered expectantly and horribly at her, "And this is where the Finance thingummy comes in. It gives you the capital to set something up. Now, here's a third question. What's the driving force in all human beings, the thing that makes them go, the throbbing power behind all of man's endeavours?"

"Fear?" Mike asked, tentatively.

"No, you berk, sex," Portia yelled, "The id, the libido, the thrusting lunge of the beef bayonet, man's eternal quest for a sodding leg over."

"Oh, that," Mike said, leering again.

"Now, do you see what I'm getting at here?" Portia asked, patiently.

Mike leaned back in what he hoped, unrealistically, was a seductive pose.

"Well, hey, baby, I don't see how you could have made it more obvious. You're a healthy, attractive woman at her sexual peak, and I'm a freelance love buffalo. Shall we do it here or in the car park?"

His mouth stayed open in a silent scream as Portia rammed her fist into his groin.

"No, you revolting creature," she whispered, "We're going to use the money to set up a service that caters for that particular need. To put it in simpler terms, we are going to establish a brothel. And we are going to become quite obscenely rich, if you'll pardon the pun. Do you understand?"

Mike nodded weakly.

"Good," she said, "Meet me in the Hertford tomorrow at six. Just you. No Andrew, no William, just you. Now, run along and have your pee. If you still can."

CHAPTER SEVEN

The network of passageways, book cupboards and boiler-rooms beneath the Victorian main block of the College was known to the students as the Underworld. It was a dark and dusty place, every cranny filled with the oppressive heat of the boiler and its constant throbbing noise. Above ground, Dr Walpurgess' expensive makeover of the 1930s Grammar school quadrangle, known affectionately as upper quad (you could tell it was affectionate as there was no definite article), and its 1970s counterpart, known, thanks to its tendency to flood, as the south swamp, had left them looking pristine and bourgeois. Bright blue signs informed the visitor of the whereabouts of the Sports Hall or the History Department, and lovingly-tended flower-baskets minced into view around every corner. Parents were charmed by the College and thought enviously of their own schooldays in the jerry-built academic gulags of the 1960s. Their children loved the Underworld.

It offered them a place into which they might escape from the relentless loveliness of the pretty Sussex town and, in particular, its pompous little college. Here there were no rules on tidying up after yourself, or not smoking, or being quiet. The underworld combined all they most loved about their bedrooms at home with freedom from what they disliked about both home and college. Its dark, untidy character mirrored the gothic squalor to which they aspired, but were forbidden by their parents to emulate. The modern child, however, is raised on double-glazing, central-heating and hi-fis. The airlessness, stifling heat and headache-inducing noise in the underworld reminded the students of what they liked about home and could not have at the College. The older classrooms were draughty and poorly heated, much to the joy of teachers like William, who had been brought up in barrack-like Manses through which the wind cut like a chainsaw and saw warmth and comfort as temptations to sinfulness. The students spent much of the day shivering and would hurtle down to the boiler-room for warmth and cigarettes at break and lunch times, cursing the antiseptic chill of the surface world.

The underworld attracted a particular type of student. The hearty lads of the football and rugby teams refused to go anywhere near the place, and their pristine girlfriends, clad in the latest fashions, were unwilling to dirty their expensive clothing in the murky labyrinth. Nor did the mafias of scientists, thesps or computer enthusiasts, who preferred to populate areas of the college closer to the amenities for learning. The principal inhabitants of the underworld were known to their fellows as the trolls, and shambled about in galumphing boots with trailing laces, their long, unwashed hair hiding their slithy, pale faces, and roll-up cigarettes dangling from their enervated lower lips. The males of the species affected black nail varnish and eye-shadow, whilst the girls, when they wore make-up at all, were inclined towards the colour purple. Despite their shabby appearance, these students were neither poor nor without academic prospects. They invariably came from well-off families in prosperous parts of town, partly because people who dressed like that in working-class areas were very quickly taught the error of their ways. The best of them worked out their angst by forming bands and spending their spare time irritating their neighbours with late-night guitar-thrashing sessions, but the bulk simply drifted through life experimenting with pretentiousness without purpose. The trolls suffered considerable persecution in the bars of the town from young men in designer t-shirts and expensive aftershave.

Attempts to relocate to more socially diverse pubs like the Hertford had resulted in their being barred for making the place look untidy and putting off the older customers. This fed their senses of grievance and superiority, and imbued in them a quite unjustified arrogance based on the notion that, as those who harrassed them were manifestly stupid, they, the trolls, must therefore be creatures of rare and beautiful intelligence. This was an attitude which did not endear them to the College staff, and led to yet more persecution. The teachers wanted to be liked, but not by people who acted like the spoilt offspring of minor European royalty and looked like creatures from an American trailer park. The tragedy for the Trolls was that they saw themselves as the equals, if not the superiors, of the staff, and deserving of their love, and could not come to terms with the fact that few of them were. Disillusionment, when inevitably it came, was bitter.

Toby Gaskett was a case in point. His coterie of shabby nonconformists were gathered in a particularly dingy corner of the underworld, drinking hot chocolate from the vending machines and spouting teenage nonsense at one another. He puffed angrily on a cigarette as he complained about the rank injustice of the system and the bourgeois attitudes of his teachers.

"Bastards," he snorted, twirling a lock of his long, straggly hair in his fingers. His girlfriend, an amiable green-haired girl from the Lower sixth with a studded dog collar about her throat and a discreet nose-ring, made a sort of humming noise in sympathy.

"They set these tests with mickey mouse questions, right, demanding petty little facts, like it's some kind of first form quiz. Then they persecute you if you don't get them right, right. But it's stupid. They don't cater for people like me who think with a different part of the brain. I like to see the whole picture, not little tiny facts. I'm not taking part in some sort of pub quiz. I'm here to get a big karmic picture of life."

"Gosh," his girlfriend said, with the slightest hint of weariness in her voice. She was actually more intelligent than he, but the trolls' demolition of social conventions had not extended so far as the notion that the female of the species could assert intellectual dominance if she was lucky enough to possess it.

"I mean, they just divide the students into two sorts of people," Gaskett continued, "There's men, right, and women."

"Yeah," his girlfriend said, not entirely inspired by this profound observation. It was not entirely accurate, for Gaskett, as a practising narcissicist, had never got round to finding out what the staff thought about anything. They actually divided the students into the interesting, the uninteresting, and the annoying, with an additional section of the fanciable for those members of staff who remained unmarried. As Gaskett fell into the third category, it was unlikely that any member of staff would have bothered to speak to him on this or any other matter.

"If you try to break down a few of those boundaries, they just don't understand. They don't understand that the blurring of gender lines in dress and appearance isn't just a surface thing. It's a reflection of the inner melding, and it means they're dealing with a completely new kind of mind, which they just can't appreciate."

There was a clatter as another troll lurched into the dark space. Gaskett looked up in irritation. He did not like his words of wisdom being interrupted.

"We really ought to find somewhere with a bit more room. This corner's crap," he observed.

"There's a sort of stockroom at the back," his girlfriend said.

The students clambered over the disused wooden seating which lined the corridors of the cellar, and tried the door of the stockroom. The handle was stiff, but it came open with a hard shove. It was evident that the place had not been used for years except as a dumping-ground for things which might one day come in useful but never had. Piles of elderly Latin primers, histories of the British Empire, abacuses and boxes of chalk lay on the shelving. A bare bulb smirked vaguely from a fitting in the ceiling, and a layer of dust lay over everything, history's smothering makeover. Gaskett looked about him.

"Hey," he said, his adolescent imagination coming to life, "There's a lock on the door. That could be useful."

"Yeah," his girlfriend muttered, trying to sound enthusiastic. After an education in an all-girls' boarding school, she had arrived at Mercier's and quickly formed a relationship with the first hippyish character who had come along. Unfortunately for her, Gaskett was incapable of true love for anyone other than himself, with the regrettable concomitant that he was convinced that if it had been good for him, that was enough for both of them. She had once observed, in one of the conversations about clitoral orgasms which for some reason peppered the delivery of the English syllabus, that it was all very well talking about that sort of thing, but most men in her experience had considerable difficulty finding the organ in question. Mike Alcock was too nice a person to remark that if she insisted on going out with a boy with a fringe of hair which rivalled an Old English Sheepdog's for length and forward visibility she had no-one to blame but herself if he couldn't find things. William and Andrew had been convulsed with laughter at this tale, much to Susan's disgust.

"There's a big box here with loads of German writing on it," Gaskett said, peering through his forest of hair at a wooden crate on the floor, "It's probably full of the Nazi propaganda that the teachers read to give them their ideas."

His disciples laughed obligingly. His girlfriend began to give serious thought to an affair with the tubby kid from Roffwater Heath who was interested in trains.

The peace which settled on the college that weekend, and indeed most weekends, made it a more restful environment than the respective homes of the various staff who worked there on Sundays. Sunshine pampered the quadrangle, making even its hideous 1965 statue of Atlas seem attractive, whilst the floral baskets, which looked so feeble in comparison with the shrieking primary colours of the students' clothing, positively rioted in their absence. Light streamed through the south-facing windows of the old building, overcoming the dormant radiators, as half a dozen staff discretely and discreetly pursued private projects, caught up on work, or found inexpensive reality substitutes.

Jane Miller was enjoying some quality time with her eleven year old son. Or rather, to be strictly accurate, she was dealing with the mountain of paperwork which was, for some reason, the inevitable lot of anyone employed by a state whose frontiers had supposedly been rolled back in 1979. Her main approach to the problem was to sort it into neat piles in her classroom, and then file it. However, by the time she had sorted out the piles, it was time to go home for supper, and the room needed to be cleared for the following morning, so the whole lot simply had to be scooped up and dumped in her office. It was a Sisyphaean task, which was relieved by bursts of creativity in which she would run about the department putting up posters. Jane was driven by a powerful sense of duty in this respect. Her colleagues did not tend to notice their surroundings and allowed huge mounds of paper to accumulate on their desks. These they left until the end of term, when all was swept into black plastic bags and burned in the middle of the playing fields in a holocaust of personal files, letters from the Department for Education, and students' essays. Jane both envied and despised them for this. Jane's son, meanwhile, stalked a supernatural castle armed with a sawn-off shotgun. A zombie emerged emerged from the murky entrails of the building and threw what looked and sounded like its digestive tract at him. The boy hit the brute with both barrels and it flopped backwards with an unearthly groan. Within seconds, it was clambering to its feet again, making a repulsive moaning noise. Of course, thought the boy, thou canst not kill what dost not live. Thou hast to dismember it. He pressed a key on the computer and a grenade-launcher appeared in his hands. Much to his satisfaction, the zombie was spattered into a collection of bright red pixels. Jane's son's ability to play the computer games which he had installed on the History Department's machine had done much to win him the admiration of the male teachers.

They too were in College, albeit oblivious of one another's presence. Andrew had hidden in an office in another wing of the building, and was working on his book. It was a point of honour for virtually all of the male staff at Mercier's that they were writing books. These rarely reached completion and saw publication even less often. They were, however, integral to the self-respect of the people who wrote them, who were keen to prove that they were not merely teachers but men of letters and intellectuals to boot. Andrew's magnum opus on nineteenth century history was his dark secret. It was the real reason why he no longer went out at weekends and went a long way towards explaining why he had not made any vigorous attempts to crowbar Susan from the boyfriend in whose existence there was little evidence (not, as Mike put it, that he had lost his bottle and was giving up the fight, leaving the field to real men like himself). His book was to be one of the most useful texts for students of the period, and incorporate his own brand of post-Marxist engagement with a creamy richness of style which ran the risk of inducing a minor heart attack. Each weekend he would sit in an office, surrounded by sheaves of paper and packets of cigarettes, and plough through chapters of what he modestly considered to be the new rock 'n' roll. This book would put the "in" into intellectual and make him a totty magnet for young female historians. His increasingly haggard appearance had been remarked upon by Jane, but neither Mike nor William had noticed, because he had simply come to resemble them. Andrew hauled smoke pleasurably into his lungs and stared at the screen, wondering if he would ever finish the blasted thing. He had to finish it before Mike finished his, but then again, Mike might never finish. It was known that Mike was writing a book, or perhaps two books, because Andrew had caught him at it. Creative stuff, probably—harder to churn out in some ways, but then again it didn't need research. Dossy

project. Andrew guessed, rightly, that William was also writing something. He also guessed that he was writing at Alice's suggestion, but
wrongly assumed that this meant that the minute he managed, whether
by verbal or chemical means, to arrange for her to go to bed with him,
he would no longer bother with the book. This was, in fact, an unlikely
scenario. Even had William been attracted to Alice, he was so painfully
shy with the few girls he liked that he required industrial quantities of
alcohol in order to express any sort of interest; too much, in fact, for
him to stay awake. For her part, Alice was a robust-minded young
woman, but even she drew the line at sexual intercourse with a small, fat
gargoyle with more bad habits than a monastery kitted out from a 1976
Littlewoods' catalogue. The key threat to William's output would actually have been his acquisition of a proper girlfriend, who might ask
awkward questions about who or what had inspired the previous three
months' worth of output. Much as she was largely unconcerned about
the possibility of a Jewish-Moslem Alliance invading Purley, Alice was
not unduly worried about the likelihood of such a relationship. Not that
she understood the contents of William's somewhat obtuse tome on the
need for a positive reappraisal of Mussolini's policy towards Abyssinia
in any case.

Andrew, meanwhile, was preoccupied with an attempt to make his
chapter on industrial relations in Bradford in the eighteen-nineties read
like the *Eighteenth Brumaire of Louis Bonaparte* without actually looking like its twin brother. He dragged savagely at his cigarette and glared
at the screen.

Mike was also staring morosely at his screen, torn between the desire
to look around the internet for women to marry and his need to get
some work done. Mike's iron resolve to stay away from the net was
driven by the knowledge that writing another chapter of the first ever
Hemingwayesque Irish novel would give him an immense feeling of
self-worth. On the other hand, being Hemingwayesque was not as easy
for him as people seemed to think it was. Whilst he had mastered the

whiskey-drinking and sexual confusion relatively quickly (a bottle of Bushmills and a pornographic magazine sat on his desk) the bull-fighting and general macho posturing had proved problematic. Nor did it help that Mike wasn't actually Irish. He just knew that Irish meant literary meant money.

"Aha," he typed, hesitantly, "You sons of bitches." He stopped. Irish people didn't use that sort of term, even if they were deliberately trying to be Hemingwayesque, which of course they hardly ever were, unless you counted Behan, and that was stretching a point a bit too far. Behan would have found Hemingway bewilderingly energetic, whilst Hemingway would probably have mistaken Behan for a hippopotamus and shot him. Then again, saying "You tossers" wasn't remotely Hemingwayesque, but it was Irish. So too was "Gobshites" but that was even less like the big lad. Why had he picked a genre whose producer had been beefy, boisterous and sporty? There was nothing there with which he could identify. If only Benny Hill had written books. Mike lit a cigarette and drank some whiskey. He closed down his file on the novel and began a new one on the dramatisation of *Our Mutual Friend*. Then he swore, remembering that he was supposed to be meeting Portia to work out more of the details of the project.

She had been remarkably persuasive when they had met at the Hertford.

"I've worked it all out," she had said, "And I used my contacts in the Social Services to get an idea of prices. All we have to do is rent a house with a few bedrooms, stick in a few slappers, issue discreet advertising and wait for the punters to roll in. You'll get your investment back in no time, and then the profits will start to mount up. You'll be rich beyond your wildest dreams, provided your wildest dreams feature sums in the region of several grand."

Mike had been faintly sceptical.

"Isn't it a bit questionable?"

Portia had looked at him dismissively.

"What do you mean by questionable? You've read Marx, you've read Adam Smith, you've lived through the 1980s. All relationships are financial; look at Jane Austen, for goodness' sake. Mister sodding Darcy would be a rather less divine love god if his breeches weren't bursting with land and shekels. Look at the Mercier's management; would anyone be married to those comedians if it wasn't for the financial and social security it gives them?"

Mike swirled the lager around in his glass, looking with apparent fascination at the suds.

"Oh, I don't know. I hear Sally's a real beast in the sack," he said.

"Well, maybe. But in general, we're just making the system a bit more straightforward. Sex and money; the two go together," Portia said.

Mike had wondered what had happened to the Portia who had comforted the sobbing girls in the office after heartless boyfriends had traded them in for better models.

"Isn't human happiness a bit of an issue too?" he asked.

"Well, of course," Portia looked at him as if he was a little simple, "We will be adding to the sum total of joy in the Hengistley district. One of the reasons why the fucking management are so bloody happy in their work and indifferent to the needs of others is because they're getting it. And one of the reasons why Andrew and William are miserable bastards is because they aren't. Our, ah, establishment can solve this problem by helping anyone who can pay to get his oats. A simple and open system."

Mike drained his glass and lit a cigarette.

"Is it legal?"

Portia waved her hands at him.

"Two hypothetical situations. One of your students sneaks into the staffroom when all the teachers are in a meeting, stashes the photocopying paper stock in his sports kitbag, and gives it to his mate to sell at a car boot sale in Crawley. Another was supposed to be in your lesson seventh period and you spot him in the pub. Who do you punish?"

"Oh, I can see where you're coming from. You don't get punished for being bad, you get punished for being stupid and getting caught. But what if we're caught?"

Portia put a comforting hand on his arm.

"Don't worry," she soothed, "Like the girls in the brothel, we'll take precautions."

Mike had been tolerably reassured. Now he ambled over to the drama studio and found her looking over an enormous estate-agent's map of the area.

"Did you put out those cards in Brighton like I asked you?" she asked, as she circled prime sites on the map.

"Yes, and I'd be grateful if you didn't ask me to do it again," he grumbled, "Leaving out these recruitment cards is almost as embarrassing as taking the advertising ones. I got a really funny look from an old lady as I emerged from that 'phone box on the sea front. I felt like a seedy old pervert."

"There's an obvious remark to be made here, Michael, and I'm not going to make it because I'm not into cheap lines," Portia said, "But I'm bound to say that a small amount of effort is going to be required to set us on the path to untold wealth. Anyway, you've done the easy bit. These girls we recruit will have to do the actual hard slog. No-one's asking you to fiddle with the parts of some frustrated accountant until they go off, or spank a member of the district council with a stick of celery whilst dressed as a nun. Never mind have a train pulled on you by the entire North Sussex rugger squad."

"True," Mike said, marvelling at Portia's capacity for rendering unusual concepts into disturbing images, "But then, I'm just a lazy bastard. Even this small amount of effort is enough to put me off any further work."

"You're as bad as one of the bloody kids," Portia snorted, "But when we interview the girlies I dare say you'll find plenty of energy."

"I'd been thinking about that," Mike said.

"Thinking, dreaming, drawing pictures, writing poetry and erotic short stories and all," Portia suggested.

"No, no, I mean, yes, but, ah, well, won't we have to er, well, road test our employees?"

"It is not wholly inconceivable," Portia said, "But these people aren't like educational book suppliers. You might ask them if they would be prepared to let you have a free sample, but I don't think it's the way they normally operate."

"How come you know so much about this?" Mike asked.

"I'm a careers adviser, and I teach personal and social education."

"About prostitution? What precisely is the world coming to?"

"No, you dozy shitehawk, I get sent information by voluntary groups and the DSS. There are some young men in that wicked, cruel world out there out there who put their girlfriends on the game to feed smack habits and so on."

"Good lord," Mike said, "That's awful."

"It certainly is," Portia said, "That kind of girl muddies the slapper market. She's got a personal loyalty to the bastard, and half the time she's bouncing around on planet chemical herself. No use in a high class venture like ours, I must say. Now, pay attention. I've identified half a dozen prime areas. We're going to go round to the estate agents of this lovely historic town and pose as a married couple. We'll see if there are any suitably furnished places for rent."

"Those are all in residential areas," Mike exclaimed, "Are you completely mad? We'll get caught in no time. What will the neighbours say?"

"They won't say anything," Portia looked at him calmly and lit a cigarette.

"How can you be so sure?"

"Because this is the 1990s. This is Mrs Thatcher's Britain, as I know to my cost. An atomised society, where each individual or family is a self-contained economic unit which moves about and carries its own social circle with it. People don't live in communities any more, Mike, or at least middle class people don't. All of our friends are the ones we acquire at work or at university or in the pubs we choose to go to—which may not be our locals. Think about it."

Mike thought. As a good card-carrying member of the Labour Party, he did not want this to be true. Portia slashed through the foliage of his self-delusion with the machete of objectivity.

"Where do you drink?"

"The Lion and Lobster."

Mike looked out of the window, thinking enviously of the people who were, as he spoke, in the Lion and Lobster, drinking beer.

"Which is how close to your house?"

"A mile. Maybe two. I always drive."

Portia raised her eyebrows. Mike did not always drive, she knew, as the police had taken an unforgiving approach to his attempt to drive from Hengistley to Brighton with four pints of lager slopping about inside him. But she let the matter pass.

"Who do you drink with there?"

"The other people from the theatre company."

Mike had a horrible feeling that he knew what Portia was heading towards, but he didn't like to say anything to obstruct the flow of what she was getting at. Portia was different these days. When he had worked with her in the old days, she had been a fluffy, cuddly sort of person, all floaty skirts and tousled hair. These days she wore suits and looked neat. It wasn't just that she had to because of her higher status in the new school, no, there was more to it than that. The suits, the haircuts, the makeup, that fucking unteachery car, were the outward signs of a new Portia, a tough and modern person who scared him more than a little.

"What is the name of your next door neighbour?"

"Don't know, miss."

"Name four people who live in your street."

"Can't."

"Name one."

Portia had a steely look about herself. Mike had a rubbery look about himself.

"Can't."

"Who are your best friends?"

"Er…Andrew, and William, and you, and…"

"How close to you does the nearest of these people live?"

"Half a mile."

"Right. Do you see what I mean? Nobody knows who their neighbours are any more. *Coronation Street* and *EastEnders* and crap like that are popular because they trade in the fantasy that communities exist where every punter knows every other punter and gives a monkey's about what they do, but let me assure you, these places are not real. That IRA geezer they lifted at Gatwick airport. His neighbours didn't even know he was Irish. He'd got a shopping bag full of semtex and a whopping great Uzi in his wardrobe and nobody knew. Why do you think child abusers and drug dealers and politicians get away with their crimes for years? Because nobody knows and nobody cares what goes on next door anymore. We could build a nuclear reactor and the neighbours wouldn't notice. Especially not in a town like this, where the insurance company reps come and go like nomadic tribes in the Sahara. William's lived here for seven years and apart from his old students he knows *five* people."

"That's William, though. He's so emotionally crippled *Blue Peter* have appeals for him."

"I am a social icon of rare charm and intellect," Portia said, "And I have *eight* friends in Hengistley."

"Bloody Hell," Mike conceded, "I see your point. But I still think it would be better to go for somewhere in a business area. A few rooms above a shop, say."

"No, you great arse," Portia yelled, "it's the town frigging centres where the life is. That's how the brothel in Horsham got snared on. Remember the headline in the tabloid that exposed it? 'Wahey! It's

Whore-sham!' Town centres hum with people in the day and at night they're full of winos. And in this town, the bulk of the winos are students from this college. So you can forget that idea right now. We're going to rent a nice detached house, away from the pubs."

"Yes miss," Mike murmured, chastened, as he followed her out to the car.

Their first attempts to find a house were relatively unsuccessful.

"The walls are too thin," Portia declared of the first place they visited.

"But it's a detached house," said the baffled estate agent, an eager young man in a Next suit with a Schaeffer protruding from his breast pocket like a discreet antenna connecting him to his mother ship.

"I mean the walls between the bedrooms," Portia explained patiently.

The young man still looked blank. Portia reflected that he had obviously not had the benefit of one of her personal and social education lessons.

"Perhaps I should elaborate," she said, silkily if less patiently, "My husband and I have just got married, and we are likely to be hosting both sets of parents for weekends. Now, I don't mind admitting that I'm a screamer. Like an electric buzz saw, in fact, or a howler monkey with its foot trapped in a crocodile's jaws. Our parents are rather advanced in years and their hearts are not in the best of nick, so you appreciate the need for rather stout walls."

The young man had turned white. Silently, he held out the details of another house.

"Ooh, that's nice," Portia said, only to reject it when they arrived there because its bedroom windows were visible from a local kindergarten.

"Kids are awfully observant," she whispered to Mike as they moved on.

Eventually they discovered perfection. The four bedroom house was old enough to have solid walls, stood off one of the main arterial roads into the town. A high hedge hid it from view, and no neighbour could possibly see in. It had been cheaply furnished by owners who were spending the year in Australia and had put their most valued possessions into storage.

"We'll be along during the week to sort things out," Portia said to the young estate agent, who had recovered enough colour to pass for someone who had not actually died as yet.

"So," Mike said, at last, as they drove off, "About that screaming."

In the garden of the house next door, a middle-aged lady was wrestling with a particularly stubborn weed when she heard the throaty sound of Portia's sports car. A yellow blare shot across her view of the road through the garden gate and headed towards the College. She wondered if it might be that teacher from the comprehensive who her daughter liked. Portia, that was it. No, it couldn't be. Coincidence, she thought. No teacher who's just bought a car like that could be looking to rent a big expensive house like the Harrisons' as well, not with the money they were charging. Mrs Jameson put the thought from her mind and went back to her gardening.

CHAPTER EIGHT

"And just how, ah, broad-minded are you prepared to be?" Mike asked, with understandable nervousness, of the young woman who sat before him in the otherwise empty house.

She thought for a moment. It was apparent that this process cost her much effort. From her first request, on being offered a drink, for a Tia Maria mixed with Bailey's, she had established herself in Mike's eyes as a woman of limited intellectual firepower. If Arthur Miller was the equivalent of an extremely large aeroplane carrying atomic bombs, this girl was like a small boy armed with a catapult. Not that this appeared to bother her, as in all other respects she bore no resemblance whatsoever to a boy, small or otherwise. Jobelle, as she liked to be called, had, relatively early in life, discovered that she could gain popularity with the opposite sex not through intellectually stimulating discourse but by offering them access to her body. This had, unlike her as yet undeveloped mind, blossomed remarkably quickly in her teens, and resulted in a great deal of attention both from her thirteen year old male contemporaries and from adults of both sexes. Indeed, her first serious encounter of a sexual nature had been with the games mistress at her comprehensive in Barking. The older woman's relative skill and thoughtfulness had had the result of not putting Joan (as she was really called; Jobelle, a name she had seen on a bottle of shampoo, sounded more American and sophisticated, she thought) off sex, whilst enhancing her curiosity about it. Catastrophic exam results, followed by a falling-out with her family, had led to the possibly unwise decision to seek out a new life in Brighton. This had initially taken the form of helping out in a dingy alternative clothing shop, which sold tee-shirts decorated with various cannabis motifs of the kind which are funny the first time they are bought by a fifth-former but tediously not so thereafter, in return for getting to stay in an even dingier flat. This had begun to pall, largely because she found the unwashed lifestyle of the Brighton alternative scene somewhat depressing.

A well brought up girl, Jobelle hated untidiness and squalor, and was unimpressed by the crusty types who she had slept with. She was sufficiently wise in the ways of the world to have come to the conclusion that sex and love were no longer the same thing. There must, therefore, be some other kind of quid pro quo. From her earliest days of sexual experimentation, she had been materially rewarded for her activity. Even the scabbiest teenage boys at school would give her cigarettes, cinema tickets and the like, whilst older admirers gave more concrete proofs of their gratitude (not that Jobelle would have phrased it like this. A concrete present, to her, was the breeze block which her older brother had dropped through the car window of a boy whose attentions she had repudiated). The Brighton hippies, whilst essentially harmless, seemed to believe that the whole concept of freedom was reward in itself for Jobelle's intimacy with their unwashed bodies. In this, they were mistaken, which was why none had slept with her more than once. Jobelle, disillusioned with life in the cosmic end of the south coast, had been about to ring her mother and ask for her old bedroom back when she had spotted Mike's card. This promised accommodation and good pay to broad-minded girls. Jobelle knew what that meant, and had rung the anonymous mobile 'phone number to arrange an interview.

And now, here she was, in front of a dishevelled-looking man with two days' growth of stubble. He did not look like what a pimp or a madam was supposed to look like, but this was not a source of much surprise to her. Everyone from Brighton was scruffy. On the other hand, this Hengistley place looked dead nice. A bit posh, perhaps, but not really up its arse the way that the little Cotswold villages her mum had taken her to as a child had been. It was certainly clean, and as for this house—well! In Brighton, a house of this size would probably have been subdivided into several flats, each of which would be inhabited by a student, or an immigrant family, or a drug dealer. Jobelle was a good girl, at least in that respect, and found such things distasteful, though again, this was not the word she would have chosen herself. The comfort of living here and being paid twenty-five quid for as many minutes' work was not unappealing.

"I've done pretty well everything, mate," she said, shrugging.

"I daresay," Mike said, taking in her tight blouse, pencil skirt and fun-fur jacket, "But, if, as you say, you've never done it for money before, you've presumably…. er…. I mean," Mike had always thought of himself as a pretty up front kind of guy about matters sexual. Certainly, compared with the nudge-nudge approach of Jonathan Bleach (in the good old days) and the monastic repression of William Fenneck, he was an open and frank discusser of such concepts as phallic symbolism in film and the sexual motif in Shakespearean text. But this was slightly different. This was not an enjoyable intellectual fondling of matters carnal in the safe and controlled environment of the classroom. He was sitting here actually trying to establish whether or not this well-endowed (in certain respects) young woman was prepared to commit sexual acts for money. It need hardly be said that he did not, in the course of his duties at the College, often find himself in this position.

"Let's try again," he tried again, "You might not always enjoy it. In fact, I can guarantee you won't."

Jobelle looked at Mike with what almost amounted to pity, an emotion which in teenage girls is always the next-door neighbour to contempt— an altogether less positive feeling which is forever popping in to borrow the sugar and twist kindness into loathing. She had encountered his kind before. The Art master at school had wanted to rescue her from the bawdy, crude, bestial attentions of the boys and give her a more sophisticated and affectionate relationship based on mutual need. Jobelle could not spell most of these words but she knew what they amounted to, and she despised it. Whatever his motive, the Art master wanted her to relinquish the power she had over the mass and confine it to him. This was not part of Jobelle's agenda, and once she had conducted her affair with the Art master long enough for it to come to the attention of both his wife and the school authorities, she had abandoned him. Jobelle did not read the newspapers, but even if she had, she would not have felt so much as a tinge of guilt to learn that he had driven off Beachy Head, leaving a note which simply said, "Fucking Bloody Bitch Women. I cannot kill them all so I'm going to kill myself. Goodbye."

Mike was clearly soft like that.

"What do you do, mate?" she asked, fixing him with pale blue eyes, and forcing him to meet them instead of staring at her cleavage as he had been doing since her arrival.

"Sorry?"

She could tell he was posh, too. Really posh. Her sort said "What?" and her mum had said "I beg your pardon?" when she was trying to be posh, but she had learned in Brighton that the real middle class were forever apologising. She did not know why. Nor, it must be said, did she care.

"I mean, for a living. You aren't a full-time madam."

"Ah, no," Mike said, realising that he was now a part-time madam, "I'm a theatre producer."

He was, too; Mike put on lots of plays in Brighton and the whole point of this sordid exercise was to fund a really big one. Just as Andrew, when he wanted to disguise what he actually did, called himself a journalist on the strength of a couple of articles in the *Law Teachers' Gazette*, so too Mike had an instant cover story handy.

People had an unfortunate tendency to switch off interest or get nasty if they discovered you were a teacher.

"Right," Jobelle said, "Do you always enjoy doing that?"

"No, of course not, it can be bloody awful sometimes. The actresses can be right prima donnas and some of the actors think they're Larry bloody Olivier playing Othello when they're actually supposed to be Bottom in *Midsummer*, but…"

"So," Jobelle had not the faintest idea what he was on about, but he seemed to be heading in the right direction. She continued triumphantly, "You still do it, though. 'Cause it's what you do. Same with me. Take the rough with the smooth, don't you?"

Mike thought about an earlier interview with a young woman who had arrived clad from head to foot in black leather and boasted of her techniques in the area of sado-masochism. One of these had involved the use of fine-grained sandpaper and a rasp file. He winced involuntarily.

"Yes," he replied, eventually, "Yes, I suppose it does."

"Well then," she said, triumphantly, "I'm a big girl," Mike took the opportunity to confirm the fact by running his eye once more over Jobelle's impressive bustline, and nodded, sagely, "I can handle meself. And other things, if you know what I mean."

With a depressing sense of predictability, Mike was reminded of bawdy Shakespearean innuendo, but refrained from saying so lest the girl misinterpret him.

"Yes," she continued, "I can do all sorts. There used to be this bloke on our estate, older guy, right, very nice to me, it was where I used to live in Barking, and he had this thing about doing it doggy style. Like it was quite funny, you know, us being in Barking and that. But the funny thing was, right, he wanted to wear a big studded leather collar, and him take the position of the dog, and I had to—"

"Quite," Mike made a mental vow that, before he went to bed that evening, he would remember to thank God for his normal attitudes and appetites. That, of course, was if he hadn't drunk himself unconscious to obliterate the horrible memories of these interviews.

When Portia arrived several hours later to take over the interviewing she found Mike in a less than positive frame of mind.

"I'm really not sure about this", he told her, "If I have to listen to just one more slapper describe what fucking horrible acts she used to carry out on her fellow human beings, and vice versa, I shall go bloody insane."

Portia examined his notes, humming and raising her eyebrows as she inspected his notes.

"Number three's certainly been around the block," she said, after whistling admiringly, "This business with the cigar; I'd read about it but I've never seen it. That's pretty impressive."

"It's put me off smoking for life," Mike moaned, reaching nonetheless into Portia's bag and extracting her cigarettes.

"Oh, don't be such a big wuss," Portia laughed, "It's all part of the rich tapestry of life. Think how boring life would be without people like this."

"I can do boring now. Boring is me, from now on. I think I'll leave Brighton and settle here. It's so lovely and quiet. Nothing ever happens here. I'll quit teaching and get a nice quiet job with the insurance company."

"And relax at the weekend with a topless hand shandy and warmed nuts at your friendly local cathouse. Remember, Hengistley isn't boring any more. It's got a sinister, sordid underside as the red hot bonking capital of the south."

"Shit," Mike said, in contravention of the rule he had been taught by his mother about swearing being the sign of a poor vocabulary.

"Now run along," she said, settling down for the next round of interviews, "And see if you can get William down to the pub for half past four, will you? I don't imagine it will be a problem. Alice has gone back to university, so he'll be pining, poor little mite. He'll be even more ready than normal for any opportunity to stick fluid down his throat. Don't tell him why. And let me do the talking."

"Yes, miss," Mike said, obediently, and ambled back to the College. He was half way there when the thought struck him that he did not know why, not to tell William why. If that made sense, which it didn't. But then, nor did setting up a brothel.

William was not, in fact, pining for Alice. He was marking essays written by his students, which he found infinitely more depressing. His cold grey eyes flickered over the teenage scrawls at high speed, catching the gist of what they were getting at. Occasionally he would circle an offending paragraph in red ink, and write 'this may make sense to you, but it does not make sense to me, so it is of no value' in the margin. With some of the students he did not even bother to read the contents and simply put a row of red ticks down the side of the page. He would draw a florid B at the end, and write 'almost an A, but needs more detail.' The essay might well have been worth an A, but William did not wish to be the agent of his students' immodesty. For what was all this talk of self-esteem, if not a pandering to the deadly sin of pride? William had spent twenty-eight years without a shred of self-esteem and it had done him no harm. All you needed was knowledge of where precisely you were in the great chain of being. William's world was a hierarchical pyramid with God and the Royal Family at the top, and the Principal just below them. He was ferociously loyal to those students and members of staff who he liked, snapped and snarled at those he did not, and bitterly fought any alteration to his routine. William would have made an excellent dog. As a Politics teacher in a classless democracy in the late twentieth century, however, his views left much to be desired.

Coming to a half page of barely literate scrawl, he stopped, and padded up to the staffroom, where he filled a coffee cup from a dispenser and lit a cigarette before returning to gaze unhappily at the script.

'Sovereignity is the Queen. It is what type of leadership is used in this country, the parliment has a lot of power and control over decisions made,' the boy had written. He was 18, not without intelligence, and a second-generation Bangladeshi Briton. William looked at the paper and then looked at the whirls of smoke dancing upwards from his cigarette. He knew, or at any rate had formed an ineradicable opinion about, exactly whose fault this was. He cursed the cowardice of an educational system which inculcated primary and secondary school teachers with a reluctance to impose English literary norms on the children of immigrants. By the time boys like this reached him, they had become the victims of those who feared accusations of racialism if they made too many demands for correct English usage. William's cigarette tip quivered as he thought angrily about the issue and dragged the smoke hard into his protesting lungs, as he considered the other criminals, the patronising leftists who believed that helping these children adapt to their host country was in some way colonialist. He spent most of his time correcting these boys' spelling, which did not leave much room for developing the niceties of constitutional theory. He hauled again on his cigarette and started work on the boy's essay, his bitterness mounting with every red correction he had to put down. By the time he had finished, the white paper looked as if it had spent the night in the Bates motel.

Mike found his colleague staring glumly out of the window in Prudence's office, a pile of cigarette ends sulking in a saucer beside him. He sighed. William was clearly engulfed in gloom as he mourned the departure of his beloved. Whilst Portia was keen on the idea, Mike did not feel that it was good for William to become as fond as he seemed to be of former students like Alice, if he got all depressed like this when they left.

"Like a pint?" he asked jovially.

"I could murder one," William growled, morosely, "It would be a humane death, though. Quick and clean. Wouldn't dwell on it."

"That's exactly right," Mike said, enthusiastically, "Nor would I. It's the natural way of things. People move on. No point getting too sentimental about them."

"I'm not sentimental about the dozy little halfwit," William snarled, "I just think it's not fair, that's all."

Mike reflected that these were harsh words to use about someone of whom William was supposed to be extremely fond. He wondered if perhaps William and Alice had had a row, as opposed to the normal low-intensity warfare which seemed to flourish between them.

"Er…well, I think you'll find it's all for the best. I mean, it's what you want for them, isn't it?"

"For the love of blinding blue sod," William yelled, "A bloke expresses a few perfectly moderate, mildy right wing opinions and the next thing he's mister prejudice. No, it is not what I want for them and it most certainly isn't for the best."

Mike wondered, not for the first time, if his colleague had lost his reason.

"I don't think I'm being unduly politically correct when I say that I really do have to disagree with you on this one," he said, nervously.

"You certainly aren't being remotely politically correct, not in the long term," William barked, furiously, "It's people like you, with your short-sighted liberal squeamishness, who are doing the National Front's work for them."

"I didn't know the National Front had a university policy," Mike mused, "In fact, I didn't know they could even spell the word."

"Of course they have, you fool. It's that none but their own sort should be allowed into them," William snapped, "And what are you wittering on about universities for?"

"Well, you know, females—ah—go off to university, and that's good, and natural, and you shouldn't go all mopey, you should be pleased and proud. Especially of Alice," Mike offered. He hoped he was being helpful but the change in William's manner from crotchety irritation to angry incomprehension suggested otherwise.

"What on earth are you talking about? What the buggery sod does Alice have to do with the Innit Posse boys from Dorkham Estate? Actually, I don't want to know. Girls these days are a hell of a lot more experimental than you'd imagine. She sets far more store by what she calls open-mindedness and I call downright filth than the Good Book would regard as healthy."

Mike thought that the human imagination couldn't possibly conceive of some of the experiments he'd just been hearing about. It also dawned on him that perhaps William wasn't talking about the opposite sex. He decided to make a clean break with things and declare a general amnesty on the conversation up to that point.

"Look, let's go up to the pub. Portia's there, and it would be nice to have a pint with her, wouldn't it?"

"Yes," William muttered, suspiciously, and followed his colleague from the room. As they made their way out, a draught scattered the marked scripts all over the floor. Neither made any attempt to recover them.

Portia was flirting idly with some of the soaks at the Hertford Arms and sipping appreciatively at a half pint of lager. Her mind was mulling over the successes of the day. A number of very promising employees had been recruited and were ready to be installed into the house in Bacons Road. Most were reasonably attractive and none were on serious drugs. She had booked them all in for medical tests to check if there was anything that they might inadvertently give to the customers which might be considered over and above the job requirements. On a beer-mat, Portia scribbled possible lines to use in an advertisement for the place on the internet. She felt a warm glow of contentment.

Portia would have felt rather less content had the last applicant been rather more honest with her. A blousy girl with dyed hair, Yvette, as she said she was called, had the lazy, half closed eyes of the dedicated slapper and a slow way of speaking. Portia sensed that the girl was not an especially happy human being, but also that she was probably quite intelligent. Had she recognised her—and there was no reason why she should have—she would have known that this assessment was correct. Sonia Thrale was indeed bright, but was phenomenally lazy and wilful. She had thrown aside a promising academic career by dabbling in drugs and swimming in alcohol, as well as pursuing endless liaisons with boys which brought her neither happiness nor pleasure. Her indifference to others now extended to indifference to herself, as she trod water at Mercier's waiting to leave. The one glimmer of hope she had was to escape England and go to New York. She was not sure why she wanted to go there, but it seemed like a good idea. In order to pay for this, however, she needed money. Hard work in the normal sense being alien to her, she had been delighted—insofar as any positive emotion ever entered her soul—to find one of Mike's cards whilst out clubbing in Brighton. Her self-image of degredation, self-destruction and unhappiness fitted in well with this new vocation. It had been pointed out that she would have made a great gay icon if it hadn't been for her fat arse. She understood this only too well, and liked the idea, though she (perfectly reasonably) deeply resented the fat arse bit. Had he been privy to the day's developments, the man who had made the comment would have warned Portia about the danger she was playing with if she pursued the employment of this highly unstable and erratic young woman. But Portia had deliberately excluded William, who had met Sonia through his students in a bar and developed an instant dislike for her, from the decision-making process, and would never get to hear this advice.

Mike and William strolled into the bar and beamed at Portia. She sighed and bought them drinks.

"William," she said effusively, "How are you, then? How's the department going?"

"As well as can be expected with me in charge of it," William said, matter-of-factly. He was not fishing for compliments. He was stating facts.

"Good, good," Portia enthused, "Look, have you come across a new thing called Democracy 2000?"

"Can't say I have," William said, after pondering the matter briefly, "But then, I get all sorts of crap sent to me. Student work, mostly. I tend to bin it."

"It's all the rage in the comprehensives."

"So's crack."

"It's designed to encourage kids to get into politics, and there's loads of European Union cash floating around for places that set up activities for pre-voting-age kids."

William's eyes flickered with interest as he gulped down his Thruttock's Old Blaster.

"What I though was, as Mercier's is the only place in the area that does Politics, you could organise something. Not only would you get the cash from the government, you'd get guaranteed future students to boost the department's numbers because of the publicity. Good, eh?"

"But what could I do, exactly?"

Portia smiled encouragingly and as she did so, the icy hand of fear gripped Mike's heart, as it had gripped so many others in the annals of bad fiction through the centuries. It had suddenly dawned on him what she wanted William for.

"Oh, I don't know. Let's think. I've got it. Tell you what. Why don't you invite down some big-name politicians—one from each party, say—to talk to the kids and take part in some suitably educational activities with them?"

"Yes," William said, slowly, "I think we could do that."

As he spoke, Mike felt an overwhelming urge to run away and hide and cry. This was all becoming large, and frightening, and dangerous, and there was nothing he could do to stop it. He hurled the contents of his beer mug down his throat with vigour, and ordered another pint. Portia was still smiling.

CHAPTER NINE

The Right Honourable Damien Sedgwick, MP, Her Majesty's Secretary of State for the Co-ordination of Information and Administration, looked intently at the letter before him. The perfectly cut Oswald Boateng suit which so precisely hung from his well-toned body seemed to ripple as thought after thought chased around inside him like demented Scalextric cars. His brain, widely regarded as one of the most powerful in the government, picked up on the revvings of these ideas and he transferred them onto his writing pad with deft strokes of his discreetly expensive roller-ball pen. Sedgwick loathed fountain-pens—messy, old-fashioned things—and biros—one had to lean so beastly hard—with equal intensity. The pen in his hand allowed him to leave his mark without causing embarrassing blots or using unnecessary pressure. Much, indeed, like his approach to government. A key confidant of the Leader when in opposition, he had persuaded the rag-bag of trade unionists, liberal intellectuals, trouble-makers and idealists which made up the Party to abandon virtually every policy which might be construed as difficult or challenging. Sedgwick believed that the era of politicians who told the punters that a bit of pain and hardship was necessary for the greater benefits to come, was over. No-one wanted that sort of thing any more. The great British public wanted a pain-free, conflict-free, guilt-free world, and this was precisely what the new-look Party would offer them. They wanted low taxes? No problem. But feeling guilty about

Health and Education? Don't worry. We care. That was all that was
needed, when you got down to it. Nobody read the small print any
more. All political equations boiled down to one thing; the popularity
or otherwise of the outcome. Would this invitation to speak to some
sixth-formers bring popularity? Sedgwick picked up the telephone and
called his ministerial adviser.

"Josh, come round here, would you? I want you to do a bit of checking up for me."

Within minutes the young man was in the Secretary of State's office,
almost panting like an eager Labrador at a shoot. The pheasant of ideas
brought down by the firepower of his master's brain had to be retrieved.

"Sir Fulke Mercier's College, Hengistley, Sussex, want me to speak to
their students. A question-time sort of thing. Here's the letter,"
Sedgwick passed it to his aide, who took in the date of the College's
foundation, the faintly obsequious tone of the address, the fact that the
Head of Politics was an M.A. from Oxford—a second rate sod who had
paid seven guineas for a bit of status, in his view. He had himself
attended a rather smart comprehensive in one of the better parts of
London and enjoyed a joyous time at the LSE.

Josh thought for a second and then made a staccato series of points,
which he checked off on his fingers as he went through them.

"Off top of head, DS, no research, need to get full details before giving really in-depth risk analysis. But here goes.

Point one. College. Students. Good. Youth. Vitality. New voters.
Possible recruitment or support, easily swayed by feelgood message.
Bound to be good looking ones—consider location—more attractive
people in wealthier area. Good photogenic stuff. But. Two key danger
areas. A. Lefties. You are the nasty fascist who sold the great traditions of
the Party down the river. Yah, boo, chuck tomatoes, look like prize berk
on six o'clock news. Do we want this? B. English Nationalists. Little
baby patriots. How dare you throw us into the arms of Johnny
European? Union jacks everywhere, possible demo by UK

Independence lads, no fun for DS, hey? So—immense potential, but also huge risk."

DS nodded.

"Go on."

"Point two, separate but equal and linked. College. Teachers. Is this place in a sector which has seen cutbacks? If so, is the profile of the staff such that they still blame the previous administration for this? Or do they blame us? Needs to be checked. Teachers can give rough time in own right, or indoctrinate kiddiwinkies.

Point Three. Sussex. Target seat area. Got some in last election—Hove, Crawley, I need not continue. Want more. Current party holding in Sussex is areas with noticeable prole or student populations. PM wants to take a constituency that's so middle class you could eat your lunch from the streets. Worth a sniff.

Point four. Hengistley itself. You know whose seat that is?"

Sedgwick looked at his aide and briefly pondered how someone with the elegant phraseology and fluid diction of a Dalek could possibly have gained a first from the LSE and a post-graduate qualification in English Literature from Cambridge. He must have been studying the works of R2D2 out of that film. The minister desperately tried to pin down whose constituency Hengistley was.

"Sorry, Josh," he conceded, "It isn't one of ours, so the need to keep an eye on it has never occurred to me."

"Only Benedict "the Brain" Wolfesbain. Shadow Home Secretary and possible future leader of his Party. Officially rated the second most intelligent man in the House, after your good self, by Mensa. A real battle of the titans there. This could be really good."

Sedgwick looked down at his well-manicured fingers and thought for a moment. Benedict Wolfesbain was a worthy opponent in a debate, and that was precisely the problem. Damien Sedgwick's career had been built on the demolition of people less intelligent than himself. With rapier intellect and clever word-play, he had slashed and parried and thrust at the arguments of clumsy, blustering old reactionaries and inarticulate, ranting radicals. In such surroundings, Sedgwick had inevitably looked good. Wolfesbain, on the other hand, was widely recognised as a bright spark in his own party, though admittedly this was not exactly a monumental achievement. He had been sufficiently astute to play the Eurosceptic card without sounding like a gibbering nationalist lunatic, and had been lucky enough to have been out of Parliament during the old administration, avoiding contamination by the sewage of corruption which had risen around the feet of the unlucky Prime Minister. He had subjected the Home Secretary to a barrage of verbal kickings over a minor scandal involving the disappearance of several Police surplus helicopters. The wretched things had subsequently reappeared in the colours of a morally dubious West African dictatorship, which used them to hose down its political opponents with machine-gun fire. And there was no juicy sexual scandal to pin on the bastard either. He was as pure as the driven mineral water

"This needs a bit of research before we run with it. Check out the College, its students, its staff, especially the comedian who invited me down there. The local newspaper will help, I should have thought. I want to know everything about the area. What sort of reception will I get? What is the chance of making an electoral impact? Go down there today and check it out. Report back tomorrow and give me a reply. I'll go entirely on your recommendations."

"Righto. Consider done," Josh said. He was not entirely pleased at the thought of having to leave London, but his master had spoken. It was, he supposed, that from such research that great electoral inroads were made. Remembering the disastrous visit of a colleague to a country village where the staple industry was beef farming and the only sport hunting foxes, he shuddered. The poor sod had been lucky to get out alive. This must not happen to DS. Josh left the building and hailed a taxi for Victoria.

*   *   *

In the saloon bar of the Hertford Arms, three men were happily discussing a mutual interest in beer. "Cowboy" Sam Avon, the manager of the local off-license, was holding forth on the beauties of his latest special offer, a new beer from the local brewery.

"I can assure you, gentlemen, that Thruttock's Pompous Heavyweight is one of the finest brews known to man. Lovely chocolate malt aroma, plenty of body without that harsh fizziness you sometimes get, and it goes down a treat. Four bottles for five pounds. And—hey—the ladies love it too. I think you know what I'm saying."

"If you don't mind my saying so," Alice's father, Henry Jameson, said, "I'm not sure that the ladies would know a good beer from a bad one."

He knew perfectly well that, whilst Sam would not mind him saying so, his wife and daughter would mind very much. Especially his daughter, who had taken to drinking beer at university and was now under the impression, as students so often are, that she knew something about the stuff. Alice would have subjected him to a vigorous tirade of abuse for this. But then, he had always encouraged her to do things she was good at.

"You couldn't say that in front of Alice," William confirmed, gloomily, "She'd bite your leg off. But Henry's right. Women know sod all about beer, even if sometimes they drink it."

"Dear dear me," Sam said, with a pitying smile. He stretched out his sparse frame, clad in a linen suit, from whose trousers protruded the Western boots which gave him his nickname.

"You really have got the wrong end of the stick. Women aren't going to notice the taste. But it's in a really pretty bottle. Frosted glass with a lovely Victorian sort of label on it. Beautiful."

"Sounds awful," Henry remarked, "Since when has beer come in frosted glass bottles?"

"Since the girlies started drinking it," Sam said, "This is a way of keeping the little woman happy whilst making sure that you have something tasty to drink."

"Goodness," Henry breathed admiringly, "It's at moments like this that you realise that socialism really was bound to fail."

"Can you lay some of it on for us next month?" William asked, "I'm arranging a kind of Question Time affair with some politicians. No-one's got back to me yet about it, but I think it's doable. It would be nice to lay on a bit of refreshment."

"If you were of a seedy turn of mind," Henry said, "You could offer them entertainment as well."

"Really?" Sam, who was of a profoundly seedy turn of mind, pricked up his ears.

"I was given a flyer by a client in Crawley last week," Henry continued, as he fumbled in his jacket pocket, "Very odd thing. Absolute disgrace in my view. I'd been installing a new driver for him and trying to sort out some damn virus problems, but that's not what the disgrace was about."

Henry was a computer consultant, and drove around the area helping people with their machines, a kind of knight-errant of information technology. Occasionally he would try to explain to William what it was that he actually did. William was immensely flattered that anyone should imagine that he had even the vaguest understanding of anything technical, and enjoyed listening to anyone who was enthusiastic about something. Working at Mercier's meant that he was surrounded by teenagers who constantly complained about life in general and teachers who regarded the management as operating a sinister conspiracy against them. Because William rarely complained—he did not understand or care enough about what was going on—the other staff regarded him as an incompetent buffoon. Henry represented a refreshing change from this treatment. He was now waving a brightly-coloured piece of paper.

"Look at this," he cried, "The Grosvenor. A massage parlour. In Hengistley. Offering extras. I don't think you need a lot of imagination to work out what that means. And the brute had the cheek to give this to me. I'm a happily married man, for goodness' sake. I'm sure my wife trusts me implicitly but I'd still rather not imagine what would happen if she found this thing in my jacket pocket before I'd had the chance to explain its provenance."

William and Sam pored over the leaflet. Sam looked up and shrugged.

"No address, just a 'phone number," Sam said, "Probably some upstairs room above a dingy shop in Roffwater Heath. A few tired old slappers with udders round their ankles, chainsmoking Lambert and Butler while they baste you down with chip fat because they've run out of baby oil. Peeling wallpaper and burst mattresses. Needle marks on the cellulite ridden thighs of the old bags. Nothing to worry about."

William and Henry looked at Sam with incredulity and distaste.

"Hey," he said, shrugging, "Managing one of Hengistbury's premier licensed retail outlets isn't all Thruttock's Pompous Heavyweight and Don Dementia Chilean Cab Sauv, you know. The sordid underside of the town is there as well. Did you know, a dozy cow came in yesterday and asked for a big bottle of Lambrusco because—now this will shock you—her husband was bringing the boss round for supper and she wanted to impress him. 'Madam' I said, 'Madam, you are a fool and you deserve the back of my hand across your chops, but I will forgive you just this once. Heed my words and buy this New Zealand Sauvignon Blanc. You will find that it appeals to your pathetically undeveloped palate, but you won't look like a tight arse for buying that fizzy Italian muck.' She was back in this morning, weeping with gratitude. It was almost embarrassing, the way she wanted to wash my feet with her tears and dry them with her hair. But—" Sam fixed the others with a steely glare "—It could all have been so different. What if some dumbarse had been behind the counter, eh? Another life ruined. That's what life's like on the sordid edges of this town."

"Gosh," Henry said. He and William, who would sooner serve water than Lambrusco, stared into the ruby light of their pints. The depth of human misery in Hengistbury had just been brought home to them.

"I think I need a Scotch," William said, "That was a nasty shock. What haven't we had on the malt shelf?"

As he peered through grimy spectacles at the pub's selection, William noticed a very smartly-dressed young man come in. He resisted the temptation to snarl, "You b'ain't from around these 'ere parts, boy," and concentrated on getting the order right. This newcomer was probably one of the young creeps from the Insurance company who tended to appear in bars at Christmas, carousing loudly and surrounded by loud, squawking female colleagues who couldn't hold their drink.

*   *   *

As he had travelled down from London, Josh had become increasingly conscious that he was moving further and further away from anything remotely approaching fashion, taste, and life. He gazed out of the window in anguish as the old train rattled out of Clapham. Even Croydon could be held to have a few attractions. But Purley! For heaven's sake, that was where they set *Terry and* bloody *June*. Josh hadn't realised it really existed. Like Surbiton. That was the *Good Life*. I'm going into the 1970s, he thought. Gradually, the suburban sprawl was replaced by open countryside. Josh winced. He hated the countryside with every fibre of his being. It was dirty, it was damp, and it was full of animals. The duty of an animal was to sit politely, seared in balsamic vinegar and dressed in pine kernels, on a huge plate in the River Café. It was not to be seen wandering about, munching grass and reminding you that it had eyes and a voice. Animals were bastards because soppy-minded, if strong-willed, middle-class women with nothing better to do with their time gave their support and energies to standing around protesting about fox crates or whatever instead of to the Party. Just because of a few photogenic veal calves and baby foxes. And they smelled. The train ambled carelessly past a field in which a girl was riding a horse. Country people. Sods sods sods. Why did they have to be such absolute yokels? The deluge of abuse which had descended on the Party when they tried to outlaw a few of the more barbaric sports and some of the more dangerous forms of meat had been terrifying to behold. Eventually, the train drew up at a dishevelled-looking station.

"Hengistley, this is Hengistley," the conductor called over the tannoy, which appeared, from the sound quality, to be made of two tins attached by a length of string. Josh got out and looked around him. The station had been built in the thirties and not, apparently, cleaned since. A spruce-looking pub lay across the road from the station entrance. Badly in need of a drink, Josh decided to go in. He could start his research there.

The back bar of the Hertford Arms was comfortably shabby and, unlike the main bar, not furnished in any discernible style. A few old horse-brasses hung from the walls and a quiz-machine winked luridly like the control console of a particularly psychadelic space rocket. At the bar, three men of varying ages were discussing which spirits to buy. They looked up as he came in, regarded him with an absence of interest, and returned to their argument.

"I still say that Greenall's gin is the best," the oldest insisted, "If you're not going to drink Scotch, of course."

"Bombay Sapphire," the youngest, and nearest to fashionability, of the three, said, "Where have you been? That is where it's at the drink world these days."

"But it's so hideously expensive, compared to the other stuff," his companion responded, "And I really am not convinced that the very slight improvement in taste is worth the extra money."

"Could I have a bottle of Sol, please?" Josh asked the barman. These people were discussing gin. How sad. It was so…so…William Hague. And if Bombay Sapphire was the cutting edge of cool in Hengistley, what did unfashionable people drink? Mead? Josh was suddenly conscious that all the attention was on him.

"We don't serve that sort of thing round here, sir," said the barman, a diminutive Liverpudlian whose black shirt, Josh was convinced, was a way of showing that he was a dedicated follower of fascism.

"But it's one of London's most popular beers," Josh replied, nervously.

"Ah, well, there we have it, y'see," the barman looked smug, "London. Fancy stuff. We have simpler tastes down here, haven't we, Mister Chips?"

"Indeed, yes, yes," the third man at the bar, brushing cigarette ash from a battered tweed jacket which simply screamed reactionary politics, said absently, "You can have bitter or lager. Simple, straightforward kit. None of your trendy London gear. You need to go to Brighton for that."

"Most of the regulars wouldn't like to drink stuff made by people who can't speak English," the barman continued, "Though we do serve Scotch, I suppose."

"Watch your bloody cheek, you scouse vermin," snorted the tweedy man, "At least we don't nick everything that's not nailed down."

"Better than bombing everybody, though," the barman commented, "Murdering animals."

"That's not us," the Scotsman snapped, "That's the Irish. Breed like rabbits and bomb like bastards. I'm a Scotsman, blast you."

"Oh, yeah, I remember, marching through Glasgow wearing dresses and supporting Celtic. Not that you could march anywhere, the state your bloody legs are in after a few bevvies."

"They're called kilts, you evil little gnome, and I'm a Ken Dodd. The good Lord has an especially hot place in the nether pit reserved for people who support Celtic and rightly so."

Hell's bells, thought Josh, this place is prejudice city. Benedict Wolfesbain only got in here because the National Front didn't have a candidate.

"Erm, I'll have a pint of whatever the locals have," he said, hurriedly

"You won't like it," the older man said.

"What?"

"Don't listen to him," the youngest said, "He has no loyalty to the local brewery."

"That's because I'm loyal to my tastebuds and my digestive system, which react with singular disfavour to the muck they churn out," the oldest explained, "Thruttock's brewery is a disgrace to Hengistley. Undrinkable poison."

"It's never done me any harm," the Scottish one in tweeds volunteered. There was a pause as everyone took in the manifest dishonesty of this statement.

"Look, I'd best be going," Josh said, "I've just realised. I've got an appointment. At the doctor's. Thanks anyway."

He bolted for the door.

"What a strange man," Henry said.

"Looked like a poofter to me," Sam said.

"Can't say I liked the cut of his jib myself," William mused, "He's not your Hengistley sort of person, that's for sure. This town welcomes virtually anyone who's white and middle class, but there was something a bit odd about him."

"Maybe he's a politician," the barman suggested.

"Oh, yeah—down to use the new brothel," Sam said.

There were loud guffaws.

Josh made his way down to the College, and stared at it for a moment. Its crumbling Victorian main block meant nothing to him, but the gleaming new sports hall and smart languages department reminded him of the fashionable north London comprehensive he had attended as a child. As he peered into the quad, Josh could see a few students sunning themselves on the picnic tables. He strolled in.

"Excuse me," he said, smoothly, "But this is Sir Fulke Mercier's College, isn't it?"

"Yes," said a girl whose blonde bob contrasted violently with her dark eyes, "But it's shut. It's half term. We're here for a play rehearsal."

"I see," Josh's mind explored different avenues, "Ah, I have a brother. Your age. Wants to study here. What's it like?"

"Depends what he wants to study," the girl said, "Drama's good."

"What about politics? Brother's a bit of a lefty."

"Depends how much of a lefty. If he's over-the-top, Mr Fenneck will pick on him. I don't think Mr Fenneck believes in anything. If you say something left wing, he'll say something right wing. And the other way about. He's probably very conservative really, but he doesn't seem to support any particular party, if you see what I mean."

Josh certainly did. His Leader's success at the last election was due to precisely this phenomenon. This was looking good.

"And how old is Mr Fenneck?"

"Late twenties. Most staff are a bit older. Miss Halsbury's young. She's nice. So's Mr. Alcock, but he's old."

Mike, had he heard this, would have sobbed aloud.

"And do they have any particular views?"

"Well, when we had a mock election, the students were split pretty evenly between the parties, and the teachers were too. Most students don't have fixed views on much, anyway."

Better and better. A young and dynamic politics department, with a student body that was in the balance, and an open-minded staff. Very photogenic kids if this little moppet and her friends were anything to go by. Josh looked around the quad. Neat, tidy, clean, attractive—this place was booming under the current government. DS could really do some good here. Possibly even swing it for the party at the next election. He put from his mind the odd people in the pub and their prejudice against London drinks. They were probably the old yokels, yesterday's men. He called the minister on his miraculously small mobile 'phone.

"DS? Josh. In Hengistley. Some real potential here. It's a yes, and I think we should ask Number ten if we can bring the media pack. We can hammer Wolfesbain on his home territory."

As Josh strode decisively out of the College, he constructed a mental picture of his boss' gratitude, and smiled to himself. This would be his next step on the ladder towards a safe seat. Josh was in an excellent mood as he picked up a ciabatta sandwich from Marks & Spencers, unconscious of the enormous bad thing that was hurtling towards himself and his master with the energy of a speeding lorry.

CHAPTER TEN

The Hertford bar was humming gently with the varied accents of its staff as Susan walked in to meet Mike for a lunchtime drink. As she spent more time at the College and found her feet, she had quickly emerged from under the wing of the English Department and asserted both Drama as a subject and herself as an individual as autonomous entities. This gained her a lot of respect but also meant that she saw less of Mike. When she did see him, she had found him subdued and furtive, very different from the flamboyantly corrupt figure of the beginning of term. Today he was sitting at one of the Hertford's bizarrely tall tables with a pint of lager and a cigarette, whose pirouetting smoke trails he was observing with dull and insipid eyes.

"Hello, Mike," she opened, brightly, as she clambered up onto the high seat as if she were mounting a horse.

"Um," he said, and stared sadly at the bubbles in his beer.

"Is everything all right?"

"Erm," Mike responded, for the sake of variety. Sometimes he did tell her his troubles, but was becoming increasingly concerned that she might come to see him as neurotic and strange, so he had stopped, pending the blissful moment of release when she agreed to sleep with him, and everything could be resolved. Not that he had any intention of telling her about this particular problem anyway.

Had Susan wanted to conduct a conversation in monosyllables with a lump of immobile and imbecilic flesh, she would have popped round to the local piggeries or gone drinking with William.

"You aren't exactly the most vibrant and colourful company for a girl, Mike," she cooed, amiably.

"Sorry," he sighed.

"You've been working very hard recently," she said, "Perhaps if I fill you in on what's going on at the College, hmmm? I mean, while you've been rushing about doing whatever it is you do you'll have missed out on all the gossip and everything, yes?"

Mike nodded listlessly.

"Well, where should I start? The lower sixth set is doing well. They still need to learn their lines for the later scenes. The big production's progressing nicely too. They've recognised the importance of mastering each dot and comma. You can't ad-lib in Stoppard."

"No," Mike sighed.

Susan ground on with the relentless optimism of a Stuka pilot.

"Andrew MacDonald's had an offer for his book, and he's got that head of faculty job in London. He starts next term. Jane and William are taking over his sets. The kids aren't pleased because they liked being taught by someone fanciable. Not that Andrew's attainable these days anyway. Did you hear he's virtually engaged to that solicitor woman who came in to do a talk on European Law?"

"Lucky old Andrew."

"Annelise Featherstone says that William was in a good mood yesterday," Susan continued.

"Lucky old William," Mike mumbled.

"She says that Damien Sedgwick's coming down to speak to the politics students."

Susan stared as Mike slumped across the table and began sobbing.

* * *

"All those of you who support the government, wait behind," William bawled as his upper sixth crashed out of his classroom at the end of another harangue on the subject of the European Union in which he expressed verbal xenophobia whilst scrawling on the board rather more balanced notes from which the students were to revise. Most of the boys continued on their way out, leaving a handful of girls and the self-appointed New Men. William was not surprised at this. The government's insistence at wrapping itself in the language of intelligent compassion put off anyone with an ounce of testosterone. Then there had been that research on "tough/tender" voting patterns in the 1980s had suggested that a new generation was emerging which would see shifts in the female vote. Though what exactly was remotely tender about women these days he had yet to establish. William found the Modern Girl a distinctly tough little bitchtroll, as he had been ordered by Jane not to say. He shuffled through his pieces of paper, looked at the boys, and decided that they were too dull to be allowed to ask questions.

"I want you lads to get a few extra punters in," he said, "To pack the hall out and make it worth the minister's while coming down. Tell them to cheer at everything he says. There'll be free drinks in it for everyone, you understand."

The boys left and William surveyed the girls. Despite his much-vaunted misogyny, he did not actively dislike them, though fear of being thought soft or, worse, predatory, meant that he would never say so.

"Erm, Sarah," he bent his head over to a forty-five degree angle as he noticed a tall blonde girl, with a faintly scatty air, standing expectantly at the back of the room, "Are you an, er, actual government supporter?"

"Oh, yes," the girl nodded enthusiastically, "I voted for them in the Euro-elections. It was my first ever vote."

"But, erm, in the last lesson, you said that you were totally opposed to European control over our internal affairs."

"That's right," she said, "That other crowd sold us out by making us join Europe."

"But things are a bit different now. I mean, that was nearly thirty years ago. The parties have realigned. Look at the single currency."

"Yes, I hate that," Sarah said, vehemently. Sarah was a bright, kind-hearted girl who worked hard and was universally adored. Unfortunately, her view of life was so surreal and eccentric that she made Salvador Dali look like a photographer.

"But the government doesn't," interjected a small, dark girl who William usually referred to as Wee Beth, or Red Beth when he remembered to remember that women these days often had their own coherent political opinions, "It likes Europe more than the opposition does. They like America, because of capitalism and so on."

"I like America," Sarah said, " I've been there. You can get jeans cheap. It's great."

"No it isn't," Wee Beth contradicted, polishing her glasses, "I've been there too and they think you're weird if you don't eat beefburgers and they don't serve wine. Not a decent glass for a fortnight. And they've got no culture. Bastards."

William felt a peculiar flutter in his chest, which he could not identify. A more sensitive person could have told him that it was affection. Insofar as he liked girls at all, William liked girls with glasses. He thought they were less vain and looked more intelligent. Bitter experience had taught him that this was not necessarily the case, but he clung to his prejudices like a comfort blanket.

"And they exploit developing nations," continued Wee Beth, the only one of William's students who also did Sociology. His heart shattered as if an iron-bound copy of *Living Marxism* had been dropped onto the glass-topped coffee table of his bourgeois values.

"The point is," he said hurriedly, "That I have, this very day, had a letter from our local MP Benedict Wolfesbain, who is going to take part in this Question Time sort of thing with Damien Sedgwick, from whom we heard yesterday. Now, we need you dedicated folk to work out questions which will really put him on the spot."

"But if he snaps back, I might cry," Annelise Featherstone said.

"If he makes you cry, my dear, I will punch him on the nose," William said. Annelise had blonde hair and *very* brown eyes. She reminded him of a baby seal.

"Oh, guess what," she suddenly flapped her arms, like a baby seal who has seen a penguin and wants it for lunch, but has not yet mastered the art of moving quickly and ravenously across the ice, "I saw a picture of that Damien Sedgwick bloke, and he was with another bloke, who was, like, his assistant or something, and I've met him."

"That'll be Josh Greze," William said, "One of the bright young things. Where did you meet him?"

"In the quad last week."

"What? You can't have done. Someone like him wouldn't come within a million miles of Sussex."

"But I did. We were taking time out from rehearsals and he came and asked about the College. Said his brother wanted to come here and asked about studying politics."

"You're sure it was him?"

Annelise opened her bag and produced that morning's *Guardian*, which she had borrowed from the library with every intention of giving it back once she had done the crossword, and pointed at a picture of a press conference at the Department of Co-Ordination of Information and Administration. Behind Sedgwick stood a fashionable young man who William recognised.

"Blast," he said, remembering where he had met him, "What exactly did you say?"

"Well, he asked how old you were, for one thing," Annelise recalled, "And I said, late twenties."

"Did you say how he dresses and acts as if he's in his sixties?" Sarah giggled.

"No, I forgot about that," Annelise said, visibly cross with herself for having done so, much to William's annoyance, "And they asked about your political views, too. I said you probably didn't have any."

"Barnaby says you're a fascist," Red Beth observed.

"That fuckwit has a beard and John Lennon glasses," William responded with what would have been a snarl had he been addressing anyone other than Red Beth, for whom he had an inexplicable soft spot the size of a dinner plate, "So his opinion isn't worth a hill of dead pigs. Those berks in sociology wouldn't recognise real fascism if it came up to them and put them in a camp, which of course is what they'd like to do to everyone else, the communist bastards. And I'd be grateful if you'd refer to him as Mister Worthington. He may teach sociology but that doesn't give him the right to indulge in this call-me-Barnaby nonsense. The sixties are long gone, thank goodness."

"And they wanted to know about the other teachers too, and the students," Annelise interjected before William could go off on one of his favourite hobby horses, "I said it was pretty evenly split between the parties. Did I do right?"

"Oh, yes, you did splendidly. How did he react?"

"He looked really pleased with himself. Went off talking into a mobile 'phone," Annelise said, "But I'm not sure I understand. What was he doing?"

"He was checking us out, probably, trying to see if it would be worth Sedgwick's time coming down, to see if he could get any new voters," William mused, "It's very interesting, I think. Devious little bugger."

"Well, he may be devious, but I'll be supporting Damien Sedgwick," Sarah said, loyally. Although she disagreed with virtually all of its policies, she knew that supporting a government which claimed to care, but didn't, was morally better than supporting an opposition which couldn't even make the effort to pretend. William found that oddly comforting.

*   *   *

Susan had given up on Mike. He had refused to tell her what was wrong and simply sat and smoked and stared at nothing in particular. This was no skin off her nose and she was not going to let it get to her. As she collected a plate of sandwiches from the bar, Portia breezed in.

"Hello, my love," she beamed, "Seen Mike Alcock about?"

"He's over there," Susan said, "But I wouldn't bother with him today. He's about as jolly and warm as the shipping forecast. He seems pretty depressed about something, but I can't get him to tell me what it is."

"Girl trouble, I should have thought," Portia said, "He's probably in love with one of his upper sixth again. If he's really depressed, it's one of his lower sixth. Even longer to wait, watching her cavort on the arms of teenage oicks, before she leaves College and he can ask her out and endure the humiliation of rejection. I'll have a word with him."

"Good luck," Susan said, "I'm just nipping into the other bar to cast my eye over some marking while I scoff these. Very anti-social, I know, but I want to be able to tell the kids something about their work during this afternoon's lesson."

"No, that's fine," Portia looked over at Mike, who seemed the very figure of despair, "I'll just go and give his problems the once over with my knuckledusters of compassion and understanding."

She bore down on Mike like a rather short galleon, her blouse billowing before her like a well-filled sail and a bloody Mary held before her like a figurehead.

"Susan's such a lovely girl," she said, "You are lucky to get to work with her. She's very concerned that you're unhappy, you know. And she doesn't understand why you won't tell her what's wrong."

"Well, for some reason, explaining to my beautiful and intelligent colleague that I am now the leading part-time madam in the Hengistley district struck me as rather difficult," Mike snapped, "And as for my growing suspicion that our mutual friend, the Head of Careers at the local comprehensive, is trying to suck prominent politicians into this web of evil via the good offices of an innocent third party, well, somehow that's even harder."

"Oh, so that's it," Portia said, mildly, "Well, for one thing, William's hardly innocent, unless you mean in the nineteenth century sense of the term. He thinks *soixante-neuf* is something to do with lefty students who missed out on the previous year. Actually, I thought you might have been in love with one of the students. Again."

"What if I was, though? Let's just suppose that I do fancy, oh, say, Annelise Featherstone, which I don't, but even so. How could I, in the eventuality of pursuing a relationship, justify this part-time entrepreneurial activity? It's difficult enough for girls who go out with teachers to explain the matter to their parents, but 'in addition to being my teacher, daddy, Mike is a pimp and a procurer' would hardly advance my cause, would it?"

"It's a bit different from your run-of-the-mill boyfriend, though," Portia suggested, not entirely helpfully.

Mike stared at her like a condemned convict.

"Anyway, I think you'll be able to live with yourself when you see this," Portia produced a fat envelope from the recesses of a bag which appeared to have no bottom.

"Satan on a skateboard," Mike breathed, "There must be a couple of grand in here. How did we make so much dosh so quickly? We've only had it running for a couple of months."

"That tractor trade fair in Roffwater Heath industrial estate netted us a fair few quid," Portia said, "One particular party of Korean businessmen was pretty generous. Came back for seconds, you know. Brand loyalty's very important to your oriental, you know. And then there was a German chap with very peculiar requirements for which he was willing to pay quite a bit extra. Jobelle was a bit miffed at the bloodstains in the carpet of her room, and the DIY shop said they'd never seen an orbital sander get damaged in that particular way before, but we made a fortune out of him."

Mike's face was as white and delicate as a little summer cloud. Portia trundled on regardless.

"Next month is looking very promising, I must say. There's a conference of tennis coaches at the leisure centre, which ought to bag us a few punters. Yvette's been building up a good forehand smash with a riding crop. You should have heard the screams from that fat bloke from the primary school when she gave him strict lessons the other day. I'll bet he couldn't sit down for a week. How's William's political shindig coming on?"

"Damien Sedgwick's coming," Mike said, morosely, "And I assume that William's best buddy, Benedict fascist bastard Wolfesbain, will also grace us with his lordly presence."

"Excellent," Portia swigged heartily from her bloody mary, "Two very senior and highly respected political figures. Just what we need to make it into the big time."

"Are you seriously proposing that we whisk these characters away after they've done whatever they're doing with William, and offer them the services of our girls?"

"More or less," Portia said, "Not all of the girls, though. Only the ones who are, or look as if they are, in their teens. There's very few of those; the majority are in their twenties, apart from that old dragon we've got on the desk, and no-one's going to want to try it on with her."

"But why the younger ones? I'm not sure I'm with you."

"It's the bigger picture. We need them to pretend to be students. Then, just think how much a national newspaper would pay for the story of senior parliamentarians in bed with teenage girls. Or how much the political parties would pay to have it suppressed."

"But that's blackmail," Mike squawked, "It's…it's…it's wrong."

This was not a word Mike normally used. A child of the sixties, "wrong" or "evil" were words he applied to things like apartheid, or war, or pollution. Individual acts of sinfulness were "mistakes" or the expression of different values. This was not. This was a great big enormous

crime, for which he could be punished quite severely. Mike was a frightened man. Less attractive blokes than him had left prison with a whole
new sexual agenda and a neurosis about using showers stamped onto
their souls.

"Oh, don't be so moralistic," Portia said, contemptuously, "What's
wrong is the catastrophically bad pay teachers get. The waste of money
by governments of either party on damnfool projects like nuclear-pow-
ered jet fighters for snooping on poll tax defaulters is wrong too. We're
going to punish a couple of the real criminals. I see us as part of a crusade for a better society. Revolutionaries, if you will."

"I'm not sure William will see it that way," Mike thought for a
moment about the likely consequences of what they were planning, "I
mean, the finger of suspicion's bound to fall on him first. He'll be livid."

"The finger of suspicion might fall on him first, but it will quickly
become apparent that he hasn't the brains to blow his own nose, never
mind cook up an elaborate plot to entrap senior politicians into being tied
up and spanked with ping pong bats by teenage slappers in a bordello."

"Why ping pong bats?" Mike asked.

"I don't know," Portia said, "It just occurred to me. I mean, baseball
bats would be a bit heavy. We don't want to break any bones or anything. Unless they're actually into that. You wouldn't believe the extrem-
ities of pain which it takes to satisfy some people. Did I tell you about
the bloke from Southurst who asked the girls to hook his parts up to a
lorry battery?"

"No," Mike shuddered, "And I'm not sure I want to know, either. But
even if William's not blamed for it, don't you think he'd be a bit hurt
that we were up to this behind his back?"

"Not William," Portia said, "For one thing, he's about as sensitive as the
packets of lard he eats for breakfast. And for another, he wouldn't want to
know. Even if he didn't regard the sexual organs as Satan's playground,
Alice won't let him get involved in something like this. If he pissed her
about, she'd never speak to him again. Provided he understood or

remembered what she said, that's one of the only things that could get to him. No, we've got to keep him at arm's length."

Whilst Portia was essentially right to suggest that William was somewhat lacking in delicacy of feeling, she had forgotten about the streak of high-minded academic rectitude, combined with low animal cunning, which had kept him in employment for more years than his classroom performance merited. Having worked out that Damien Sedgwick was almost certainly going to try to use his appearance at the college to promote himself, William was seeking ways to counter him. William loathed Sedgwick's media-obsessed, valueless attitude to government, and the progressive posturing which characterised modern politics. He yearned for the grand intellectual jousts of the past, when the Commons resounded to the elegant speeches of Gladstone and Disraeli rather than the politically-correct soundbites of the present day. Sedgwick represented to William all that was banal and trite in the modern life he despised. Whilst he disapproved of Wolfesbain's views, he felt that the opposition politician was at least honest about the cynicism of his vision. He pondered for a while how best to turn the minister's visit against him, and rang another of the former students with whom he maintained contact. Like Portia, William was friendly with some of the people he used to teach. As a habitue of the town's bars with no interest in forming regular friendships, he couldn't really afford not to be. His circle had been nicknamed the SA by Barnaby Worthington, who believed that William shared the blasé approach to political indoctrination common in the Social Science Faculty. Luke Wallace was, it was true, one of these young men who, out of a mixture of gratitude for William's loans of the right sort of literature and pity for his social ineptitude, went drinking with him at the Conservative Club. William's interest, however, lay in Luke's other skills. An enthusiastic Media Studies student whilst at College, Luke was rapidly making a name for himself at university as a producer of plays which owed as much to the big screen as they did to the great traditions of the English stage. His production of *Frankenstein* demonstrated at least a nodding acquaintance to Fritz Lang, was socially friendly with the film noir genre and had vigorously snogged Paul Verhoeven. It had impressed William enormously, though, admittedly, so too had the caretaker's new dog.

"You've got the cameras in there," he said to Luke, "Sedgwick wanting to look good in front of them, here in his enemy's heartland. How do we rig things so that he looks like the ghastly little creature he is? I want him humiliated."

"Difficult questions from photogenic girls?" Luke mused, "It would look really good if he could lose his temper and make one of them cry. I mean bad. For him."

"Problem there," William pointed out, "Most of the girlies are pro-government. And Sedgwick doesn't tend to lose his temper, I've noticed. Always smooth and unruffled. In any case, I'd rather we attacked him on substance, getting behind the soundbites to expose the poverty of his thought."

"Protest against some aspect of government policy," Luke declared, "That's the one. There's bound to be something—peculiar stuff to do with crops, dodgy road building schemes which destroy the habitat of endangered newts, new brands of eye shadow tested on bunny rabbits. Ideally, this is done by a company which has links to the Party, the government or the man himself. We could get a few banners knocked up, or perhaps a gauntlet of demonstrators, with a few pretty girls to shout abuse. Bingo. That sort of thing hits him on the left-wing credibility level. I'm sure we could get a load of sociology students to be a pain in the neck outside the lecture hall. Meanwhile Wolfesbain goes out and makes an announcement to them which calms them down and sends them on their way rejoicing. He ends up looking like Gandhi or Martin Luther King or something."

"We'd better not use sociology students, then. They'd try to tear Wolfesbain limb from limb, and do it badly, which could be embarrassing.

Have a scout round the town and recruit a few ex-students. We can script them and they won't have any ideas of their own. But overall, I think this has promise. We're going to show the watching millions that some smooth-talking apparatchik is no match for well-informed students with a taste for blood."

CHAPTER ELEVEN

Portia settled into her chair in the Hertford Arms and shuffled through the accounts from the Grosvenor. She opened her bag and produced a packet of cigarettes, one of which she lit. The smoke gushed from the tube of tobacco in her lips and forcefully entered her pharynx, thrusting down into her trachea and filling her left and right bronchi. Portia's bronchioles were caressed by the burrowing column of smoke as it moved deeper and deeper into her, penetrating the alveoli as it broke through to her lungs. It burst forth inside her and coated the delicate tissue of her lungs with a coating of tar, simultaneously bringing a rictus smile to Portia's face and damaging the gene which was doing its best to defend her against cancer. Portia felt fantastic. She leaned back in her chair and grinned the broad grin of the recently-gratified smoker at the frankly bizarre statuary which had been placed in her favourite corner of the bar in a less successful aspect of the Hertford's refit. Four two-thirds size negro jazz musicians stood frozen into a variety of funky positions, two on either side of the fireplace. The saxophonist, trumpeter and singer all had their eyes closed in sweet musical ecstasy, but the bass player had his eyes wide open and his teeth bared. He stared down at her with a fixed, wide-eyed gaze, rather like a psychopath, albeit one the height of an eight-year-old child. This somehow made it worse. His almost demonic grin made him look like one of those fertility idols Portia had seen in a programme about foreign lands and funny ways when she was a small child. The double bass he was strumming had not featured in any of the cults in the programme, but doubtless there was a folk religion somewhere for which that instrument had a particular significance. Wherever it was practised— New Orleans was a possibility—the Hertford Arms, Hengistley did not seem a likely cultic site. The town had all the soul and groove of a Volvo estate. Portia reflected that perhaps the people who had put these rather peculiar statues in the Hertford wanted to transform the town into something rather more hip and trendy. Their aim was probably to reinvigorate the town. If so, they had failed. Despite the presence of the coolest four foot high statues of negro jazz musicians to be found anywhere in the south-eastern region, Hengistley had remained obstinately moribund. Had it been Lazarus, Christ would have had to put a lot more effort into bringing him back to life. It was a matter for discreet pride on Portia's part that, within a few weeks, she had done more to enliven the town than any number of funny-looking statues. She smiled to herself, remembering of the small boy who had, that morning, used an unconvincing collision with a table to stumble into her capacious bosom, then ran out into the corridor yelling "ten points." He would be a client in the years to come, she thought, and did a few calculations.

✳   ✳   ✳

    In the Grosvenor, the security company had finished its job. Cameras now lurked in all of the bedrooms, and each was wired for sound. All the girls were out shopping in London, with the exception of Yvette, who was catching up on some History homework in the library at the College. Portia had decided that it was probably not necessary to tell them about the arrangements that she had made.

"What sort of thing you hoping to do, mate?" the curious electrician asked as Mike nervously put used banknotes into his hands.

"Not sure yet," Mike said, untruthfully, "It's all a bit hush hush. Government, and so on."

The electrician looked at Mike dubiously. His client was wearing an old leather jacket and a woollen cap. He looked jumpy and frightened, like a woman riding on a stagecoach in Indian territory in them westerns. In the electrician's experience, governments did not employ people like this to do delicate hush-hush jobs. Or indeed any jobs. Money, however, was money, and he was happy not to ask awkward questions in return for plenty of it.

Mike was, in a way, in a similar position. Except the awkward questions were those which he should have asked of himself, and he was not especially happy. For most of his career he had enjoyed robust discussions about matters sexual in the classroom. He had never, unlike some, decried the folly of romantic love as an illusion to mask the baser desires, but he was perfectly happy to accept that base desires could operate on their own. His genial post-Freudian analysis had annoyed the students, who preferred not to see a sexual metaphor behind every church steeple or lurking within every railway tunnel. Neither of these images appealed to him now. His work solely in the field of base desires was bringing him very little satisfaction. Only the thought that there was growing interest in *OMF* and almost enough cash to form the nucleus of the production costs kept him going. He slouched moodily away from the house and up to the Hertford to meet Portia.

*   *   *

Alice was on the telephone to her mother.

"I have a seminar on Milton next week," she was saying, "But before then there's an excellent party at the lads' house. James Bond theme. I'm going as a villainess in a slinky ballgown, with a gun and a bottle of Bailey's."

"How lovely," her mother said, more worried about the bottle of Bailey's than the gun. Her memories of the teenage sick she had had to clean up after Alice's school parties, at which the wretched substance was all too prevalent, still occasionally caused her to sit bolt upright in the middle of the night, screaming for Jeyes' fluid.

"Have you seen anything of William?" Alice asked.

"Your father and I are having supper at his flat next Friday," Mrs Jameson said, "But he's been keeping a bit of a low profile recently. Cowboy Sam told your father that he hasn't even been in the off-license for a fortnight. Apparently he's busy on some sort of project."

Alice was immediately suspicious.

"Does anyone know what sort of project?"

"No, not really. He's being pretty secretive. You of all people ought to know what he can be like if he wants to hush something up. It takes several months for anyone to find out about deaths in his family."

"Hmmmm…" Alice mused, making a noise like an electric engine. She did not trust the little fat man. Not in the sense that she thought he would ever do anything to hurt her, which he probably wasn't up to, but insofar as he could be guaranteed to do something stupid at the drop of a hat.

"Is there any other gossip?"

"Oh, well, yes. The strangest thing. Your father was given a flyer for a brothel the other day."

"A brothel?" Alice squawked, deafening her mother, "In Hengistley?"

"Yes, dear, a house of ill-repute. Daddy was rather shocked, as I'm sure you can imagine."

"Do you know where it is?"

"No, the flyer just gave a telephone number. But I'm sure one could find out with a minimum of effort, if one was thus inclined. But I do feel that if you want to be a teacher, you should try to find a rather more edifying summer job."

"Mother, I have a boyfriend. I don't think he'd be too keen on me plying my wares in a bawdy house."

"I read in the *Telegraph* that some men these days are rather attracted to seediness in all its forms," Mrs Jameson said.

"Yes, but they're sad, inadequate, twisted men like Michael Alcock and William Fenneck," Alice snapped.

And then an enormous and horrible thought fell upon her, and she felt as if a giant black bat had wrapped her in its wings, and she was being smothered by it.

*   *   *

"The basic principle of the thing is pretty straightforward," Portia was explaining, "After the politicians have finished their talks, we have a kind of ambush party waiting to meet them on their way out of the assembly hall. I assume that's where William's going to put the bastards?"

"Yes," Mike said, "He's getting quite excited about the whole thing, you know"

Portia raised her eyebrows. The thought of William excited was not appealing.

"There'll be reporters from the local press there, and civic dignitaries, and the senior management of the College," Mike continued, "More guests than politics students, actually."

"That wouldn't be difficult," Portia commented drily. Since William had inherited the politics department from its energetic and agreeable founder, numbers had plummeted, especially of girls. His predecessor had enthusiastically recruited them with promises of debates and discussions, whilst William dourly steamrollered through the syllabus in the same traditionalist way in which he had been taught. "I don't care what you think," had become one of the most overheard phrases in the College, as he bellowed it at any hapless teenager who ventured some sort of opinion during a lesson. Perhaps unsurprisingly, the Politics department had dwindled to a hard-core of boys from the local comprehensive who recognised in William a kindred spirit, another insensitive and chauvinist bully with limited imagination and boundless arrogance. The few remaining female students either loved the subject enough to ignore William or persisted with the notion, common in young women, that their influence could reform even the most stony-hearted curmudgeon.

"There may even be tv cameras. He's not sure."

"Well, no matter. The important thing is that we're ready and waiting to move in there as they come out. We have a couple of cars waiting to take them to a 'reception'," Portia waggled her fingers in the nationally-recognised and annoying signifier for inverted commas, "And then we ply them with drink and let the girlies do that lovin' thang."

"I don't see what loving's got to do with it," Mike pondered, morosely, "This is a shabby and sordid enterprise in which I am ashamed to be taking part."

He lit a cigarette and puffed on it with little enthusiasm.

Portia looked at him evenly. Mike knew that he was going to be hit with the full force of her rhetoric and erected buffers of his own.

"No, really. I do think that this is wrong. I'm a member of the Party, for God's sake. I don't believe in this, I don't like it. Damien Sedgwick may be a twat but he's one of our boys and at the end of the day that counts for something. What we are doing is profoundly illegal and if we get caught we'll be in for the fucking high jump. I don't know how many years you get for this sort of thing but I'd rather not do any, thanks all the same. It's all very well teaching the kids in Personal and Social Education lessons that exploring their sexuality's a good thing, but I don't fancy mine being explored by the twenty-stone axe murderer with whom I have to share a cell in Strangeways."

"Oh, come on," Portia chaffed, "Where's your sense of adventure?"

"That's a bit rich coming from someone who has an airbag in her car."

"Don't be childish. Anyway, we won't get caught. If the going does get rough, we've got a lot of dosh salted away and we can just burn up to Gatwick and be out of the country before anyone spots us."

"Are you serious?" Mike stared at her, "Are you actually saying that we should just leave everything and bugger off?"

"Only in an emergency situation. But would it really be so bad? We could live pretty well in most places on the dosh we've got so far. By the time we get to the big day itself, there'll be nearly two hundred grand in the kitty, on current performance."

"How the hell are we getting this money?"

"It came to me as I read a book about one of the more corrupt ministers in the last government. Apparently he used to fix up rich Arabs with white girls to help with arms sales to the Middle East. So I put an ad in the in-flight magazine of one of their airlines, and contacted the sales division of the aeroplane factory at Dunsfold. Prince Ali has been particularly generous. The girls were a bit repelled by him at first, in their racist way, but they've come to find him relatively charming. He gives them little presents and so on. And his father's bought half a dozen jump-jets, so I think," Portia's voice became firmer here, "That instead of constantly talking down the enterprise, you ought to be dwelling on how it's good for Britain. It's people like you who create economic depressions and unemployment. Do you want that on your conscience?"

"I will not be told that it is my patriotic duty to run a whorehouse," Mike yelled. He drank, angrily, pulling the beer into his mouth as if it might otherwise try to escape.

"Suit yourself," Portia shrugged, "But you really shouldn't worry. Relatively few people will actually connect you with it. Even if they do, you can always play dumb and look stupid. I imagine you'll convince most people that way. Your main role on the big day is to keep William out of the way whilst we get his politicians out to Bacons Road. Even you can manage that, I think."

Mike nodded, numbly.

∗   ∗   ∗

The Trolls were gathered in the underworld for their customary lunchtime cigarettes and communal grievance exposition.

"Fucking Alcock," a boy with a number of metal adornments in his face snorted, "He rang my parents just because I didn't hand in an essay. It was just about Shakespeare. I mean, why can't we do *the Catcher in the Rye*?"

"We've already done it," Toby Gaskett's girlfriend said, "We can't do it twice. It's not Alcock's fault."

"Yeah, well, there's bound to be something else that's decent," Gaskett said, "That little Scotch bastard Fenneck's getting on my wick at the moment. He just can't stop sneering every time I enter the room."

"He's not like that with everyone," his girlfriend said, wondering if perhaps Mr Alcock had told Mr Fenneck about the clitoris thing.

"Listen to Miss Teacher's pet," the boy with the metalwork jeered, "Any other fascist bastards you'd like to stick up for?"

"Piss off, scab face," the girl snapped.

The boy shoved her.

"Don't talk to me like that, you bitch," he said, manfully.

"Don't push my bird," interjected Gaskett, who saw that particular privilege as reserved for himself alone. He poked the metal-faced boy listlessly, and was rather surprised when the boy fell over and splintered the top of the big packing-case with the German writing on it.

"You bastard. You've ruined my trousers."

"They're grunge trousers, you twat. They're supposed to look like that."

"Shut up and get out of the way. What's in that box?"

The students lifted the broken wood off the top of the box and peered inside.

"Fucking hell," Gaskett ejaculated, crudely but unsurprisingly.

*   *   *

Alice was curled in a chair in her student digs. Normally, this was quite an arresting sight for her flatmates, or would have been had they been male. Alice was so feline that she made most cats look like elephants, and could drape herself over a piece of furniture more fetchingly than a damask tablecloth. Today, however, she was like a coiled cobra, ready to spit venom at whatever crossed her path. Her flatmates sensed trouble and steered clear of her. She was emanating harmful energy like a leaky atomic reactor and the walls of the room positively glowed with it.

Alice was alight with anger and needed to express it. William had betrayed her. She, the only person in the world who understood him and cared for him, had been spurned, her advice rejected. His sick and seedy little mind had brushed aside the warnings she had given him like an Israeli tank division driving past UN checkpoints en route to the Lebanon. All he wanted was the money he could get from exploiting some whores. A secret project indeed! He would probably have tried to persuade her to work in the beastly place. Alice seethed with fury and unhappiness. How could she have been so stupid as to trust someone so manifestly questionable? She had ignored his own advice to her—"Never trust anyone"—so why should she expect him to take hers? Angry with herself and filled with volcanic loathing for William, Alice uncoiled from her chair and advanced on the telephone like a panther.

*   *   *

Cowboy Sam's off-license stood on one of the arterial roads leading into Hengistley. He enjoyed his job and had a good relationship with his customers, many of whom listened to his pronouncements on drinks as if they were the sayings of a mystic sage. Typically for a Mercier's old boy, Sam often made these up as he went along, but this did not trouble his clientele.

Today he was plying William with a new Spanish red which was, he insisted, the next great little number that would take the market by storm. They were perched on stools in the office at the back of the off-license, with a bottle of the wine and a calculator on which William was working out how much of it he could afford to buy out of his departmental budget in order to impress the MPs when they came to talk to the students. An enthusiast for partnership between local enterprise and the College, William had irritated his less well-funded colleagues by hosting a drinks party for the parents of his students, primarily designed to give them the impression that he was a dedicated and caring individual, and that in the event of a conflict between their offspring and himself, they should automatically believe and support him. Refreshments for this had been arranged by Cowboy Sam's off-license. Dr Walpurgess had almost had apoplexy when he saw the publicity photographs in the local newspaper, which prominently featured an enormous banner cheerfully declaring that the Mercier's Politics Department and Avon's Wine Merchants were building a better Hengistley together.

Sam and William finished their third glasses and pondered the idea of comparing different grapes. Another two bottles were fetched from the store and they set to work.

William eventually stumbled into his flat, accidentally scattering the elaborate pyramid of empty beer tins which he had constructed with Mike as a drunken expression of modern art and a possible low-budget skittles game. He saw the little red winking light of the answering-machine but did not check it because the alcoholic auto-pilot in his brain told him that there was no point, and he might accidentally erase the message. The auto-pilot also told him to drink some water and take an aspirin as well, so he did, following them down with a final cigarette before he removed his suit, curled up beside the childhood teddy-bear which was his only sleeping-companion, and fell into the last untroubled sleep he would have.

And so it was that William was relatively sober when he checked the answering-machine the next morning. He was naked and unprotected by the warm padding of alcohol when Alice's words erupted into his little dining-room like the thunderbolts of an angry Calvinist God.

"You bastard," the familiar voice spat, shaking with a passionate bitterness William had not heard before, perhaps unsurprisingly as he had never provoked a passionate anything in people, "You filthy, evil, treacherous little bastard. I know what you're up to with your fucking project. I hate you, I hate you, I hate you. I never want to see or speak to you again as long as I live."

There was a click as the receiver was replaced. There could be no mistaking the tone of Alice's message. There was a finality about this which entered every corner of William's being like a hyperactive computer virus.

The next message was from the gas board, threatening to cut him off. William wished that he could have had a hangover. At least then the day could have got better. He looked into a long, dark tunnel which he did not understand and from which he could see no escape.

CHAPTER TWELVE

Susan had been thrown in at the deep end somewhat when Mike asked her to direct the College play, but found it oddly therapeutic. *Arcadia* was a bitch to explain to sixteen-year-olds, but it was a brilliant piece of writing and it tested the students' abilities, which was, presumably, the point of doing it. Listening to the tantrums and watching the flounces of the Theatre Studies students made a refreshing change from staff meetings. There were tantrums and flounces in staff meetings too, but they were controlled, rather Teutonic affairs, not easily observable to the untrained eye. It often had to be explained to her that so-and-so was clearly in a state of extreme wrath, because he had asked a question directly to the Principal instead of dropping a note to his secretary. The staff were a bit opaque in their emotions and expressions. The students, by contrast, whinnied and pranced and stamped like prize Lippizaners, which was infinitely more entertaining. They were also genuinely talented and put a great deal of effort into what they were doing, which is more than Susan could say for some of her colleagues. The chief shadow cast over all this was the not infrequent presence of both Mike and William in the hall during rehearsals.

Susan supposed that Mike could make some sort of contribution, being of a theatrical turn of mind himself, but William clearly only came for someone to talk to. Neither was known for enjoying the presence of outsiders in his lessons, so Susan found their cavalier approach to hers both hypocritical and off-putting. The rare occasions when they had let other people into their classrooms were widely known throughout the College. An attempt to give Alice work experience by letting her sit in on the activities of the English and Politics departments had ended in chaos after the over-hormonal boys from the rugby team had spent every lesson slavering over the young woman who was sitting taking notes at the back of the room. The female students were less appreciative. They had deeply resented her, as they did any outsider. The nicer ones were protective of their teachers and jealously guarded access to them. They had subjected Alice to a barrage of black looks and furtive whisperings about an imagined past. The less nice simply believed that they, and they alone, should be the object of the boys' lust, and were just plain rude. Although Alice, who had been a sixth former herself not too long ago, understood this perfectly and did not take the hatred personally, the lessons had ended in near-riots and the experiment was not repeated. Despite this, Mike and William felt perfectly entitled to come and sit either on the floor of the drama studio or high on the terraced seating at the back of the Clutterbuck Hall, where rehearsals took place. They compounded their offence by cadging cigarettes from the students and drinking bottles of wine, whose contents they rarely, if ever, shared around.

Mike was alone today. He stared from his seat at the back of the hall, virtually immobile. For half an hour, he sat perfectly still as Susan gave briefings to each member of the cast in turn, chivvying the line-forgetters and soothing the ruffled feathers of highly strung young artistes who had been upset by enormously traumatic events such as being made to sit in the back of the car during the morning school run. Susan found this faintly unnerving. Normally, Mike was a bundle of nervous energy, full of helpful suggestions for the young actors and warm encouragement for Susan. Today he was like an avant-garde sculpture as his highly-trained mind experimented with different possibilities for blocking Portia's lunatic plan. He thought that if he sat without moving for long enough, all the negative ions would drain from him and be replaced by the power of pure mental energy. He had read about this in the *Guardian*, or somewhere like that. Apparently Bob Dylan used the technique to write songs. This would enable him to come up with the way to prevent a potentially messy kidnap and blackmail operation which would end in his arrest and brutal molestation at the hands of more deserving prison inmates. If it was good enough for recorded music's greatest living legend, Mike reflected, it was good enough for the morally questionable Head of English in a Sussex college. Irritatingly, the process did not seem to be working, no matter how still he sat. He was not assisted in his quest by the peculiar looks which Susan kept directing at him. Hadn't she ever seen anyone go into a trance before? Probably not, he thought; she had only been to one staff meeting so far, and had never heard the Principal speak. A further distraction was the play. Normally, Mike found these affairs comforting and soothing. However, when the seventeen-year-old Annelise Featherstone, playing the thirteen-year-old Thomasina asked her tutor Septimus about the meaning of the phrase "carnal embrace", Mike squirmed uncomfortably. Wearing a long silk night-dress, the girl entwined herself around her chair in a masterly portrayal of unknowing eroticism. Mike wrapped his legs over one another in ecstasies of guilt and thought that now he knew what Catholicism was like. There was something unhealthily interesting—and he used the word advisedly, even in his mind—about the experience. He fixed his eyes on a spot in the middle of the table on the stage and thought about rotting vegetables.

This task was made easier by the arrival of William, who entered the hall as attractively as a dose of mustard gas. He nodded glumly at Mike as he sat down on the uncomfortable high bench seating which was the college's concession to the assembly hall's main use as a theatre. After a day spent drifting unhappily through lessons with only the hope of opening time to sustain him, William had popped in to the rehearsal to be with normal human beings for the long and depressing hour until the Hertford was prepared to wrap him in its comforting embrace. His relationship with Alice had been perfect. No romance, no sex, no love; above all, no potential for the infliction of pain. Unwilling to risk more ear-bashing by telephoning her to ask what the matter was, he had searched desperately through the tattered rags of his alcohol-ravaged memory to find what he could have done which would have offended her so much, and had found nothing. Not apart from the usual, anyway, and she had always put up with that in the past. He had, therefore, been forced to the conclusion that Alice was just a stupid, irrational cow like the rest of her sex, and the idea depressed him even more than the thought that she hated him for something. William deeply disliked being wrong about things. He had never agreed with the idea that teachers were facilitators who lead children to the thresholds of their own learning; he saw himself in a priestly role, filling empty vessels with the rich wine of his infallible wisdom. The discovery that he had made a mistake undermined this assumption, and with it the little self-confidence remaining to him in a world of efficiency gains and key skills which he found both repellent and terrifying. He passed a paper cup full of claret to Mike and watched Annelise being precocious on stage.

Her scene over, Annelise skipped over to Mike and William. She held them in the kind of peculiar affection that young children will sometimes bestow on pet woodlice.

"What did you think?" she asked brightly. Annelise did most things brightly. She had been a logical choice for the character of Thomasina, and a career in children's broadcasting lay prostrate at her feet.

"It was awfully good, Annelise," Mike said. He was a strong believer in giving credit where it was due. As an incurable optimist, he hoped one day to find someone else who believed in this creed. That way he would get some too.

"Yes," William echoed, tiredly, "Ever so good."

"I'm trying to make her as bubbly as possible in the scenes where she's thirteen," Annelise went on, "Does it work? Only I'm not used to being thirteen. I haven't been for ages."

"Four years," Mike said, "Which is rather less time than it's been since m'colleague and I were thirteen. But then, I don't suppose we were very bubbly at thirteen. Boys aren't. Except facially."

"Yuck," Annelise grimaced.

"You, however, were incredibly bubbly. You could carbonate water," Mike continued.

"Oh, good," Annelise thought for a moment. Beneath her blonde mop, her concentration was leaping around like a lunatic on a space hopper and landing on different areas of subject matter. Finally it bounced onto the one she wanted.

"You know little Beth?" she asked.

Mike thought for a moment.

"No," he said slowly, "But make that a yes if she's one of my students and I've forgotten her, in an uncharacteristic moment of amnesia."

"I don't think you would know her. She does Politics and Sociology and that. I meant Mr Fenneck. You know little Beth, don't you?"

"No," William, coldly said. His austere Caledonian mind refuted the concept of banal introductions to sentences, and, as a consequence, he hated being asked what he interpreted as pointless questions. This often made him unnecessary enemies, as when, in response to being asked what he was drinking, he had snapped "Blackcurrant juice. What does it look like, you moron? It's bitter. What business is it of yours, anyway?"

Annelise had forgotten this trait, but she remembered that William was appallingly absent-minded.

"Oh, you know little Beth. She sits beside me. Next to your desk. Dark hair..." "Yes, yes, dark hair, some freckles, big green eyes, wears goggles, pretty, about five foot two," William snapped, "Of course I bloody well know who little Beth is, you dozy bat. She's sat in front of my desk for two years. What about her?"

Annelise was unfazed by this abusive tone. It was relatively polite by William's standards. She was interested to note that he had absorbed some detail about little Beth's appearance, and filed the information away for future use. She would have been less interested had she known that he, like most of his male colleagues, could equally easily have rattled off a description of her or any other upper sixth girl he considered remotely attractive.

"Who's in a mood today?" she asked, archly. William snarled at her, a harsh, canine sound, accompanied by a baring of teeth. Mike had often wondered why William always refused to consider the theories of evolution. It was quite obvious that he could have made an absolute fortune proving that human beings were descended from bears or wolves.

"What about little Beth, then?" asked Mike, who could sense that, for some reason, William was not in the mood to be teased. Annelise, at this precise moment, resembled a small child with a sharp stick, with which she was poking a mangy old Rottweiler. Mangy, yes, but a Rottweiler nonetheless. Mike was good like that. He was capable of picking up on the unhappiness of others and treating them with the appropriate sensitivity. William did not deserve him. He needed to see someone in tears before he would realise that there was something wrong, and even then his response tended to be to wander off until whoever it was had finished crying and could talk properly.

"Anyway," Annelise bounded on cheerfully, "I was talking to little Beth today, and you know the way she's very left wing, yeah," (William nodded, with a fixed smile which did not extend to his eyes. Little Beth was indeed more left wing than most of the other students, but in the great scheme of things was essentially a Social Democrat. By Hengistley standards, however, this was tantamount to Leninism), "Well, she says that the Sociology teachers say that that Damien Sedgwick is some sort of fascist, and they should demonstrate against him."

Annelise looked pleased with herself. This was a very long thing to remember, what with her lines and revision and so on.

"The *teachers* are saying this?" William ruminated, "Poo and bother."

"Isn't he a fascist, then?" Annelise asked.

"Compared to them he is," William sniffed, "But then, compared to them, I am."

"But William, you *are* a fascist," said Mike, gently.

"Well, not quite," William mused, "I have a number of reservations about fascism, actually. And anyway, I'd rather be fascist than a twat. But did Beth say what specifically was fascist about him?"

"Some sort of thing with a third world country. It's in the papers. I don't know the details. But they want to have a demonstration. With banners and everything."

William looked worried.

"I don't bloody *believe* it," he muttered to himself, as he ruffled through the tattered school exercise-book he carried everywhere, and which contained the addresses and telephone numbers of everyone who had ever meant anything to him. It was not a large book and it was by no means full.

"Oh, but you *must* believe it," Annelise teased, "Little Beth told me and she's *ever* so pretty with *big* green eyes."

William looked up, uncomprehending.

"What?" he asked, in some confusion. He found it difficult at the best of times to follow women's leaps in logic and subject matter.

"What the screaming toss do wee Beth's eyes have to do with anything?"

Annelise was swinging from the railing at the side of the seats. If it was possible for a girl to leer, she was doing it now.

"Don't worry, your secret's safe with me," she trilled, "I can't quite make up my mind whether I think it's sweet or yucky, an old man like you fancying a young girl like her. It's probably a bit yucky, really. After all those years telling us you hated girls, eh?"

"Don't be stupid," snorted William, "The girl does sociology. I find that deeply unattractive in a person. It's a sign of feeble-mindedness, as the Führer used to say. And I am not old."

"Annelise!" Susan called, "We need you for this bit."

"Coming!" Annelise cried, and skipped away, grinning knowingly at William, who glared back with highly distilled venom.

"Little Beth, eh? You're a dark horse," Mike sniggered, naming only one of the many members of the animal kingdom with whose backsides William had been compared, "And there was us thinking you only had eyes for the lovely Alice."

"I never want to hear the name of that lunatic witch again," William spat, and stomped off in a huff to check the papers and 'phone Luke Wallace.

If William was livid, Mike was overjoyed. His escape plan was now clear. If the sociologists were going to mount a demonstration against Sedgwick, it would be much more difficult for Portia and the whores to get hold of the poor sod. His bodyguards were sure to put a tight cordon around him the minute they saw the herd of bearded leftists and their raggle-taggle student supporters. Anyone attempting to abduct him would have to brave the demonstrators and then the policemen. The presence of television crews would make it doubly difficult to get near the politician, and making off with him would be downright impossible with a crowd of irate troublemakers, journalists, and policemen in hot pursuit. Portia's scheme with the aircraft factory had netted him all the money he could possibly need, as well as covering the initial borrowings from the English Department funds, so he could afford to get out of it. He smiled broadly down at Susan, who looked up at him in confusion. Susan really was a very lovely and beautiful woman, he thought. He wondered how he could possibly persuade her to go out with him.

*　　　*　　　*

"Not fun, agree, DS," Josh Greze dropped the *Times* onto the pile of newspapers which so spoiled the look of his master's desk.

"Not fun? It's not even torture. It's worse than that. Cut out the well-bred understatement, you odious little mollusc, or you'll be looking for another host organism off which to leech," bawled Damien Sedgwick. The normally immaculate minister was as ruffled as a piece of 1970s shirting and his hand shook as he pointed at the lead story in virtually every newspaper.

"Sedgwick In Friendship With Dictator Scandal" the *Times* announced. "Top Labour Fixer's Links With South American Despot" the *Mail* trumpeted. "Queen Mother's New Love : Pictures" the *Mirror* squawked, helpfully.

"Need you to be honest with me, DS," Josh said, untroubled by the politician's anger, "Is it true? I mean, can we plausibly claim that these people have the wrong end of the stick?"

"We met at a party, if that doesn't sound too corny. He's a nice bloke, and the wife's a really lovely woman. I stayed with them a few times at Santa Christina. I know there were a few human rights abuses in the early years of the regime, but, hey, there were guerrillas in the hills, and is our own record so squeaky clean? Can we afford the luxury of moral superiority when we have Bloody Sunday and, erm, the Glencoe massacre on our hands, eh? Answer me that if you will."

"Glencoe massacre was in seventeenth century, DS," Josh replied mercilessly, "Bloody Sunday occurred under Conservative administration. New Labour does not "do" human rights abuses."

"Yeah, right," Sedgwick scoffed, "Like the electrified police batons we're exporting to the Saudis are going to be used for decoration."

"You aren't convincing me, DS," Josh heaped up pressure on the minister like a JCB confronted with a pile of cow manure. He saw it as his duty to test his master every so often.

"Well, look at the economic growth his country's experienced," Sedgwick came out fighting, "Poverty tackled, streets safe to walk at night, unemployment rate lower than, er, ours. No guerrillas any more. Tell you what, he's one of us. Tough on crime, tough on the causes thereof."

"You're telling me he's tough. Amnesty International have written the encyclopaedia of violent aggro based solely on the accounts of people imprisoned by him."

"Tish and pish," Sedgwick sniffed, "Troublemakers. People with no vision, who were unable to see the path of greatness on which Julio was leading them. Carping reactionaries and so on. Forces, if you will, of conservatism. They make that stuff up, anyway."

"What about the economic exploitation stories?" Josh demanded.

"Oh, for goodness' sake. Now this is getting silly. When the PM attracts big foreign companies to set up shop in this country, thus creating lots of jobs and sticking up two fingers to that crowd of blue-rosetted cretins in the opposition, who couldn't attract iron filings even if their arses were magnetised, he is, quite rightly, hailed as a hero, the saviour of his people. Julio does the same thing in San Isodoro and suddenly he's Mr Nastypants. I mean, what's wrong with these people?"

"The General seems to have attracted multinational companies which torched the rain forests and paid their workers a pittance."

"Oh, look, really. I'm getting just a tad fed up here. Have you ever seen a rain forest? No, I bet you haven't. Well, I have, thanks to Julio, who kindly took me along to see the work in progress on one of his new hydro-electric plants, and let me tell you this. They're stinking malarial sweaty hell holes. Not a wine bar for miles, and the air choc-a-bloc with the densest clouds of insect life this side of the eternal pit of Hades. Massive great stinging buzzing things, big as your fist. Tiny little sods that nip up your trouser leg and inject you with itchy stuff that makes the retention of any kind of dignity during the evening's banquet a tad difficult, I may say. And then the middle sized ones that are just plain off-pissing. Snakes, too. Anacondas that would make Linford Christie weep with envy, and little poisonous weaselly horrors, like the creeps who wrote those articles. And don't ask about the barbed sheatfish."

"Is that the one which swims up your…"

"That's the boy. Julio was doing the world a very big favour tearing down those miserable disease factories, and don't you forget it. He brought a lot of employment to areas in which the population would otherwise just have sat around on their undernourished arses being bitten to death by the aforementioned insects whilst waiting for a visit from Sting or a photo-op in *Smug Internationalist.* Don't talk to me about exploitation, matey."

Josh, his thumbs hooked in the pockets of his waistcoat, turned on the politician like a particularly florid barrister, and produced another damning charge.

"The General's links with Soviet Russia?"

"We forced him into it, dumb arse. If the west, thanks to a few whingers, won't sell him arms, he has to go to our Slavic brethren to the east. And let us not forget that his armed forces now buy British, thanks in no small part to the efforts of yours truly," Sedgwick was in control now, his breathing even and his hands rock-steady, "No-one is going to touch me on this one. No-one."

"Well done, DS," Josh said, "But need suitable platform to launch counter-attack. My feeling is use College speechy thing day after tomorrow. We lay down key facts before appreciative audience. Local media less probing and skilful than national. Put case across and get pictures with photogenic young students. I've seen them. Very nice. Perhaps not enough ethnics to be truly Cool Britannia, but daresay we can find some."

"Nice one," Sedgwick poured himself a cup of coffee, "I think we're going to be all right."

*   *   *

"I just thought I'd make it authentic," Luke protested, as William's fifteen minute blast of swearing came to an end in an eruption of vigorous coughing, "Alice said she saw Sedgwick with General Domingo at one of those Irish Embassy parties you take her to, and so I said to a mate whose dad's at the *Express...*"

"I might have known that evil bitch was involved somewhere," William snarled, "She seems to be determined to ruin my sodding life."

"I thought you and she got on rather well," Luke protested.

"No, we don't. For some reason best known to the malevolent hag, she's decided she hates me. I've no idea why, but I can assure you, that spiteful little cow is out to get me."

"There must be some rational reason, surely?" Luke was bemused.

"Ah, the innocence of youth. I'd been hoping to spare you this until you were older, but you might as well know now. It is a truth universally to be acknowledged, if you will, that where a set of circumstances suggests a logical and rational assumption or course of action, you can take it that the female of the species will do the complete opposite. She will ignore the path of reason and sense and assume, say or do the most fucking ridiculous and annoying thing imaginable. Take it from me, they're insane, the lot of them."

Luke said that he couldn't see what the problem was with the Sedgwick thing, and immediately regretted it when William exploded again.

"The fucking Sociology, Cannabis and Beanbags Department are going to picket the event," he screamed, "Have you any idea what those people are like? They're died-in-the-wool malingering Marxist lunatics. We have absolutely no control over them. They might try to kill him for all I know. I thought we were having our own stage-managed protest?"

"Ah," Luke said, nervously, glad that there was a telephone line between himself and his old teacher, "This will make you laugh."

"Ten pounds says it won't."

"Heh, heh," Luke said, feebly, "Well, the thing is, I was down at the Conservative Club, and I saw Peter Drake, and Billy Tharpe, and Johnny Ferral, and a few of the others who work for the supermarket and the insurance company. And I explained that we wanted them to pretend to be left wing protesters. And…"

"Oh my dear sweet Lord. Oh, great thundering nonce. You didn't. You absolute cretinous piece of plankton. I am going to rip your liver out and feed it to the College cat," William's voice was altering pitch like a jet fighter heading for take off. In a few moments, he would begin to break panes of glass. He had taught all of these young men, and the experience had scarred him mentally. Indeed, if Johnny Ferral had been a little quicker with a pint glass one evening in the Hertford Arms, it would have scarred him physically as well. "You told the most right wing people in Sussex that Sedgwick was coming and that they were going to pretend to be lefties?"

"Erm, well, more or less."

"Pretend to be lefties? Some of that lot can only just pretend to be human," William shouted, "I'm convinced that if we go back a generation or two, you'd find tails and the ability to hang from trees by the feet. As for being lefties, they're the kind of people who used to get booted out of the SS for having unacceptably radical opinions. What did they say to your kind offer?"

"Um," Luke muttered, "They sort of told me to stick it up my arse and said they were going to do a nationalist demonstration with Union Jacks. They're going to burn him in effigy on the College lawn. I can't really stop them."

"Oh, bollocks," William said.

There is a school of thought which says that it doesn't matter what life throws at you so long as you have friends. William had not attended it, and even if he had, its teaching was of little value to him now that Alice had steamed off for whatever reason it was. William attached much more importance to earthly material things, like his salary, and the thought which had occurred to him the previous night, a possible glittering future as a Conservative MP. If his morning had been made unpleasant by Alice's call, his evening was becoming an unremitting hell as he pondered the likelihood of losing it all. He swore a few more times and went to the pub.

*   *   *

The Head of Media Studies looked at the post-war British cinema shelf for the third time. He still couldn't find what he was looking for.

"Edward," he called to his colleague, "Have any of the students booked out any tapes recently?"

Edward emerged from the Editing Suite with a clipboard.

"Don't think so," he said, "Oh, hold on, yes—*Metropolis* is out, and *2001*; that red-haired kid's doing a comparative essay on science fiction allegories."

"Nothing taken from the British section, though?"

"No, doesn't look like it. Why, is something missing?"

"Yes," the Head of Department said, "We really are going to have to get that lock fixed. Some little bugger's made off with our copy of *If*."

Chapter Thirteen

Had Mercier's been a normal institution, its staffroom at lunchtime would have been a babel of conversation marbled with cigarette smoke. But Mercier's wasn't normal and its staffroom resembled a half-empty airport lounge, aseptic and cold. Middle-aged female staff sat and talked about their children, whilst two men played a desultory game of chess in the corner. Rehearsals over, Mike strode in, with Susan trotting pertly behind like a Jack Russell.

"Has anyone seen that prize noddy Jason Hinge?" Mike bawled, with unnecessary volume, across the room. The older women looked at him disapprovingly. He was not wearing a tie. Again. They smiled pityingly at Susan.

"No," was the general response from those colleagues who bothered to reply, sometimes following it up with the deeply unprofessional addition, "Thank God."

"That's it, then," Susan said, "He's in College, you know. He's been seen. One of the lower sixth girls says he's out in the park, picking flowers and talking about poetry, sex and, as per usual, his psychological problems. We have to contact his parents, don't we?"

"Excellent!" Mike cried, "You catch on quickly. Now, this is a useful piece of what the Americans in Vietnam called Hearts and Minds operations. Watch and learn, my cherub, this will be an act of masterful pastoral care."

Jason Hinge had rapidly emerged as the biggest thorn in Susan's side. A sensitive and not unintelligent child, he had left Woodlands comprehensive school for boys, an institution notorious for its hearty football-playing laddishness and casual brutality, in the hope of finding more amenable companions, preferably of the opposite sex, at Mercier's. He had naively bought the College propaganda that Mercier's was a bit like university and one could find oneself there. Jason had eagerly gone in search of himself, and soon developed a reputation for introspective pretentiousness that made Jean-Paul Sartre look like Baby Spice. He had grown a pony-tail, and would have attempted a beard had his chin been up to the production of more than a few lonely tufts of hair which resembled marram grass on a sand dune. His clothes were flamboyantly odd, to say the least, varying from velveteen smoking jackets to luridly-coloured sarongs, and attracting the hostility of the more testosteroned lads. Susan had to endure him more than most because, not unnaturally, he had found in Drama and its highly-strung practitioners an ideal milieu in which to preen and camp. Always a delicate boy, and now surrounded by equally fragile girls, his discovery of subjects like Psychology and Sociology had taught him a number of extraordinarily dangerous lessons. From Sociology he learned that absolutely nothing which happened in life could possibly be one's own fault, or even just bad luck. There was a reason for everything that went wrong, and that reason was upbringing, or society, or capitalism, or the weather. It was most emphatically not Jason Hinge and his personal inadequacies, selfishness or stupidity. Psychology had provided him with a rationale for the increasing dislike which both students and staff displayed towards him. It also enabled him to establish himself as a self-appointed psychoanalyst to the various flakes, sentimentalists and prima donnas with whom he associated. This gave him considerable self-gratification, as well as an excuse for missing lessons. If he was not having a crisis of his own, he was counselling some other mimsy babe in the wood who was having a bit of a bad time of things.

Susan had inherited the pastoral care of this deeply precious and problematic child from the previous Head of Drama, and he was a source of constant irritation to her. His absences from lessons annoyed her colleagues, who vented their frustration on her—some occasionally hinting that Hinge's behaviour was a result of the absence of suitable discipline by his form tutor—and undermined the general morale of the department. This meant that she had to corner him and discuss matters, which she disliked, for he thrived on attention. He liked nothing better than wittering away, in his thin, piping voice, about the injustices of the world, whilst he played coyly with his pony-tail. Disciplinary meetings merely gave him another platform and a different audience for his camp performances as Woody Allen without the jokes. Attempts to pin him down on one piece of work would lead to a swift change of agenda as he announced that he had completed others—usually poems about tortured adolescence which no-one had asked him to write. It was becoming increasingly apparent that the one thing Jason Hinge had in common with his teachers was that none of them particularly cared about his A level results.

Susan was fed up with him, and had come to her Head of Faculty for support. Mike, who was in a good mood since he had learned that morning of the impending disaster facing Portia's plan, was eager to help. Especially since Susan was wearing a particularly fetching summer dress.

Mike went to the 'phone and dialled the Hinge residence. There was no reply so he let it ring for several minutes and then put it down.

"Now, here is real psychology at work," he said, "Mrs. Hinge has had some sort of nervous illness, and sleeps during the day. She doesn't know that I know this. One of the cleaners told me, the hippyish one. She's in a Tibetan prayer circle with Mrs. Hinge. Anyway, I have just woken her up, and she will not be very happy. Now for phase two. Can you pass me that file?"

Susan handed Mike a bulky file which was crammed with the crimes and misdemeanours of Jason Hinge. He rummaged through it and extracted a card, marked "Emergency Contact Only".

"Now this is the nuclear attack button. It's his uncle's mobile," Mike sniggered.

"He hates his uncle, doesn't he?" Susan remembered a lengthy discussion with Hinge in which the latter's Hamlet complex had played a prominent part, despite the fact that his uncle would sooner have cut out his own spleen with a hacksaw than married a woman who had produced a moron like Jason.

"That's right. The soppy little sod hangs off the apron strings of his mum, who indulges him something chronic. Uncle Ian acts as emergency contact and also stand-in for his brother, Jason's dad, who's away most of the year servicing aeroplanes in Kuwait. He's a vicious and unforgiving bastard."

"Jason says that if he'd gone to boarding school, he'd probably have ended up hanging himself," said Susan, thoughtfully.

"Yes," Mike remembered the conversation. William had been in the room at the time.

"Do you remember what William said?"

"Oh, God," Susan blenched, "I don't think I'll ever forget. That man is such an evil bastard. I mean, I know he's your friend and everything, but he's utterly devoid of human sympathy."

"I wouldn't go that far. He seems to get on all right with Alice. Sometimes."

"And who else? One ex-student does not a warm and compassionate personality make. Telling Jason Hinge that nature has to weed out the runts somehow was not the act of an understanding and charitable person. And as for asking if he was bullied enough here, would he kill himself—for goodness' sake, Mike, he shouldn't be allowed near teenagers. He's a sick man."

"Maybe so, but he's not our problem. Young Jason is. Now I'm going to ring his uncle. Watch and learn."

He consulted the Emergency Contact card and dialled Mr Hinge's mobile number.

"Hello," he said suavely, "Michael Alcock, Mercier's College. I'm looking for Mrs Evangeline Hinge."

There was a burst of what sounded like verbal gunfire from down the 'phone line.

"Oh, I am sorry," Mike continued, "It's just that Jason's missed a few lessons and we were wondering if he was ill. I've obviously got the wrong number from the file."

There was another burst of noise and Mike nodded.

"Thank you, Mr Hinge. I'll try his mother's number. Sorry to bother you."

He replaced the receiver and grinned.

"Right. The cat is now amongst the pigeons and having a gay old time. He will almost certainly ring Mrs Hinge and give her an earful. He regards the boy as a lily-livered nancy, if I may quote directly, and takes the line that even if he is ill he should still go to lessons. But he's probably skiving, and this is her fault because she's too soft on him. We have already woken her up on a fruitless call to get to the 'phone before it stops ringing, so she's gone back to bed and will now have to get up again. They will argue and she will be put in a bad mood, and will want her revenge on the boy for letting her look bad."

"That's very clever," said Susan, who actually felt that it was cruel and unpleasant to exploit family divisions. She had heard that this one made the San Andreas Fault look like a crack in a paving stone. Uncle Ian, a former Parachute Regiment Sergeant-Major from the Gorbals, had strongly disapproved of his brother's decision to marry the pretty but vacuous air stewardess he had met at Gatwick, and by all accounts took every opportunity to bully the hapless woman. He had wanted Jason sent to the most savage boarding school possible to have his delicate arty-farty ways beaten out of him and believed that, like all boys, he should then should do National Service at the age of sixteen. He had expressed these views forthrightly to Susan at one of the many meetings about Jason's future which the College, in the absence of a sufficiently ruthless expulsion process, had been obliged to host. Mrs Hinge retaliated by pandering to the boy's every whim and taking a perverse pride in lavishing her husband's vast salary on all manner of eccentric hobbies which Jason would adopt and discard like paper handkerchiefs.

"Oh, that's not the half of it, babe," Mike leaned back in his chair with irritating smugness, "In half an hour, we will hit mummy again. We'll try the 'We're just concerned. Is he ill?' line, and let her admit that he isn't. Then we give her a few salient facts about the bugger's academic performance. She'll be reeling on the ropes by then. When Hingey-boy comes traipsing in, she'll have his guts for garters."

"I suppose we have to do this," Susan reflected sadly, "I mean, it's in his interests, isn't it?"

"That's right, O beauteous colleague," Mike lit a cigarette and grinned happily, "And it's very rewarding for us."

*   *   *

In the Social Science Faculty, the banners were being readied for the great anti-Sedgwick protest rally. They announced strident principles in primary colours.

"Sedgwick : the Butcher's Pal." "New Labour Camp." "Sedgwick : Agent of Fascism."

The Sociology students chattered and shrieked as they drew lurid representations of the Minister in Nazi storm-trooper uniform, grinding his heel onto a prostrate South American peasant.

"Now, remember to make sure that there are plenty of leaflets kicking around the College, yah?" Barnaby Worthington shouted over the din, "We want everyone to know just what a monster this man is."

He hefted a large box of luridly-coloured leaflets which detailed the crimes with which the Politics Department's guest was associated onto his desk. The more energetic students grabbed great handfuls and tore off round the College to distribute them or leave them in prominent places from which the cleaners would, later that day, take them away to be recycled.

"Erm," Beth Seymour said, nervously, "Does Mr Fenneck know about this? I have a lesson with him next period, and…"

"William is a fascist, yah?" Mr Worthington, as she had to remember not to call him, declared passionately, his beard trembling as he spoke, "He deserves everything he gets for bringing that swine into the College. We've got to show our resistance, yah? He's giving a platform for a man who condoned the massacre of Santa Vera in 1978. Do you, like, want to accept that or demonstrate that you feel solidarity for the members of that workers' guerilla movement, gunned down by Damien Sedgwick's friend?"

Wee Beth felt guilty. She had not been born at the time of the Santa Vera massacre of 1978. She tried very hard to feel solidarity with the massacred workers' guerillas, but it was not easy. She wished she could. Barnaby was so enthusiastic about it all. Mr Fenneck was never enthusiastic. He was bitter and cynical.

"The massacred workers? My arse they were. Bunch of poncy middle class posers who'd read a few too many stupid books at university and decided they were revolutionaries, not unlike certain other people I could name. I've no time for el Presidente but Latin America was better off without that pack of tossers," he had snorted, derisively, when she had raised the subject, "If you're interested in socialism I'll lend you a book about Clem Attlee and Ernie Bevin. Or I've got something about Uncle Joe if it's Marxism you're after."

"Right, everybody," Barnaby continued, "It's time to work on our chants. Remember, William Fenneck's invited down the capitalist media to show off his fascist friends, and we're going to show that there's no welcome here for people who torture innocent workers and revolutionaries. Anybody thought of one?"

"Chanting, banners, bloody slogans," Toby Gaskett sneered, "This bastard is friends with a murderer and does trade deals with him. We want direct action, not a bit of a demo that'll make Sussex Today on BBC Radio Bourgeois, and then be forgotten."

"Hey, man," Barnaby actually spoke like this. Members of the Mathematics department did not. It was part of the job description and was on his cv.

"I understand your feelings, yah? This guy is a dealer in death, and we don't want him here. Not the other creep, either, Benedict "Hitler" Wolfesbain—hey, did you vote for him? I certainly didn't."

There was a ragged cheer. Wee Beth reflected that if Mr Fenneck was here, he would make some kind of nasty remark about how Barnaby couldn't vote for Wolfesbain, or against him for that matter, because he lived in Brighton, well away from the daily lives of the students entrusted to his care. For a professional cynic, William took surprising pleasure in having a mortgaged occupation of this particular piece of moral high ground.

"I sympathise with your views, Tobes," Barnaby continued, "If it was up to me I'd stick a gun against his head and show the world that some people have just had it up to here with racism and fascism and imperialism and all that other shit that they feed us."

"Yeah," Toby Gaskett said, somewhat strangely. The other Sociology students cheered again. Nobody ever cheered in Politics.

Wee Beth went to her lesson with William feeling depressed.

*   *   *

Jason Hinge had been sitting under a tree in the park, looking at a flower and hoping that one of the other students would notice him doing it. They had, but refused to take the bait. Most of his peers regarded him as a weird and ridiculous boy, chiefly because he was one. Teenagers are not totally stupid. Hinge was writing poems in his head and thinking about which of the three girls having cigarettes by the duckpond he would try his counselling skills on if she had a problem. They were all bound to have problems. Everyone did. Some people just repressed their difficulties. With his sensitivity and growing knowledge of the easier bits of the psychology textbook, he could bring these problems to the surface and give comfort and succour. One of the girls had a pierced eyebrow and a tattoo. She was presumably rebelling against a strict parental regime. Hey, he'd been there. Another had dyed her hair blonde—to flee from reality? Understandable. It sucked. Then there was the one who looked vulnerable and scared and in need of protection. Hinge pondered for a moment and decided to counsel the one with pierced eyebrow and the tattoo. She had the biggest tits.

He was just getting up to lope across to the girls when a familiar figure hove into view.

William Fenneck was returning from his liquid lunch at the Hertford Arms and was still in a filthy temper. Jason Hinge had missed his lesson that morning and now, by the grace of the vengeful Old Testament God William worshipped, he had found him. He could not make the Sociology Department suffer for the disaster that Thursday was undoubtedly going to be, but he could make Hinge suffer. He liked doing that. William was a product of the old school and believed that to take time off lessons for anything other than life-threateningly serious illness was an act of cowardice. After Alice pointed out that he became maudlin and emotional after two bottles of white wine, he never drank it again, believing that to show weakness in front of a woman was a crime equivalent to wearing clip-on ties or invading Belgium. His contempt for

Hinge's touchy-feely sensitivity was almost boundless. And the little creep was wearing pink taffeta loon pants and a multicoloured dressing-gown affair. William wished he could have dropped the simpering little twat down a well like they did to that similarly-attired oddball in the Bible.

"Mister Hinge," he bawled across the park, jabbing his cigarette at the boy as he advanced, puffing like an elderly and much-vandalised steam engine, "You are a useless piece of scum."

The blend of polite formality and splenetic distaste which characterised William's relations with the students was widely studied by the English Language teachers as a cultural oddity.

"There's no need to talk like that," Hinge bleated, defensively.

"You were not in my lesson today," William carried on, a bulldozer in corduroy and tweed making its way through a sensitive, intellectual, blancmange. Like Susan, he was always secretly relieved when Hinge didn't turn up for things, as it meant he didn't have to listen to the boy's voice, but appearances had to be maintained.

"There was a very good reason," the student whined.

"No there bloody well was not," William yelled, drawing closer to the boy and circling around him like an old, vicious tabby toying with a mouse. He rarely looked his victims in the eye when he was administering a bollocking. This was usually because he was much shorter than they were. Hinge was a small boy but William wasn't going to give up the habit of a lifetime. By now, a small crowd of onlookers, students who had come to the park to sunbathe and smoke, had gathered.

"I was helping a friend who had some personal problems she needed to sort out. She'd been really traumatised by hearing about the suffering of the little animals in the veal trade."

"Don't give me that mimsy old cobblers. I've told you about this before, Mister Hinge. If your friends are weak and feeble, drop them. Let them wallow in the mire of their own inadequacy. Pass by one the other side like a bad Samaritan, and laugh at their pain. Learn to despise them as the rest of us do. Don't fall for their sob stories. They're vampires, sucking life from everyone around them. They're the undead. They're socially useless. And as for the fucking animals, you want to get a few priorities right, sunshine. I've seen you and your ghastly chums in McDonald's. Take that bloody plank out of your eye before you criticise the nation's farmers."

"That isn't fair. What about caring?" Hinge didn't understand the plank reference but was given courage by the presence of the girl with the pierced eyebrow and the tattoo and the rebellion complex. And the large breasts.

"Don't use that word in front of me," William snapped, with contempt that would corrode human flesh if picked up without protective gloves, "Caring went out in the sixties. This is a post-Thatcherite world of competition and domination. We are all animals, struggling to survive. They are the crap beasts, at the back of the herd. They will fall further and further behind, victims of their own pathetic weakness and frailty. Then the hyenas will get them. They are going to get you too, Mister Hinge, and when they do, I shall laugh."

Hinge was angry but he knew that he was impotent. Among the onlooking students were some of Fenneck's pet thugs from the rugby team, who were sniggering at the spectacle. If he laid a finger on Fenneck—which he could easily have done, as the teacher was clearly about as fit and healthy as a piece of three-day-old roadkill—he would immediately be beaten to a pulp.

"If everyone thought like you do," he sniffed, "The world would be a horrible place."

"It already is one, you ponce," William snarled, "And yours is becoming more so. I'm going to hang you out to dry, you see if I don't. Mincing great faggot."

He stomped off, trailing clouds of smoke and feeling rather better. Acts of malice always made William feel better. He went to his lesson with Wee Beth determined to concentrate on the fact that she had big green eyes and not on the possibility that, if granted executive power over the country, she might round up what remained of his family and nationalise their property.

Hinge stood forlornly as the other students laughed at him. One day he would show this choleric little bastard what he was made of. He sighed and went to sit down under his tree. Looking at the flower again, he pulled out a mobile telephone and called his mother to ask her for a lift home.

*   *   *

Toby Gaskett was marshalling his troops in the underworld.

"This is it," he breathed, "Our big chance to really make a statement. To tear down this bourgeois Wendy House and show the world that the kids have had enough."

He looked lovingly at the grenades and the machine-pistols.

"Erm...isn't it dangerous and illegal?" his girlfriend asked.

Gaskett looked at her pityingly. Sometimes he wondered what he saw in her. Usually he remembered that it was the way she was young and impressionable. Today he had forgotten that bit.

"You're just falling for their lies" he jeered, "their conformity, their clapped out bollocks. We are going to have a revolt against this system. The revolution will be televised. There will be cameras there, and the other kids will rise up following our example. They'll watch us on tv and we'll be famous."

"Are you sure?" the girl was sceptical. She had made up her mind that she was not going to go out with Toby any more. He was just too weird.

"Of course I am. Every student in this stupid place resents the power structure really. They just need their latent feelings of frustration brought out. Those that don't can pay the price. We're going to bring the whole rotten edifice of Fulke crappy Mercier's College crumbling down, and take out these so-called politicians with it. It'll trigger a chain reaction across the country. The reactionaries have been pushing and pushing at anyone who's the slightest bit alternative. We've got to snap sometime. We've got to say that we've had enough."

"But surely Damien Sedgwick will have bodyguards?"

"Not necessarily. He isn't senior enough. Fenneck says that only the really big bastards like the Home Secretary and the Defence Secretary have proper protection. A couple of plod, maybe, but we can take them out with the sniper rifle. Who wants to do that?"

"I do," a voice from the darkened corridor intruded. Toby jumped, nervously. Jason Hinge was standing in the gloom, looking depressed. He often did this, but it made a refreshing change for him to offer to shoot someone with a high-powered rifle, instead of attempting to embrace every girl in sight on the off-chance that she might have some sort of trauma with which she wished to be helped.

"Erm, right, ok then, Jase," Gaskett said, "We'll have to work out a suitable place for you to shoot from, though."

Gaskett was delighted that Hinge wanted this role. It would keep him away from the centre of the action, where Gaskett needed to be, leading the youth revolution against the government and its hired agents in the academic establishment. Hinge would undoubtedly fancy himself as a leader of men as well. It was good that this way, he could be kept out of camera vision.

"Up on top of the old building," Hinge said, in an unusually flat monotone, "There's a balcony there that connects it to the newer block next door. It has an uninterrupted view of the quad and the entry into the assembly hall. You get to it through the caretaker's flat, and there's a back staircase from here to there which isn't used much."

"Hey," Gaskett said, impressed, "You've thought about this."

"I've been thinking about it for the past hour," Hinge replied, still in his flat monotone, "And I want to shoot Alcock and Fenneck."

"Well, I don't see why you shouldn't," Gaskett said, breezily, "They're agents of oppression, too."

Hinge did not appear to hear him. He continued to speak, rambling gently.

"Thanks to them, my mum's chucked me out of the house. I'll have to live with my uncle. He makes me swim in the sea off Brighton every morning, regardless of the weather. He puts salt in my porridge. He spars with me and lands heavy blows on my chest. He'll make me cut off my pony-tail and wear Aran sweaters and other types of what he calls heterosexual clothing. My life is going to be hell because of them."

"Shit," Gaskett said, "That's heavy stuff. You're going to want to pay them back for that one, I bet."

"Too right. I'm going to spread their brains all over the hall."

Jason Hinge smiled for the first time that day.

CHAPTER FOURTEEN

Portia bustled about the Grosvenor like a woman possessed, which was, interestingly, what Dr Walpurgess had once called her. She frantically wiped the tiniest specks of dust from every surface and emptied each ashtray. These tended to get rather full as both she and the girls smoked heavily. They preferred it to eating. It required less energy and involved fewer calories.

"If you have to smoke today, do it in the garden," Portia commanded, "I want this place looking clean and sophisticated for our honoured guests."

"I don't see what's so special about these ones," pouted Jobelle, whose favourite hobby was to lie in front of the Jerry Springer show with a packet of Embassy and a large bottle of Diet Coke, "No-one's ever complained before."

"They'll be paying a lot for this," Portia said, reflecting that this was not merely a financial statement, "And we're going to give them their money's worth."

The girls went out into the garden and started smoking. Portia dashed round all the rooms to make sure that the cameras were in full working order. She had conducted an experiment with Mike the previous evening to see just what their fields of vision were. Mike had been in a surprisingly exuberant mood after his defeatist sogginess earlier in the month. Portia had no idea why, not being privy to the fulfilment of his

treacherous desire to nobble her little venture and his successful persecution of Jason Hinge. But she wasn't complaining. Mike, bouncing
around like a hyperactive chimp, had insisted on checking out every
possible corner of the room whilst making quite lurid suggestions
about the positions which could be adopted in them. By the time they
had got to the third room, Portia had been faced with a choice between
punching him in the face or calling his bluff. She chose the latter and
was pleasantly surprised to discover that Mike was both willing and able
to put some of his more sordid ideas into practice. This was a side of
him which Portia had never seen. Indeed, she was soon to see virtually
every side of him, and from angles which she had never previously considered. He was clearly in better physical shape than she had supposed,
and Portia found herself wishing that she could give up smoking in
order to keep up with his energetic performance. She was not easily
embarrassed, but an asthma attack on the dining room table after an
hour and a half of Mike's vigorous attentions was not the greatest
turn-on she could have offered. Still, at least they had proved that the
cameras worked, though annoyingly they could only be accessed
when whoever was in the room had finished whatever they were doing
there. She called the girls back indoors.

"You're quite clear about how this afternoon works?" she asked, in
her best schoolmistressy way.

"Yes," Yvette sighed wearily. They had been through this six times
already. Jobelle might be a dumb blonde but Yvette resented being
treated like a half-wit. It was why she didn't enjoy life at Mercier's.

"So recite it for me," Portia said, in a tone that couldn't quite make up
its mind whether to patronise or menace.

Yvette adopted a sing-song voice, like a small child repeating its
tables.

"I infiltrate audience for talks. Meanwhile, Jobelle chats up chauf-
feurs and explains to them where to take the VIPs. We have a revised
itinerary which says that the reception's going to be here rather than at

the College. At the end of the talks, I make sure the VIPs go to the cars. We get into the cars with them and pretend to be students. Then we head back here. Glasses of champers all round and then we gradually lure them into our rooms with our feminine charms."

"Well done," Portia said, drily, "But remember to keep it vaguely innocent. Don't put all your wares on show at the outset. We'll get more money if you pretend to be sweet little things who were seduced by these nasty middle-aged men. They won't go for straight, up-front give-us-the-dosh-and-get-yer-lad-out stuff. Part of the fantasy of the whole thing is that you're schoolgirls."

"But we're College students," Yvette objected, and hurriedly corrected herself, "Supposed to be, I mean. We can't exactly wear school uniform. Makes it a bit less kinky, doesn't it?"

"Then wear something that approximates to uniform. Not too short a skirt, and no low-cut tops. You're healthy enough girls not to need wonderbra-ed cleavages to announce what produce you've got on sale. They're politicians, remember. They have enough imagination to work out what's going on in there. The less up for it you look the more interested they'll be when you look fascinated by them. It also gives you credibility when, at the end of a five round sparring match, you turn round, burst into tears and do the old how-could-you-you-brute routine. But play it by ear; you know men well enough to be able to work out what will appeal to them."

The girls went off to change and prepare themselves for the afternoon's work. Portia went out to her car, then paused. A nagging doubt was lingering in the back of her mind, like a stubbed out cigarette that has fallen onto the carpet; it might be irrelevant but which needed to be addressed for complete peace of mind. She went back into the house and emptied the safe. Then she took all the cash and cheques and put them into what she had told Mike was a joint account at Barclay's. Portia parked her car outside a pub close to the house, where she could watch the comings and goings. She had several hours to spare, and so she went into the pub and ordered a baked trout for lunch. Portia loved fish and thought about it with eager expectation. Funny how you could still enjoy the idea of the simplest things even when was involved in great and weighty matters.

The Principal was also looking forward to lunch. It was his best time for ambushing the teachers, who tended to avoid him if at all possible when he prowled the corridors, looking for someone to talk to. He found Mike and William racing through plates of spaghetti bolognese in the canteen, as the customary student riot took place around them.

"Michael," he nodded, "William."

"Good afternoon, Headmaster," William oozed, unctuously, bowing his head. Mercier's had not had a headmaster for twenty years, but William still used the term because his colleagues regarded it as sexist. The Principal liked this because it showed proper humility on William's part. William, unlike most of the staff, who addressed him by his Christian name, realised that he was but a cockroach on the hearthrug of the Principal's genius.

"How are preparations for the great debate going?" the Principal asked.

"Jolly well, Headmaster," William rubbed and intertwined his hands like two small snakes writhing in agony. Mike was reminded of Uriah Heep. People often were when they saw William with the Principal.

"The cameras are set up in strategic positions in the Hall, and we will have a photo-shoot in the foyer for the press. You will want to be in that, of course."

"Really? I hadn't actually given it any thought. If I'm free at the time I'll pop over," said the Principal, who had in fact thought of little else for the past week, and had cancelled several appointments in order to be present.

"It would be awfully nice if you could," William gushed, "And of course we'll be wearing gowns for the shoot. It will look rather good with all the suits. I'll get some local dignitaries to join in. I believe the Mayor is coming with his chain thingy. It's a good opportunity to establish ourselves as the big beasts in the community."

"Splendid, William," the Principal beamed, "Are there any problems which remain unresolved? Anything you'd like me to deal with?"

"Well," the Head of Politics squirmed slightly, "One doesn't like to criticise a colleague, but I fear that Barnaby Worthington wants to hold a demonstration against the Minister. Forgive me if I'm speaking out of turn, Headmaster, but I do rather feel that it might not be the best image to present to the world, which will no doubt be watching, if we have the sociology students leaping about outside and chanting what I am very much afraid may prove to be Marxist dogma."

"Indeed," the Principal nodded sagely, "You do understand that I cannot be seen to favour your chosen method of political discourse over his?"

William didn't. He considered it perfectly obvious that given the choice between people with beards and Marxist views and those without them, any sane person would support the latter. But he knew better than to ask questions of the old man, who frightened him. So too did the *Wizard of Oz*. He nodded like a fluffy car dog and repeated "Absolutely, headmaster" several times.

The Principal thought for a moment.

"Leave it with me, William, and Michael and I will come up with something together."

Mike cursed inwardly. He had been hoping to catch the cricket scores in the staffroom, and, in any case, it was in his interests to see that the great sociology demonstration went ahead as planned, so as to prevent Portia's plan to lure the unfortunate Sedgwick into the arms of her slappers. William bowed and smiled gratefully, like a peasant granted a plot of land by a mediaeval monarch, and scurried off to see Cowboy Sam, who was in charge of the post-debate refreshments.

*　　　　　*　　　　　*

At the railway station, Alice was descending from the London train. Impending exams, rows with her flatmates and boyfriend, and a bout of 'flu had driven her home for a week's quiet revision in the bosom of her family. She was quite looking forward to curling up with Milton and her mother's chocolate pudding. Her father collected her in his car. The journey home took them past the College. Henry Jameson glanced at it as they drove under the windows of William's classroom, which looked blankly down from the first floor of the Victorian grammar school building.

"Cowboy Sam says William's roped him in for this big project of his," he said.

"Oh, God," his daughter said, miserably, "He has to drag everyone down with him, doesn't he?"

"Steady on," Henry liked William, who shared many of his opinions and was therefore an alternative punchbag when Alice went into one of her periodic anti-men moods. William had tried to explain to him that Alice's complaints were perfectly tolerable provided one didn't actually listen. "It's going to put the College on the map, apparently."

"I'll bet it will," Alice snorted, "And put William in prison, where he should be."

"You are unkind sometimes, darling," Henry observed, mildly, "He's not doing anything wrong."

"That's a matter of opinion."

"Well, I don't know all the details, but I don't think it can do any harm, and it's giving William something to do with his time, and it might do some good. I think you're being unfair on him."

Alice thought that her father had been hanging around with William too long. He had begun to lose the moral sense which she had once looked up to, even if she found it infuriating. She sighed and nestled down into her coat.

*   *   *

In the College canteen, the Principal turned to Mike.

"The problem, as I see it, is to how resolve matters without explicitly ordering Barnaby not to have his demonstration," he said, spearing a piece of mushroom with his fork.

"Indeed, Basil," Mike said. He desperately wanted to get away. For one thing, yesterday's exertions with Portia had left him with a bad back and sore legs. Mike wanted to lie flat on the Drama Studio table and be pampered by Susan. He suspected that she would be altogether less energetic than Portia, whose asthma attack had come as something of a relief to him. Yesterday's victories had been so exhilarating that he had felt obliged to celebrate it somehow, but he had quickly come to regret this particular choice. He felt as if he had been in a prolonged wrestling match with an extremely powerful creature, which, in a way, he had.

"I think we need to adopt a two-pronged approach. I shall find something which will keep Barnaby occupied at the time in question, whilst you head off his students and give them something to do. A drama workshop, perhaps."

"A fascinating idea," Mike said, "But I'm not sure that I can just ask a baying mob of sociology students to come and do some drama."

"Why ever not?" the Principal asked, "You're a popular member of staff, widely known for your amiability. Students will believe, and do, what you tell them." "Erm," Mike knew better than to be disarmed by the Principal's flattery. It was a potent weapon but it was not based on objective reality as most rational adults understood the concept. Whilst Mike's name did not evoke the same virulent hatred as William's when mentioned to the students, he was still pretty certain that if he asked a load of unknown teenagers to come and act out a few scenes from *A Streetcar Named Desire* they would respond with the calculated jeering at which young people seemed to excel. They might even beat him up. New teachers were still told the chilling story about the time Jim Speer was almost scalped by a homicidal Home Economics class which he was supposed to be lecturing on waste disposal contractors.

"Or you could simply ask them to disperse. With no member of staff to accompany them, the formation of a picket would represent a breach of College regulations."

This was rather more like it. Mike could ask them to disperse, and they would refuse, because kids were like that, and he would be off the hook, because at least he'd tried.

"Yes, Basil," he said, "That's a good idea. I'll do that."

Barnaby Worthington came in and sat down beside them with a vege-burger. The Principal smiled at him indulgently.

"Ah, Barnaby, just the fellow. You may not yet be aware that the Vice Principal had an excellent idea last week. About the refurbishment of the Social Sciences block."

Barnaby looked at the Principal suspiciously and chewed on his vege-burger. The Principal was a prime example of the fascist ruling class and never to be trusted. His daily work revolved around confirming in the young minds under their tutelage the notion that individual effort, rather than collective solidarity, was the key to success, and he enforced disciplinary regulations which were bourgeois in the extreme. The fact that the Principal had been a scholarship boy from a two-up, two-down in the East End whereas Barnaby was the scion of a well-to-do Bishop's Stortford mercantile family which boasted three knighthoods and more Swiss bank accounts was of little relevance in this. Each, in his own way, was betraying his class, with Barnaby, of course, on the right side.

"Yes," the Principal continued, smoothly, "Your hard work in building up the Sociology Department has not gone un-noticed, Barnaby. It's been a hard struggle but you richly deserve that hundred per cent pass rate. We wish to reflect that in a smart new suite of rooms, equipped with whatever you and your colleagues feel you need."

Mike listened in disbelief. The Principal was widely known to regard the Sociologists as a crowd of subversive oddballs, and the entire staff was well aware of his belief that the subject could be taught by a glove puppet on a stick provided its students could understand Marxist theory and apply it to more or less any social circumstances.

"That's very kind, Basil," Barnaby remained suspicious but was slightly mollified. Even to the most blinkered, small glimpses of reality may occasionally be given. The Principal was clearly waking up to the fact that Sociology was where it was at.

"Yes, well," the Principal nodded, generously, "I need you to go and see Dr Walpurgess this afternoon to draw up the plans with him. About two o'clock. Shouldn't take more than a couple of hours."

"Ah," Barnaby said, "Bit of a snag there, Basil. I'm busy this afternoon."

"Really?" the Principal frowned, "But if I remember rightly, you don't teach on Thursday afternoons."

"Er, well, no," Barnaby thought desperately, "But I was going to a meeting."

"Oh, of course," the Principal smiled, "You'll have been wanting to go to William's little debate. An admirable display of support for a colleague, don't you agree, Michael?"

Mike nodded, reflecting that this was about as likely as Barnaby turning up to show solidarity at one of the British National Party coffee mornings some of William's ex-students were rumoured to attend.

"Well, I'm afraid I'll have to disappoint you there," the Principal said, "It's vital that you see the Vice Principal today to sort these plans out. We need to have a definite proposal with the governors by the end of the day. The money is coming from a special trust fund linked to the Mercier bequest which only becomes available every thirty years. We need to seize this window of opportunity while it lasts. Applications need to be in very soon. I'm sorry about the short notice, but it's one of the funny little eccentricities of the old legacy."

Barnaby could believe anything about the anachronistic feudal system, with its proto-capitalist elements, on which the college was based. He also realised that his colleagues would never forgive him if he turned down the chance to have their tatty rooms refurbished.

"Of course, Basil," he replied.

Barnaby looked around the room for one of his students. A leader-figure, ideally, who could galvanise the revolt. Obviously, only he was really suitable as a proletarian vanguard, but for a small demonstration a proxy would have to do. Toby Gaskett was lounging by the pool tables. He was not an ideal choice, Barnaby felt—his affectation of nail varnish was a tad bourgeois-revisionist—but he was at least passionate. Barnaby escaped from the Principal, who had now launched into a monologue about the College's only original title deed, which lived in a bank vault in London and he, alone of all the staff, had seen, and went across the canteen to Gaskett.

"I'm not going to be there this afternoon to lead the demo," he said, conspiratorially, "Can you get people together and take charge yourself?"

Gaskett was delighted. He was fairly indifferent to Barnaby, but at least he wasn't actively unpleasant the way some other teachers were, and it would be better if he wasn't caught up in the crossfire if force had to be used in what they had decided to call the Rainbow Revolution.

"No problem, yeah," the boy said, "When everyone assembles I'll lead them out and we'll show the fascists that they can't mess with us."

"Right on," Barnaby replied, somewhat predictably, and went to have some trifle for his pudding.

*   *   *

"Looks like a brothel," Cowboy Sam sniffed, as he gazed around the Conference Room, "You can just imagine some bosomy slapper with one foot on a chair, hollering for clients. I wonder if this is where the town facilities are."

"Interesting thought," William said, " Do we have all the wine and whatnot?"

"Yes, it's all under control. It would be nice to have people to serve it, though. Can you lend me a couple of reasonably capable students?"

"I don't see why not," William mused. He ambled down to his class-room and summoned two of the more loyal girls. His misogyny was not an all-embracing principle, and was tempered with the knowledge that the female students were infinitely less likely than the boys to steal his drink.

"This is Annelise and this is Beth," he said, "Ladies, this is Mr Avon from the off-license. At the end of the debate, you will come here and help him to serve wine to our guests."

"Fine," Annelise said, "But have you seen some of the students? They're in a really funny mood. They're a bit nervous about asking questions to such important people."

"Yes," Beth added, "Some of them are saying that they won't do it."

"But they've bloody well got to," William panicked, "It'll be really embarrassing if they just sit there like a bunch of cabbages and stare at the MPs. It'll make me look like I didn't teach them anything. I'll look like a proper arse."

"Why don't we perk them up a bit?" Sam asked, "I've got a bottle of vodka here. Mix that with orange juice and they'll feel a good bit more confident."

"Excellent," William said, grabbing a large jug and pouring in the vodka, "Annelise, get the orange juice and mix it in, then give it to the jumpy ones. Not too much, though. I don't want them asking Benedict Wolfesbain if he wants to step outside and say that."

"Why don't we script questions for the really nervous ones?" Beth offered, brightly. She knew she was under suspicion as a sociology stu-dent and was keen to prove her loyalty.

"Well done," William cried, "I'll scribble some down on this bit of paper and you can give them that."

He seized a sheet of A4 from a pile at the side of the room and scrawled down half a dozen questions which managed to tread the fine line between being insulting and being banal.

"Right. Give them that. At two o'clock, I want all the students moved round to the hall. They're to be ready and in their seats for a quarter past. That's when the Head and I are having our pictures taken with the bigwigs."

"Not everyone's here yet," out Annelise pointed.

"Well, we can wait a minute or two for them all to arrive," William had sampled a few glasses of the vodka mix and was feeling much more relaxed than he had been ten minutes previously. He smiled warmly at Annelise and Beth and ushered them back to the classroom. Downing his drink, he headed off to his office to put on his gown.

One student who had no intention of going to William's classroom or the Hall was Jason Hinge. He had waited by the entrance to the underworld until he saw the caretaker take his dog for its customary post-prandial walk. He went into the cellars and collected the Mauser with the sniper scope, wrapped it in a bin-liner, and went up the back stairs to the caretaker's flat. He could hear the voices in the meetings room as he passed by the first floor of the old building. One of them sounded like William, barking orders at the girlies, as he chauvinistically called them. Jason smiled grimly at the thought that soon his tormentor would be dead, along with that other bastard, Alcock. When he reached the door to the caretaker's flat he found it unlocked.

"Dear me," he said, "And in today's crime-ridden climate, too."

He slipped inside. Along a small corridor decorated with pictures of the College in its grammar school days lay a living-room with a large French window. This led onto a stretch of flat roof, with railings on each side, which covered the modern languages rooms that had been built into the archway connecting the old building to the social studies block. Hinge giggled. From here he had a perfect view of the entrance to the Clutterbuck Hall, where the staff would be waiting to fawn upon the mighty politicians. Suddenly, he became conscious that people in the quad, if they chose to look up, would also have a perfect view of him. He nipped back into the caretaker's flat and collected some cushions. Re-emerging carefully onto the roof, he put he cushions on the ground and lay flat on top of them. He peered through the sniper scope and focused on the Hall. A beautifully clear view. Casting his mind back to the Lee-Enfields of his unhappy days in the cadets at secondary school, Hinge then set about working out how to operate the rifle.

CHAPTER FIFTEEN

The government Jaguar had finally broken free from the death grip of the London traffic and was hurtling towards the Surrey-Sussex border at a fine rate of knots. Damien Sedgwick flicked idly through the morning's papers to see if there were any difficult issues on which he could be ambushed by his student inquisitors. There had been a particularly vicious assault on an old-age pensioner in Worthing, business was complaining about the pound, and a bomb had gone off in a small town in Pakistan. A war veteran had been arrested for threatening some vandals with a walking stick and several terrorists had been let out of prison early. New statistics showed that the European Union was about as popular with the voters as pubic lice. Unemployment had risen. All of these things could be brushed off with relative ease. It was one of the supreme ironies of modern life that, just as the state withdrew its responsibilities from so many spheres of activity, so the ridiculous notion that "the government ought to do something about it" had become more widespread among the public. If they wanted the government to do things, they shouldn't vote for low-tax parties, Sedgwick thought. The rare occasions when the government had felt able to do something in response to public pressure had been disastrous landmarks in the history of democracy. The Dangerous Dogs Act; there was a supremely dozy bit of legislation, stuck onto the statute books to appease a moronic electorate who'd been whipped up into a frenzy of bovine idiocy by the jackal press. Policemen wasting their time rounding up suspicious-looking animals, which turned out to be the much loved pets of elderly ladies who subsequently died of loneliness. For heaven's sake. Meanwhile the real crooks got away because everyone was scared to tackle the real issue. Teenage yobs got big dogs as virility symbols and encouraged them to develop as many anti-social tendencies as they themselves had—and, surprise, surprise, the hairy brutes bit people. Everyone with half an ounce of wit knew that it wasn't the fault of the bleeding dogs but of their parasitic lumpenproletariat owners, people who even dear old uncle Karl had written off as "social scum." But it was a political death sentence to say so. Sedgwick had been terrified that the press would interview his parents on the subject; they still lived in the suburban semi in Edgbaston in which he had grown up, and openly espoused toe-curlingly right wing opinions.

"String the bastards up," his old man would snort, polishing the collection of National Socialist memorabilia which he kept in a glass case in the dining-room, "and give the rest of the buggers national service. A few years in the army would cut the nonsense out of these child molesters and pit bull terriers."

He winced, and remembered his own speeches on the subject, lambasting the then government for its sloth in dealing with "this plague of nightmare creatures, straight from the horror films of Hollywood, which are preying upon the nation's children." What a load of codswallop. It had gone down well in the tabloids, though, especially his bit about how the then government, with their hunting and shooting mentality, probably thought there was nothing wrong with natural predators taking their pleasure thus. Well, his was a civilised party, not living in neanderthal times, and it demanded that something be done. Oh, yeah. Back in the twenties it wasn't a crime to suggest sterilising the wretched creatures. It was positively enlightened, for heaven's sake. Every progressive government in Europe was doing it, and the Webbs wanted it adopted as Labour policy. Was it so very wrong? Sedgwick banished the thought from his mind. You couldn't even think that sort of thing these days. Headquarters would be monitoring their brain waves next. It was ironic that he, who had encouraged much tighter control of the Party, should now be conscious of the dangers of his own ideas.

"Ten miles, DS," Josh's faintly metallic voice cut into the politician's reverie.

"Eh? Oh, right, yes," Sedgwick peered out at the agricultural land on either side of the dual carriageway as the Jaguar lunged effortlessly southwards. A farmhouse stood amongst fields of oilseed rape, small islands of hard-edged red and brown amongst the undulating bright yellow. He chuckled to himself as he remembered an intervention by one of his colleagues during agriculture question time a few years previously. The minister had innocently announced that rape was becoming increasingly common in the countryside and that, whilst some concerns had been expressed, the government saw no reason to take immediate action. The opposition MP, who was something of a law and order buff, had exploded with fury and castigated the minister for his cavalier approach to public safety and the general morality of rural communities. The minister, a somewhat dim patrician of the old school, grasped hold, in turn, of another end of this particular multi-pronged stick and suggested that whilst it was a bit unsightly, one soon got used to it and there was nothing specifically unsafe or immoral about making a few quid. His opponent had become virtually incandescent by this stage and said that if people were making money out of it they should be stopped forthwith. The minister expressed sly surprise that a party supposedly committed to private enterprise was so opposed to farmers making a bob or two. Sedgwick was impressed with this response, which he felt would scupper the career of his colleague and rival.

"We support free enterprise, but not crime," the MP shrieked.

"Rape is not a crime," the minister barked live on *Today in Parliament*, losing his patience, and, shortly afterwards, his job. Sedgwick marvelled at the ways of politics and continued to stare at the blaring yellow fields until they passed out of sight, replaced by a singularly unappealing piggery.

"Entering enemy territory, eh?" Josh offered, cheerfully.

"Yes, I suppose so," Sedgwick said, absently.

"Caught you out, DS," Josh grinned in triumph.

"Bollocks," Sedgwick knew that Josh sometimes tested him. It was annoying, but, as Josh pointed out, it kept him on his toes. The next time, it could be a tabloid reporter.

"We govern in the interests of all the people. We are a big-tent government. Come into our inclusive new third way of political dialogue. Even you rustic fascist peasant rabble," Sedgwick paused, "Satisfied?"

"It'll do," Josh settled back, happy, and watched the chauffeur nimbly slide the car off the dual carriageway and onto the road into Hengistley.

Sedgwick's opponent, Benedict Wolfesbain, had already arrived at the College, having strolled across the town park to it from his constituency office. A tall, sparse, angular man, he was accompanied by Luke Wallace, who was nervously explaining that there might be a few demonstrations at the College, but there was nothing to worry about. Wolfesbain was not especially worried in any case. He had served in Indonesia and Aden and was perfectly well aware that there was nothing the pampered bourgeoisie of Hengistley could throw at him with which he couldn't cope. As they entered the College gates, they were met by the first demonstration. Peter Drake, Johnny Ferral and their colleagues were gathered in the car park, clutching Union flags and placards denouncing the European superstate of which Damien Sedgwick was a puppet. When they saw Wolfesbain, they cheered loyally. Most of them had canvassed for him in the elections. If he was in any way disconcerted by the display, Wolfesbain did not show it.

"Hello, lads," he said, genially, "Here to show Sedgwick that Britons never shall be slaves, eh? Jolly good, jolly good. Where do I go from here, then?"

The patriots were all former students of Mercier's, and knew their way around. So did Wolfesbain, but he liked making people feel useful and important. Peter Drake pointed through an archway to the upper quad, where a large classical portico, incongruously tacked onto the gothic old grammar school building, marked the entrance.

"If you go up there," he said, "I imagine Fenneck will be waiting for you. Sedgwick isn't here yet."

"Splendid, splendid," Wolfesbain beamed, and loped through the quad to the College entrance. Around him, television crews from the local stations bustled in and out of the Hall on the other side of the quad, and journalists stopped photogenic female students to ask them what their feelings were about having such great men come to visit. As most of the students who had any idea about the visitors were already tucked away in William's classroom or in the hall, the journalists got a variety of answers, few of which made sense. One bemused chemistry student got Damien Sedgwick mixed up with a recently-gaoled murderer and said that it was disgusting that he'd been let out but she wouldn't put anything past that Mister Fenneck, he was a right little shit he was. Another was aware that there were politicians coming but knew only that he had been ordered to stay well away from them because of his extensive collection of body-piercings. William, who was wearing a suit of a cut which would have been considered old-fashioned before he was born and a black gown sprinkled with scurf, greeted Wolfesbain at the door.

"Mr Wolfesbain," he virtually curtsied as he spoke, "So kind of you to come. Do pop upstairs for a glass of sherry before we get to the big event."

"Lovely, lovely," Wolfesbain said, "I've already met some of your old students. They're having a Euro-sceptic demonstration down by the gates."

"Oh, yes," William said, through clenched teeth, looking at Luke with irritation glowing in the grey clinker of his eyes, "I'd forgotten about that. Very patriotic, I'm sure."

He ushered Wolfesbain upstairs to the meetings room. The Principal, gowned and jovial, was already there, enlightening Cowboy Sam about the provenance of sherry.

"Looks like a brothel," the MP commented.

"Indeed," William smiled sycophantically, "Most droll, Mr Wolfesbain. You've met our Headmaster, of course?"

"Of course, of course," Wolfesbain turned the warm glow of his charm onto the Principal, "Basil, Basil, how marvellous to see you again."

"Indeed, Benedict," the Principal replied cheerfully; unlike William he was not one of life's cringers, and addressed the politician as an equal, "For the last time, I fear. I shall be retiring soon, and another will be here to greet you. My successor is coming along for a meeting at five. If you're still around you might like to meet him."

"You'll be missed, Basil," Wolfesbain said, "You've seen the College through some rough times."

"Quite," the Principal said, "Most of them while your party was in office."

Wolfesbain laughed uproariously. He was well known at Westminster for his ability to laugh at himself, and indeed anything else. This had almost caused a momentary dip in his fortunes; someone had told him a rather good joke in the lobby as he was entering the House, which had just heard the momentous news from the Prime Minister that a minor celebrity had died in a yachting accident and was consequently in a fit of hypocritical silence. Fortunately, Wolfesbain had realised not only that he had made a gaffe but that it had almost certainly been picked up on the microphones. He had sprinted unnoticed for the exit and the intrusive guffaw was attributed to a blameless Welsh Nationalist.

William had sloped off to the car park with Luke Wallace.

"How many of them are there?" he barked.

"Five," Luke said.

"Blast," William snarled, "If there were more, it would look like an impressive demo. But a small, scruffy one makes the College, and, by implication, me, and the town, and, by implication, our Honourable Member, look like arses. We've got to get rid of them."

Luke nodded, vigorously. Out of the corner of his eye he could see more camera crews going into the Hall. They arrived in the car park and strode up to the gates, where a motley collection of placards and flags announced the presence of the Great Anti European Show of Strength.

"Hello, chaps," William opened, nervously.

The patriots gave an uncertain cheer. A pile of empty beer cans lay on the ground close by and William realised to his horror that most of them were drunk. Repressing the desire to get drunk with them, he decided to go for the straightforward approach.

"I'll give you a case of wine if you'll naff off," he said.

"No," one of the defenders of Britain said, "Fuckin' Sedgwick's coming. We're going to show him that Hengistley isn't some dumbarse little shithole that's going to let the Germans take over."

"And an admirable cause that is, I agree," William adopted a glassy smile, "But it just isn't terribly convenient. I could get into a lot of trouble over this, and we wouldn't want that, would we?"

"You'd put your cosy little job before sticking up for your country?" Peter Drake asked, derisively.

"Lads," William opened his hands in a faintly Semitic gesture, "Lads, lads. What did I teach you? What values did I encourage you to develop and keep close to your hearts, in those politics lessons, so long ago?"

"Look after number one and never trust a woman," his former students chorused.

"Well then," William said, "You see my point. I will give you vast quantities of booze if you piss off."

The lads went into a huddle to discuss the issue. As they did so, Luke tugged at William's sleeve like a nervous child. Coming towards them were Benedict Wolfesbain and a camera crew.

"Arseing bum," William said.

"William, William, my dear chap," Wolfesbain called, "I got a bit bored with your Principal. He kept banging on about Napoleon in that way of his, you know?"

The protestors nodded. They had been to the Principal's assemblies in their Mercier's days and they all knew.

"Anyway, thought I'd take a wander about, and I found these chaps. They were taking atmosphere shots in the quad, and I thought perhaps they'd like to see our Eurosceptics."

"The lads were just going, Mr. Wolfesbain," William said, who could not think what on earth had possessed the MP to do this bizarre thing.

Wolfesbain drew level with him, out of earshot of the camera crew.

"My sentiments exactly," he whispered, "But the ideal scenario is that they go because we encourage them so to do. Makes us look like conciliatory types. Good for both of us, eh?"

The MP winked at William, who was overcome with a tidal wave of relief that things might sort themselves out, if a little annoyed that this variant on his original plan was not one which gave all the credit to himself. They went over to the gang and Wolfesbain outlined his ideas.

"Essentially," he said, "There aren't enough of you to put the frighteners on him properly. So we're going to pretend that you're the advance party of a larger anti-Euro crowd. And we're all going to say on television that thanks to the persuasive skills of Mr. Fenneck and myself, you chaps are going to show that Hengistley is prepared to welcome even a treacherous brute like Sedgwick into its bosom, by clearing off."

"What's in it for us?" Johnny Ferral was blind drunk, but retained enough of his suspicious nature to be dubious.

"I'll buy you a pint," the MP offered.

"As will I," William interjected.

"Me too," Luke said.

"Oh, all right then," Peter Drake and the assorted protesters trudged over to their car. They stopped by the camera crew and Johnny Ferral peered into the lens.

"Is that thing working?" he asked, belching flammable vapours at the reporters, who confirmed that it was.

"In that case," he said, drawing himself up to his not especially great full height, "We wish to make a statement. We are the Hengistley Young Conservatives and National Freedom League and we were going to demonstrate to Mister so-called Sedgwick our undying hostility to his disgraceful unpatriotic views on Europe. But Mr Wolfesbain and Mr Fenneck, who we respect a great deal and who contribute a great deal to this town, have suggested that we should withdraw our protest so that this communist bastard gets a warm Hengistley welcome when he arrives. We are doing so because we respect Mr Wolfesbain and Mr Fenneck a great deal and they contribute a great deal to this town."

He paused and thought for something else to say. Wolfesbain and William prayed silently that the Good Lord would not see fit to allow Ferral further inspiration.

"Oh yeah," Ferral brightened, and muffled swearing was audible on the evening's broadcast, "But if Damien Kraut loving Sedgwick tries it on here just once—juuust once—(Ferral swayed as he jabbed his fingers, which held a smouldering cigarette, at the camera) we'll 'ave 'im. We will find a way, and we will have him, as the old song by Animotion puts it. Though not in the same way, obviously. There's no poofters in Hengistley, eh Fenneck?"

William whimpered like a beaten puppy as the camera swivelled to focus on him.

"Yeah, some of the teachers here are right lefty bastards, but not Fenneck. He tells it like it is. Straight right wing propaganda. No commies, no arse-bandits and no fucking feminists allowed in his lessons. That's why me and the lads are devotees of eighties music, you know. It's a reminder of a golden age."

"You're on your own now, pal," Wolfesbain muttered out of the corner of his mouth, as William tried to suggest, by hand gestures, that he had no idea what Ferral was talking about.

"Mr Wolfesbain. What a fucking brilliant MP," bawled Ferral, who wasn't finished yet, "How many elected representatives these days have enough of a sense of humour to tell a few gags about our immigrant friends, eh? And dykes. What was that one you told at the Christmas Party? Fuckin' hilarious, it was. Something about how they're ugly with no sense of humour. Can't remember the punchline but it was bloody brilliant. And very true, you know."

Wolfesbain stared up at the sky in despair. Above him, an aeroplane was climbing upwards as it left Gatwick. He did not know where it was going, but he wished desperately that he could be on it.

"Anyway, must be off," Ferral grinned horribly at the camera. He clambered into the back of a bright red Ford Escort, wound down the window and put his Union flag through it.

"Wahey!" he yelled, apolitically.

The driver revved the engine and spun the wheels, making a profoundly unpleasant noise. The car jolted forward, showering the onlookers with gravel, and shot out of the car park onto the main road.

"Go on, welly it," Ferral bawled to the driver, "I want to get to the pub to drain my spuds."

"Fuck that," said the driver, a rather odd young man known in his College days as Hannibal Lecter, "Look who's coming."

"Faaackin' 'ell," Ferral shrieked, "It's a government Jag. It must be Sedgwick. Play chicken with him."

*　　　　*　　　　*

The drive from the dual carriageway to the College was not a long one, and Sedgwick's car was now nosing its way down the long, tree-lined road on which the College had been rebuilt in the nineteenth century. It had taken the big Jaguar a mere ten minutes to lope past the 1990s executive housing estate on the town's perimeter, past the 1980s executive housing estate slightly further in, and past the 1970s executive housing estate that was far enough removed from the town centre to warrant suburban status but not so far removed as to warrant its own 'bus service. Josh and his master stared out of the windows like curious children, soaking up all the details of the place that they could as they drove though. This was an electoral tactic which normally served them well. On their way to an engagement, they would spot some chronic example of urban decay—a closed hospital, a vandalised school, an old lady being mugged; anything would do. In his speech, Sedgwick would attribute this to the previous government and promise that things were different now and it would all be sorted out, even if he had to intervene personally to do it. Hengistley, unfortunately, offered no such specimens of social blight. It was irritatingly well-kept and clean, with manifestly wealthy inhabitants who were walking their pedigree dogs or trundling about in the kind of chunky four-wheel-drive vehicles that the middle class seemed to find indispensible on primary school runs and journeys to Tesco's. No homeless people sat disconsolate on the roadside benches or begged by shop doorways.

"Telling these people that we're going to take them out of their misery doesn't strike me as a potentially successful message, Josh," Sedgwick commented.

"So we don't give that one, DS. Give the your cash is safe with us number. Or the clamping down on dole spongers one," his assistant said, "True, they don't have any social problems, but they think they do. Play on their unwarranted fears."

"They may not have any problems," the chauffeur interrupted, "But we do. Some berk's driving head on at us."

Sedgwick and Josh looked up from their notes and papers. A Ford, with several clearly inebriated young men protruding from its windows clutching Union flags and lager tins, was driving down the wrong side of the road straight at them.

"Get out of the bloody way!" the chauffeur yelled at the unhearing driver of the other vehicle, waving his free arm frantically. The other driver responded by making a gesture with the first two fingers of his left hand.

"Do something, for God's sake," Josh yelled. The red car was almost upon them.

"He's not going to budge," the driver shouted, "I'm going through that hedge."

He hauled vigorously on the steering wheel, dragging the big car out of the path of the speeding Ford, across the road and through the hedge. The hedge separated the Mercier's rugby pitch from the road, but also disguised the fact that the two were on different levels. The rugby pitch was a good four feet lower that the road and a steep bank down to it was invisible from outside. The Jaguar smashed through the privet and hurled itself from the top of the bank onto the field below. It hit the iron-hard turf with a metallic smacking noise and skidded sideways. Students who were wont to use the upper rugby pitch as a safe haven for smoking, working on the assumption that the staff would be too lazy to walk all the way up there to identify and persecute them, scattered in panic. Hannibal Lecter laughed maniacally and swerved across the road after the Jaguar, not bothering to slow down for the bank, despite knowing it was there, because he simply didn't care. Sedgwick's chauffeur wrestled with the slewing Jaguar and spun it round to face the pursuing Ford.

"Right, you little bastards," he screamed, "Do you want some?"

He plunged his foot to the floor and drove straight at the other car.

"Bollocks," Ferral yelled, "He's coming for us. Ram him, for fuck's sake."

Hannibal Lecter needed no encouragement. He smashed the Ford into the side of the government car with a cry of animal joy. Pressing hard on the accelerator, he pushed the Ford up the playing field towards a ramshackle cricket pavilion, inside which a couple of students were taking part in a rather intimate biology revision session. The Jaguar hurtled after them and shunted the Ford into the pavilion, demolishing it and revealing the happy couple before skidding backwards into a rugby post, which it also destroyed.

"Like that, you bastards, eh?" the chauffeur shouted, "There's more where that came from."

"Die, communist scum," Ferral replied, waving a placard, which depicted Sedgwick carrying out an act of fellatio on the President of the European Commission, with one hand and hurling a beer tin with the other.

"Bollocks to you, you little turd," the chauffeur slammed the Jaguar into the Ford again, laughing hysterically.

Sedgwick was enjoying himself rather less.

"What the hell are you doing?" he shrieked, "Get us out of here, now."

Through the window, he could see what seemed like a host of howling demons grimacing at him and bawling offensive messages. For the first time in his life, he had an insight into teaching.

The chauffeur was reluctant to abandon the duel with the red Ford, but orders were orders. He turned the Jaguar towards the car park and drove across the dusty rugby pitch towards it at high speed.

"Should I follow him?" Hannibal Lecter asked.

"Best not," Ferral said, "We've had our fun, and we did promise Fenneck an' Wolfesbain. I hope they didn't see that. We might lose those pints."

CHAPTER SIXTEEN

In the Social Sciences Faculty, high above the car park, Toby Gaskett looked on with interest as the battered Jaguar limped off the rugby pitch and shuddered to a halt beside the team from BBC *Sussex Today*, who swarmed round it like vultures.

"This is a very promising start, I must say," he remarked, "The camera crews are really excited. We'll get loads of coverage now."

He turned to the assembled students and gave his orders.

"Barnaby can't come on the demo. He's in a meeting. But he's asked me to get everyone down into the quad to show our resistance, right. So you lot with the banners go down and wait outside the Hall. I'll get some extra bods and join you in a minute."

There was a general movement for the door, punctuated by moments of low comedy as placards got stuck in it and long banner-poles prevented people from getting out. Much giggling ensued.

"Don't titter like that," Gaskett snapped, "You're supposed to be protesting about a serious issue. It'll look bloody crap if you're poncing about giggling like schoolkids."

The students sniggered even more. An uproariously funny remark was made about where the poles could be inserted. Gaskett sighed and followed them out. Revolutions sometimes needed to be manned by less than heroic elements, but why did he have to put up with people who'd been influenced by the wrong Marx? He made his way down to the Underworld, where his most trusted lieutenants were waiting with the guns from the German arms cache.

"They're very heavy," complained a particularly scrawny boy with a dose of acne which could be heard seething from across the room. People on telly seemed to chuck guns about as if they were made of feathers, but this beastly thing was made of wood and metal and weighed a ton. He was not used to effort of any kind, let alone the struggle of carrying big guns around.

"Stop moaning. This is important. We've got to hide the guns under our coats and whip them out at the right moment, right," Gaskett was, again, becoming increasingly aware of the immense difficulties which faced all the great leaders in History. Not that he could think of very many, as he didn't do that subject and the thought of reading about it to enhance his general knowledge had never occurred to him. Che Guevara, presumably, had had problems whipping his Cuban revolutionaries into shape, and doubtless Charles Manson was not unfamiliar with idiot subordinates.

"What sort of gun do you want?" asked an excitable boy who was making desperate attempts to grow a beard and succeeding only in creating a fine haze which made his face look blurred. The teachers did not bother to enforce the no-beards rule in his case because they could use him as a terrible object lesson to other boys who might be tempted to try this particular act of rebellion. Gaskett looked into the box. A rifle was too long and obtrusive, but a pistol was only little and people might not think it was real. The light machine-gun, which was actually rather heavy, was being wielded unsteadily by an unnaturally pale young man with dreadlocked hair and a Rastafarian tea-cosy hat. A machine-pistol, of a kind familiar to Gaskett from the war movies his father had made him watch as a child, remained. That was ideal. Not too heavy, but hard as hell. He picked it up and inserted a stick of ammunition into it, like Clint Eastwood had done in *Where Eagles Dare*. He smacked the magazine in hard and looked at his colleagues.

"Right," he said, "Let's go to work."

           *   *   *

Damien Sedgwick emerged from the rumpled Jaguar with as much dignity as he could muster, and gave a watery smile to the cameras as he did so. The local news team which had been filming Wolfesbain and William had been joined by photographers and reporters from the hall as word filtered through of the demolition derby on the rugby pitch. The minister was deluged with questions about his experience and what he intended to do now. Sedgwick thought quickly and decided to turn the situation to his advantage.

"As you can see," he announced, "My car came under attack from a racist mob. These people were clearly members of the National Front, and whoever put them up to this will be found and punished."

The local news team's camera swivelled onto Wolfesbain, William and Luke, who tried to apportion blame by looking at one another suggestively and succeeded only in resembling a nervous menage-a-trois. Sedgwick was momentarily disconcerted but carried on.

"But we in the government are not easily put off by minor intrusions such as this. I intend to carry on with this engagement and not let down the students of this excellent educational institution."

William stepped forward nervously, his head low and his body almost weaving, like a terrier which wishes to ingratiate itself with a new master. He gathered his gown around him like a shroud.

"That's, ah, awfully good of you, Minister. My name is Fenneck. I am the, ah, Head of Politics here. Welcome to Mercier's."

He caught sight of Josh. The two recognised one another instantly. Josh decided that he knew exactly who was behind the car incident and glared at William, who averted his gaze.

"Photo-op here, I think," said Sedgwick, who had not noticed. He arranged William and Wolfesbain on either side of himself. Spotting Annelise and Beth, who were trotting out to fetch William, he summoned them and added them to the group.

"This should make a nice shot for the papers, shouldn't it?" he smiled helpfully at the photographers. Sedgwick then put his arm companionably round William's shoulder. William froze.

"Get your fucking arm off me or I will break it," he hissed through clenched teeth. Only Alice was allowed to touch William, and even then only on the understanding that she had no amorous intent. William had a heightened sense of disgust at his own appearance and regarded with immense suspicion anyone who wanted to make physical contact with him. This made sex somewhat difficult, and at least one promising relationship had foundered because William, who wasn't very good at affection, found the girl's advances disturbing. Only someone with a very sick mind indeed would want to sleep with him, presumably out of some perverted craving for rotting flesh, he reasoned, and he had no desire to go out with a girl with a sick mind. The thought of physical contact with a stranger made him ill, and he looked at the politician with concentrated malevolence. Sedgwick hurriedly removed his arm and draped it around Annelise, who was not especially keen on the proximity of a questionable old man (Annelise was seventeen. Most people over twenty-five were old in her world.) William sensed her discomfort.

"And no touching up my students either," he snapped.

The group stood stiffly as the shutters clattered and snapped around them. A sickly hissing sound came from the car and an even less healthy swearing sound came from the driver.

"Right, that's enough," William barked, "Let's go to the hall. Are the students there?"

"Erm, yes," Annelise said, "But there's something I ought to tell you."

"I don't want to know," William said, "I really do not care any bloody more."

"You might," Beth said, agitatedly, "If you knew what it was."

"Elizabeth," William fixed her with a bloodshot stare, "For two years you have managed, uniquely among your peers and among your sex, not to annoy me particularly. Let us not spoil that record."

Beth and Annelise exchanged looks. The politics students who had been missing earlier on had arrived. The girls really felt that he ought to know that a number of them had made their own arrangements about overcoming nervousness. The Hertford Arms had connived at this with a rather irresponsible special lunchtime promotion of double measures of spirits at very reasonable prices, and the students had invested heavily in this generous offer. When Beth and Annelise had gone into William's classroom, they found a scene of disorder which made *Lord of the Flies* look like the Trooping of the Colour. A gang of boys from the rugby team were exposing themselves to passers-by in the road outside, whilst a studious boy who was expected to read Law at Cambridge was leaping from desk to desk like a gibbon. Some of the desks had been overturned and made into a fort, wherein several teenagers, thanks to the effects of any number of double whiskies on empty stomachs, were in advanced states of asocial paranoia and were convinced that their classmates wanted to sacrifice them to Wotan. The girls concluded that giving out any more drink might be counter-productive but were mobbed before they could give the spiked fruit juice back to Cowboy Sam. The drink was gone in seconds and the now dangerously inebriated students had lurched boisterously over to the hall, ready for anything. They were now sitting on the upper levels of the tiered seating, like the mob at a Roman Circus, ready to express their semi-coherent views on the issues of the day. But if William didn't want to know about this, that was his problem. Annelise and Beth had done their bit.

William ushered Sedgwick and Wolfesbain towards the Hall, with Josh snapping at their heels like a sheepdog. Luke and the girls ran ahead to ensure that all was ready and to try to limit any possible damage.

*   *   *

Mike had arrived at the exit from the Social Studies building just as those students whose protest was confined to unarmed sloganising reached the foot of the stairs.

"I'm sorry," he said, "But the Principal has decided that you are not to go ahead with this protest. We want to give a warm welcome to our important guests and not spoil the day for the Politics Department."

The sociology students, leaderless, paused. Mike was a little disappointed. He had been hoping that they would simply shove him aside and charge into the quad, forcing Sedgwick's staff to drag him away and saving the politician from a fate worse than death at the hands of Portia's whores. A pixie-faced girl with a stud in her nose and an unappetisingly vomit-coloured tie-died shirt emerged from the huddle.

"Why?" she asked, simply.

"Erm, well, ah, that's a good question, isn't it? And in a way, that's why we're all here. To learn about asking questions. To find out what sort of things we want to find out about. To look for answers and so forth," Mike babbled.

"But you," the pixie-faced girl observed, with perfect reason, "Are paid to answer these questions."

"Yes," Mike chuckled sagely, "And no. There are some questions which can never be answered, aren't there? Like about the origins of the universe, and the nature of love, and why Noel Edmonds got that second series."

"But this is a reasonable question," said the girl, for whom Mike was developing a degree of respect. It was a pity that she resembled a malign spirit with regrettable dress sense, really. Had he been younger, he would have considered her potentially attractive. Mike liked bright, sparky women. They were so much more interesting than the prim little middle-class miss types who tended to study English. Rebellion in the teenage years was a normal part of growing up, he felt. In Jonathan Bleach's heyday, or better still in the seventies when everyone was doing it, the customary way to rebel against established structures was to break down traditional staff-student barriers. Perhaps over a few cans of lager, an intimate curry *a deux* and a mutual exploration of the finer points of Far Eastern body massage, featuring baby oil and oddly-shaped vegetables. He banished the thought from his mind. Today's interesting rebellion was tomorrow's pain in the arse.

"It is," he conceded, "You're right there. I'm merely procrastinating."

"So tell me the bloody answer," the girl yelled.

"Could you remind me of the question again, please?"

The girl stamped her foot.

"Why should we give a warm welcome to a man who legitimises dicta-torship and why should we not spoil the day for the politics department?"

"Oh, yes. Well, because we have no proof that Mr Sedgwick legit-imises dictatorship, have we? I mean, you've only got your teacher's word for it, and I wouldn't go by anything he says. He doesn't know his *Lear* from his *Leviathan*. And the politics department wouldn't spoil it if *you* had a big day."

"Yes they fucking would," the girl shouted, "Bloody Fenneck hates sociology. Barnaby says he's a nazi. And after Politics lessons Beth Seymour turns up for our lessons spouting crap out of the Labour Manifesto because he's indoctrinated her with his fascist views."

Mike reflected that, even if William had been in the habit of promoting the Labour Party, which he very much doubted, only in the fetid atmosphere of the sociology department could quoting that organisation's policies be considered an act of fascistic deviance. But he did not say so. It was in his interests to end this debate as quickly as possible.

"Oh dear," he said, "You seem to have me bang to rights."

"Right," the pixie-faced girl said triumphantly, "We're going in."

"Strictly speaking," said Mike, who had spent a rather difficult term at Cambridge being taught by a logical positivist, "You're going out, as we are within the Social Sciences block at the moment."

"That," the girl sniffed, "Typifies the bourgeois-reductionist attitude of this college to the struggle for the liberation of third world peoples."

She and her colleagues surged out into the quad and charged towards the Hall, determined to create a scene and prevent the oppressor Sedgwick from getting in.

"Dear me," Mike mused ironically to himself, "I appear accidentally to have let them out. Do forgive me, William. I am so sorry, Principal. But I do you a great service of which you have no comprehension."

But he hadn't. Whilst Mike had been arguing with the girl, William had hustled his guests into the hall unseen from the Social Studies block. The only person to witness this was Jason Hinge, high in his eyrie on the caretaker's flat's balcony.

He had become rather bored sitting there waiting for something to happen and had taken out the little notebook in which he wrote poems. He liked it to be known that he wrote poetry as it set him apart from the other students and made him sound more intelligent than actually he was. He was blissfully unaware that every educational institution in the country has a frustrated adolescent poet knocking about somewhere. Unlike most teenage poets, however, he did not write sentimental, derivative love doggerel to the unlucky female who was the object of his affections. This was partly because he had decided that week to be bisexual and had taught himself to have a crush on the captain of the College football team, a boy so singularly unromantic that he made breeze blocks look delicate. Chiefly, however, it was because Hinge was unable to focus more than token amounts of adoration on other people. A towering passion, his self-indulgent idolatry of his own genius had filled notebook after notebook as he poured it out like so much effluent. The thought of this reminded him of another reason why he wanted to kill Alcock and Fenneck. He had gone on a joint Humanities trip to the battlefields of the Somme, and had been taken to an enormous crater which was the result of a bomb being set off under the German lines inside a tunnel dug by the British. Half way down the slope of the crater he had found an unexploded mortar shell, and had sat down beside it to write a moving eulogy hymning the great loss to society which would have occurred had he been killed in 1916. As he did so, one of Fenneck's thugs from the football team had emerged from a clump of bushes at the crater rim holding a suspicious-looking object.

"Sir," Joe Allen had yelled, "I've found a German grenade."

He had waved it enthusiastically in the air.

"Put the beastly thing down, you arse," Fenneck had shouted from the other side of the crater, "Those things are extremely dangerous. I don't want to get sued by your parents because you've lost a hand."

"I'll send it over to you, sir," Allen replied, and lobbed it high into the air. It described a graceful parabola and headed down to where Hinge was sitting with his mortar shell and his poetry.

"Bollocks!" Fenneck shrieked, and, turning to his Oxbridge candidates who were standing beside him, added, "Get away! The bloody thing could go off!"

Alcock had simply flung himself flat behind their coach, doubtless reflecting that hazards like this were unknown on the English trip to Stratford-on-Avon.

The object had bounced off Hinge's head just as Allen had yelled, "It's a stick."

Fenneck, lividly angry, had stomped off to swig Scotch from his hipflask. Alcock gave Allen a stern talking-to for exacerbating the heart conditions of the staff and imperilling the Oxbridge candidates. Not a word was said about the nasty bruise which Jason Hinge had sustained. He was particularly hurt as he considered himself, by virtue of his superior intellect, to be an equal with the staff, and was offended by their indifference to his welfare. When an old shell did go off, about a hundred yards away, Alcock had looked at Allen with a degree of disappointment, as if to imply that he had been on the right lines first time around. Hinge was furious.

Well, now he had his chance. The men who had shown him such contempt would learn what it was to trifle with a sensitive genius. He scanned the quad for signs of Alcock and Fenneck, and saw nothing. In the distance, he could hear screaming engines and the clatter of metal, but dismissed it as the post-modern social dialogue through road rage which was common amongst the testosterone-fuelled teenage drivers of the College. It soon died away. After a few moments, he saw them. Fenneck, with his long black gown, puffing along with Sedgwick, Sedgwick's assistant, and Wolfesbain. But where was the demonstration? Where were the banners decorated with Amazonian tribal symbols? And where was Michael Alcock? Hinge was confused. His shots were supposed to spark a revolt, but apart from the plants in the shrubbery and the hanging baskets there was no organic life in the quad on which to build a revolution.

Hinge's confusion was heightened by a strange breathing noise close to him which he could not quite identify. Peering through the sniper-scope as he was, he had no peripheral vision and could not see that the caretaker and his dog had returned from their walk. The caretaker was making a cup of tea, but the dog had decided to investigate the strange boy smell which had been left in his territory. The dog, an enthusiastic labrador-rottweiler cross called Beelzebub, usually shortened to Bubbles, liked boys. They played football with him on the College pitches and even the older ones like William and Mike were always ready to throw sticks or offer chocolate. Mike found the dog an ideal accessory for his Hemingway moments. He could wrestle with the big animal and play with a ball which had been confiscated from a pupil in 1978 and had remained there ever since. William liked the way the dog adored him in an uncomplicated way, never asking him what he was thinking, demanding to go shopping or trying to discuss "the relationship". As Alice had put it, "Dogs don't know you're ugly and horrible. They just know you like them." This was the basis for a perfect friendship.

Jason Hinge, on the other hand, hated dogs. A creature of self-advertised complex emotions himself, he did not understand the straightforward feelings which animals have and distrusted them accordingly. Dogs were large and unruly beasts, whilst cats gave off an air of suave superiority which he felt was his own prerogative. Cows might well turn out to be bulls and horses were just bloody enormous. Hinge looked up to see the slavering jaws of Bubbles the labrador just inches from his face.

"Fucking hell," he shrieked, and leaped to his feet.

Bubbles was delighted. A boy with a big stick was here to play with him. He bounced and pirouetted around Hinge in eager anticipation, barking cheerfully. To Hinge, this was like a savage wolf, circling its prey. He was reminded of how William had recently cornered him in the park. Nervously, he moved away from Bubbles.

"Nice doggie," he begged, then, his rational mind taking over, continued, "You're actually a stupid big brute and you don't understand a word I'm saying, do you?"

Bubbles barked loudly and enthusiastically in reply. His master had been thinking about problems with the boiler system as they were out walking, so the dog had not had much conversation recently. This boy was prepared to talk to him. Bubbles barked more to signal his pleasure and leaped up at Hinge to show how keen he was to play.

Terrified, Hinge edged backwards. He fell over the railing and dropped three storeys onto the unforgiving quad.

CHAPTER SEVENTEEN

Situated on the north-west side of upper quad so that it caught the afternoon sun, the Clutterbuck Hall sat smugly opposite the old grammar school building in which the staff of the Humanities Department plied their trades and the Principal governed through eccentric power-broking. It had a broad frontage of white stucco and a wide paved area, surrounded by ornamental shrubs, spread out before it like a small plaza. On warm days, the students liked to sunbathe there, and the space was used at weekends by local youths who skateboarded along it and performed ingenious tricks until ordered away by the caretaker. It was the jewel in Dr Walpurgess' crown as manager of the College site. Built in the 1960s from the legacy of a former pupil, it had been extensively modernised under his stewardship and was, he felt, the envy of every academic institution in North Sussex in general and in the Hengistley district in particular. The battered old metal entrance doors, whose movement went from a loud, irritating rattle in the slightest breeze to a positively homicidal flapping in a stiff wind had been torn out, replaced by smart blue-framed affairs with chunky brass handles; a clever, almost ironic, reference to the colours of the old grammar school tie. The new doors were mounted on springs and required an almighty effort to open, but at least they did not leap back into other people as old ones had, and they closed with a satisfying hiss, a bit, Walpurgess felt, like those sliding things on space-rockets in science fiction films.

Inside, a snugly carpeted reception area, featuring a mahogany cash desk and bar for such times as Mike and Susan put on plays, had replaced the lino-covered East German prison lookalike. Guests could wipe their feet on welcome mats with the emblem of the College, a drippy-looking sixteenth century virgin clutching a lily, woven onto them, and gaze in wonder at a huge mosaic featuring the same device and the legend "The Clutterbuck Hall" picked out in blue and gold on the wall which faced them as they came in. On each side of the mosaic, short flights of steps with brass rails led up to the Central Auditorium Area, as the Vice Principal's plans referred to it. Here, an enormous metal box could opened out into twelve tiers of elegant, and painfully ill-designed, seating, which consisted of long rows of narrow padded benches with very low and small back supports. Comfort could only be acquired at the expense of dignity, through draping oneself diagonally over the bench like a baboon lounging in a tree. The best seats, as on an aeroplane, were at the sides on the structure, where one could lean with slightly less agony against sturdy metal railings.

All of this was new, the result of months of painstaking work carried out at great expense at precisely the same time as the College had been making redundant several of its staff as a cost-cutting exercise. Portia, who normally had to pass the Clutterbuck Hall to get from her class-room in the old grammar school to visit friends who taught biology in a building in the corner of the lower quad, had rearranged her route to avoid looking at the new monument to posterity which Walpurgess was fashioning. She developed a deep and abiding hatred for him, and help-fully passed it on to her students, who impeded the building project by making off with expensive construction equipment. Replacing this, and installing video-cameras to prevent more thefts, had driven costs up so much that another teacher had had to be culled. Fortunately, it had been a PE teacher who Portia had not much liked, so her conscience—never an organ which she was going to wear out through over-use in any event—was untroubled. The Hall, for Portia, represented all that was worst about the College, with its pretentious little corporate-branded details, and the fact that students were discouraged, by order of Walpurgess, from going anywhere near it—except to hear the Principal's words of wisdom during the excruciatingly tedious assemblies which he liked to inflict on them in order to qualify for additional funding units. For a long time, she had harboured a fantasy about blowing it up. She had a chemistry A level. The College labs were unguarded and there was all sorts of stuff lying about with which she could have cause highly satisfactory mayhem. But revenge, she considered as she tucked into a positively depraved chocolate pudding, was a dish best consumed out of the fridge with a bottle of nicely chilled Chablis. The humiliation which the exposure of the politicians would bring would be reflected back onto the College, and the Hall in which their slide into disgrace began would endlessly be shown on television stories about the scandal. The institution would become a laughing stock, and it would serve the bastards right. Portia paid the barman for her lunch and bought a lager shandy. She went outside and sat at a picnic table in the beer garden with a packet of menthol cigarettes and a folder of year eight History projects. Keeping a weather eye on the house, she flicked through her pupils' work appreciatively and smoked, excited but curiously content.

Facing the seats in the Hall was a large podium, about a foot off the ground. This normally acted as a stage for plays but today had a long table on it, where the politicians were to sit with William and take questions as he acted as chairman. They had still not arrived. As the audience waited, they grew restive. The assorted parents and local dignitaries at the front were not as young as once they were and more than one was complaining volubly about the merry hell which these bloody seats were going to play with his dodgy hip. Others were fed up with being asked to move by journalists and cameramen who wanted to be in the best spots to catch the famous Damien Sedgwick being wrong-footed by some teenage lovely over his questionable deals. The arrival of the students, however, had been the icing on the cake. They had stumbled into the building shouting and laughing like football supporters, then staggered up the steps at the back of the seating to take their places on the topmost benches. Here they divided into two groups, and amused themselves as they waited by chanting football slogans at one another.

"Come on ye re-eds," the students on the left bawled.

"You're going home in a fuck-in' ambulance," their counterparts on the right jeered.

"Can you hear the Tories sing? No-oo, No-oo," the Labour students carolled, unmusically. The New Men had supplemented their generally meagre numbers by promising free drinks and an afternoon off lessons to anyone who would attend, and had taught them a few basic facts about what being a Labour supporter meant. The colour of the party, its leader, that sort of thing.

"He's bald! He's white! He's fuckin' dynamite! He's William Hague," the young Conservatives responded with more imagination than conviction.

"We got one, We got two, we got two hundred and fifty more than you."

"You're so vain, I bet you think this song is about you," the Tories roared, holding up a picture of the Prime Minister, captured in one of those gestures of his which resembled the Roman salute.

The camera crews annoyed the grown-up guests still further by clambering over the front benches in order to get newsworthy shots of what promised to be a very entertaining riot. They were rather disappointed when Annelise came running in, shouting, "Sir's coming! With the Principal! Shut up, shut up, please shut up."

Annelise was a pretty and well-liked girl, so the students' cat-calling subsided to muttered threats and obscene hand gestures. The camera crews sighed and turned back to the front, where they were briefed by an agitated Luke to try to work out if Mr Fenneck had a good side, and then film it.

The soundproofing on the doors of the auditorium, coupled with his premature deafness, meant that William did not notice the noise from the students when he came into the reception area with Wolfesbain and Sedgwick. Even as they entered the auditorium, he was oblivious to anything being awry; it smelled like him. The one thing which was readily apparent to him was that Luke's enthusiasm for Film Noir had coloured his ideas for lighting the hall. As the party moved along the sides, tall, sharp shadows were cast on the wall beside them. The podium was lit by a singe bulb, which dangled above it, shadeless. On the table, there was a bottle of bourbon and a cigarette, whose smoke spiralled gently upwards into the high, dark ceiling. William grabbed Luke and snarled orders to get the place back to normal.

"Don't you want to look like Humphrey Bogart?" asked Luke, who had also been influenced by the knowledge that in pure light William resembled an orang-utan.

"You'll look like James Dean if you don't sort this out," William barked, "The way he appeared after the accident."

Luke scurried off to the lighting booth and soon the hall was bathed in a brightness which stunned the audience. Blinded, the speakers stumbled forward into a glaring void.

Sedgwick, who was neither a smoker nor a heavy drinker, had been hit immediately by a cloud of alcohol fumes. The sickly vapour hung in the air like a gas attack at Ypres. The minister had a horrible flashback to the time when he had addressed a working men's club in Burnley on the need for more middle-class southern types, particularly women, in the party. The air had been thick with the fug of tobacco and bitter, and it seemed like an olfactory realisation of the atmosphere of hostility which had washed over him that night. The podium party was passing along the right-hand side of the benches to get to the front, and Sedwick could now see a host of unhealthily flushed faces peering down at him with somewhat out-of-focus hostility. It was going to be like that club all over again. One boy, whose head protruded from between the safety railings, appeared to be a kind of guacamole colour, and Sedgwick hurried along to get out of the way in case he found himself the victim of whatever it was the teenager had consumed. Josh, following behind, was less fortunate. The boy, whose name was Campbell, moaned softly and retched copious amounts of luridly coloured vomit from a height of ten feet onto the head of the Party researcher.

"Bloody hell," Josh spluttered, perhaps understandably.

The teachers and politicians turned and looked at him. His suit—expensively tailored from an expensive new fabric by an expensive new designer who was due to be given a peerage for his support for the party of the working man—was doused in the contents of Campbell's stomach. The minimalist, but stylish, hairstyle now featured identifiable chunks of vegetable matter from the microwaved curry the boy had guzzled for his lunch and washed down with several double vodkas mixed with a frighteningly-coloured drink whose manufacturers claimed it transmitted energy. Certainly, if the force with which the stuff had hit Josh and the surrounding floor was anything to go by, Campbell's stomach muscles had been mightily assisted by something. The Principal looked up at the boy, who was now unconscious. His face had a strange serenity about it, if one discounted the stream of purple drool seeping from the side of his mouth.

"Dear me," the Principal said mildly, "What a to-do. This is somewhat unfortunate, isn't it, William?"

"Quite, Headmaster," William fawned, ever the whipped cur, "As always, straight to the heart of the matter."

"Tory boys can't hold their drink, doo-dah, doo-dah," the Labour supporters chanted to the tune of the *Camptown Races*.

"Quiet up there, you commie bastards," William barked.

"What are you going to do about my researcher?" shouted Sedgwick, whose day was going from dreadful to downright horrible, "He's covered in sick."

"That, I fear, is only too obviously the case," William turned to the minister and adopted his usual posture of cringing servility, "And you may rest assured that I shall do everything in my power to put matters right. Lads, give Campbell a beating."

There was a flurry of feet and fists as half a dozen rugby players took out their adolescent angst on the recumbent body of their classmate under the excited gaze of the television cameras.

"No, no," conscious that the cameras were drinking all of this in with the same delight that had brought Campbell to his present sorry state, Sedgwick, somewhat to Josh's annoyance, squawked orders to stop the attack, "My Party is opposed to corporal punishment."

"Why do you allow the IRA to do it in Northern Ireland, then?" a young Conservative with a planted question and a burning desire to ask it yelled.

"Well said, that lad, well said," called Wolfesbain, who was also well aware of the cameras, "This is an issue which the government consistently evades."

"For goodness' sake!" Josh shrieked, "I'm drenched in spew here. Can you argue about that some other time?"

"Quite," the Principal said, genially, "Here comes Mr Alcock. He'll take you away and get you cleaned up."

Mike, who had just poked his head inquisitively round the door and had been so overwhelmed by the acrid stench and general Will Selfishness of the scene before him that he was about to poke it away again, nodded sycophantic assent.

"Yes, indeed," he said, "Come on up to the staff bogs. Then I'm sure we can get you some new kit out of the Drama Department dressing-up box."

"Blech," Josh said, morosely, and squelched after him.

Mike was conscious of a new possibility now. He did not know who this young man was, but assumed that he must be something to do with the politicians. If he could keep him occupied, then the others wouldn't leave without him and Portia's sinister designs would come to naught. The sociology students had proved highly disappointing. Mike had found them on the steps of the hall, deliberating over whether or not to go in.

"It's a bit like barging into a lesson, isn't it?" a weedy-looking specimen with a truly unfortunate nose was saying, "You know how embarrassing that is. Everyone looks at you as if you're a twat. It's pants."

"Everyone looks at you anyway, Concorde," the elfin girl snapped, displaying the kind of tact and sensitivity which would one day make her a hated and feared junior minister in the Home Office, "And what's the point of having a demonstration if you don't want people to look at you?"

"But these are Politics students," the boy whined, "They're right bastards. They take the piss out of everyone."

"Yeah, but from a fundamentally unsustainable position of bourgeois liberalism which is based on a limited, essentially capitalistic, concept of negative freedom," his leader pointed out, hoping that she had remembered Barnaby correctly.

"Not flying the flag for Mercier's radicalism, then?" Mike demanded with a jocularity he didn't really feel.

"They've already gone inside," Concorde mumbled.

"And you're not going in to express your views to them?" Mike asked.

"Probably best not to," the boy muttered.

Not for the first time, Mike was annoyed by the cowardly conformity of some Mercier's students. Saying so might well be a mistake, however.

"Well, I must say I'm glad," he breezed, patronisingly, "It was always a silly idea anyway, your little protest. Just nonsense. We really don't want to mess up the image of the College by doing daft things like that, do we? And those South American Indian tribes who were cleared off their land by that state-owned conglomerate to which Mr Sedgwick is an adviser were probably asking for it."

"No way," the pixie-faced female said, "We're going in whether you say so or not."

"Oh dear," Mike said, "Must you?"

He had scampered into the Hall with the Sociologists in hot pursuit, and was confronted with the bile-drenched Josh. As he led the unfortunate researcher out into the quad, he was annoyed to discover that the students had again halted and were engaged in another vigorous debate. Shaking his head in sorrow, Mike ambled over to the staffroom, feebly attempting to make conversation with Josh.

"Apart from, er, you know," he said, "What do you think of the place?"

"It's a very interesting institution," Josh replied, making a mental note to pop in and see the Minister of Transport as soon as he got back to Westminster. These bastards wouldn't be so cocky when a dual carriageway was built over them. He looked back at the entrance to the Hall.

"What are those people doing with those banners?" he asked.

"Oh, they're protesting against Damien Sedgwick's links to repressive regimes in Latin America," Mike said, "I hope you don't mind."

"Not at all," Josh had expected something much worse, though it had not occurred to him that worse might entail being chased by a carload of nationalist lunatics or doused in the contents of a teenager's stomach.

"Yes," Mike thought for a moment. Living in Brighton as he did, he was aware that it was difficult at the best of times to make conversation with an angry political activist, but when the activist was covered in sick things took on an even greater challenge.

"Erm..." he continued, hesitantly, "Look, here are the College flowerbeds. The roses are looking jolly splendid this year, I think. Um...there's a red one, and this one, as you can see, is pink...ah...The groundsman says that every week we use several gallons of chemicals for this area alone, you know."

"What's *that*?" Josh demanded, his voice suddenly rather shrill. He pointed at a crumpled form lying at the back of a row of sulky-looking geraniums.

Mike looked at it.

"Oh," he said, "That's Jason Hinge. He's a rather odd boy. Writes poetry and strikes all sorts of pretentious poses. I imagine he's showing off. Hoi! Get out of that flowerbed!"

Hinge did not move. Mike and Josh drew closer.

"Should his leg be at that angle?" Josh asked.

"I'm not sure," Mike said, "I'm an English teacher, you see. But I don't think so. It doesn't look very natural."

He fumbled in the pockets of his jacket and produced a pencil. Conscious that there was probably a better way of approaching the problem, but unaware of what it was—teacher training had never specified how to deal with this sort of thing—he prodded Hinge with it. The boy did not move.

"Oh, dear," Mike stared unhappily at the student, "I suppose we'd best call the authorities."

"But what about me?" Josh cried, "I've got vomit coming out of my ears."

"Oh, yes," Mike remembered, "Well, let's get you cleaned up first. He's not going anywhere for a while."

In the Hall, a semblance of order had been restored as the teachers and politicians took their seats on the podium. William made the introductions.

"On my left is the Right Honourable Damien Sedgwick, MP, Her Majesty's Secretary of State for the Co-ordination of Administration and Information. A rising star in the firmament of his Party, he was first elected in 1983, on the basis of a manifesto whose commitments he subsequently devoted himself to abandoning. The post he now holds was created especially for him and gives him wide-ranging powers to interfere in the activities of his ministerial colleagues, one of whom, doubtless unfairly, was recently alleged to have called him an 'oily, patronising, double-dealing creep.'"

The good burghers of Hengistley tittered appreciatively. Sedgwick smiled grimly. This fat oaf would learn the hard way not to piss him off. It occurred to him that anyone who could preside over a festival of idiocy such as the one which he had just witnessed would surely benefit from a dawn raid by one of the Department for Education 's new teaching hit squads.

"His reputation for unerring political judgement took something of a knock recently when he was exposed as having links with the South American dictator, General Julio Domingo. We all knew the government had moved to the right a bit but this seems to be going a bit far." There were more loyal sniggers from the audience. The cameras drank it all in and panned from William, who was wearing an expression of high minded innocence, to Sedgwick, whose rictus smile clearly masked a burning desire to commit acts of violence, to Wolfesbain, who was grinning broadly.

"And on my right is our own Member of Parliament for Hengistley, Benedict Wolfesbain."

There was an eruption of polite applause, which degenerated into raucous cheering as the Tory students got carried away.

"Mr. Wolfesbain has represented us for several years now and I think we're all agreed that he does it very well. He combines the job with being Shadow Home Secretary, advising a number of large and successful industries, and doing charity work which is disgracefully underreported."

Wolfesbain smirked modestly.

"Right," William said, uncharacteristically businesslike, "Let's have the first question."

*   *   *

Toby Gaskett emerged from the underworld and blinked as the bright spring sunshine caught him unawares. The machine pistol, which hung from his shoulder underneath his shabby gabardine, was reassuringly heavy, and he felt a sense of power. One of his lieutenants muttered an oath.

"What is it?" he said.

"Look in that flowerbed. It's Jason Hinge."

They walked over to the body. Gaskett nudged it with his much-scuffed boot.

"Stupid sod must have fallen off the roof. What an arse."

"There's been no shooting. Alcock and Fenneck must still be alive."

"Yeah," Gaskett thought for a moment, then looked over at the Hall. On the steps, the other Sociology students were still arguing.

"Let's get this show on the road, lads," he said, and trudged over to the demonstrators.

"What are you doing waiting here? Let's go for it!" he cried.

The students charged into the building to challenge the power elite. The revolution had begun.

CHAPTER EIGHTEEN

The full and frank exchange of views in the Clutterbuck Hall was becoming fuller and franker by the minute. Damien Sedgwick was beginning to lose the imperturbability for which he was justly famous and the raucous cheers of the students every time he fluffed an answer were not helping. It was quite unfair, Luke Wallace reflected from his seat next to the ITV cameraman. Poor old Sedgwick had been chased around the rugger pitch by a lunatic in a car, and then seen his researcher covered in spew from a drunken student. It was bound to knock someone off the top of his form. Even David Niven would have been kicked into a screamy stampy fit after that sort of thing. But that was the idea, wasn't it? The whole thing was a set-up, designed to make the Minister look bad and show that slick stage management wasn't everything. Obviously, it was a bit of a pity that both William and Wolfesbain seemed likely to get their fingers burned, which had not been the intention. Still, William didn't like teaching anyway and Wolfesbain could probably get over it. Luke watched the podium with interest as the politicians fielded their questions. Sedgwick was clearly getting the worst of things, and even the government supporters amongst the students were deserting him. This was not surprising. Students reacted as a pack to weakness, falling like hyenas onto a wounded beast, even if it was one of their own, which Sedgwick most definitely wasn't. Opening with a lame joke about crusty old farts and

implying that he wasn't one, Sedgwick had made the fatal mistake of trying to patronise them and was immediately worried like a rat at a terrier
convention. Used to the company of party hacks and sycophants,
Sedgwick disdained the bear-garden of Westminster, preferring to com-
mune with the masses via the internet and other forms of electronic
democracy. He was ill-prepared for the savagery of the Mercier's students.
Wolfesbain, on the other hand, remembered the students from the
General Election and knew that the first priority was to establish precisely
who was boss. There was no point pretending to be nice with these buggers. A few sternly-expressed big words and personal recollections of life
as a minister had set him up as the dominant one, the greatest ape in this
particular jungle. He commanded respect and fear. No student would ask
him a silly question. He sat securely at the front of the Hall, ramrod-
straight in his chalk-striped suit from Savile Row, his hawk-like features
surveying his questioners with the air of cold arrogance which had helped
him lose his original seat in 1992.

Sedgwick was sweating, irritable and worried. He needed Josh to be
feeding him lines, and he wanted this musty relic beside him to calm his
students down and give the Tory a hard time for a change. It was almost,
but not quite, a relief when the doors on either side of the back wall of
the Hall burst open and the Sociology students charged in.

"Sedgwick is a murderer!" the sociologists yelled as they ran up to the
podium with their banners. Or at least half of them did, for those who
had chosen the passageway in which Josh had been deluged with vomit
had skidded in the wretched stuff and slithered into a sprawling heap at
the foot of the podium. There they lay, swearing and groaning, whilst
the politics students jeered unsympathetically. The adults in the audience looked on in horror. Wee Beth pondered that it was now distinctly
possible that William would refuse to teach her or any other sociologist
ever again. Benedict Wolfesbain settled back in his chair and watched
with pleasure as those protestors capable of standing upright gathered
in front of Sedgwick and started yelling, "Scum! Scum! Scum!" over and

over again. Now the smug bastard knew what it felt like to be a Tory, Wolfesbain thought. Sedgwick himself adopted an expression of aggrieved dignity and hoped for the best. The Principal looked at William.

"This isn't anything to do with you, is it?" he asked.

"Absolutely not, Headmaster. Look at the length of their hair," the Head of Politics protested.

"Quite so," the Principal agreed. He peered at the nearest protester.

"Who is in charge of you, young man?" he enquired, gently.

"Barnaby," the boy said.

"Mister Worthington to you, you unwashed lout," William snapped, "And you will address the Headmaster as Sir or Doctor Godley."

"It's all right, Mr Fenneck," the Principal said genially, or as genially as he could given that he now needed to shout to make himself hear above the chanting sociologists and the jeering politics students, "We must have a little diversity. It makes the College a more interesting place, as I'm sure you'll agree."

"Absolutely, Headmaster, a most sensible policy, if I may say so," William gave words like 'servile' connotations of dignity and self-respect.

"Do you want to step outside, then?"

"I could have you any time, you long haired tosser."

"Don't talk to me like that, you fat bastard. I'll pull your head off and crap down your neck."

"Your mother won't recognise you after I've finished with you, you little faggot. I'll rip your spine out."

"Yeah, yeah. Hope you like hospital food."

William's heart sank as he contemplated this exchange between a sociologist and what he presumed was one of his own students. Then the crowd parted slightly and he realised that the boy was actually addressing the Mayor of Hengistley.

"I'm going to stick my boot into your middle wicket," the Mayor shouted, and, rising from his seat, proved as good as his word. The student crashed to the floor and whimpered.

"Does anybody else want some?" the Mayor yelled, waving his fist at the students, "I can have any of you little bastards."

"I must say, that's very impressive," the Principal said, "Especially for a Liberal Democrat."

"Is he a Liberal?" Wolfesbain asked, in surprise. Then he laughed.

"Hey," he said, "Shows you how much I know about the constituency, eh?"

Sedgwick had a momentary flashback to the time when, aged seven, his Cub Scout pack had been ambushed by a homicidal gang from the Boys' Brigade. That feeling of fear and confusion was with him again today.

Mike had rummaged through the *Arcadia* costume collection, and had found an old pair of trousers, a dinner jacket and a dress shirt which fitted Josh reasonably well.

"There," he said, cheerfully, "Quite the thing, I must say. You could be going to an early eighties New Romantic concert."

Given that Josh had spent the eighties in impotent fury as the Party was steamrollered beneath an invincible government, this was perhaps not the most fitting analogy. Josh felt that the New Romantic movement represented the high point of the period's vulgarity. His indignation was compounded when, in order to get rid of the all-pervasive aroma of stomach contents, Mike had sprayed him down with a brutally masculine deodorant borrowed from the rugby team's changing room. It seemed only polite to take the unhappy researcher along to the Conference Room, where Cowboy Sam fixed them up with bracing gin and tonics.

"How are things going over there?" he asked.

"I'm not sure," Mike admitted, "They sent me away with Josh here as soon as I arrived."

"I've seen you before," Sam announced, looking Josh up and down, "You came into the pub looking for silly beer. Are you sure you want a gin and tonic? I've got some alcopops here if you'd like one. Or you could have a mixture of cranberry vodka and orange juice. We call it a pink poofter."

"That's not very nice, Sam," Mike admonished.

"No, it's not," Sam agreed, "But then you and I have robust manly tastes which not everyone shares."

"I do," Josh said, coldly.

"Good-oh," the off-license manager smirked, "I'm only being helpful."

Josh looked around the room.

"Looks like a brothel."

"Wish it was," Sam remarked, jovially, and was rewarded with another glacial look. Mike shuddered.

They went over to the window, from which the Hall entrance was visible. Despite the soundproofing, there were faint sounds of yelling coming from inside. A shot rang out, followed quickly by another, and then silence. A minute later there was more shooting.

"Bloody hell," Josh gasped, "Someone's started shooting. Got to get back. DS is in there."

"And so's a looney with a gun," Sam observed, "I'd leave it if I were you. It'll sort itself out. Things like this usually do, you know."

"The students," Mike croaked, "There's nearly a hundred of them in there. We have to do something."

"I'll put on some Elvis," Cowboy Sam offered, ambling over to a portable hi-fi which was kept in the room to record meetings, "I find that often helps with the thought process. And if it gets really difficult, we'll try Bob Dylan."

The opening bars of "Jailhouse Rock" filled the small room.

"Shit!" Mike cried, "Susan might be in there."

"True," Sam observed, "Who's Susan?"

"You don't know her," Mike said, "She's our new drama teacher."

"Well, let's ask ourselves the important questions. One. Young? Two. Pretty? Three. Goes like a mule?"

"One, yes, two, yes, and three I'll never find out if somebody shoots her, so I'm going over there to get her out."

"Wahoo!" Sam shouted, "Go for it, my son."

Mike charged down the stairs and into the quad, closely followed by Josh. He was just entering the Hall when it occurred to him that a mule probably wasn't a very nice thing to go like.

Susan was indeed in the Hall. She had gone to William's meeting to ensure that the building wasn't too badly damaged by the politics students. If it was wrecked, the performances of *Arcadia* would be set back by at least a week. Susan had sat in mute despair as the rising tide of chaos had lapped about her feet. Positioned in the front row next to the Mayor, she had politely rebuffed his generous offer, made as he sat down, flushed with violent bravado, of a good seeing-to in the stock cupboard. The Mayor had quite forgotten, in his testosterone-fuelled excitement, the presence of his wife on the bench next to him. She had pulled him to his feet and punched him hard in the face.

"I'm sorry, my dear," she said to Susan, "You'd think at his age he'd learn. But he reads about that Peter Stringfellow and suddenly he's as randy as an Italian rabbit on Viagra. Normally I put things in his tea, but I forgot this morning's dose."

"That's quite all right," Susan said, nervously.

The Mayor staggered to his feet and spat out a bloodied tooth.

"There was no need," he said, plaintively, "For that sort of violence."

"Ooooh!" his wife shrieked indignantly, "That's rich, coming from the Karate Kid Part III here. You laid that poor teenager out flat."

"More'n I've ever done to you," the mayor muttered bitterly.

Their discussion was interrupted by Toby Gaskett.

"Shut up, you bastards," he yelled, waving his arms about. The mayor, who was standing next to him, did so, though admittedly only in order to draw breath prior to calling him a cheeky long-haired little fairy. No-one else did. They were all too busy with their respective quarrels. Gaskett tutted in irritation and nodded to two of his henchmen. From beneath their baggy overcoats they produced rifles and, pointing them at the ceiling, fired.

The brawling, shrieking, caterwauling mob stopped.

Sixty-three politics students, ten parents, five teachers, six members of the district council, the mayor, his wife, Luke Wallace, four cameramen, three photographers, a handful of journalists, thirty-seven protesting sociologists and two Members of Parliament stared at Toby Gaskett. It was the best moment of his life.

"That's better," he said, and began to take the manifesto of the Rainbow Revolution from his pocket. His lieutenants lowered their rifles and pointed them, casually, in the general direction of the audience. The Principal leaned over to William.

"Are *they* anything to do with you?" he asked.

"Certainly not, Headmaster," William snorted, "Look at the way that mimsy little woofter's holding that rifle. One of my students would hold it like he was a man and it was a weapon, not as if he was a big girly and it was a knitting needle."

"Barnaby Worthington again, do you think?"

"I fear so, Headmaster. As I've said before, one doesn't like to say it about a colleague, but I fear he's not quite sane."

"On the other hand, it could be a piece of performance art by the Drama Department," the Principal said. He looked over at Susan.

"Are these people anything to do with you?"

"I told you bastards to shut up," Gaskett yelled. He gestured to his aides and more shots were fired. Plaster and debris rained down from the damaged ceiling.

Susan felt an overpowering desire to smoke.

"Are those cameras on?" Gaskett asked.

The journalists nodded.

"Right," the boy said, "We're the Rainbow Revolution, right."

Some members of the rugby team sniggered audibly. Gaskett decided to ignore it for the time being. He didn't want to have to do it, but if the time came to execute hostages he knew which bastards were going first.

"We represent all the alternative viewpoints in this country and in the world," he continued, "Viewpoints that you and you don't represent."

He pointed at Sedgwick and Wolfesbain.

"What about us?" the Mayor asked, indicating himself and his colleagues, "We're Liberal Democrats."

"You don't either, you old bastard. No mainstream politician, with his boring, safe, bourgeois view of the world, can hope to understand what it's like to be young and radical and alternative."

"Oh, I don't know," said the Mayor, who wasn't going to let this little whelp make the running, "I went to a Hendrix concert once."

"Who's that?" Gaskett asked, derisively, "Bloody classical music. You still don't represent us. You're still Mister Square. And then there's the other scumbags, who try to keep us down with their old-fashioned educational methods. They teach us nothing about life, man, nothing about what it's really about."

He stared at each member of staff in turn, finally reaching the Principal.

"This one," he pointed at the Principal for the benefit of the cameras, "Has absolutely no idea how to relate to the thousand teenagers he's in charge of, man. He's living in a previous era."

The Principal smiled amiably at the journalists.

"Well, the time has come," Gaskett announced, "Young people from the radical alternative fringe have had enough, right."

Mike and Josh crept in at the back, drinking in the student's every word. Recollections of his childhood came flooding into Mike's mind. He remembered during one of the school holidays in 1968, seeing, on his parents' prized new television set, young people in America who were dressed exactly like Gaskett was now. They had the same hairstyles, the same huge, flapping trousers, the same selfish, petulant idealism. It was Gaskett who was living in the past, not the Principal. Even his vocabulary was quaintly dated. No-one spoke like that any more. Gaskett might as well have been conducting a revolution in the name of the Indian Raj. Mike moved quietly up the steps at the back of the seats and slipped into place beside the BBC cameraman.

"We're doing this live on television so that the world can see what we stand for, and so that young adults round the country can rise up spontaneously," Gaskett continued.

"He isn't, you know," the cameraman whispered to Mike, "It's all being recorded. We don't do live broadcasts of things like this. I wish we were, though. I could get a fucking BAFTA for this, especially if there's a bit of serious aggro."

"Just supposing," Mike muttered, "A bit of aggro could be arranged. How would that help the career of the chap who organised it?"

The cameraman looked at him and grinned.

"Oh, I see. We'd have ourselves a national hero, if that's what you're getting at. Who are you trying to impress?"

"Good enough for me," Mike whispered, ignoring the question. He turned to Wee Beth, who was staring transfixed at her fellow-student as he rambled nonsensically about his vision of a better world, which appeared to feature the Glastonbury music festival being held more or less weekly.

"Do you reckon they'll actually use those guns?" Mike whispered to her.

"I'm surprised they know how they work," she said, "That crowd are all stoned half the time. And all they've shot at is the roof. That's pretty easy to hit, isn't it? And they aren't holding the rifles properly. It would be easy enough to disarm them. Though I'm not volunteering to do it myself."

"My thoughts precisely. Now, in a minute, I'm going to cause a diversion, and I want you to take the female students off the seating by the steps at the back, then get them out of the Hall. Can you do that?"

"I can try," Beth whispered, dubiously.

"I'm sure it'll work. Let's face it, with hair that length they'll never be able to see out to shoot straight."

He inched slowly over to where the rugby players were sitting in sullen silence, swigging from their lager cans and looking with undisguised contempt at Toby Gaskett. Mike took a tin from someone's bag and opened it matily.

"Oi," a tall youth said, "That's mine."

"I'll replace it if you just follow along with what I'm about to do," Mike said, "We're going to cream these hippy bastards."

"We have a list of demands," Toby Gaskett was saying, "And we will not release our hostages until our demands are met."

The Head of English stood up.

"Bollocks," he said, with a confident contempt he did not feel. Thinking about it, he supposed he felt the contempt part. Better than nothing.

Excitement and anxiety rippled through the hall as if a breeze block had been dropped into the stillness.

"Sit down," Toby Gaskett commanded, realising what it must be like to be a teacher dealing with annoying children, though not, of course, imagining that he could be categorised in that way, "I haven't finished yet."

"You're talking balls and we're all bored with it, aren't we, lads?" Mike turned to the rugger team and they growled their assent. The captain stood up and pointed at the sociologists, encompassing both the armed and unarmed varieties.

"Kill the trolls," he yelled.

The rugby team and those other male politics students still capable of movement surged down the gangway. The few sociologists with weapons had only a few seconds to work out how to use them before they were overwhelmed by the mass of flesh that was William's upper sixth. Clambering over the selected guests in the front rows, they pelted Gaskett with beer tins and attacked his supporters. The revolutionaries retreated towards the back door of the Hall as the assault on their crusade continued. Mike made his way into the morass of struggling bodies and found Susan.

"Susan," he cried, "You're safe. Come with me, quickly."

"Mike?" Susan stared at him, "What on earth are you *doing*?"

"I've, er, come to, ah, well, rescue you," he said, blushing as he realised how toe-curlingly corny this sounded.

"You patronising chauvinist bastard," Susan said, "But thank you. It's awfully sweet of you to think of me."

"That's, er, all right," Mike said, blushing again, "No problem. All in a day's work as, ah, Acting Head of Faculty. Perhaps we should get out of here, though."

"You're going nowhere," shouted a boy with greasy dreadlocks, a faded purple shirt, a Luger, and memories of innumerable bad films. He pointed the pistol at Susan.

Mike hit him with a chair. It was not a cinema prop chair and didn't break wittily on the lad's head, but it had the desired effect. The boy yelped and fell to the floor.

"What did you have to do that for?" he whined as blood poured from his nose.

Grabbing Susan's hand, Mike ran from the room. The thought that he was rescuing his beautiful colleague from the slack, gum-chewing jaws of teenage death was the icing on the cake of the knowledge that the chaos in the Hall would almost certainly have prevented Portia's plan from coming to fruition. Mike had a warm sense of personal redemption.

"You bloody neanderthal," Susan said, "You hit a boy with a chair. That's no way to solve arguments. And it's an appalling example to set to the kids. If you think that kind of old-fashioned approach impresses me, you're wrong."

Nonetheless, she embraced him tightly. Annelise, making good her escape via the same route, caught Mike's eye and winked at him. Mike gave her a thumbs up sign behind Susan's back. He tried to remember if he had changed his socks that morning.

The Principal, William, Wolfesbain and Sedgwick were edging towards the Fire Escape.

"Things do not appear to be going as planned, William," the Principal observed.

"No, indeed, Headmaster," William wheezed, "I am monitoring the situation and I can assure you that the malefactors will be punished most severely."

A gang of politics students had grabbed a sociologist by the feet and were bouncing his head off the floor like a pile driver.

"They, for instance, are going to be given an extra essay to do," William offered. Despite his protestations to the contrary, he quite liked his own students. However, he found it difficult to regard teenagers he didn't know as human beings, and this particular boy was wearing one of the oversized jackets associated with American rap musicians. William felt he was learning a valuable lesson.

"That seems fair," the Principal said.

The female students poured into the quad, followed closely by the adult guests and observed from above by Cowboy Sam, who cranked up the volume of the meetings-room cassette player and held the speaker out of the window. He opened a bottle of Champagne and swigged it from the neck as he sang along with Elvis. Several sociologists dashed out of the Hall, fleeing from the violence in disarray. A few armed revolutionaries also made good their escape, and tossed a grenade behind them to cover their retreat. The foyer of the Clutterbuck Hall blew outwards in an eruption of smoke, broken glass and unpleasant sound.

From the other side of the college came the cadets, a relic of the grammar school days which virtually everyone, with the unsurprising exceptions of the Principal and William, loathed. Delighted to be able to demonstrate their skills, they broke out their rifles from the armoury and charged at the revolutionaries with enthusiasm.

In his office, overlooking the quad, Dr Walpurgess surveyed the destruction with horror. He rounded on Barnaby Worthington in fury.

"Look at what your bloody students have done, you communist halfwit," he yelled, "They've blown up my Hall."

"My students are pacifists," Barnaby protested, "They fight for peace."

"And I suppose they shag for chastity too," the Vice Principal shouted, "Look at the Hall, you berk. It's on fire. Your students did that. I saw the little long-haired commie bastards and I'm going to have their pocket money docked until they're drawing the sodding pension if that's what it takes to repair that building."

Elvis informed Dr Walpurgess that he gave him strength to carry on.

Walpurgess took another look into the quad. Toby Gaskett's urban guerrillas were heading towards the old grammar school building, pursued by a motley army of cadets and rugby players. Sporadic shots occasionally rang out over the sound of screams and breaking glass. The Police needed to be contacted and, on reflection, it seemed like a good idea to drive up to the station rather than to 'phone. The Vice Principal had just bought a new Porsche and he wasn't going to have that blown up as well.

"I'll see you later, you fucking lunatic," he snapped, and stormed out. Barnaby Worthington looked at the quad and saw a colossal fight taking place between his own students and William's. A couple of casualties lay propped up against the trees, and black smoke gushed from the Hall. Mike and Susan were trying to usher non-combatants out into the car park. They kept exchanging meaningful looks. Camera crews circled the action like vultures. Barnaby could not understand what was going on, but he had a horrible suspicion that somehow his mission to inculcate progressive thinking amongst the young people of Hengistley had failed. He was too bewildered to appreciate that in a way he had entered Mercier's history by being the first person to get the Vice-Principal to show some human emotion.

*   *   *

Jobelle had been unable to find the Minister's limousine. The only big car she could see was a very scruffy Jaguar which looked as if it had just been in a fight with a lorry. She wandered about the car park and looked for someone interesting to talk to. A brightly-coloured Volkswagen with enormous spoilers was parked near the exit, the rhythmic thuds of teenage music hammering from its speakers. Jobelle walked over to it, chewing listlessly on her gum. A boy in a bulky jacket sat inside.

"Awright?" he said.

"Yeah. You a student 'ere?"

"Yeah. S'borin'. You ain't a student. I'd 'a recognised yer."

"Naw. I work over there," she gestured vaguely in the direction of Bacons Road.

"Watchoo doin' 'ere, then?"

"Came to see the politicians."

"Sod that," the boy said, "Me'n the lads, we're goin up to Crawley. Clubbin'. Want to come?"

"Might do," Jobelle said.

The first sounds of gunfire and chaos reached them.

"Oh, blaady 'ell," the boy said, "It's some sort of ruck. I can't be doing with that. The Bill will be down in a minute, and they've got it in for me. Hop in if yer comin', 'cause I'm off."

Jobelle did not actually sniff the air, but she sensed that there was a new atmosphere in the campus. People were running, and she could hear screams and bangs. She got into the car. As it roared flatulently off up the road, she did not look back.

*   *   *

Inside the Hall, the Principal looked at his watch.

"My successor is due to come and see me any time now," he said, "Would you like to meet him, Benedict?"

"Lovely, lovely," the MP replied, "I'd be delighted."

"William, you can sort things out here, I'm sure," the Principal smiled winningly at his subordinate as he set off for the old Building, "Perhaps you could organise a cleaning-up party for that explosion in the lobby, and discipline any particularly persistent offenders."

"Absolutely, Headmaster," William looked at the scene of devastation as the remaining revolutionaries, cornered in the lighting booth, fired off occasional shots from their weapons and tried to blind their attackers with a spotlight. The politics students were preparing to burn them out with bottles of ethanol looted from a nearby chemistry lab.

"Just leave it all to me," William said, reassuringly.

He picked up an abandoned rifle and looked at it with interest.

"A Mauser 98, Headmaster," he said, "Waffenamt stamp, 1940. Standard Wehrmacht issue. Beautiful condition. You could kill an elephant with one of these."

He chambered a round and aimed the weapon at the lighting booth, nestling the butt comfortably into his shoulder.

"Handles marvellously, Headmaster," he said, "You must have a try. Almost as good as the Lee-Enfield."

Sedgwick felt faint. He was reminded of a study visit he had once had to an American congressman who had insisted on showing him the family weaponry collection in the back yard and refused to take no for an answer when he offered Sedgwick a go with a pump-action shotgun. There was a loud bang as William fired the rifle at the spotlight, which shattered and showered the students with broken glass. The sound of screams and swearwords drifted down into the hall. William looked to the Principal for approval, like a child which had mastered a particularly challenging piece of long division. The old man smiled.

"Do try not to kill any of them, William," he said, and wandered off.

"But what about me?" Sedgwick bleated.

Josh appeared at the back door, dressed, for some unaccountable reason, for a nineteenth century dinner party and accompanied by a girl.

"DS," he yelled over the cacophony of breaking glass, moaning and foul language, "Over here. Yvette here says she can get us out of this awful place."

Sedgwick needed no further invitation. He ran to the door and followed Josh and the girl down the fire escape. William gazed after them indifferently. He wondered for a moment why Sonia Thrale was calling herself Yvette, then put the rifle down and ambled over to ask his students if they wouldn't mind not blowing up the sociologists with ethanol.

CHAPTER NINETEEN

Bubbles was disappointed. The boy who he had hoped would play with him had gone. But he had left his unusual stick behind, which was nice. The big yellow dog subjected it to the thorough scrutiny which is the hallmark of his species. It didn't smell like sticks from the park, but Bubbles was not unduly bothered by this. He was an easy-going animal, who had always believed that variety was the spice of life. He picked up the stick with his teeth. It was surprisingly heavy. Perhaps his master would be interested in it. His plumy tail wagging vigorously, Bubbles ran towards the narrow door into the caretaker's flat.

Below him, in the quad, Mike had successfully herded several dozen students away from the pandemonium of the Hall, watched by several camera crews whose movements were being co-ordinated by Luke Wallace. He was also observed by an admiring Susan. She had not seen this side of him before. Nor indeed had Mike, who was not entirely clear about what he was doing.

"Go to the rugby pitch, like in a fire drill, and wait there for your form tutors," he shouted, as the screaming girls fled from the burning building. Mike hoped that the form tutors themselves were somewhere to be found. The revolutionaries had disappeared and no-one was particularly keen to look for them. A group of rugby players followed, carrying two sagging bodies as trophies.

"Look, sir," their leader said to Mike, "We've captured these communists. Do you want us to lynch them from the lamp-posts like they did in Romania?"

"For the love of bloody hell," Mike shrieked, "The telly people are filming all this. We'll all go to prison if you do anything like that. Call an ambulance and chuck the stupid sods into the back. I'll tell the journalists that you rescued them."

Disappointed, the boys did as they were told. Suddenly, a shot rang out from the top of the old building. A bullet whined and cracked as it ricocheted around the quad.

"Arse," Mike yelled, "They're still out there. Everybody down, now."

The students obeyed, but the camera crews remained alert, greedily drinking in Mike's heroism as he inched towards the entrance of the Victorian grammar school. Suddenly, the caretaker appeared on his balcony, holding a rifle.

"Sorry about that," he yelled, "Bubbles tried to run through a three foot wide door holding a four foot long gun. It went off. Scared the living daylights out of the poor brute. Do any of you know anything about this thing? What's it doing outside my flat?"

Collective sighs of relief rose from the quad. The last person to emerge from the Hall was William, his face blackened from the explosion and fire which had been the perhaps unsurprising result of his students' all too successful chemical experiments.

"There's no-one left in there," he spluttered, and coughed up a thoroughly unpleasant-looking substance.

"Where's Sedgwick?" Mike demanded.

"One of the girls took him away. Sonia Thrale. Calling herself Yvette for some reason."

"Yvette?" Mike squeaked.

"Mmm. Strange bint."

William coughed some more, then asked Mike for a cigarette. Mike fished in his pocket for a battered metal cigarette case. It had been the property of Limping Taff, an elderly Latin master at Mike's grammar school, who had fought in the war. Limping Taff had reminisced to his pupils that everyone in the desert hoped to cop a Jerry bullet on the cigarette case worn next to the heart. This was, however, insufficient protection against an Italian land mine if you trod on one, as Limping Taff (known until that point as Footie Taff) had done after an over-enthusiastic celebration of the victory at El Alamein. When the old man died, his property had been auctioned off, and Mike had kept the famous, if ineffective, cigarette case as a reminder of the cruel nature of fortune. He thought about this as he watched William inhale. Just when everything was going so well, poor Sedgwick had been kidnapped by one of the slappers. Mike was morally opposed to violence towards women, but at this precise moment he felt that Lady Luck could do with a bloody good back hander. How devious of Portia to employ one of the students as a whore. How could she live with herself? But then, why hadn't he tried to find out who the bloody whores actually were? Then again, if Yvette was actually a student, there'd have been hell to pay if she'd discovered that one of her bosses was a teacher at her own College. Bad thoughts crammed impatiently in the thoroughfares of Mike's mind like a traffic jam on the M25.

"And you didn't stop her?" he asked, nervously.

"Of course not. She was taking him to safety."

"That's what you think," Mike muttered.

*   *   *

Damien Sedgwick sat in the back of the car with Yvette. Despite the battering it had taken on the rugby pitch, it was still running reasonably. It slewed out of the car park, watched by the evacuated students, and turned right towards Bacons Road.

"The local party members have laid on a bit of a reception for you at the constituency chairman's house," Yvette soothed, "You can have a glass of champagne, relax, unwind, take your mind off what's happened."

"That sounds marvellous," the minister sighed.

"I can take the car to a garage while you're there, minister," his driver said, "And borrow a vehicle from the police station to take you back up to London in."

"Excellent idea," Sedgwick agreed, "Josh, you go with him. Sort out the paperwork and make a statement to the plod about what went on in there. Then bring them round to the house and I'll speak to them."

"There's no need to bring the police to the house," Yvette said quickly, "We'll bring you round to the station. The constituency party chairman lives in quite a posh area, and I don't think it would do his reputation much good if a police car was to be seen going up the drive."

"Absolutely. I can see the point of that," said Sedgwick, who didn't relish the thought of being seen to be taken away from someone's house in a panda car. He would not have put it past some of the nut-cases in the College to arrange for *Sun* photographers to capture the moment.

The government Jaguar, battered and scuffed like an eight-year-old boy's school shoes, slid past the pub and turned off the road into the driveway of number twenty, Bacons Road. From the pub garden, Portia watched it with pleasure and anticipation. A couple of minutes later, it nosed out onto the road again, minus Yvette and the minister, and headed towards the town.

"Welcome to my pleasure dungeon," Portia giggled.

Inside the house, Sedgwick took in the deep carpets, the pleasant furnishings and the complete absence of people.

"Where are the other party members?" he asked, "And the constituency chairman?"

"They'll be along shortly," Yvette said, "I imagine they've been held up by that riot at the College."

She disappeared for a moment, going into what was presumably the kitchen. She emerged clutching a bottle of champagne and two glasses.

"This will make you feel better," she said, "I found a message on the answering-machine, by the way. The others have been held up at the College. The police are questioning everyone. It'll be at least an hour before they're back."

Sedgwick was curiously relieved. Pleasant though it would have been to mingle under normal circumstances, he was happy to wait for a bit and let the tension flow out of his soul. This girl seemed pleasant enough and she was looking after him nicely. Of course, compared to the other people he had met that day, anything short of a wrestling match with an alligator would have been a light diversion. He accepted another drink and sat down in a Swedish armchair.

"The constituency chairman says that you can use his jacuzzi if you want," said Yvette, who had read an interview with the minister in which he had confessed that he found the things immensely comforting after a hard day slaying Whitehall dragons, "It's upstairs. I imagine you deserve it after a dreadful experience like that. I find them awfully relaxing myself."

"Yes, they are, aren't they?" Sedgwick replied, his judgment slightly dulled by the champagne, for which he had a limited tolerance and which he had gulped back rather quickly. Its effects were more marked thanks to Yvette's thoughtful addition of some harmfully strong Polish vodka from Cowboy Sam's off-license.

"Shall I sort it out for you, then? You've got at least an hour before the others come back. I'll clean your suit up while you're in the tub thingy."

"Oh, you *are* an angel," the minister sighed, "You've no idea just how perfect it all sounds. Are you sure it isn't too much trouble?"

"None at all," Yvette dashed off to make the necessary arrangements.

*   *   *

Wee Beth returned from the rugger pitch and reported to Mike that all the female students were safe, except for Sonia Thrale.

"She's taken the minister away," Mike said with some bitterness, "She's safe."

Beth looked at William with concern. A peculiar charred stench came from his clothes, mingling unattractively with the tobacco and whisky smells with normally clung to him.

"Are you, er," she asked. Beth was still worried that William might blame her for the antics of the other sociology students.

"I am quite all right, thank you," William said, politely, "Your loyalty has been noted. I trust that today has been a useful lesson to you in the inadvisability of the socialist policy of attempting by direct action to restrict freedom of speech. Do you have any cigarettes?"

Beth gave him a Silk Cut. Mike repressed his desire to shout at William for being such a right wing bastard and took one as well. Beth sighed. Her mother had always told her that men were only after one thing.

"Well done, thou good and faithful student," William said, "But I think you'd better get away from here. There could be more explosions. Some of the lads were chucking half the contents of the chemistry lab around. Made a hell of a bang. It's amazing what we've got in there."

Amazing it may have been, but there was little left of it as the fire spread to the laboratories next to the Clutterbuck Hall. A succession of explosions tore the Hall's doors from their hinges and reduced the expensive tiered seating to matchwood. The windows of the labs blew out in a carnival of noise and coloured light. A horrible chemical smell lingered over the quad.

"Bloody hell," Mike said. It seemed like an accurate description.

"I'm really sorry," William said to Susan, "I fear that *Arcadia* may have to be set back by a week or two. It's the fault of those stupid sods from sociology, of course. I shall see to it that they apologise."

Susan said nothing. The College's very own arcadia was lying in tatters all around her. Dr Walpurgess' carefully modernised grove of academe was burning, holed by bullets, doused in vomit or just plain wrecked. She looked across the quad and watched what looked like a rugby scrum demolishing the flowerbeds as the competing values of social protest and political reality were earnestly and physically debated. Barnaby Worthington came running out of the old building and tried to separate the combatants.

"Hey, like, guys," he said, "Surely we can sort this out like rational adults. I realise you've got a lot of anger, yah. Everyone has. It's, like, society. Hey, even Dr Walpurgess has a lot of repressed tension at the moment, and he's, like, fascistville."

"Piss off," one of the students yelled.

"Don't talk to me like that, you little ponce," Barnaby snapped, and was immediately dragged to the ground by several boys and pummelled vigorously. The Vice Principal appeared, having sensibly left his car at the police station. He was about to intervene when he saw who the boys were thumping, and went inside, sniggering malevolently. He stopped laughing when he found that his office had been redecorated by a hand-grenade and was now open to the elements on one side. Above it all, Elvis declared that he had a dream in which all his brothers walked hand in hand and demanded to know why it could not come true.

"It's like a post-modern hell," Susan sighed.

"Where did, er, Sonia, take Sedgwick?" Mike asked.

"No idea," William said, "And I don't care either. Big lefty woofter can take care of himself."

"What?"

"He can take care of himself. He's a minister of the Crown for good-ness' sake."

"No, the other bit. What do you mean, lefty woofter?"

"You know perfectly well what I mean by it," William growled, "Don't go all politically-correct on me just because you live in Brighton."

"You mean Sedgwick is gay?"

"I prefer not to corrupt that good old English word to mean a sodomite," said William, who in fact regularly used it, invariably followed by the word 'bastard', just as the word 'woman' was usually preceded by 'bloody'. He tended to employ it as a term of abuse for male students who took more than two days at a time off sick, "But yes, he is a lifter of the shirts of other chaps, a player with the parts of his own kind, an arse bandit, a mincing queen of the non-royal variety."

"There's been nothing in the papers," Mike gasped.

"Well, no," William said, "He hasn't annoyed the press yet. But if he did, his repulsive bum-chummery would be all over the shop. It's one of those open secrets that everyone in Westminster just accepts."

Mike began to laugh. The world seemed bright and gay. In the sense in which William claimed to use the word, of course.

*   *   *

Sedgwick settled into the warm, oscillating waters of the jacuzzi and closed his eyes in placid contentment. He sipped from the glass of champagne and allowed the day's horrors to wash out of his system. His trim frame accepted the ministrations of the bubbling fluid as he concocted revenge scenarios for the College. A visit from an Education Department action squad would be too minor a punishment, but then, what could he do to the College that it had not already inflicted on itself? The wretched place was burning when last he'd seen it. Still, there would be no harm in applying a bit of pressure on the civil servants. With any luck they could get the place shut down.

He was lost in these thoughts, creating fantasy images of the Principal and William arraigned before a rigged tribunal accusing them of gross educational malpractice, and did not notice Yvette as she padded silently into the room. Her hooded eyes took in the naked form in the jacuzzi, and she decided that she was not unimpressed. Most of her clients were physically unexciting, if not actually repulsive, and it would make a nice change to pamper someone who didn't resemble a circus exhibit. Sedgwick clearly kept himself in shape. It was a pity he wasn't the Home Secretary, she thought, but you couldn't have everything, or indeed everyone. Yvette had a thing about the Home Secretary. The smack of firm government could mean something quite different if she had her way. The girls in her class, much to William's disgust, had once discussed which politicians they would most like to bed. The PM was too squeaky clean and boring, and the Chancellor—well, maybe—that stern Calvinist rigour would be fun to corrupt, but he was a bit podgy. No-one could understand the thrill appeal of the Foreign Secretary. The Scottish Premier was, well, too Scottish and looked about as cheerful as a Methodist minister in a clap hospital. His Northern Irish counterpart was red-haired—a genetic time bomb—and no-one could remember who the First Minister of Wales actually was. The Leader of the Opposition resembled a lightbulb and the leader of the Irish ultra-nationalists' beard would tickle, even if he didn't kneecap you halfway through the process. Sedgwick had come quite high on the acceptability list. She knelt down beside the jacuzzi, artfully arranging her silk bathrobe, and asked if the minister was feeling any better.

"Er, yes," Sedgwick, startled, opened his eyes, "Absolutely fine."

"Good," Yvette smiled at him, "Is there anything I can get you?"

"No," Sedgwick squeaked.

"You aren't, ah, uncomfortable with me being here like this?" Yvette asked, as smoothly as she could, "I mean, we're not like the other lot, all hung up and starchy. The New Britain is all about freedom and stuff, isn't it?"

She draped herself across the rug at the side of the jacuzzi in what she had found from experience to be a seductive fashion. Not that most blokes needed seducing. A half way decent-looking bit of tottie with plenty of flesh on offer was more or less all they required.

"Indeed," Sedgwick said, "People should, er, liberate themselves. We mustn't be bound by stuffy conventions."

"At the College, you know, the Principal and Mr Fenneck are still living in the past," Yvette cooed, guessing that the teachers' stock was not especially high in Sedgwick's eyes, "They're part of old Britain. They don't let you express yourself physically or emotionally. But I'm so glad that you understand people's needs."

Sedgwick was obviously delighted that this young woman was so keen on the government's liberal agenda but profoundly uneasy about the direction the conversation was taking.

"Some people's needs are normal, some people's are strange," Yvette breathed, conversationally, "I know a chap who gets turned on by having lots of millipedes walk over his naked flesh. It takes all sorts. You look like a baby oil man. Lovely skin like that doesn't grow on trees."

"Well," he said, nervously, "I must say I'm pleased that you're with us on the, ah, issue of personal freedom. Anyway, what would you like to do after you've done your A levels?"

"I was thinking of getting involved in politics," Yvette said languidly, "You know, that's an awfully big jacuzzi and there's tons of room. It's been such a trying day and I've got a bit of an achy back. You don't mind if I join you, do you? We're both broad-minded people, after all."

She did not wait for a reply, but doffed her robe and slipped into the jacuzzi, sitting opposite Sedgwick in the round tub.

"Erm," the Minister said.

Yvette's rather obvious physical charms faced him in the water, as threatening as icebergs.

"This is nice, isn't it?" Yvette smiled.

"Yes." The sound resembled an elderly maiden aunt reluctantly cajoled onto a rollercoaster at Alton Towers, scared out of her wits but too polite to say she'd sooner be fighting giant ice bears at the North Pole.

Yvette stretched out her legs and rubbed her right foot along the minister's calf.

"Perhaps there's not quite so much room as I thought," said the girl, coquettishly.

"Would you like me to get out, then?" Sedgwick bleated.

"No, no," Yvette said, edging closer to him, "It's rather cosy like this, don't you think?"

Sedgwick made a high-pitched gurgling sound.

"An interesting prelude to me going into politics," Yvette looked straight at him and adopted her huskiest voice, "Would be a bit of politics going into me. I think you know what I'm saying, Damien. I can call you that, can't I? Now that we're, so, well, intimate?"

Where this girl got her chat-up lines was a mystery to Sedgwick. Perhaps there was some female version of Barry White. He made a bleating noise again and looked around for the door. Yvette was now virtually on top of him, her hand inching up his leg beneath the surface of the warm water like a determined crab in a rock pool.

"And what have we here?" Yvette raised her eyebrows and smiled roguishly. Her smile faded somewhat when she discovered that she had not even remotely excited Sedgwick in any way. Yvette was more than a little irritated. Not every politician got the chance to be joined in a jacuzzi by a busty eighteen-year-old bird who was clearly up for a spot of ministerial probing. Her attempts to induce greater enthusiasm on Sedgwick's part using one of her tried and tested techniques met with an even more disappointing response.

"Christ on a bike," he screamed, leaping out of the jacuzzi and running down the stairs.

"Come back," Yvette yelled, "It'll be good. Wait 'till you see what I can do with a loofah."

She put on her bathrobe and ran after him.

In the pub car park, Portia was just on the threshold of getting bored when she saw the Secretary of State for the Co-Ordination of Information and Administration run out of the house and into the road. He was dripping wet and stark naked. Something was clearly very wrong. Portia wondered if Yvette had gone over the top with an electrical appliance again. That girl was going to have to learn that there were some men who wanted you to be gentle with them.

"Oh, dear," she said. She got into her car and started the engine, watching the minister carefully all the while.

Yvette came out of the house, wearing a bathrobe and flip-flops. Sedgwick looked at her in terror and ran off. A car-load of students passed him, tooting and jeering. Sedgwick ran up the drive of another house and hid behind a bush. Yvette, standing on the pavement, could not see where he had gone. Portia gunned her engine and shot out of the car park. She hurtled down the short stretch of road and went through the gates of no.20, known to the district's pervert fraternity as the Grosvenor. Yvette trudged back up the driveway to see her.

"He's run off," the girl complained, "I don't know where he's got to. He can't get far, though. He's in the nip."

"I know," Portia said, "What the hell did you do to him?"

"We just shared a jacuzzi. I was about to tickle his fancy a bit when he ran off. Fucking weirdo."

"Right," Portia had made up her mind. This was crunch time.

"We're getting out of here. Get your things together quickly. Where's Jobelle?"

"I'm not totally sure," Yvette admitted, "She sort of disappeared."

"Never mind," Portia dashed upstairs, "Just get dressed, get your stuff and meet me in the car in five minutes."

She ran into the jacuzzi and took down the huge mirror which overlooked it. Opening a small door built into the wall, she extracted a cassette from the miniature video camera behind it, and put it into her bag. She went downstairs and took all the champagne from the kitchen and loaded it into her car. There was no point in going on the run without adequate sustenance. Yvette might not have been the ideal choice as Thelma to Portia's Louise, but she would do. The two women got into the car and roared off in the direction of Glasgow.

*   *   *

Alice was nestled in an armchair reading the annotated works of John Donne. Like a slim young ocelot at rest, she seemed moulded to the contours of the furniture as her brown eyes soaked up the text. Donne was one of her favourites. As she reflected on his poems about love and friendship, she thought that perhaps she ought to give William a call. Maybe she had been a little hasty in jumping to conclusions about him. She didn't have any actual proof that he was running a brothel. He was so emotionally and sexually repressed that he made John Major look like Keith Richards, so he was hardly likely to try to make money out of it. He was too innocent and too stupid. In any case, he had always been kind to her personally, even if he was unpleasant to virtually everyone else. And he could make very nice soup. Her thoughts were interrupted by a nervous tapping at the window. A naked man stood there. Alice shrieked and hid behind a chair.

"Please don't be frightened," the man begged, "I can explain, honestly."

Alice peeped up and looked at him. He seemed in pretty decent physical condition, she would tell her friends later, and she seemed to recognise him.

"My name is Damien Sedgwick," he said, "I'm in the government."

"I know," Alice said, "I saw you at a party. At the Irish Embassy."

"Now you know who I am," Sedgwick pleaded, "Please will you let me in? I'm stuck out here all wet, with no clothes."

"I can see that," Alice said. She went to the bathroom and fetched a towel, then went to the door and let him in.

"Thank you," Sedgwick gasped.

"I'll just go and find you some of my dad's clothes," Alice said, "You're about the same size."

She returned with an old jumper and a pair of trousers.

"What happened?" she asked, "Where have you come from?"

"Next door," Sedgwick said, pulling on the trousers, "It was awful. Some godawful tart tried to rape me in a jacuzzi."

"But what were you doing there in the first place?" Alice could not quite accustom herself to the idea of a politician not being in London. It was a bit like seeing Sooty's legs.

Sedgwick's voice was muffled as he put his head into the jumper.

"She lured me round there after some evil little swine called Fenneck got me to come down to that ghastly College to talk to his maniac students. I'm going to nail that odious bag of lard if it's the last thing I do."

His head emerged, tortoise-like, from the jumper. He looked up to ask her if he could use a telephone, but Alice had gone.

If Alice was full of righteous indignation as she marched round to the College to give him a piece of her mind, William himself was imbued with a sense of general doom. He trudged down the corridor that led to his office and his drinks cabinet singing a Noel Coward song which cheered him up at times like this.

"There are bad times just around the corner,

There are dark clouds hurtling through the sky...."

"Fenneck!"

Like a surly Pit Bull disturbed at its dinner by a child with a hammer, William turned and snarled, an animal sound full of unpleasantness. He hated being interrupted.

Toby Gaskett stood at the end of the corridor holding a German machine-pistol.

"I couldn't get the politicians but I can get you, you fascist bastard," the boy shouted.

He pointed the gun at William and pulled the trigger.

Nothing happened. He pulled it again and again, and again and again nothing happened. He stared dumbly at the weapon. William looked at him with disgust, and walked slowly and deliberately up to him. Gaskett pulled the trigger once more; there was a feeble click.

"You really are a twat on a ladder, aren't you, Gaskett? A useless, clueless berk," William snapped, contemptuously. He snatched the gun from the student's hands and inspected it.

"This is an MP28 machine pistol, a favourite with the Waffen SS, an organisation which would have had great fun dealing with your poxy little revolution this afternoon," said William, whose encyclopaedic knowledge of National Socialism was a source of some concern in the College, "It has a magazine containing thirty nine-millimetre rounds and a safety catch here. If you do not take off the safety catch, the weapon, funnily enough, won't work."

He held the gun up to Gaskett's face and depressed a small lever beside the trigger.

"But then, I wouldn't expect a total cretin like you to work out a simple thing like that," William continued, "Despite it being a regular plot device in films. Nor indeed to have cocked the weapon, thus sticking a round in the chamber and making it ready to fire. This is how you do that thing."

There was a harsh clacking sound as William cocked the weapon. Then he put it into his shoulder.

"Observe," he hissed with a thoroughly nasty smile, and pointed the gun at Gaskett's kneecap.

"Christ, no," the boy screamed.

William calmly and deliberately fired a single shot into the thick wooden flooring. He gradually raised his eyes upwards, taking in the damp patch on Gaskett's trousers where the boy's fear had made itself physically manifest. Tears of bitter humiliation pricked Gaskett's eyes. William noticed this too.

"You tragic, worthless piece of scum," William said, loathing oozing from every pore of his being, "You big poof. Stop whingeing. You're male. Boys don't cry in this College. And while we're on the topic, get your ridiculous girl's hair cut, clean that nail varnish off your paws, and piss off out of my sight."

He thrust the machine-pistol into Gaskett's hands, turned on his heel and stalked off.

The boy stared angrily after the retreating figure. Rage boiled inside him rather as acne did on the outside. He had never hated anyone so much in his life as he hated William now. He pointed his gun up the corridor and emptied the magazine in William's direction. Toby Gaskett had not fired a gun before and the shots sprayed wildly around the walls, chipping plaster and wood and glass everywhere. Two rounds found their mark. They smashed hard into William's back. He staggered, and then, like a wounded hippopotamus, crashed to the floor, and lay still.

Chapter Twenty

"In all my years as a news journalist, I have rarely witnessed heroism of this nature," the reporter from *Sussex Today* gabbled to the viewing millions. In all his years as a television journalist, the most exciting moment had in fact been a ride on a green goddess during the firemen's strike, so this was perhaps a little hyperbolic. Luke Wallace and Beth Seymour were scurrying about like sheepdogs, finding for the news crews people with interesting stories, or at any rate a reasonable degree of sobriety and coherence, and had given Mike to the local man.

"Michael Alcock, the Head of English and Combined Humanities at Mercier's College in Hengistley, risked his own life in a daring attempt to ensure the safety of students and politicians being held hostage by a terrorist gang."

"Oh. Gosh. It was, erm, nothing, ah, really," Mike murmured modestly.

"But you stood up to young toughs armed with military grade weapons," the reporter enthused, "And that's pretty heroic in my book. What was going through your mind when you stood up and confronted the terrorists?"

Mike was unwilling to reveal that the first thing he had noticed when he got to his feet in the Clutterbuck Hall was that from that position he could see down Susan's blouse. Not for the first time, he embraced his old friend dishonesty.

"Well, I'd be lying if I didn't admit to being just a bit nervous," he said, "But my main thought was for the safety of the students. Hey, everything we in the teaching profession do is ultimately for them. They are always our first priority, whether there are terrorists around or not."

He smiled winningly at the camera. By lunchtime the following day, he would be a hero.

Any further observations were drowned by the arrival of another ambulance, which wailed into the car park like a fat white banshee. A panic-stricken Toby Gaskett, fleeing from what he knew to be the wrath to come, accidentally ran into its path and was smacked vigorously into the air. Contorted, and indeed dressed, like a broken rag doll, he was pitched into the air and landed horribly on the bonnet of a police car. The unpleasant thudding, squelching sound was picked up by the sound recordist who was interviewing Annelise Featherstone. She was putting in some groundwork for her future in the media and was distinctly unimpressed when Gaskett's body interrupted her career development.

The prompt action of the Fire Brigade had ensured that physical destruction was largely confined to the Clutterbuck Hall and the two chemistry classrooms next to it. Nonetheless, the pristine symmetry of the quad had been ruined for the foreseeable future. The white stucco of the Hall's frontage was smudged with smoke and black holes stared out blindly where once there had been windows. The labs were desolate, the explosions having torn them apart in a series of convulsive chemical belches. Their blinds flapped feebly in the afternoon breeze, pathetically trying to beckon onlookers inside. The Vice Principal stared at the wreckage of his architectural dream and stomped angrily over to the shrubbery, where Barnaby Worthington was curled up in the foetal position under a damp bush. A centipede was inquisitively pottering about in his ear and a line of ants was marching in military formation up the leg of his trousers. He looked up.

"Have they gone?" he whispered.

Walpurgess looked at him with distaste.

"I assume you mean the students of that other moron Fenneck who were beating seven shades of crap out of you earlier," he said, "And making a jolly good job of it, I must say. Well, yes, they've gone. But they might come back. You never know. I'd say you're safer in there. Best to stay there for at least another couple of hours."

"Thanks," Barnaby said, "I owe you one, man."

"Strictly speaking," Walpurgess replied as he went back to his ruined office, "You owe me about two hundred thousand."

The Police were busily stuffing male students into vans and driving them to separate stations, where they would spend long and miserable hours being interrogated. Those Rainbow Revolutionaries not beaten up by the politics students and subsequently arrested went into hiding behind a compost-heap in a distant corner of the rugby field. They frantically stuffed the weapons, whose use they had never really understood, deep into the smelly pile. They then sat back and gulped down lungfuls of aromatic smoke from a hastily rolled joint. This calmed them down somewhat, which was fortunate as it made them more docile when the police were led right to them, alerted by the furious barking of their sniffer dogs.

*   *   *

Inside the old building, which had escaped the damage, the Principal looked around his office wistfully.

"It seems strange to think that in a few weeks I'll be gone," he said, "Twenty years is a long time, Benedict."

"Yes, yes," Wolfesbain, too, surveyed the room, which Dr. Godley had restored to its Victorian splendour in the late seventies. His first act as Principal had been to order a skip and dispose of the egalitarian modernist furniture which his predecessor had installed in order to lull government inspectors into the erroneous belief that the College was in some way progressive. Dr. Godley had known which way the wind was blowing, and he knew his market well. Parents who were ushered in here were awed by the William Morris wallpaper and the large mahogany desk, behind which they would find the Principal, inscrutable and delphic, uttering words of wisdom they could barely comprehend. Civil Servants, sent to impose the whims of ministers with right-wing populist agendas, would be impressed at the quality of the refit, seeing here a no-nonsense approach to traditional values. The discreet whirring of a computer in the corner of the room reassured everyone that the present day was also very much a part of life at Mercier's.

"What's your successor like?" the MP asked, "I just can't see how they'll be able to replace you."

"Nice chap," the Principal ruminated, "Head of one of the better comprehensives in Cambridgeshire. Young family. MBA, whatever that is. Seems to count for something these days, though I must say I regret the fact."

"I fear we shall have to disagree on that one, Basil. Business management is where it's at these days, you know."

"Actually," the Principal remembered something, "We've been conducting an experiment along those lines for the past couple of terms. You remember those reforms in the Civil Service designed to make the chaps more businesslike and responsible?"

"Oh, yes, oh, yes. Ran some of the early ones through myself. Quite effective, you know."

"Well, indeed," the Principal commented, "We've done the same sort of thing here. Each Department is managed entirely by its senior tutor—salaries, equipment expenditure, the lot. We should be getting the preliminary results through today."

There was a knock on the door and Jonathan Bleach came in.

"Mr. Wolfesbain," he said smoothly, "How lovely to see you again. Principal, we have the reports of the Departmental Finance Initiative. And your successor is waiting in reception. Shall I bring him in?"

"Do, yes, Jonathan," the Principal took the printed pages from his subordinate and glanced through them. Bleach left and returned a moment later with the new Principal, an efficient-looking man in a suit.

"James Osgoode, my successor," Dr. Godley said, "James, this is Benedict Wolfesbain, the town's MP. The Shadow Home Secretary, as you are no doubt aware. They always are, I'm afraid. We were just going to have a look at the results of our Departmental Finance Initiative."

"Do carry on. I should like to know what the financial health of the College is going to be," Osgoode suppressed a desire to scream aloud a torrent of questions about the large number of emergency vehicles in the car park, the absence of several buildings which had been here on his previous visit, and the all-pervading stench of chemicals.

"It's remarkably good, Principal," Bleach said, "Er, Principals. And, ah, Mr. Wolfesbain."

"And did you ever think it would be otherwise?" Dr. Godley asked.

"Oh. Er, well, no, I mean, we always knew the DFI would be a roaring success, Principal, naturally," Bleach panicked, "I mean, it was such an inspired idea."

The Principal beamed modestly around the room, a Buddha-like figure behind his desk of power.

"Most Departments are financially stable," Bleach continued, "They've managed their resources reasonably well and broken even, often making slight profits. The Home Economics ladies, for instance, have revealed something of a talent for playing the stock exchange. Their office is next door to the Sociology classroom, so they just listen in to find out where the repressive regimes are, find out which British companies are supplying them with arms, and invest in them. Rather clever, I thought."

"You say 'most'," Osgoode interrupted, "Are there exceptions?"

"Well, er, yes," Bleach said, "And that's the peculiar thing. Some Departments have actually made quite substantial amounts of money." The Principal continued to smile benignly. Bleach wondered if perhaps the old man's grin would remain after his departure, like that of a Cheshire cat. Had the old sod known all this from the outset? The DFI had been assumed to be camouflage for who was responsible for the impending ruin of the College, at least in the minds of his colleagues on the management team. Its success would have been nice but it was not actually believed to be remotely likely.

"Um, the Humanities Faculty," he pointed to the relevant graph, "Several Departments in there are doing incredibly well. Initially, because of the substantial cash payments to an off license, we thought William Fenneck was simply using the Politics Department budget to drink himself to death. But then we noticed a pattern of payments in and out, which means, I think, that he has set up a wine-trading enterprise. These cheques are the same surnames as our students, so he must be buying the stuff cheap somewhere and flogging it on to parents. Add that to this input from the European Union for today's, er, conference, and there's a tidy profit of about three grand."

"Splendid," the Principal said, "And are there any more success stories?"

"Well, Principal, Fenneck's achievement pales into insignificance compared with the English Department. It's got as much money as it had at the start of the term, and Michael Alcock doesn't appear to have paid himself any salary. Which means a profit of twenty-five grand in real terms."

"What?" Osgoode was incredulous, "How the hell can that happen?"

"I'm not sure," Bleach admitted, "But looking at the expenditure pattern, there was a big payment to an estate agency at the start of term. This was repaid within two months and since then the only money going out of the English Department has been on book purchases. Alcock's found some way of making the money work for the

Department which means he's been living off some alternative source of income, but I don't know what it is."

"These are the kind of chaps I need on my team," Osgoode declared, "They're obviously wasted in lessons."

Jonathan Bleach was about to interject that Mike and William were regularly wasted in lessons but the new Principal carried on.

"I want to meet these guys. They're obviously pretty dynamic and go-ahead, ready to respond to the challenges which face us. And, let's face it, now that someone's seen fit to blow up half the College—I *did* notice that, by the way, and I'd like to talk to you about it later—these challenges are greater than ever before."

"Shall we go to find them, then?" Dr. Godley suggested, "It's such a lovely day, it would be a shame to spend it all in the office."

*   *   *

Like an old dog which crawls back to its favourite haunt to die, William limped back to the Wolfschanze. He was not in as much pain as he thought he ought to be. Shock, perhaps. He lurched up the stairs of the Victorian grammar school building to the untidy room in which he had gone through the motions of teaching for the previous six years. He collapsed into the chair behind his desk and gingerly opened his suit jacket. The shirt which stretched across the lower half of his abdomen was soaked in blood. William tutted weakly. He regarded the wearing of primary colours by anyone other than cardinals or peers of the realm as vulgar. Removing his gown and the punctured, bloodstained jacket of his suit, he reached behind him for the old tweed sports coat which he kept on the back of his chair to promote the illusion that he was always in the building but was temporarily unavailable. William carefully put on the tweed jacket and gown, which he wrapped around himself, and

took a bottle of whisky from his desk. He poured some into a grubby
wineglass and drank it slowly as he wrote out his last will and testament.
Wheezing like a rubber dinghy slashed by a knife, he scrawled his
demands onto a student's essay.

I have been shot by that little creep Toby Gaskett, he wrote, *and it is my
dying wish that he should be excluded from the College. I wish patriotic
music to be played at my funeral, including the national anthem. All staff
must attend, wearing gowns. I particularly request that Barnaby
Worthington, who bunks off the Christmas Carol Service and Founder's
Day Prayers pleading atheistic convictions, be there. I leave all my worldly
goods to my ex-girlfriend Calpurnia Woodard, because this will annoy
Alice Jameson.*

The door burst open and Alice strode in, a fierce young tigress in
search of prey to dismember. She looked him up and down with embit-
tered fury.

"You bastard," she hissed.

"I see the anger management course worked well, then," William
murmured.

"Don't try to be funny," she snapped, "It doesn't suit you."

"I never stopped you trying to be intelligent."

"Fuck off. Just fuck off. You really disgust me. A government minister
has just appeared in my front garden stark naked and why? You set up a
brothel, not just anywhere but next to my house, you sick bastard. After
the loyalty I've shown you. More than anyone. And then what do I find
when I come round to the College? It's like a bloody war zone, and don't
try telling me it's nothing to do with you. You make me sick."

William looked at her through a tired haze as he thought about
things to say. One by one, the biological systems which kept his body
going were breaking down. He could not afford the time to say a great
deal. She had quite clearly got the wrong end of the stick about something, but that was women for you. It was too late to put in the effort to
disabuse her. He hated arguing anyway. Alice usually won. She stood by

the door of the classroom, not coming too close to the desk lest his corruption infect her. Her slender frame was taut with fury, her dark eyes lit up, burning at him. She was curiously beautiful when she was angry.

Suddenly, it hit him. Alice was actually beautiful all the time. It had never really occurred to him before. She was all right, really. He had never understood this, so had never told her so. Well, there was no point in trying now. If she believed him, it would inflate her ego, and if she didn't, she would regard it as an attempt to curry favour with bad chat-up lines. To express his feelings would, in any case, be emotional self-indulgence, which William despised. He had managed to achieve a stable, if not exactly happy, existence through the rigid suppression of sentiment and ruthless adherence to duty. Probably best to act normally, he thought, not pausing to consider that being normal was rarely on the agenda at Mercier's.

"We all make mistakes," he ventured, "I'm only human."

"You're only just human, you evil sod," Alice screamed, hysterically, "How could you do it?"

"You're so bloody ungrateful sometimes," William said, " You'll laugh about this some day. It'll make a great story down the pub."

"You bastard," she shouted, with startling originality.

Alice stalked out, slamming the door. She clattered down the stairs and out of the College.

The College cat came through the window into the room. It moved sinuously through the gaps in the furniture and leaped up onto William's desk. There were sometimes scraps of food here if he forgot to eat all of his lunch. William looked at the cat with tired affection. It was a delicately-featured grey-and-buff tabby with white paws.

"Hello, furry boy," he said, vaguely, using his childhood word for animals. The cat, which was actually a girl, looked at him suspiciously. William had never been nice to it before. He was clearly a dog person. The cat had seen him with the caretaker's labrador, throwing sticks for the slobbering yellow brute. But the cat was prepared to forgive. It pressed against William's outstretched hand, and purred as he stroked it with the backs of his fingers.

"She's like you, furry boy," William said, "Soft and silky and so on. So very beautiful, and nice when she's not being shouty. Perhaps not very clever, but she is a girl, after all. Can't help that. She's a decent enough wee lassie really. Are you a decent sort of lassie, furry boy?"

The cat purred on. William could talk whatever nonsense he liked so long as he gave it attention. It undulated beneath his caress.

"But I don't think I should tell her so. It would make her big-headed. It was nice to see her."

He ran his fingers slowly and gently along the supple little animal's flanks.

With his free hand he crossed out the reference to Calpurnia Woodard, and inserted

to Alice Jameson, who, although pig-headed and foolish, typically of her sex, has some not unreasonable qualities. He thought how convenient it was that he had only now realised how he ought to feel about Alice. It would have been so terribly awkward before. William was very happy. The Principal came in, with Bleach and Mr Wolfesbain and the strange new man whose arrival William feared. He struggled to his feet.

"Well done, William," the Principal said.

"Thank you, Headmaster," William smiled weakly. He wondered how the Principal knew about his good fortune in discovering the truth about Alice. The old boy really was awfully clever. "She's got such very lovely eyes, you know."

He slumped forward onto the desk. Alarmed, the cat leaped away and ran out the window.

"Sorry," Bleach said to Osgoode, "He's often like this after lunch."

*   *   *

Damien Sedgwick had just finished calling Josh and arranging to be picked up when he heard a car pull into the drive. A middle-aged man got out and came into the house. He looked Sedgwick up and down.

"Hello," Alice's father said, "It's Mr Sedgwick, isn't it? You were on television yesterday."

"Yes," the minister said.

"I don't mean to be rude," Henry said, "But would you mind telling me why you're wearing my jumper and my trousers? And indeed what you're doing in my dining-room. I mean, I'm sure there's a terribly good explanation, but I would like to know what it is."

"Ah. Yes. Quite," Sedgwick said, "My, er, clothes are next door. I was taken there by some evil woman. She tried to molest me in a jacuzzi."

"Why on earth would anyone want to do that?"

Alice's father had an abiding suspicion of all MPs. He ran a small business and was distinctly unimpressed by the disparity between the assistance politicians claimed to offer people like him and the hindrances they all too frequently put in his way. He was automatically distrustful of those like Sedgwick who were particularly notorious for propagandising.

"I'm not sure. It's probably got something to do with a nasty little sod called Fenneck. He teaches at that wretched College round the corner and lured me down to this beastly town. The whole thing reeks of perversion."

"Aha!" Henry had caught the politician out, "That wretched College, as you call it, provided my daughter with a good education. And I know William Fenneck and he'd never be a party to molesting people in jacuzzis. He's perfectly normal. In fact, I don't imagine he even knows how jacuzzis work. He wouldn't have anything French in the house."

"I think that the word jacuzzi is Italian," Sedgwick said.

"You seem to know a disturbing amount about our continental friends and their filthy foreign practices. What are you really up to?"

"It's the truth, I'm telling you. Ask your daughter. She gave me these clothes. I was in the garden with nothing on."

"Good grief, man," Henry exploded, "If anyone reeks of pervsion round here it's you. Cavorting about in the garden without any clothes on? I thought we'd put an end to that sort of nonsense when we got rid of the last bunch of criminal incompetents. And where is my daughter?"

"I don't know," Sedgwick whined, edging towards the front door, "She just disappeared."

"Don't be ridiculous. Twenty year old girls don't just disappear. Not unless they get kidnapped by sex perverts. I can't say I've ever liked your crew anyway, and I must say it wouldn't surprise me if this was one of those kinky sex games that you Westminster wierdoes play. What have you done with her?"

Sedgwick was almost at the door when Alice swept past him and stormed upstairs to her bedroom. She slammed the door, flung herself on the bed and burst into tears. Alice wept bitterly for the destruction of the College where she had been given the enthusiasm to teach and for her stupidity in giving her loyalty to an undeserving William. The long and elegant figure for which he had chastely repressed his affection shook and shivered as she was racked with angry sobs. Her eyes, normally a warm, translucent brown and in William's view her most striking feature, reddened as she cried without consolation and resolved to become an accountant. Downstairs, her father turned on Sedgwick with renewed indignation.

"Look at the state of her. She's distraught. What have you done? How could you do this to the poor girl? What kind of monster are you?"

"It wasn't me. She was perfectly all right earlier on."

"Yes, until you turned up in the garden without any clothes on. I'm calling the police."

A beige Rover hurtled up the drive and screeched to a halt. Josh got out.

"Quick, DS," he squawked, "We're being pursued by a load of journalists. Got to get in. Get on dual carriageway. Out of here. Back to London."

Sedgwick ran for the car. He was just about to get in when another vehicle turned in to the drive and drove hard up against the Rover, blocking its escape. A handful of seedy-looking men got out, some armed with cameras, others clutching small tape recorders.

"Mr Sedgwick," a particularly sordid individual in a grubby raincoat shouted, "Gareth Strongbow, *Daily Express*. What do you know about Mr William Fenneck, Mr Sedgwick? Someone has shot him, sir, shortly after you were overheard saying 'I'll kill the bastard'. Would you like to say anything about this?"

"What?" Henry yelled, "This is ludicrous. First he does something beastly to my daughter and then he murders William. He isn't fit to be a minister of the Crown. He ought to be strung up."

Sedgwick flung himself into the Rover and locked the door. He curled up into a little ball and whimpered. In the absence of any coherent speech from the minister, the journalists clustered around Henry, who gave them the benefit of his strongly held views on the subject of Damien Sedgwick and, while he was at it, the tide of bureaucracy which made life difficult for small businessmen in the electronics industry in the south-eastern region.

In the car, the driver's mobile telephone trilled. He pressed a button and listened intently.

"As you wish, Prime Minister. Thank you, Prime Minister. You're very kind, Prime Minister. Tony, then. Thank you. Goodbye."

He turned to the cowering minister.

"Which would you like first; the good news or the bad news?" he asked.

"Let's get bad news out of way first, eh, DS?" Josh suggested.

"The PM wishes to see you as soon as we get back to London. A draft letter of resignation will be ready for you there. He's sure you'll understand."

"How can there possibly be good news after that?" Sedgwick moaned.

"Well," the driver said, modestly, "The PM was watching the telly, and he saw the way I handled the motor when those little hooligans in the Ford Escort tried to play dodgems. He was very impressed and wants me to be his personal chauffeur. Bit of a step up, eh? No offence."

*   *   *

Portia was now on the other side of London. She listened with mounting disbelief to the reports on the radio of carnage at Mercier's. Never in the wildest fantasies of revenge had it occurred to her that this was possible. Walpurgess and the Principal must really be livid, she thought, with grim satisfaction. As the tales of Mike's heroism were built up through the course of the afternoon, Portia smiled. It was nice to think that he would do all right out of it. She just hoped that he had remembered to cover his financial tracks and muddy the waters by keeping money constantly moving in and out of the English Department accounts. Beside her Yvette looked through the CD rack for something more soothing to listen to.

"Where are we going, exactly?" she asked.

"Stranraer," Portia said.

"Where's that?"

"West of Glasgow. It's the main port for Northern Ireland."

"We're going to Northern Ireland?" Yvette shrieked, "What the hell for?"

"Because it's the last place anyone would think of looking for us," Portia explained, "It will come out, sooner or later, what happened today. And people will realise that we've buggered off somewhere. They'd expect us to hole up in London or maybe to nip across the Channel to Belgium or France. So we wrong-foot them. We go to Belfast, wait there a few days while we sort out new identities, then nip down to Dublin. From the Republic we can get a ferry to Spain. Easy, eh?"

"How do we get new identities in Belfast?"

"Ah, well," Portia said, "One of those farmers at the agricultural show turned out to be from Ulster. He had some, er, well, friends, let's say. He was very taken with the services we provided and gave me a 'phone number to ring in emergencies. Turns out to be a commandant in some, ah, organisation. They're used to sorting out false I.D.s for people. They can get a respray and new plates for the motor, too."

"Bloody hell," Yvette was both horrified and amazed.

"And while we're there," Portia said brightly, "We can go and see the Ulster Folk and Transport Museum. Really interesting place. It's got loads of old houses from all over Ireland, you know, rebuilt so that you can see how people lived in the past. Fascinating stuff. I've always wanted to see it."

"Bloody hell," Yvette said again, "Has anyone ever told you that you sometimes sound just like a History teacher?"

Portia looked at her. She pulled the car over to the hard shoulder and got out. She lit a cigarette and stared up the motorway into infinity.

*　　　　　*　　　　　*

In the English Office, Mike and Susan were gazing into one another's eyes and making plans together. Their conversation was punctuated by light and affectionate kisses and soppy smiles.

"We could get a place together. Save on the, er, living and travel expenses."

"In Hengistley? Or in Brighton?"

"Not Hengistley. It's a bit dull."

"Yes. And besides, now that you're a big hero, you'd get mobbed by screaming fans wherever you went."

"Oh, I'm not a hero."

"You haven't heard the radio broadcasts. And anyway, you're *my* hero."

"For goodness sake. You're a drama teacher. That's such a corny line."

"But it's true."

"I'm only a hero because I've got someone worth being heroic for."

"You're so sweet."

The door opened and the Principal came in with his retinue. Mike and Susan scrambled to their feet and smoothed their hair.

"Ah, Michael," the old man smiled warmly at his Head of English, "And Susan. How lovely. I do like to see close co-operation between my staff."

"Quite, Basil," Mike said, nervously.

"You've met Benedict Wolfesbain and James Osgoode, of course. Jonathan here was just telling us all about your great triumph."

Mike looked at Bleach suspiciously. So far as he was aware, the Under Vice Principal had spent the entire duration of the riot hidden under his desk clutching a bottle of Jack Daniels. What the hell did he know about what had gone on in the quad?

"Just doing my duty, you know," Mike said.

"Every member of staff in the College did his or her duty," Osgoode said enthusiastically, "But you went over and above that. Your achievement is a shining beacon to everyone in the profession."

"If you say so, Mr Osgoode," Mike replied, politely.

Susan gazed up at him in admiration.

"When I take up the reins of the College in September, I want you to be by my side, as Vice Principal in charge of financial restructuring. It's a substantial promotion, and you'll maybe put a few backs up amongst the existing nonentities on the management team, but from what I've seen, you're the man for the job."

Mike went pink with embarrassment whilst Jonathan Bleach turned an unpleasant shade of green.

"The first piece of good practice I want you to share with us," Osgoode continued, breezily, "Is how you managed, in effect, to double the money of the English Department budget."

This time it was Mike who turned an unpleasant shade of green. He swallowed.

"Susan," he said hoarsely, "I think you'd better wait outside."

ABOUT THE AUTHOR

Douglas Maddon was born in Ireland and educated at the Belfast Royal Academy and Merton College, Oxford. A former journalist, he has been a college lecturer since 1993. In an ideal world, he would be living in an attractive Tudor manor house in Sussex with his beautiful, accomplished wife, their three talented children and their Labrador, Disraeli. Sadly, as this is not an ideal world, he lives alone with his large collection of whisky and a dwindling supply of Prozac. Douglas Maddon enjoys the theatre and pottering about in public houses.

The English Department's Whores is his first novel.

Printed in the United States
144633LV00003B/87/A